Knight Tir
By Katy
Edgecombe Publishing

Copyright © 2024 by Katy Berritt

All rights reserved.

No part of this publication may be reproduced, distributed, or transmitted in any form or by any means, including photocopying, recording, or other electronic or mechanical methods, without the prior written permission of the publisher, except as permitted by U.S. copyright law.

The story, all names, characters, and incidents portrayed in this production are fictitious. No identification with actual persons (living or deceased), places, buildings, and products is intended or should be inferred.

Published by Edgecombe Publishing 2024

Cover Design by Candace Lucas

Table of Contents

Knight Time in Texas 1
Prologue 3
Chapter One 17
Chapter Two 31
Chapter Three 47
Chapter Four 55
Chapter Five 69
Chapter Six 85
Chapter Seven 99
Chapter Eight 109
Chapter Nine 119
Chapter Ten 131
Chapter Eleven 143
Chapter Twelve 159
Chapter Thirteen 175
Chapter Fourteen 193
Chapter Fifteen 205
Chapter Sixteen 231
Chapter Seventeen 245
Chapter Eighteen 259
Chapter Nineteen 279
Chapter Twenty 289
Epilogue 305
Chapter One 311

Other Romantic Comedies by Katy Berritt
The Candy Capers
Baby and the Bank Robber
Lucky's Ladies
Love & Laughter
A Wild and Wooly Texan
Tangled Up in Texas

Prologue

April 20, 1891—New York City

"Dr. Knight!"

Eli's hand jerked at the sudden interruption. After throwing a furious look over his shoulder at his nurse, he took a deep breath to calm himself. "Adelaide. I've told you never to interrupt me when I'm in surgery."

"I'm sorry, Doctor, but—"

"Not now." Returning his gaze to his patient, he readjusted his grip on his scalpel and quickly scanned the man's arm for any nicks or cuts. Thankfully, the patient appeared unscathed, but Eli wasn't. His hand still trembled from the fright. He needed calm. Closing his eyes, he took another deep breath and held it.

One. Two. Three. Exhale. He repeated the exercise, focusing on slowing his heartbeat and steadying the hand holding the razor-sharp scalpel. Finally, believing he was relaxed enough to do his job properly, he opened his eyes and slowly drew the knife across the swelling on the man's arm. It made a clean cut across the reddened lump and the skin parted, revealing a pocket of infection that needed to be drained.

"But Dr. Knight. There's this man. He won't go away. He says he needs you right now."

"I'll come out when I'm done here," he muttered. Keeping his eyes on the now open wound, Eli gently applied pressure to force the infection out, then dabbed it with a gauze square. Press, dab, press, dab, until all that oozed out was a thin flow of nearly clear liquid tinged slightly with red, a sign he'd managed to clear the wound of infection, at least for now. Tipping a bottle of carbolic solution, he soaked a large gauze square and laid it across the open wound.

"Dr. Knight!" Adelaide's voice shook. "Please come now. The man has a gun!"

"What?" The bottle slipped from Eli's hand, spilling across the white sheeting covering his unconscious patient. He slewed around to face his nurse. "What do you mean he has a gun?"

Her trembling hands gripped the front of the white cotton apron she wore to protect her clothing. "He has a gun and he says you need to come right now or he's going to start shooting things and those things might be one of us." She blinked behind her spectacles.

A gun? Here, in his office? On Park Avenue? Damnation.

"I'll come right out." He picked up the bottle he'd dropped and handed it to Adelaide. "Here, finish sterilizing the wound then sew it up. Bind it tightly. Stay here until I return." Standing, he left his surgery. He and the gentleman were about to have a few words about bringing a gun into a medical office.

He surveyed the man dressed in blue serge trousers and a white collared shirt with a tweed jacket over it. Medium height, craggy faced with a thick dark mustache that spread the width of his face and joined his bushy sideburns. Most prominent was his bulbous nose and small black eyes so piercing they sent a momentary shiver down Eli's spine.

The gun Adelaide referenced was nowhere in sight but if that face didn't say thug, Eli didn't know what did. "How can I help you?" Eli said through tight lips. The anger coursing through him made it difficult to address the man civilly.

"You gotta come right now."

Eli stared at the man. A doctor needed patience and fortitude, and Eli possessed both of those in abundance but there was no way he would allow this man to bully him into going anywhere until he knew the why and wherefore. "I don't *gotta* anything," he said after a minute passed.

The thug's gun reappeared. Damn! Fear made his heart lurch but he pushed the fear aside. After five years serving in the Dakotas as a military surgeon, he'd faced death before. He'd learned to handle fear. "Are you going to shoot me?" he asked. "Because if you do, you'll need to find another surgeon."

"The boss don't want another surgeon. He wants you. Word is yer the best in the city and Morgan only hires the best."

At the name Morgan, Eli inhaled sharply. Clevon Morgan was the cruelest, most corrupt crime boss in the city. If a vice existed, Clevon Morgan was involved in it. Rumor said he ran gambling rings, drug houses, prostitution rings and claimed responsibility for at least ten murders.

The last thing Eli needed was to get involved with the man. Once involved, he might never get free again, because that's how Morgan operated.

"Sorry, but I can't leave right now. I have a patient in my office in the middle of surgery and appointments directly after that. I can't leave." And if Eli had anything to say about it, he'd have *appointments* for the rest of his life.

The man's hand tightened on his long-barreled gun. "Look, Doc, I gotta bring you. Mr. Morgan's kid's been shot. He's real bad off. We already done brought another doctor in who said he wasn't able to help. He said the only one he thought could do it is you."

Son of a bitch. A kid. How could he not help a child, even if that child was the son of a monster? He closed his eyes, wishing he could say no, knowing damned well he was about to say yes.

Damn him for a fool. "Let me get my bag." Turning, he returned to his surgery. Adelaide sat next to his patient who was awake now but groggy. She stared at Eli, her blue eyes wide and questioning.

Pulling his medical bag from a closet, he filled it with what he thought he might need. "Adelaide, I'm going with the gentleman. I have no idea how long I'll be gone. You'll need to send Herbie to my other appointments and tell them I'll have to reschedule. Suggest that Mrs. Bright go to Doctor Cannon for her goiter surgery and reschedule Jake Updike to my father for the knee surgery. Dad's in Boston until fall but the Mr. Updike's knee can wait until then."

Her face went white. "Dr. Knight. No. Don't go. I heard who he works for. You don't know...he could...oh, please, don't go."

He gave her a lopsided smile. "It'll be fine. When Mr. Larson here leaves—" He gestured at the groggy patient. "Close up my offices and go home. I'll send a message when it's time to return. Oh, and also send Herbie to tell Helen and her husband I won't be joining them for dinner tonight." His sister was used to him canceling at the last minute due to emergencies so she wouldn't be surprised.

Together, he and the gentleman—Eli used the term loosely—left the townhouse where he maintained his practice on the ground floor while living in the top two floors. The man gestured at the hansom cab sitting at the curb and they climbed in. They were both silent during the short ride to reach their destination near Washington Square where they stopped in front of a large brownstone. Disembarking, they climbed the wide stairs to the front door the butler opened.

Eli blinked. The foyer was massive, with black and white marble checkerboard floors, walnut wainscotting, a wide staircase that bisected the lobby, and several crystal—electric—chandeliers, still a rarity in Manhattan. Apparently, crime paid.

His friendly neighborhood gangster grabbed his arm and dragged him up the staircase to the second floor where he flung open a door and pushed Eli inside.

"I got him, boss, like you said."

Lucky me.

A bull of a man stood up from the chair where he sat and swiveled around to face Eli, a black scowl on his face. Over six feet tall, Clevon Morgan possessed the body of a stevedore, wide shouldered, broad chest, ham-like hands. His face, crisscrossed with scars, provided evidence of his rise to power in the criminal world. An older woman who appeared to be a maid stood behind him. She ducked her head when she saw him looking.

The room smelled of blood and fear and desperation. "Save my son," Morgan said, his three words part plea, part command. He stepped aside so Eli could see the patient on the bed.

Son of a bitch. This was no kid. This boy—man—appeared to be close to twenty, was probably six feet tall and sported the traces of a mustache on his upper lip. Christ. He'd been duped. Fury settled in his chest, hot enough he was tempted to spin on his heels and leave but he'd taken an oath as a physician to save lives and no one, not even the son of a crime boss, deserved to die. Eli didn't deserve to die either and he was pretty sure if he left now that he'd be dead within hours.

He set his bag on the bed. "What happened to him?" he murmured, removing his coat and rolling up his sleeves.

"Damned foreigners. Making trouble. Always making trouble. Like I give a fuck they couldn't afford their rent. What did they expect, that I was going to let them stay out of the goodness of my heart? Not Max's fault that Irish bastard's wife fell down the stairs. She shouldn't have resisted."

Any sympathy he previously held for the young man disappeared. The problem was, it wasn't necessary for a physician to like their patient, or to approve of their actions. His oath required that he heal the sick and wounded.

"His name is Max?"

"Maxwell. But we call him Max." Morgan's voice was thick with concern.

Eli focused his attention to the still figure lying on the bed. The sound of the young man's harsh, erratic breathing warned him of what he would probably find but he needed to see for himself.

He laid a gentle hand on the young man's shoulder. "Max, I'm Doctor Knight. I'm here to help you," he said in the calm voice he used when dealing with patients. Running his gaze over the young man, he quickly assessed the young man's shallow, rapid breathing and abnormally pale sweaty face. Carefully pulling the bedcovers down, Eli bared the young man to the waist, exposing a bandage wrapped around his chest and soaked in bright red blood. He reached into his bag, found a pair of scissors, and snipped through the bandages until he could clearly see the wound.

A hole perforated the patient's chest a few inches above his heart. Blood bubbled up into the bullet hole, ebbing and flowing in time with his breathing. The bullet was in his lung.

He'd read of cases where victims survived gunshot wounds to the chest, but the survival rate went down significantly if the lung collapsed. The young man was alive so the lung was still inflated but was likely filling up with blood and might collapse at any time.

"I'm going to turn you over, Max, so I can see your back." Max didn't respond but Eli didn't expect him to. Cautiously inserting his hands under the young man, Eli tipped him till he could see his back. There was no exit wound which meant the bullet was probably still inside. Reaching into his medical bag again, he withdrew his precious stethoscope, a gift from his father upon his graduation from medical school, inserted the ear tips into his ears then laid the diaphragm on the young man's chest. The sound of wheezing and crackling reached his ears. Underneath the crackling, he could hear a rapid, irregular heartbeat.

Damn it. Cold trickled through Eli's veins. This was not good.

"You will save my son," Morgan said, and this time there was no plea in his voice, only command.

What to say? Eli didn't have much hope. What he had was fear. "I'll try. But...I can't make any promises... The bullet...I believe it's in his lung. It has to come out, but...if the lung collapses..." Eli's throat tightened, making it impossible to continue.

Morgan laid a hand on Eli's shoulder. The hand tightened and Eli winced. "My son is not going to die. You're going to save him. Because you won't like it you don't." He stared at Eli, and in his eyes Eli saw the bright light of a madman, a man who reputedly set fire to a warehouse, burning five men to death because the workers tried to unionize, a man who let nothing, and no one, stand in the way of getting what he wanted.

But in this case what Clevon Morgan wanted meant nothing. There was only so much Eli was able to do, the end results were up to God. But Eli didn't think Clevon Morgan would accept that. What did he get himself into? He should have listened to Adelaide. Too late now.

He began to unpack the things he'd need to remove the bullet. Placing everything into a small metal basin: tweezers, forceps, clamps and scissors, he then poured a chlorine solution over the tools to sterilize them. Lastly, he dropped in several sponges, a needle and thread then pulled out an ether mask and a bottle of ether. He set those on the nightstand.

"I need to wash my hands."

Morgan's eyes narrowed. "The other doctor didn't waste time with this garbage. You're wasting time."

Eli ground his teeth. What kind of idiot medical practitioner didn't wash their hands before touching a patient with an open wound? Everyone knew it was standard practice. "If you want him to have the best chance for survival, everything needs to be a clean."

Morgan hesitated, his gaze boring into Eli. Eli could see the doubt, the rage, burning inside the man but finally, with a wave of his hands, the crime boss directed Eli to a washstand in the corner where he was able to wash his hands with more solution then held them up to dry.

He returned to bed. "Someone needs to assist." He focused his gaze on the woman still in the room. "All I need is for you to hand me things if I ask. Can you do it?" She mumbled something under her breath that he took to mean yes. "Good, then go wash your hands with soap and water and come back. Don't touch anything once you've washed your hands. Stand next to me and wait until I tell you what to do."

From that point Eli focused entirely on the work at hand. Although the patient was unconscious, the last thing he needed was the young man waking in the middle of surgery and struggling so he placed an ether mask over his face and dripped ether onto it until he believed the patient was deep asleep. Occasionally, he asked for assistance.

"Sponge off the blood."

"Hand me the other forceps."

"Tweezers." He used them to pick bits of cloth from the wound.

"Sponge again. Make sure it's a fresh sponge."

The bullet was deep inside the young man's chest. Working carefully, Eli finally located it with a probe and extracted it with forceps "Chlorine solution." She handed him the bottle of solution and he poured some into the wound. "Hand me the threaded needle." He pointed at what he needed and used it to pull the wound closed. It was a matter of six quick stitches to close the hole after which he added a few drops of collodion sealant to form an airtight seal over the wound, and seal off the lungs, hopefully giving it time to heal. Lastly, he wrapped the wound tightly.

"He's going to live, right, Doctor?"

Eli shrugged and sent a silent prayer up to heaven. For everyone's sake, he hoped so.

But there was nothing to be done except wait for nature, or God, to decide Max's fate. He settled at the young man's bedside. Over the next few hours, he monitored the patient's breathing, his temperature, struggling to stay awake, barely taking the time to drink a cup of coffee and bolt down a pastry. A fever soon spiked and no matter Eli's efforts it didn't go down. The boy's breath grew shallower. His pulse grew slow and sluggish. Morgan hovered at his son's bedside, his face growing grimmer and grimmer, his eyes, when not on his son, on Eli.

"If he dies..." The remainder of Morgan's threat remained unsaid. Not meeting the man's eyes, Eli checked the boy's heart beat again, pretending that everything was fine but he knew it wasn't. Fear burned in his stomach as time passed and his patient deteriorated.

More hours passed. Dawn came, the day passed and evening fell. Eli's eyes grew gritty from the lack of sleep, his back ached, his hands trembled from exhaustion but he continued to swab the patient's body with alcohol, to pack ice next to him to bring down the fever and to check the wound periodically for infection. The young man's harsh, wheezing breath was the only sound in the room.

And then the breathing ceased.

Eli's heart stopped. God, save me. Save Max. Bring him back. He covered his mouth with his hand, trying to decide. He'd read of...in a medical journal...but could he...? With a chest wound...?

Nothing to do but take a chance. He placed his hands on the patient's chest and pressed down, counted to three, released then pressed down again. He'd read about the treatment but the article in the medical journal included no details of the procedure so he had no idea if he was doing it correctly.

He repeated the motions, again, again, praying, praying, but the patient's chest didn't rise on its own and the ruddy color of fever slowly bled from his face until it was the waxy ashy gray of death.

Eli closed his eyes. His hands stilled. He straightened. Unwrapping his stethoscope from around his neck, he placed the diaphragm on the patient's chest and listened. Nothing. No heartbeat. No signs of life. The boy was dead. For all his effort, all his prayers, the young man died. He stepped back. Shook his head.

Morgan slowly stood. "No. No. He's not dead." He looked up at Eli, his eyes red-rimmed, disbelieving. "Save him."

Eli shook his head again. There was no saving a dead man.

"No!" the man howled. "No!" Grabbing the water basin sitting next to the bed that Eli had used to hold cold water, he hurled it against the wall, shattering it. "No!" The anguish in his voice sent shivers up Eli's spine.

Morgan fell to his knees beside his son's bed and spread his arms across the still form of his son. "Max. My son." Sobs broke the silence. "They killed you. Those fuckers. I'll make them pay, Max. I swear I'll make everyone pay. All of them, everyone who did this to you, will pay, if it's the last thing I do," he moaned.

Eli's blood turned to ice because he realized that eventually he was one of the people Morgan would seek revenge against and that if he didn't leave now, he would not be able to. Leaving his coat, his bag, all his surgical equipment where they lay, he slowly backed away from the two people hovering at the young man's bedside until he reached the door. He carefully twisted the knob, opened the door and slipped through. The door clicked shut behind him. He sprinted to the staircase then leaped down the stairs, two at a time.

The butler jerked awake from his spot by the front door. "Sir—"

"Mr. Morgan needs you. Go. Now," he ordered, pointing up the stairs. The butler blinked. Taking advantage of the man's confusion, Eli yanked the front door open and clattered down the front stairs to the sidewalk. He turned left and headed crosstown towards Third Avenue at a trot. The stethoscope flopped up and down against his chest. Yanking it from around his neck, he stuffed it into his pants pocket, fearing people would remember it and report to Morgan. With dusk settling in, the streets were darkening but people still strolled through the nearby park, wagons and carriages still rattled over the cobblestone.

He continued to the next avenue and thank the lord a streetcar arrived the second he reached the stop. Jumping aboard, he dropped his nickel into the slot with a trembling hand and shoved past several passengers until he was deep inside, hidden from casual view. The streetcar slowly made its way north. Eli grasped the strap over his head with a trembling hand. Nerves crawled up his spine, the sense that a bullet from an unknown assailant could strike him in the back at any moment making his heart race.

"Thirty-Fifth Street," the conductor called. Pushing his way to the exit, Eli jumped off, jogged across the street and continued another half block until he reached a narrow white townhouse. He bounded up the stairs and pounded on the front door.

"Dr. Knight," Flint, his sister's butler said, appearing startled when he opened the door.

"Where's my sister. I need her now." He shoved his way in and slammed the door behind him which caused Flint to gasp.

"Eli, what's going on?" Helen asked, coming down the stairway from the upper floors. "Where have you been for the last several days? Adelaide said you couldn't come for dinner but—"

"Not now, Helen. Never mind where I've been. I need money, as much money as you can give me."

She paled. "What? Why? What's going on?"

"I don't have time right now. I'll tell you the whole story later...at another time. Right now, I need to get out of the city."

Her husband opened his office door and stuck his head out. "What's wrong?"

"I need money, Ned. I have to leave the city right now."

"Why? What's happened?"

"Clevon Morgan."

Ned's eyes widened. "Damn. Come inside, quickly." Spinning, he went back into his office. Eli followed with Helen right behind. Within minutes, Ned opened the safe hidden in the wall and pulled out a slim bundle of cash. "A hundred and twenty dollars. I'm sorry, but this is all I have on hand. I wish it was more." He handed it to Eli who tucked it inside his shirt. "I can have my carriage ready in ten minutes. Let me take you to the waterfront. From there I can take you across the river to Hoboken in the *Florence*." His small sailing craft named after their daughter, Eli's niece. "You can catch a train at the station in Hoboken."

"No, it's too risky. He probably already has men searching for me. I'm sure he'll have men stationed at the ferry depots and the nearby piers so I'm going uptown to Harlem. He won't think to search there right away. I'll find someone there to take me across."

"How will you get to Harlem?" Ned asked.

Eli shook his head. A million thoughts swirled crazily through his brain, making it impossible to think clearly. "I don't know. Walk. Catch a cab. I don't know. I'll find a way."

"I'll take—"

"No! You can't be seen with me. If anyone asks, I wasn't here."

"Eli, how will we contact you? How will we know if you're all right?" his sister asked, her face pale with anxiety.

"I don't know. I don't know where I'm going exactly. I'll contact you when I can."

"Oh, Eli." A tear dribbled down her cheek. "Please be safe."

"I'm sorry. I'm so sorry. But thank you. Thank you both. Remember, you haven't seen me. I'll...I'll get in touch. I'll send a telegram. Uh, from Ulysses." He gave a passing thought to having someone warn the poor Irish immigrants Morgan mentioned but realized it was futile. He didn't have a name or even an address.

He didn't wait for her to answer. Instead, he gave Helen a brief hug then left Ned's office, walked through the house to the back door leading into the alleyway and headed uptown.

Chapter One

April 27, 1891—Texas
"Buck, I need you to go on out to the pasture behind the stables and shoo in a couple of those calves into the corral so we can start the castrating. Jud, you can help me with the castrating."

Jud's eyes widened and a hand flew over to cover his pants fly. "Aww, shucks, Miss Tillie," he said. "Do I have to? Can't you get Buck to help with castrating instead of me and I'll shoo in the calves instead? You know I hate castrating." He shuddered.

Tillie Buchanan gave the ranch hand a flat look. Men and their gonads. You'd think those darned dangly things between their legs were pure gold the way they acted. "No. Buck has two broken fingers and can't do that kind of work right now and the rest of the crew are all out in the north pasture rounding up strays to brand so there's no one else to help except you. We're already behind schedule so unless you want me to kick your lazy ass off Buchanan Hollow, you'll help me."

The cowboy shook his head back and forth then up and down then shook it back and forth again.

Punching her fists on her hips, she glared at the cowboy. "And don't you be shaking your head no at me. Git."

Jud got.

She sighed. Lazy ass bum. Some men weren't worth a hoot when it came to hard work. If it weren't for the fact that most women weren't strong enough to do the job, she'd fire half the men working for her and hire women. They knew what hard work was.

It wasn't that she didn't like men; she did. She liked them rather a lot, actually she found them fascinating with their deep voices and the way they strutted around like they owned the world. Which, when you thought about it, they more or less did. Didn't mean she wanted one in her life right now, not when she needed to retain control of the ranch.

Maybe she'd get married someday. If she ever met the right man. She thought of the book lying open on her bed. *Ivanhoe*. Maybe if she met a man like that.

"Hey, Miss Tillie," Buck yelled. "We're coming in. Open the gate."

Buck waved his arms and hazed a small group of calves towards the corral while she rushed to open the wooden barrier and hold it open. After allowing two calves to enter, she swung it shut then grabbed the castration pliers.

"Jud, come on in here and help." After a few moans and groans and a lot of foot dragging, Jud climbed the fence, helped her tip the calf over onto its side and held it down while she snipped off its testicles.

The calf bawled loudly and Buck let out a mewl of distress.

"Geezwax, Jud," she said. "Stop being such a baby."

"I can't help it, Miss Tillie. It purely makes me sick to see the poor thing's manhood whacked off like that."

For crying out loud. After pouring some alcohol on the small cut, they let the calf up and it scurried away, no worse for the experience. Jud grabbed the next calf and they repeated the process. More calves were shooed in. The sun beat down on them, sweat rolled between Tillie's breasts and dripped off the tip of her nose, her back ached and her hands cramped from holding the castration pliers, but by midafternoon they'd managed to castrate eleven calves. She called it quits and Jud wobbled off to the bunkhouse, probably to throw up.

She cleaned off the equipment and put it away for the next batch they'd need to do in a week or so then washed her hands and swiped them dry on her dungarees.

"Hey, Miss Tillie."

She spun around. "Hey Joey, what's up?" she asked, delighted to see the old fellow who taught her almost everything there was to know about ranching. "You doing okay? Working hard?"

The old man grinned a toothless grin at her. He was eighty if he was a day, small and wiry and weather beaten as an old barn but he refused to settle back into a comfortable old age even though Tillie promised she'd continue to pay him for the rest of his life.

His response to the offer was the sooner he stopped working the sooner he died so what was the point which explained why he still worked on Buchanan Hollow, doing what he could even though what he could do wasn't much.

"I'm good. Ma joints hurt but what are you gonna do, huh? So, yer pappy wants you up to the house," he said then hawked a huge glob of saliva onto the ground.

She flinched. Ugh. Okay, so it was irrational that she could spend all day cutting off cows' testicles and not turn a hair but someone spitting made her nauseous. She might spend her day wearing pants but she was still a lady and a lady needed standards, and not spitting was one of hers.

"Know what he wants?" she asked, a curl of dread running up her spine. The last time her Pops called her in like this, it was because he'd drained their bank account dry. Which was when, and why, she took over the bank accounts in addition to managing the ranch.

"Nope, just he needs to talk to you."

Talk. That's what her Pops liked to do. Talk. He was big on talking. What he was short on was working.

With a sigh, she made her way to the house, a long, low ranch house painted white with a wooden porch that spanned the length of the building. Back in the day, her great granddad built what was a four-room cabin but he prospered and added on, then her grandfather added a few more rooms. Finally, her father, with his grandiose dreams, added on a bunch more and now the house was sixteen rooms that included eight bedrooms, two offices, a sunroom and a ballroom, for cripes sake. A ballroom. Like Tillie ever wanted to hold a ball. It did make a good place to store her books though. She did purely love to read, so she owned a lot of books.

She climbed the stairs, walked inside then strode back to her father's office. "You wanted me, Pops?" she said, anxiety burning in her chest like a canker sore.

Her father grinned at her, exposing large white teeth underneath his pure white handlebar mustache. She didn't grin back, simply ran her gaze over his tall, skinny body and shook her head. He was up to something. The man was a weasel. On second thought, not a weasel. That was an insult to weasels and she happened to like weasels and their cute little faces.

No, her Pops was a coyote. The Navajo believed the coyote was a trickster, a troublemaker, and that was her Pops, a man with more lies and tricks up his sleeve than a flim-flam man. Trying to keep up with his constant schemes was a full-time job.

"Tillie, my girl. I want you to meet someone." He waved at a dark figure standing near the back window, his face in shadow. The man stepped forward.

Her heart leaped. By the good Lord Harry, the man was a god. Tall, lean, and broad shouldered—which was great and all, but that didn't matter all that much since Texas laid claim to a lot of men with that description. What made this man so godlike was all the stuff above his shoulders. His hair was dark, not black but close to, with a slight curl at the ends which right now was a little longer than it should be. He possessed a straight, narrow nose, a perfect nose, like the one she'd seen in pictures of that statue of David. Now she thought about it, he might have modeled for the statue. Sharp blades for cheekbones. Square jaw. Wide mouth, full lower lip, mobile....

Kissable...

His eyes met hers and her heart leaped again. He sported the bluest eyes she'd ever seen in her life. Texas sky blue. She wanted to fall into those eyes and fly up to heaven.

Whoa, Nelly. There wasn't going to be any flying up to heaven nor kissing either. Not if she could help it. Kissing was for fools and those floofy girls in town who thought of nothing other than catching a husband.

"Tillie, this is Eli Knowles. I heard you need more help so I hired him."

She swung her gaze over to glare at her father, anger surging hotly through her veins. "You what?"

He stuck out his narrow chest, his face flushed with irritation. "You heard me. I hired him."

"Pops, you can't go hiring men without my say so."

"I can and I did."

She didn't lose her temper but it was a close-run thing. She loved her Pops but the man didn't know his ass from a hole in the ground. Up until she took the reins nine years ago when she was sixteen, the place was bleeding money but that didn't stop him from constantly meddling even now.

"What do you know about him? Where is he from? What are his skills?" She studied the man, taking note of the expensive trousers and fine white linen white shirt covered by a cheap, ill-fitting coat. Which was strange. Expensive or not, all this clothes appeared to have been slept in for the last week. Her gaze dropped to his hands. Pale with well-kept fingernails. And not a callus to be seen. Fah. Useless, like her cousin Orson, the last city slicker to visit Buchanan Hollow. She still experienced nightmares about the week he visited when she turned thirteen. The last thing she needed was another Orson in her life.

"Can you even ride?" she asked, eyeing the man's expensive shoes and soft hands.

The man's jaw tightened. "I've ridden since the age of three."

She snorted. "One of those pancake saddles where you pop up and down like a darned jackrabbit?"

He didn't say anything.

She glowered at her father. "Get rid of him. He obviously isn't used to hard work and he probably doesn't have enough sense to spit downwind. I've got no use for him."

"Now wait a cotton-pickin' minute, young lady," her father sputtered, his face getting redder than ever. "This is my ranch and what I say goes."

"You may own it but I do all the work." This was an old argument, one she was determined to win, because, in the long run, the ranch would be hers, and she believed in the maxim it was important to start out like you mean to go on.

"You listen here, Matilda Rae!" Pops shouted then stopped. His eyes widened, then he took a deep breath, took a step backwards and collapsed into the cowhide covered chair in front of his desk, his hand clutching at this chest.

"Pops!" She rushed forward, falling to her knees in front of him. "Pops, what's the matter? Are you okay?" Her stomach spasmed over at the thought her father might be ill.

The other man, that Eli Knowles fellow, knelt down next to her. "Let me look," he murmured, and took hold of her father's wrist.

She thrust an elbow into the fellow's side. "Stop that. What are you doing? Leave him alone."

He ignored her, instead he pressed his fingers over the inside of her father's wrist and counted under his breath.

She whacked the man on the arm. "Stop!"

He flicked her a hard look from the corner of his eye. "I'm trying to help. I...um...have a little medical training so..."

She sat back on her heels. "How much medical training?"

The air seemed to go out of him. He sighed. "Enough. I...uh, worked in a hospital back home."

She returned her attention to her father who was still breathing hard. "Pops?"

"Let him look, Tillie," her father whispered hoarsely.

"His heartbeat is a little fast. Is there somewhere he can lie down?"

She pointed to a settee in the corner. "Lay him there."

Rising to his feet, Knowles scooped her Pops up like he didn't weigh an ounce and carried him over to the settee where he laid him down. Kneeling next to her father, he unbuttoned the top buttons of her father's shirt and pulled the edges aside, baring his chest, and laid his ear down to listen.

"What? What's wrong? Can you tell? Is he going to be all right?"

Eli stared down at the floor for a minute, trying to gather his thoughts. What should he tell the girl? What *could* he tell the girl? Possibly Buchanan suffered from angina pectoris but without a sphygmomanometer to take his blood pressure, and without a stethoscope to listen to the man's heart, he couldn't tell for certain. He still possessed his stethoscope, the only medical equipment he still possessed because it was draped around his neck when he fled, but now it was hidden inside his knapsack and he dare not admit it.

Because letting this girl—who already seemed to hate him—know that he owned the instrument would be like admitting he was a doctor. Being exposed as a doctor would be dangerous. Even doing what he'd done so far might give away his identity.

He rubbed a hand over his mouth. The problem was, he *was* a doctor, and he'd taken an oath. Behind him, the man's daughter paced around the room, throwing him a distrustful glance every time she passed by.

He put his ear to the man's chest again. The heartbeat was slow and steady and strong. He picked up the man's wrist again, checking his pulse. It seemed fine now. His color was good, he was breathing fine, his pulse was normal and he didn't seem to be in pain.

Eli leveled a narrow-eyed stare at the rancher. Buchanan looked back at him, his eyes wide with innocence, a smile on his face like the cat that ate the canary. Then he wiggled an eyebrow. And winked.

Okay, what was going on? Rising to his feet, Eli said, "Um, Miss Buchanan. I, uh, would like to examine your father a little more. I may need to... Maybe you should leave the room."

"What?" she yelled. "No, I'm not leaving him with you. I don't know you from an organ grinder's monkey. I'm going to get Dr. Peterson." She swung around to leave.

"Tillie, no. No need," Buchanan said, his voice now sounding perfectly healthy, and sat up. "I'll be fine. Just need a minute to rest. I'm sure it's only a touch of heartburn but Knowles here can check me out to be sure."

Eli winced at hearing himself referred to as Knowles. It grated to have to hide who he was but there was no way of knowing whether Morgan sent people searching for him. It was possible, even this far away, that people might recognize his name, which had often been in the newspapers due to his prominence in New York City society. Using his real name would be foolish.

"Check you out! Are you batty? You need a real doctor."

Buchanan's face reddened. "He is a real doctor. He's even got a ste—!"

"Mr. Buchanan—" Eli blurted, but anything more he wanted to say got cut off when Buchanan kicked him in the shin.

"Never mind, young fellow. No need to explain," the rancher said.

Eli clamped his mouth shut. There was every need to explain but apparently he wasn't going to get a chance to do it.

"It's why I hired him on. It'll be good to have someone around on a regular basis who has a little medicinal expertise."

"I only worked at a hospital. I'm not a—" Eli interjected, trying to save the situation but they both ignored him.

"But Pops. He says he's not a doctor," Tillie said, scowling at Eli.

"He knows where my heart is. That's good enough for me. Now git so's he can take a looksie at what's going on with me."

"Fine." She slapped her hat back on her head and slowly walked to the door, peering back over her shoulder and glaring daggers at Eli. The door slammed.

He glared at the rancher. "All right, Buchanan, what's going on? You're no sicker than I am. And I'm not a doctor." It burned his mouth to be forced to deny what he was.

The man curled his mouth up into a rueful smile. "Well, you said you worked in a hospital back in New York so that's good enough for me."

"And what if you'd been really ill? If you were really having a seizure of some sort?"

"Ahh, I just have a touch of heartburn. Had it before, I'm sure I'll have it again."

Eli snorted.

The rancher gave Eli a look of disgust. "The least you could do, man, is play along with me since I'm giving you a job."

"Doesn't sound to me like if I'm getting a job regardless. Your daughter doesn't want me."

"Well, if you weren't such a dumb bunny, you'd have played along about being a doctor so my daughter would have been convinced I need you, that you'd be real handy to have here on the ranch. Left me in a bind, you being so dumb and all."

He couldn't believe what he heard. The man was a maniac. Especially the part about pretending to be a doctor...even though he really was a doctor. "Why do you even care? What does it matter if she won't hire me? If she turns me off, I'll simply have to find work somewhere else." Although finding work elsewhere wasn't a certainty. Since arriving in Texas three days ago, he'd tried a number of places without any luck, making the possibility he'd run out of the money Ned gave him a reality. After bribing someone to take him across the Hudson River, and putting a little aside for food, he was left with only enough money to pay for a third-class train ticket as far as Texas. Heck, even the coat he wore and the knapsack he carried he'd stolen from a poor drunk sleeping on a bench in the train station.

"Listen here, young fella. My daughter does a damned good job running this place but until I die, it's still my ranch and sometimes I get tired of her telling me what's what. Once in a while I like to have a say-so in things and if I want to hire you, I'm going to hire you."

So this entire scene was nothing more than a turf war between Buchanan and his daughter which left Eli in the uncomfortable position of being resented and possibly fired for any number of minor infractions at a later date. But beggars can't be choosers.

"Now, check me out, like I said, and tell her I got a touch of heartburn."

He narrowed his eyes at the man.

Buchanan sighed. "Okay. Fine. All you have to do is say I'm fine. I'll take it from there. But mind, until I say different, you're hired. Got it."

After another stare-down, Eli jerked a short nod.

"Now tell my daughter to c'mon back in."

Eli pulled open the door and allowed Buchanan's daughter back inside. "It appears to be a touch of heartburn. I'm sure he's going to be fine," he told her through tightly clenched teeth.

Her gaze went to her father. "You sure, Pops? I can send for Doc Peterson to check you out. He could be here in a couple hours."

"Naw, I'm fine, like he said."

"Pops," she said, her face wrinkled with worry. "I really think—"

"No! I said no and I mean no." He got to his feet and strode over to his desk where he picked up a spur that sat on top and idly spun the rowel. "I'm fine. Fit as a fiddle."

The girl rolled her eyes. "Fine, now about this fellow—" she said.

"He's staying," Buchanan barked. "Don't argue with me or who knows, I may have another attack of heartburn."

Her lips tightened. She and her father stared at each other for a full minute while Eli mentally shook his head. Evidently this wasn't the first time they'd have a similar disagreement. This was not going to end well.

After another full minute of visual sparring she spun on the heel of her high-heeled cowboy boot and strode out the door. "Follow me."

Jim Bob collapsed back into his chair with a grunt. Well, that didn't go quite the way he planned it. Of course, a lot of his plans didn't work out the way he planned them which is why once his daughter got old enough to run the ranch, he let her do it. Her plans tended to work out a lot better than his plans.

Still, Knowles was here, and it seemed like he was here to stay which was a good thing since he liked the fellow the minute he'd met him during a poker game with a bunch of other ranch owners in town. Jim Bob had no idea if Buchanan Hollow needed more hands or not but the young man needed a job so why not hire him on? He owned Buchanan Hollow, even though he didn't run it, and if he wanted to hire someone, he would.

Although, it wasn't like he really had a choice, what with losing the poker game the two of them partook of, but that was a piece of information he didn't intend on mentioning. Tillie didn't approve of his gambling. She didn't approve of his drinking either. Or his smoking. She also didn't much like Norma Lee, his lady friend over to Pearsall. Or Flora in town. Or Maria Cruz...

Honestly, all his little hobbies got Tillie's bloomers in a twist but over the years he'd done lots of exasperating things and somehow she always eventually forgot about them—okay, she never really forgot about them, it was more she forgave him—and life went on like usual. He counted on her forgiving him this time too.

Fact was a lot of times he wasn't a good man. Regardless, he was what he was, and at the age of sixty-two he was too old to change now. Not that he wanted to. He liked his life. He liked to gamble even though he almost always lost. Which was why when he saw Knowles trying to pawn that stethoscope with the thing on the end he called a diaphragm made out of pure silver all beautifully carved like an ancient Medieval goblet he purely wanted it. He tried to buy it but instead, when the man offered to play a round of poker for it against a job at Buchanan Hollow, well, he would've been a fool not to take him up on it.

Turned out, Jim Bob was the fool because Knowles was one fine poker player so even though Jim Bob hid an ace up his sleeve and marked a few cards, Knowles left the table with the stethoscope and the job both.

But having to justify his decision by faking a heart attack made him think. What if the seizure was real? What if something happened and he died? It would leave his daughter, a beautiful young woman, running this ranch on her own.

It wasn't that he didn't have confidence in her abilities. He did. She'd proved herself more than capable over and over. But she was still a woman. A lot of men refused to do business with a woman, which was one of the few times he needed to step in and assist even though he never knew what the heck the girl was dickering about with those men since he didn't have a head for business…or numbers…or negotiating. According to his daughter, about the only thing his head was good for was a place to keep his hat but Jim Bob realized that, as a man, if he said to those reluctant fellas they needed to negotiate with Tillie, they did. Which might not happen if he wasn't around.

And there was the problem of the girl living by herself surrounded by a bunch of raunchy, vulgar cowboys. Nobody set a foot out of line now because they understood damned well Jim Bob would shoot their randy asses full of buckshot if they did but once he was gone, then what?

His daughter needed a man. Now, all he needed was a plan.

Chapter Two

"All right, City Slicker," the girl said, the words *City Slicker* stressed and not in a friendly fashion. "C'mon. I'll show you around."

If Eli realized Buchanan planned to hand him over to this ornery girl, he might have thought twice about winning that last hand. Although, what choice did he have? He was down to his last twelve dollars which, at the cost of food and shelter, wouldn't last long. So, like it or not, he was stuck with it. With an inward sigh, he followed the girl out of the house.

She walked across the yard, her strides long and confident. "Knowles, huh? Eli Knowles?"

"Yes," he said, hating even the sound of his alias. Would he ever get used to lying?

She snorted. He trailed after her into a long, low wooden building. Inside were ten narrow beds made of wood with thin mattresses atop them, none of them occupied at the moment. Small wooden trunks sat at the foot of each bed.

"You can bunk here," she said, pointing at one of the cots. He swallowed his protest at the thought of his aching back. "The trunk at the end of the bed is yours. Go on and put your things away."

Opening the lid, he tossed in the cloth bag that held all his belongings, which weren't much. A straight-edge razor, soap brush and soap mug, two clean pairs of underdrawers, one pair of woolen trousers and one clean shirt. Spending even the few dollars it took to buy those items was painful but the idea of not having clean underclothes or being unable to shave was even more painful. The fact that he owned so little depressed the hell out of him.

Together they trooped outside. She pointed at the stables. "Barn."

He shot her a look. It was obvious she thought him a useless city dunce. Little did she realize he'd spent those five years in the Dakotas while in the army taking care of his own horse, often living in a tent, or worse. "Oh," he said, drawing the word out, injecting just enough sarcasm to snag her attention. "I see. A barn."

She narrowed her eyes at him. Her eyes were unusual, light blue with a dark ring around the irises. "We keep our breeding stock in the barn," she muttered in a low voice. "But right now, all the horses except my mare Daisy, are out into the field out yonder right now." She pointed to the field in back of the barn. "Daisy's in foal and due to deliver any time so I keep her close. Other than the breeding stock Pops's horse is the only other horse kept in the barn. Not that he spends all that much time in the saddle."

"Tool shed, training corral, feed barn, holding pen," she continued, pointing each out in quick succession, an expression on her face that said *How come I'm the one that got stuck explaining things to the dummy?*

He forced a smile onto his face. He got the sense the less he said, the longer his employment would last, and until he could figure out his next move, he needed this employment to last as long as possible.

She surveyed him up and down. "Those clothes all you got?"

"I have another shirt and a pair of pants." Sadly.

"Well, they're not gonna last long out here doing the kind of work we do. Soon as you get paid, I suggest you buy some dungarees."

Sure, right after he bought more underclothes. He'd gotten tired of continually washing the same two pairs of drawers.

"C'mon, let's put you to work." Leading him to the tool shed, she opened the door, and pulled out a bucket, a bristle brush, and a tub of soft soap. She led him to a water trough that stood in front of the barn.

She handed him the brush. "Algae," she said, pointing at the trough. "Dump out the water, scrub it down real good then refill it using the pump. Make sure you don't leave any soap in the trough." She jerked her chin at the pump. "When you're done, come find me. I've got more work for you to do."

I bet you do.

He took the brush and watched her walk away, his gaze on her backside. It was a very nice backside; indeed, it was a rather superior backside. A man didn't get to see too many female backsides these days, not with the current women's dress styles. Full skirts hid a lot of flaws; wide hips, fat buttocks, flabby flesh, but Miss Buchanan's tight denim pants revealed everything, a trim waist and a nicely rounded ass he wouldn't mind fondling.

But intriguing as her backside was, her front was even more interesting. Like her eyes, her face was unusual. It was not a traditionally pretty face, soft and pink and vaguely unformed. No, her face consisted of angles, a small, pointed chin, wide cheekbones, straight eyebrows several shades darker than her hair, a short narrow nose. It should have been a severe face. But it wasn't. Because of the freckles. Her nose, and those wide cheekbones were covered in freckles. They were erotic, enticing...lickable. If only...

He sighed and put aside his forlorn hopes. He was fairly certain that any attempt to taste one of those freckles would see him face down inside this watering trough, not cleaning it.

Grabbing the side of the trough, he tipped it over and let the water run across the ground. Brush in hand, he knelt and began to scrub. It didn't take long before his back ached, his hands cramped, and his arm trembled with exhaustion. It wasn't the only time he'd done work like this but the last time was four years ago while he was in the army, and he'd grown soft.

But damned if he'd let that prickly little miss get the best of him.

He scrubbed and while he did, she walked back and forth across the wide space between the house and the barn a number of times. It seemed almost like she was seeking an excuse to watch him. Every once in a while, he'd glance up and catch her eyeing him from wherever she was. Every time, she'd quickly look away, pretending that she wasn't watching him the whole time. It made him redouble his efforts simply to prove he could.

Backbreaking as the work was, it did have one benefit; it took his mind off his worries.

The sun beat down. And the lady boss walked past the water trough again, still pretending she wasn't watching him. What was she seeing? He grinned to himself. Maybe he should give her something to really look at.

Straightening from his kneeling position by the trough, he stretched, first putting his hands to his back, and twisting back and forth. From the corner of his eye, he saw her pause on her journey, then resume walking. Next he raised both hands over his head, thrust out his chest and took a deep breath.

Again, she paused for a split second before resuming her walk to the barn. She disappeared inside. He sensed her peeking through the crack in the door. So he kept stretching. Lift one arm up. Stretch. Lift the other. Stretch. Bend over, touch his toes, straighten and reach for the sky. Eyes on the barn door. Stretch again.

The big wooden door swung opened and she strode out, heading for the shed on the other side of the corral.

Even from where he stood, he saw the side-eye she gave him. Time for the next step. Unbuttoning it, he slid it off and tossed it aside.

"Eek!" she yelped and stumbled over nothing.

Hah. He covered his laughter with a cough and a hand over his mouth. Now to up the ante. He stretched one more time, drawing out the motion for a long minute before leisurely kneeling again to resume washing out the trough.

With one last glare, she stomped into the house and loudly slammed the door shut.

The sun continued to beat down on him and he felt his skin start to fry. New York City didn't have this kind of heat, or sun. His city skin wasn't used to it. Maybe it wasn't such a good idea to take his shirt off. Reaching for it, he slipped it on again. Before he could button it, an enormous fly landed on his chest. And bit him. Good gravy. Even the flies were out to kill him. He swatted it away.

After more than an hour of cleaning, the trough appeared pristine enough to refill. He pulled himself to his feet, his knees cracking and every muscle in his body protesting. Going to the pump, he pressed the handle. Again. And again. And again, until the trough nearly overflowed with clear, sparkling water. Done, he sagged against the pump, almost comatose with exhaustion. He'd viewed that poorly stuffed mattress on his new bunk with disdain, but at this point, falling into it and tumbling into unconsciousness might be a blessing.

Unfortunately, the trough cleaning wasn't the end of the torture Tillie Buchanan had in store for him. Per her order, he climbed the stairs leading up to the front door of the house and knocked. It opened immediately.

If he wasn't so exhausted, he'd laugh. Obviously she was watching him. "I'm done."

Shutting the door behind her, she strode across the porch, down the stairs and across the dirt yard. He watched for a second, not for the first time admiring the way her long blonde braid bounced on her back and the sway of her slim hips, and slowly followed. His legs protested the movement, his back complained and he sensed he had one hell of a sunburn. He hoped to hell the next chore wasn't outside.

She disappeared into the barn and he followed to find her waiting with a shovel and a rake in hand. She thrust them at him.

"Clean all the stalls. Manure goes out back. Use the wheelbarrow over by the door. Fresh hay for bedding. After that, refill their water buckets, give each horse a square of alfalfa—I hope you know the difference between alfalfa and bedding straw—"

"Yes."

"Good. Hay and alfalfa are in the loft." She pointed upwards. He sighed. Damn. It meant climbing up into the loft. He wasn't sure if his poor legs could handle it.

"Give each horse a scoop of oats. Oats are in the feed room by the door. When you get to Daisy, give her an extra helping of oats. She's my baby."

She walked out. Not even a good-bye. Hell and damnation, working for Tillie Buchanan was going to be so much fun.

At least he was indoors out of the sun, and at least the work was with horses. He enjoyed working with horses and always loved the horse he owned while serving in the army.

Grasping the wheelbarrow handles, he wheeled it over in front of a stall and pulled the door open to observe the horse inside, a beautiful chestnut mare, bright as a copper penny, with a white blaze and four white stockings. Stocky, with a massive chest, solid shoulders and a short neck, a prime example of a quarter horse. She also sported a significant bulge in her belly. She looked back at him with large dark eyes and snorted.

Reading the name carved into the wooden plaque affixed to the stall door, he confirmed it was Miss Buchanan's mare. "Hello, Daisy. Nice to meet you," he said, giving her a pat on her muscular neck. "Just going to clean things up a bit. Don't mind me. And don't kick or bite me, okay?"

The mare shook her head, which he took to mean she agreed. He went to work, shoveling the dirty bedding into the wheelbarrow. Once he was done, he wheeled it out back and dumped the soiled bedding into the existing pile. Returning inside, he repeated everything with the next stall, empty like all the others, moving on to the next and the next, until he'd cleaned out all ten stalls. Climbing up into the loft, he dropped down bales of straw and added the bedding to each stall.

Done with cleaning the stalls, he began refilling the water buckets from the pump out front and adding oats to the troughs. Blisters formed on his hands, sweat ran down his face, his back, under his arms and made his sunburn burn like fire. What was he thinking, taking his shirt off in the blazing sun? Ego, all ego. He sure hoped the lady enjoyed the show because he was paying for it now.

He stopped for a minute, leaning against the wall to catch his breath. It was growing late. He'd not eaten all day or taken a break. The horses still needed their cubes of alfalfa. Which was in the loft. With a sigh, he climbed the ladder again, barely making it up the last two rungs his legs shook so badly.

He needed to sit down and rest for a moment. The horses were all still out in the field so would have no idea that he didn't fill their manger right away. Surely sitting for two minutes wouldn't hurt. Only two minutes. That's all he needed. He collapsed onto a bale of hay, leaned back against a tall stack of bales and closed his eyes. Just for a minute.

The sun sat on the western horizon, an enormous orange ball surrounded by long streamers of orange and pink and yellow. Tillie pulled her watch from her dungaree pocket and checked the time. Seven-thirty. Hmm. The last time she'd seen that yahoo from back east was a little after three when she'd carefully poked her head inside the barn to make sure the idiot wasn't doing something stupid like putting alfalfa down for bedding and feeding the horses straw but, surprisingly, he seem to have the hang of things. Around five, she saw Joey bring all the horses grazing in the pasture back into the barn and put them up for the night. But that was over two hours ago and the city slicker should be done by now. So where was he?

She peered over her shoulder at the house. Inez, their housekeeper would have dinner waiting for her but she didn't want to get settled in until all her responsibilities were completed. Including the city slicker. Was he still working on the stalls? How could it take so long?

With a sigh, she strode into the large structure. The stall doors were all closed and she could hear the sound of the horses grinding up their oats. Hmm. Maybe he was inside one of enclosures although the wheelbarrow sat over by the back door in its usual place. Opening the door to the tack room, then the feed room, she checked inside.

Nothing. Huh.

"Hey, City Slicker?" she called. All was quiet. "Slick?" she said, louder this time. Still no response. Lordy, did the man call it quits and take off without her seeing? It was possible but highly unlikely since she'd pretty much kept her eye on the barn for the entire afternoon, not trusting that prissy city fellow any farther than she could throw him. Although probably it would be better if he did. Even thinking about him made her tingle in parts that shouldn't tingle.

She took a moment to stop at Daisy's stall and give her an apple before walking up the aisle again but still no city slicker in sight. Puzzled, she opened the door to each stall but all the horses were peacefully eating their supper with no dude in sight. What the hell?

She looked around before a thought struck. Setting her foot on the bottommost rung, she climbed the ladder to the loft.

"Sli—" She stopped. The man sat on a bale of hay, half-hidden in the gloom, sound asleep, head tilted back against another bale exposing his neck. And what a neck it was, strong and muscular with a prominent Adam's apple. She stared at him, her heart dancing a little two-step in her chest as she followed the line of his neck down a perfect angle to meet wide shoulders. Her gaze fell to his chest, rising and falling with each breath he took. Under his thin cotton shirt, she could see the outline of his pectoral muscles. Shoulders and chest all narrowed down to a trim waist and slim hips.

She banged a fist on her sternum to restart her heart while taking a deep cleansing breath, for all the good it did. Because she continued to eat him up with her eyes. Because the man was truly a sight that made her catch her breath. And that was before her gaze dropped to his lap to the buttoned flap closure of his trousers and noticed the bulge. Damn! She wondered if it was all him or...

Down, girl. You've got no business wondering anything about the hired help.

Which didn't stop her from taking a second look and a third.

That was when she saw his hands, propped on his knees, palms up. Blisters. Dad blast it. What was the man thinking, for goodness sake? There were several pairs of gloves inside the tack room. Didn't he see them?

Kneeling, she touched his hand, waiting a moment to see if he awakened. When he didn't, she uncurled one of his hands to better see the blisters. Hm, bad.

Blisters often were dangerous. She heard of a ranch hand who got a blister on his heel from new boots and died when it got infected. Letting Slick die would purely be a waste of a fine figure of a man and no one ever accused Tillie Buchanan of being wasteful. Rising, she went back down the ladder and walked to the house.

When she entered, her Pops sat on the bench by the front door, brows furrowed. He sighed. Loudly, because that's what Jim Bob Buchanan did. Everything he did must be bigger than life, his voice, his sighs, even his damned farts were bigger than life.

She rolled an inner eye. Rolling her eyes for real would earn her a lecture on what an undutiful daughter she was. Yeah, she was so undutiful she only worked eleven hours a day instead of thirteen.

"Is something the matter?" she asked, hating herself for asking because asking simply opened the door for a discussion on all kinds of things she didn't want to talk about.

He sighed again. "No." Pause. She waited. "I'm fine." Another pause. She dipped her chin, hoping this was the end of it. But, of course, it wasn't.

"A mite peaked, is all."

Her heart skipped a beat. "How peaked? Is it your heart, your stomach? What?"

"Oh, I'm sure it's nothing," he said in a die-away voice. "I'm sure I'll be fine."

"Pops, this is beginning to worry me. I should send for Doc Peterson."

"Oh, no, don't do that. I'm sure it's indigestion, like before." He gave her a smile.

She narrowed her eyes at him. She didn't trust that smile. It was too charming, too innocent, too...too...too Jim Bob Buchanan. "I think we should get the doc."

He bounced to his feet. "No need. I'm better already. Just a touch of dizziness, but it's passed. I'll be fine." He beamed another smile on her and strolled into his office.

Stubborn old goat. She loved her Pops but damn, the man was a trial. She hoped he wasn't really ill. Aggravating as he was, she'd hate to lose him.

Leaving the foyer, she walked back to the kitchen. "Inez, put my dinner in the oven to keep it warm. I'm going to be a while but you can go on home once you're done," she said to their housekeeper. Walking into her own office, she pulled out the bag of medical supplies she always kept on hand because accidents were common on the ranch and went back to the barn.

She climbed the ladder for the second time, knelt in front of her Pops' latest mistake, placed a hand on his knee and shook it. "Hey?"

His chest rose from the deep breath he took but he didn't awaken. She repeated her actions but all that happened was his chin drooped down onto his chest. With a shake of her head, she took out a bottle of iodine. The iodine might wake him since it would sting a little but if it did, she'd make some excuse for why she was helping, fix him up proper, and send him to bed. If he didn't awaken, she'd fix him up anyway and leave him to sleep in the loft.

Using the little glass wand, she spread the orange liquid across the popped blisters. He slept through it. She wrapped gauze around each hand. Done, she got to her feet and stared down at him. Still sleeping. Yep, exactly what she thought; the man was a citified pantywaist and didn't belong on a ranch. But she was stuck with him. For now.

Which didn't mean she couldn't torture him a bit more.

Because...maybe if she tortured him enough, he'd quit. Yeah, because if he did, she might be able get through the day without thinking about that magnificent chest she'd seen when he removed his shirt. And how about his shoulders? And his dark hair with that bit of curl on the ends. And his smile.

Shaking her head at her folly, she climbed down the ladder and stomped back into the house to eat, undress and get ready for bed. Like all days on a ranch, today was long, hot and exhausting so she figured she'd fall asleep the minute she fell into bed. But she didn't. The events of the day reeled through her mind, her worry about her Pops—was it really only heartburn, or was it something worse, something possibly fatal—but what her mind went to over and over was the memory of her new employee's chest.

Hmph. Why did she waste her time thinking about the man? She'd seen plenty of male chests. She's seen Buck who walked around shirtless any time it got hot—of course, he had a chicken chest, bony and pale. She'd also seen Joey's torso, leathery like an old saddle. And there was her Pops who tended to forget about clothes altogether, but blech, he was her father never mind the fact he possessed a pot belly that resembled a woman six months gone with child.

City Slicker's chest was a completely different thing, firm with a light coating of hair between the bulge of his pectoral muscles that led down to the waistband of his pants and what lay right beneath.

The thought made her hot all over.

After relighting the kerosine lamp on her bedside table, she picked up *Ivanhoe* and opened it to her marked page, but after rereading the same paragraph five times she realized it was a lost cause and returned it to her nightstand.

Her thoughts were fixated on that man, and his chest. And now she really couldn't sleep. She pushed the covers aside, rose and went to the window. Was he still in the loft, sound asleep, or did he wake up and go back to the bunkhouse for the rest of the night?

Did he sleep in his drawers? Or did he sleep in the nude. She shivered.

Something moved in the dark. She squinted. There, by the barn, a shadow near the door that blended into the wall until it moved away and walked further into the yard. Slick.

She gripped the windowsill. What was he doing? Where was he going?

He walked over to the horse trough he'd spent the day cleaning and stopped. Staring down at the water, he did something, she couldn't tell what. His shirt came off over his head.

Oh my! There was that chest again. It gleamed smooth and pale in the moonlight. Her breath caught in her throat. His hands moved again and he dropped his pants to the ground, toed off his shoes and stepped out of his trousers.

Son. Of. A. Texas tornado.

Like that statue of David she'd compared him to earlier today, he stood tall and straight and gosh darn it, perfect, in the moonlight. Long legs, slim torso, broad shoulders. Taut, muscular butt. Dadgum it, the man was perfection, and while she watched, all that perfection stepped over the edge of the water trough into the water and sat. He slid down and his head disappear from view.

What in the holy heck!

Racing to her closet, she grabbed her robe and drew it on over her nightgown. Lastly, she grabbed her Webley Bull Dog pocket pistol. Rushing out the front door, she marched over to the trough.

He lay face up, the only thing not covered by the water were his nose and closed eyes. Even his mouth was underwater. His white cotton drawers clung to his hips, and his thighs, with that other part of him that said he was a man clearly outlined.

She stared at the bulge, heat rampaging through her. Hoo boy. She wondered where her breath went because it wasn't in her body. Did the sight of him in all his glory strike her dead? She pinched her wrist. Nope, she was definitely alive, simply stunned senseless by his male wonderfulness. She'd seen plenty of male balls and male cocks on both cows and horses and she'd seen both species mate, so she knew the mechanics, but this was something different. This she'd never seen. She wondered...

Get a grip, girl! Pointing her gun at him, she kicked the side of the trough. And his eyes sprang open.

"If you pee in that water trough, you're fired," she roared.

He practically flew out of the trough to land, feet in a puddle, next to it, his eyes wide with horror. He looked down at himself, gasped, "Good gravy," and covered the front of his drawers with both hands.

"What are you doing out here in the middle of the night?" he demanded.

She shoved her gun into her robe pocket. "Me? I think the question is what are you doing? In my water trough? In the middle of the night?"

One hand left his nether regions and rose to his chest where it frittered around uselessly, like it sought a perch to land on but unable find one. "Sunburn," he muttered.

Even in the dimness of the night, she could see his chest, neck and shoulders were bright red. Idiot. That's what he got for showing off his chest and baring skin previously unexposed to the Texas sun. He'd learn though.

She rolled her eyes. "Wait here," she said and walked back into the house, retrieved her medical supplies for the second time that day and returned. Digging through the bag, she pulled out a crock and handed it to him. "Here. Use this until the redness goes away."

Having said her piece, she spun around and retreated into the house again. No way would she help him spread that lotion on his body. It was all she could do not to leap across the expanse of the trough into his arms and attack his lips. Oh, boy. She was in so much trouble. She needed to get rid of the man, and soon, before she forgot that she had no use for men at this time. And maybe never.

Chapter Three

Eli burned. First because of the sunburn. Even two days after his stupidity, his skin still shrieked with pain from his clothing rubbing him raw every time he moved. Then there were the blisters. His palms, his fingers, his thumb, all were covered with blisters. Hell, even his blisters had blisters.

But those burns were purely physical. It was the mental burning that threatened to kill him each time he thought about that blasted termagant Tillie Buchanan. Unhappily for him, the Tillie burn came in two forms. The first was the embarrassment of standing in front of her in his wet, nearly transparent drawers, trying like hell to cover himself, knowing she'd seen it all.

But the other burn was the worst one, the one where he couldn't forget the image of her upturned nose dotted with tiny freckles he'd been able to see even in the moonlight, and the sardonic tilt of her luscious mouth after she'd yelled, "If you pee in that water trough, you're fired." Thinking about it gave him a cock-stand he couldn't control. Damn, he liked a woman with a smart mouth. Even so, the entire episode was embarrassing and damned awkward.

He shifted uncomfortably on the wooden box he'd set up inside the barn, out of the sun. Bending over his task again, he scooped a dab of saddle soap onto a cloth and stroked it over the bridle he was almost finished cleaning. Lucky him, there were only ten more bridles to clean after this one. After which he got to start on the saddles.

He gave the saddle sitting on the nearby sawhorse a jaundiced look. It was no simple English saddle, or even a basic cavalry saddle. The damned thing was the size of Rhode Island, and with all the carvings, and flaps and long strings hanging from it, it might take him the rest of the morning to do more than one or two.

Several flies buzzed around his face, seeking a juicy spot to feast off. Damned things. He swatted at them. At least he wasn't working in the hot sun. He wasn't basking in a trough of cool water either—his preference—although the cream Tillie handed him the other night helped some.

Sighing, he went back to work. Cleaning tack was boring, tedious work which gave him entirely too much time to think. About his loneliness. And his worry for his sister and her family. And the nagging fear that Morgan would arrive anytime.

What he refused to think about was what Tillie's hair looked like when out of its braid. And there he went, thinking about her again. Stop. No thinking about the termagant.

He forced his thoughts away from the woman. Would he ever be able to go back to New York? Was Morgan searching for Eli? Knowing Morgan, he'd have a dozen men searching. He told himself he was safe because Morgan's men would be searching for a doctor named Eli Knight, not someone named Eli Knowles on a ranch in Nowheresville, Texas. But the fear was still there.

If only there was a way to learn for sure but he didn't dare send a letter or a telegram. A good investigator could track down the source and lead Morgan straight to Eli.

Anger burned his stomach at the situation, the injustice of it all. He missed his life. He missed his patients but mostly he missed his sister and her family. Helen practically raised him so they were closer than most siblings.

But instead of being in New York with the people he loved, he was stuck in godforsaken Texas. The worry and frustration clouded his mind and compressed his chest to the point he felt almost unable to breathe. The not-knowing was a heavy weight.

At least his father was in Boston, teaching at Boston University until this fall, hopefully out of Morgan's reach.

He glanced up when Tillie walked into the barn. Her hips swayed and her breasts pushed out the front of her blue plaid shirt when she strode by. Fifteen minutes later, she exited leading a saddled horse. Opening the gate to the corral, she led the horse inside and mounted. With a nudge of her heels, she moved the horse into a trot, then a canter then back to a walk. Sitting still in the saddle, she neck-reined the horse to the right, then a quick rein to the left. Right, left, right left, making the animal pick up its feet like a dancer. The only part of her that moved was her braid bouncing against her back and her breasts shifting under her top.

His mouth went dry. Heat shot through his body, making him sweat. She was magnificent. Like Aphrodite on horseback.

It might be there were a few compensations to being in Texas, after all.

Noon arrived and Tillie put the horse away in its stall and went inside the house, leaving Eli still with half a dozen saddles to clean and nothing exciting to look at. Losing sight of her was almost like losing a limb.

Joey Newton, the old man who was their cook, shuffled outside and handed Eli a cheese sandwich and a jug of water. Still five saddles to clean. Dinner rolled around and so did the rest of Buchanan's hands, riding into the yard where they unsaddled, curried their horses down and turned them loose in the far pasture. The dinner gong rang. He rose stiffly from his perch, put the supplies away and started towards the bunkhouse. His back hurt, his arms hurt and he was exhausted. Bedtime couldn't come soon enough.

"Goin' in to dinner?" a young fellow said with a sly grin when Eli passed the group clustered next to the front door of the bunkhouse.

He nodded wearily in response.

"Well, have a good trip," Jinx Horton, the ranch's foreman, said and stuck his foot out as Eli walked through the door. He tripped and went sprawling.

He lay on the floor for a minute while the men walked around him. Finally, he hauled himself back to his feet. A few chuckles made him study the men clustered around the dining table, their heads turned away to avoid his eyes but their shoulders shook with laughter.

It wasn't the first time one of the hands tripped him. And probably wouldn't be the last. "Thanks for the assist," he said, forcing down his desire to beat the crap out of someone. "Out of curiosity, who's supposed to clean the floors?" He knew that was Jud's job. "They look like crap."

The man named Buck snickered. Jud glared at Eli, clearly angry at Eli's criticism but Eli ignored him, his attention focused on Jinx, the bullyboy of the bunch. Like a lot of bullies, he was bigger than most other men, using his six-foot height and two hundred plus pounds of muscle to intimidate. Small blue eyes smirked back at Eli from under thick black eyebrows that were incongruent with the thinning hair atop the bully's head.

Eli clenched his hands into fists at his side. If it weren't for the fact that fighting would cost him this job, which he needed, he would slam a fist into Jinx's jaw. Instead, he walked past the foreman, careful to avoid the foreman's outstretched leg, and sat on the end of one of the benches at the long kitchen table. Within minutes, Joey exited the kitchen and set a bowl of some unidentifiable mess of something buried in brown gravy down on the table. Everyone, including Eli, helped themselves.

"So, the stew's good tonight, huh?" Jinx asked, his question directed at Eli.

In spite of how it looked, it was pretty tasty. The meat was a little tough but hungry as he was, he wasn't going to be picky. He said nothing since remaining mute seemed the best way to avoid conflict.

"Yep, rattlesnake is a real delicacy around here."

Hell's bells. He stared at the brown mess in his bowl. The rattlesnake threatened to come back up again but he reminded himself food was food, whether on the hoof, or slithering on the ground. Gritting his teeth, he gave Jinx a flat stare, swallowed the bite in his mouth, stabbed another chunk and ate it simply to prove he could. In spite of his determination, his stomach still roiled.

Joey edged up next to him. Bending, he whispered. "That there's beef."

Sighing in relief, Eli ate the remainder of his meal. Afterwards, he fell into his cot, still wearing his clothing.

"Get up!" someone yelled in his ear. He sprang out of bed, still half asleep and stood, wobbly, next to his cot.

Tillie. Of course it was Tillie. Who else would barge into a bunkhouse where half a dozen men currently walked around in their drawers, scratching their armpits, farting loudly, and using the foulest language he'd ever heard? Who else would use it as an opportunity to torture him?

"Get dressed," she said. "Then come find me by the tool shed and I'll tell you what I need done today. Ten minutes."

He checked his hands. All the puffiness around his blisters was gone and the blisters were well on the way to healing which meant her task could be anything. She waited for him to agree but when he simply stood and stared at her, still disoriented from his rude awakening, she marched away. He watched her exit out the door. Damn. That butt.

Nine minutes later, he joined her by the shed. Hah, take that Tillie Buchanan. Nine minutes. Of course, he wasn't able to shave nor eat or, now he thought about it, he wasn't even able to take a piss but hey, he was here, and in only nine minutes.

She indicated he should follow her with a jerk of her head. Okay. Fine. She was the boss. Sigh. Walking behind the barn, she stopped to point out a plant she called locoweed. Apparently locoweed did bad things to animals. Men too. After slapping a pair of leather gloves in his hands, she set him to work with instructions to pull up every weed near the house, the barn and the small pasture. "When you're done, take everything out back to the fire pit so we can burn it."

Lucky him. Now he'd have blisters on his knees to match the ones on his hands.

"Any questions?"

He rapped his heels together and snapped his hand to his forehead in a salute. "No, ma'am. No questions, ma'am."

She sucked in a breath and her mouth puckered up. He could tell she wanted to say something but what could she say? He'd been polite. Hadn't he?

They stared at each other, Eli keeping his face impassive, Tillie visibly grinding her teeth. Finally, she spun around and stomped off.

He grinned and returned to work.

Lunch came around and he received another dried cheese sandwich. He ate it while kneeling in the garden behind the house because it was too much effort to get to his feet. He'd only have to get down again in about five minutes and he didn't think he could manage it.

Dinner time came and the dinner gong sounded. He tried to get up so he could go into the bunkhouse and get something to eat but he couldn't make his legs hoist him to his feet and he was unable to straighten his back. The whole thing didn't seem worth the effort simply to get handed a bowl of slop. He rolled over onto his side and fell asleep.

"Oh for pity sakes," a voice said in his ear, right after a foot poked him in his ass.

He opened his eyes. Tillie. Of course it was Tillie. It was always Tillie. Tillie the tyrant. Tillie the torturer, dressed once again in her nightclothes, probably to torment him.

"What in the Sam Hill are you doing?" she barked.

"Dying," he mumbled, and closed his eyes, not that closing his eyes made any difference since the night was dark as pitch. What time was it? How long had he slept?

She threw a bucket of cold water over him.

"Shit!" He leaped to his feet, sputtering and gasping. Somehow, when assaulted by cold water, his back and knees found the strength. "What the hell! For Christ's sake. What the hell?"

"You're not allowed to die, not on my payroll. I'd have to call the doc out. There would be paperwork and I don't like paperwork, especially when the subject of the paperwork is dead. Complete waste of my time. Then we'd have to dig a hole to plant you in and it's too damned hot to dig. Heck, we'd probably have to call out the reverend. You seem like that kind of fellow who'd want a reverend."

Water dripped off his nose. He could really learn to hate this woman.

She thrust a sandwich wrapped in a napkin at him. He took it without thinking. Shoulders stiff, she tramped away, her backside doing that thing that made him stand at attention. He waited until she entered the house before unwrapping the sandwich, expecting another hunk of cheese stuck between two slices of dry bread. He blinked when he saw thick slabs of fresh sourdough bread holding two inches of thin sliced roast beef, a slice of tomato and some lettuce, all slathered with mustard. Manna from heaven. Okay. He could really learn to lo...okay, not love. But he might learn to like her. A little. Well, maybe they could settle for tolerate.

He bit into it, chewing slowly while he walked to the bunkhouse where he stripped out of his wet clothes and fell onto the cot, stark naked and exhausted for the fourth day in a row.

Chapter Four

Tillie slipped on her Levis, buttoned them up and buckled her belt then walked to the window to peer out at the lemon-yellow sun rising on the Eastern horizon. Where was he? Was he still snoozing in his bed? When she'd walked away last night, he was sopping wet so that raised the question; did he go to bed wet or did he take everything off. What if he did, and what if she woke him up again? Would she get to see that chest again, in addition to other parts? Not that she had any use for those other parts. Remember, she was the lady who snipped those parts off yearling horses and young calves.

Still...

She smiled to herself. She wouldn't wake him up this morning but it didn't mean she wouldn't continue to make him earn every penny she would pay him because of her father's idiot mistake...even though it was really her father who deserved to be punished.

She shook her head in disgust. How much torture would the man endure before he left? If he was anything like her sissy cousin Orson, probably not much more, at least that's what she hoped. Because if he was gone, maybe all her heart palpitations and jangling nerves would go away.

Buttoning a clean red shirt up over her camisole, she tucked it into her pants and tugged on her boots. Lastly, she tucked her handy revolver into the holster on her belt and left her bedroom, making a detour to the dining room to grab something to eat. When she entered, her father was at his usual place at the table. He started at seeing her, hesitated, then his face twisted and he groaned.

"Pops! What's the matter?" She rushed to his side.

He waved her away. "Nothing's the matter, little girl. Stop fussing. I'm fine."

"But you groaned."

"It's nothing. Just got things on my mind."

"But Pops. How do you know? It could be your heart. You're no spring chicken, after all."

His face flamed the color of a tomato. "You watch your mouth, young lady. I'm not old and don't you be saying I am. I'm fine. You get your breakfast and go on about your business, you hear?"

Men. Grabbing a tortilla, she loaded it up with eggs and tomatoes and hot sauce and left to walk over to the bunkhouse, finishing it up in three bites. When she arrived, Slick was seated on the tree stump by the door, his shoulders sagging, faint circles under his eyes and his mouth set in a tight line. Under the red of his sunburn, he appeared a little pale.

She stopped in front of him.

He gave her a tight smile. "Good morning, Miss Buchanan, ma'am. What's on the schedule for today? Cleaning the outhouse? Slaughtering some chickens. Or give a goat a bath, because I hear you've got goats so surely you'd want them bathed?" A sardonic gleam shone in his eyes.

Yes, they owned goats. Angora goats produced wool that was made into mohair, a fine wool in great demand. They also produced goat's milk which she sold. Both goat products were very profitable and both were her idea, one she was proud of.

She shook her head. "Nope, no goat baths today."

He sighed. "Please don't tell me you have pigs stashed somewhere that I have to clean the sties."

She couldn't stop the chuckle. The man possessed a sense of humor. Maybe he deserved a break. Possibly she'd regret it later but right now, she felt a little sorry for him, and she couldn't think of anything to torture him with anyway.

"I need to ride out to check on Buck and Kermit, see how they're doing with the branding. You can come with me." She headed towards the barn then looked over her shoulder when he didn't follow.

"Well, git a move on. If you want to come, you need to get a horse and saddle up."

He stared back at her, skepticism on his face. She lifted her hands in a 'what?' gesture. After another second, he rose to his feet and followed her into the barn. She pointed at one of the stalls. "That's Chessy. Take him. He's easy to manage and has a nice steady trot. His saddle and bridle are in the tack room with his name on the saddle rack."

She saddled up Buster, the gelding she rode now Daisy was with foal, any minute expecting the man to holler for help with his saddle being the dude that he was. However, when she exited the stall leading her horse, he was waiting in the aisle with Chessy all saddled and bridled.

Not that she didn't trust him...but she didn't trust him. He was a citified dude. What the heck did he know about horses and western saddles? Flipping up the fender, she tugged on the cinch. Huh. Just right. She checked the cinch connector—the knot could be complicated—but he'd done that perfectly too.

Hmmm. Maybe there was more to this city slicker than met the eye. Or maybe not. She'd have to keep her eye on the man.

Leading their horses outside, they mounted up. He mounted easily, and with the motions of a man who had done it many times before. More to wonder about.

They rode alongside Duggan's Creek, with her acutely aware the entire time of her newest ranch hand's presence next to her. When they reached the pasture, Buck and Kermit were already hard at work separating the calves from their mothers, leading the bawling youngsters to the fire where they laid the BH brand on their hindquarters and notched their ears with a sharp knife.

"Everything going okay?" From the look of things, it appeared they might be close to done which meant time to get them riding the fences.

Tucking his knife away, Buck walked over to meet Tillie, hat in hand. "Nearly done, Boss Lady. Maybe four more calves."

She gave him a thumbs up in approval. "If you get finished with that before noon, ride the fence line." Buck worked for Buchanan Hollow for the last ten years so he always took pliers and a little extra wire with him to fix any breaks in the fence. He also was smart enough to take food in case he couldn't make it back for meals.

Reining her horse around, she headed towards the north pasture where they kept their extra saddle stock. Knowles followed.

"Why do they cut the calves' ears?" he asked after they'd ridden for a few minutes. "Seems painful for them."

She studied him, wondering if he was trying to butter her up, but he seemed sincere. "Not much feeling in their ears. We brand too, but brands can be changed with a simple running iron and the only way to tell it's been changed is to kill and skin the cow, which would be stupid, so we also notch their ears. Doesn't completely eliminate the risk of rustling but it helps."

He went silent. Which was too bad. She kind of enjoyed showing off a little, showing off her knowledge. They rode a little further till they reached the fence line then stopped to view the dozen quarter horses grazing in the field.

"So how big is your ranch?"

Hmm. Was he sizing things up? Again, he seemed sincerely interested but you could never tell about people. For all she knew, the man could be some kind of con artist wanting to take advantage of their wealth. She'd give him the benefit of the doubt for now, but she wasn't going to let her guard down, not yet.

"We own about two thousand acres. Some of it's not good for raising cattle. It's one of the reasons I brought in the goats. They can survive on almost anything, although we make sure they get plenty of hay and other roughage to keep them healthy. Healthy goats make good milk and healthy hair. Come on, I'll show you." She reined Buster around and headed towards their pen.

"Sounds like Buchanan Hollow is a profitable enterprise. Other than cattle and goats, what else does the ranch do?" He idly swiped at a fly buzzing around his head.

"Mostly cattle, but I also breed and train quarter horses and sell them as cutting horses." Why all the questions? Nothing about him made sense. He wore a cheap coat but his trousers fit him like a glove, obviously tailored to his body, and his shoes appeared to be made of the finest leather with the thin soles only a rich man's shoes would have rather than the thick soled boots a working man would require. And his speech was that of an educated man. What was he doing working for peanuts on a ranch far from civilization?

Maybe she should ask a few questions of her own. "So, where are you from?"

They rode for a few minutes before he answered. "Philadelphia."

He didn't look at her. He was lying. Why? "Philadelphia's nice." She had a distant cousin there and enjoyed a week visiting with her when she was fifteen. "Where in Philly?"

He cleared his throat and she prepared herself for another lie. "Rittenhouse Square."

It was a nice neighborhood, suitable for someone like Slick. Who was still lying. "What did you do there?"

Another long silence followed. She wished he'd hurry and answer since they'd soon be to their destination and her opportunity to ask him questions would be lost. "So?"

"Like I said before. I...uh...worked in the medical field."

"As a doctor?"

He laughed under his breath. "Hardly. Your father likes to make things up. I worked in a hospital. As an orderly."

Bullshit. But she could tell he wasn't going to elaborate. "How did you end up in Texas? And not working in a hospital?"

He inhaled a long slow breath. "I...needed a change of scenery," he said then clamped his lips shut.

There was more to the story. "Your family must miss you, being so far away."

He shrugged. Which told her nothing. "No family?"

"A sister," he said tersely. "And my father."

She wanted to learn more but wasn't sure what else to ask without it seeming like she was interrogating him.

Since the goats were kept close to the house, they soon arrived at the large, fenced enclosure. Inside, two dozen adult goats rambled around while a number of kids frolicked across the field, bleating and kicking up their heels while they played with each other.

"See how long their coat is? We shear them every spring and the fur is shipped to a buyer in Houston. In addition, Joey milks them every morning and one of the hands takes the milk into town to one of the grocers."

"Very smart," he said to her but his gaze never left the baby goats at play.

"One more stop." She headed towards the windmill a mile or so away her grandfather erected to pump the water that filled several ponds for the stock to drink from. Someone needed to check on it regularly to make sure it was still pumping and that the pipes weren't leaking or gotten clogged.

After getting down from her horse and checking everything was working fine, she remounted. "Okay, let's head home."

They rode the rest of the way in silence although there were still a million things she wanted to ask. "Why—" she started but at that moment, the barn came into view and Slick kicked his horse forward into a canter, leaving her behind, her question unanswered.

Damn it. She still had questions. But she wasn't done investigating.

She unsaddled and brushed down her mount and turned him out into the pasture then pulled Rowdy, the bay she was training for sale out of his stall, saddled and bridled him. Taking him into the corral, she worked with him to accept a rope being flung over his head. The entire time, she could sense Slick's eyes on her, who was back to work cleaning tack, watching her every move until she burned.

Noon arrived, time for lunch and she was never so glad to have an excuse to flee into the house.

"Tillie? Is that you, darlin'?" her father called from his office, his voice sounding strangely wobbly and hollow.

She made a sharp left and walked into his study. "Do you need me? Is something wrong?"

He waved a hand, brushing away her concerns.

"Pops?"

"Sit down, Matilda. I need to talk with you."

Matilda? She was getting Matilda'd? She only got Matilda'd when she was in serious trouble. A cold sweat broke out on her forehead. "What? What's wrong?"

He sighed. "I'm fine... Well, mostly fine...but...I've been thinking...ever since the other day..."

Her heart thumped in her chest. "The other day?"

"Oh, you know, the day when I had that little..." He patted his bony chest and gave her the pathetic look of a beaten cur. "Incident."

"You mean the heartburn."

A shaky smile appeared. "Yes, that day. It got me thinking."

"Thinking?" Drat. She hated it when her father thought. Jim Bob Buchanan thinking somehow always ended up with Tillie having to clean up his messes.

"Yeah, you know. About me. And you. And the ranch. Yeah, the ranch." He sighed.

Damn it, Pops, get to the point! Cold sweat now enveloped her entire body and she felt slightly nauseous. "What!"

A tear formed in the corner of his eye and terror washed through her. "Pops!"

"I've been thinking, Matilda, what with all this heartburn I've been having—not that I'm sickening or anything but it does make a fella think, you know—what's going to happen when I'm not here anymore."

Shock rattled through her. They'd discussed that situation several times already. He'd shown her his will. They'd made plans, so it was all settled. Wasn't it? "I'll run the ranch the same way I do now," she growled.

He shook his head slowly and tsked. "Tillie, those twinges got me thinking, that and the fact we got a new man and we don't know for a fact who he is. Not that I don't like him and trust him, you hear, but it got me thinking about you here all alone with a bunch of men..."

He stopped, put his hand to his chest and gazed at her sadly. "I know what I said before. But it won't do, Matilda. You need a man to—"

She leaped to her feet. "What! A man! You think I need a man? I don't think so. I haven't needed a man in the last ten years and I won't in the next ten years either."

"Hush!" he yipped, sounding a lot healthier than moments before. He pointed a finger at the chair she'd just vacated. "Sit!"

She sat, alarmed. Pops never ordered her around. He knew better than to try to tell her what to do, mostly because what he wanted her to do was usually wrong and she didn't listen anyway. But this sounded serious.

"Young lady, you can't run this ranch by yourself when I'm gone. You can't live here alone with a bunch of randy cowhands who might not respect you, never mind that without my influence, you'll have trouble getting contracts to sell our beef."

"I got that contract for the goats," she protested. "And I've closed deals with cattle buyers for the last ten years."

"With the goats, you were dealing with that fool Latimer who'd do business with the devil if it meant he could make a profit. But the beef buyers are another story. They bought our beef on my say so but without me backing you up, most of them won't do business with a woman and you know it."

She clenched her hands in her lap, her insides burning with fury and resentment. Damn this being a woman. It wasn't like she wanted to be a man, she didn't, but she hated that life didn't treat women fairly. In the eyes of wealthy men, women were simply ornaments. Poor men considered women nothing more than a drudge and breeding stock. All men, rich or poor, thought women too dim to exist without a man to tell them what to do. "So what are you saying?"

He smiled. "You need to get married."

The bottom dropped out of her world. No! Getting married meant some man would have every right to take over her ranch, and her life and her body. She always planned on getting married at some point, but not now. Not for years. And she hadn't met a single man that she'd consider marrying. "No. I won't."

Jim Bob's face hardened. "I already asked Warren Trinkenschuh out this morning and changed my will. Unless you're married, you don't get the ranch."

"No!" The words burst from her, her sense of betrayal like a hot poker in her heart.

"No use arguing, girl," her father said. "It's done. You've got one month to find a husband."

She shook her head, her brain still reeling at what her father sentenced her to. "No. You can't do that to me."

"Daughter, it's for the best. You need a man."

"I don't need a man. I don't want a man!" She did want one, someday, but she sure as hell wasn't telling her Pops that.

"I don't give a hoot what you want. It's what you need. One month."

"Well, what if I plumb refuse?"

That foxy look he got whenever he came up with a new scheme crossed his face. "Well, then your cousin Orson will get a nice inheritance."

Her mouth fell open. "You'd leave Buchanan Crossing to that weak-chinned, sissified, lisping little girly-man?"

"You're darned tootin' I would, unless you get married."

"But Pops. He wouldn't even know what to do with the ranch. The man's about as useful as a pimple on the backside of a Billy goat."

One corner of her father's mouth twitched and for a moment she thought she had him but no. "You have one month."

Shock and agony tore through her. Everything she loved, everything she'd ever dreamed of, was about to be taken away, all because of something she couldn't help, and couldn't change, her femininity. "I can't possibly find a husband in one month. If there was a husband worth having around here, I'd have already found him but there's not. It's slim pickings and you know it."

"Aw, come on, Tillie, that isn't so."

She glared at him. "Who then? Phil Perkins over to River Ranch, fifty years old with his pot belly? Curtis Lockner, who owns the general store, the man who can't count to twenty even with his boots off so he can use his toes? Or how about your lawyer fellow, Warren Trinkenschuh, the man who's probably taken every woman in the county to bed, even the married ones?"

Her father cast his eyes towards the ceiling, refusing to meet her gaze. "Well...."

"Or I suppose I could marry Felix, that fellow who hangs out at Danner's bar all the time, drunk as a skunk."

He cleared his throat. "Okay, I admit those fellas you mentioned aren't suitable."

"Of course they're not suitable. And there isn't a man within a fifty-mile radius who is suitable." Those floofy girls in town already snapped up the good ones. The leftover men weren't worth having.

"Well, if not men like them, what in tarnation do you want?" he said, his voice impatient.

Her mind went to the book lying on her bed, page one-fifty-one marked where she left off last night. That's what she wanted. She wanted someone like Ivanhoe. Someone gallant, someone brave, someone who adored her enough to go to the ends of the world for her. Not that she would tell her father so. He'd laugh her out of the room. His opinion of love and romance started and ended with the buttons on his pants fly.

"I don't know," she muttered, lying through her teeth rather than admitting she was a romantic at heart. "I only know there's no one around here that'll do."

Her father tapped his fingers on his desk. His face brightened. Oh no. Damn. The man thought of another new idea.

"I've got it! You could advertise for a husband."

What! "Advertise? Are you loco? You want me to advertise for a husband like I'm some kind of for-sale item at Lockner's General Store?"

He huffed. "No, not like that. Like the fellows that use to advertise for mail order brides back in the day...only in reverse..."

Anger and confusion and resentment swirled through her. Advertise? What kind of man would answer an ad like that? Some low life searching for an easy mark, that's who, certainly not a knight in shining armor. Not that she wanted an actual knight in shining armor but she'd always hoped the man she eventually married would have a few knightly qualities, like Saint George with his quest to kill the dragon.

A quest. That's what she wanted. She wanted a man who would go on a quest for her. If some strange man was going to step into her shoes and take over her life, why shouldn't he have to work for it? Why shouldn't he have to do something knightly to earn the right to her ranch, her life...her body.

Ideas start to buzz through her head. She stared at her father, those ideas spinning faster and faster until something gelled. "Okay. I'll do it."

A huge smile blossomed on his face. *Go ahead, Pops, smile all you want. Now.* "That's more like it, little girl. Now you're—"

"On one condition."

The smile disappeared to be replaced by a well-justified suspicious expression. The problem with their relationship was her father knew her as well as she knew him. He was perfectly aware she could think rings around him. But for some reason, he always forgot which was why she was able to pull the wool over his eyes over and over again.

Still, this time he didn't seem completely convinced. "What's the condition?"

"There's going to be a lot of men who might want to win my hand so I want to make sure whoever wins it is worthy of being my husband. I deserve someone smart, someone brave, someone who'll work to win me. The only way to test their mettle is to set a task for the competitors to complete. A quest, if you will, like the knights of old."

He groaned. "Geezy peezy, Tillie. This isn't Merry Old England and any man who competes for your hand isn't going to be Sir Galahad or whatever."

She narrowed her eyes because no matter what she said, he was sure to argue against it, which is why she drew a line in the sand. "That's my condition. Otherwise I won't agree to this."

"And what happens if no one wins this here quest thing?" he asked, his eyes flashing with doubt like he believed she was up to something. Well, she was but she certainly wasn't about to tell him.

"Then all bets are off and things return to normal."

"Normal? What normal?"

"Yes, normal. You know what I mean. I go back to managing the ranch, by myself—"

"Now wait just a cotton-picking minute—"

"That doesn't mean I don't intend to get married. I'll simply get married on my own schedule, like say, a year from now when I find someone I really want to marry."

"Geez Louise." Her father screwed up his face with displeasure.

"Either take it or leave it or…"

"Or what?" he growled.

"Or I'll marry the first saddle tramp that passes through. Pops, I at least deserve the chance to find someone I want to marry. You need to be fair."

He rolled his eyes to the ceiling and sighed. "Lordy. Fine. Do the quest. Find someone who deserves you. You have one month."

"Six months. I have to organize this and advertise it and give the men time to get here, time to complete the task after which I'll need to arrange a marriage. It can't be done in a month."

"Two months."

"No. Four months. That's only fair, right?"

He narrowed his eyes at her. "Nope, two months, no more. My last offer. I want this settled sooner rather than later."

"Fine." She stuck her hand out.

Her father took her hand. "Deal," he said but his face didn't say deal, it said, *maybe I should rethink this*. He rubbed his temple. "So this quest thing. What exactly is a quest? Is it like a competition? Like a rodeo, or something like that?"

"Sure. Like a rodeo." Laughter bubbled inside. "Or something like that," she said under her breath and smiled. Because she knew something he didn't.

Chapter Five

Several days passed. Although none of the jobs Little Miss Tyrant set him to doing caused a sunburn or blisters, she seemed to take a special delight in finding unpleasant tasks for him to do while pointing out every mistake he made, then howling with laughter at his failure, like when he was sent to feed the goats and one of them sent him flying when he turned his back.

He guessed, being low man on the totem pole, it made sense he would be the one to do the scut work which included cleaning the outhouses and kitchen duty with Joey. The other men were seasoned hands who knew what they were doing whereas he didn't have a clue about cattle. But he meant to learn, and damned fast, because he didn't want to get assigned to latrine duty on a permanent basis. So he set to work asking questions and watching how things were done.

But even so, when he thought about his life in New York City, he got damned depressed. Dishpan hands versus hands that used to do the most delicate surgeries. Lord help him.

He still worried that Morgan was a threat, and fretted he'd put his family in New York in danger. Most nights he stayed awake for hours worrying and wondering if he should simply return home and find out. But the fear that returning would only expose his family to risk was always in the back of his mind. He was like a duck without a pond.

One day his tormentor declared she was going into town and might be gone overnight. It didn't mean he got off easy from work.

"While I'm gone, I want you to paint the shed out back."

Damn. He held back his sigh, instead saying, "Yes, ma'am. Whatever you say, ma'am," and tipped his hand against his forehead in a salute.

A glare sparked in her eyes. She realized he was goading her but as usual, she couldn't protest when his words were so polite. "We need another outhouse. Shovel's in the tack room. Make sure the hole's at least four feet deep. There's wood on the other side of the shed that you can use to build the structure. I assume you can handle that, right?" One corner of her mouth tipped up in a challenge.

He nodded, not letting the fact he was grinding his teeth get in the way of his smile. "I'm sure I can handle it just fine, Miss Buchanan, ma'am. Anything else, Miss Buchanan. I'm here to serve, Miss Buchanan."

With a glare, she stomped away, neither one of them having won. Which didn't stop him from admiring the sway of her slim hips.

Unfortunately, the instant she disappeared over the horizon, the hands decided it was only right to really *'break in'* the new fella. It started the first morning. Tugging his shirt off the bedpost, he thrust his arm into the sleeve. Or tried to. Because he couldn't get his fist past the cuff. Thinking the sleeve got tangled, he took it off, shook it out and tried again but still couldn't get his hand through.

He took it off again. In the background, he could hear snickers while he examined the garment. Damn it, the cuff was sewn shut. Furious, he looked up. Five pairs of eyes quickly swiveled away, avoiding his. Son of a bitch. He pulled his only other shirt from his wooden trunk, checked it thoroughly to make sure it didn't also have something wrong with it, and slipped it on.

He went about his day. That evening, exhausted, he walked back to the bunk house, interested in only two things, a hearty meal and sleep. He walked to the dining table. Stopped. Because six butts were parked on the benches, spread out so there was no way he could find a place to sit. He cleared his throat. Nobody responded. Nobody moved. "Excuse me?"

"Oooo," Jinx said. "You need something?"

"A place to sit?"

Jinx ran his gaze over the other men sitting at the table. "What do you think, fellas? Think there's room at the table for the city slicker?"

Like their heads were all attached to the same string, they shook their heads in unison.

Damn it—

From behind, Joey nudged Eli and held out a plate filled with mashed potatoes, fried chicken and white gravy.

"Thanks," he said with a sigh and took it outside where he sat on the old tree stump by the door to eat his meal and worry about his situation. When he was done, he set his plate in the big tub of soapy water in the kitchen before heading for his bed. After stripping off his pants—leaving his shirt on for fear what might happen to it—he threw the covers back and climbed into—

Soaking wet sheets. "Fuck!"

Laughter broke out. He slept in the barn that night.

He woke up the next morning, determined not to let them get to him. Starting a fight would only get him fired, and he couldn't afford to get fired. Maybe after he got his first—hopefully last—paycheck, he could use it to escape this cursed place and travel on further west, but for now, he was stuck.

After helping Joey dish scrambled eggs and sausage onto serving plates, he sat at the end of the bench and waited for Joey to bring out the food.

Kermit approached. "Hey, Knowles. Sorry about last night. We was only having a little fun, you know, and it got out of hand. Let bygones be bygones, right? Here, to make up for it," he said, and set a cup of coffee in front of Eli.

"Sure. Bygones." he said and took a sip. "Jesus Christ," he yelped and spit it out. The coffee was loaded with salt instead of sugar. He rushed into the kitchen and took a long drink of water from the pump while the men laughed.

Okay, he got it. He was the new man. He wasn't from around here, and he wasn't a cowhand, so he got that he would be subject to a little harassment, but Christ, this was getting a little old. He couldn't wait until Tillie got back so their pranks would go back to tripping him when he walked by.

Unfortunately, it didn't end there. The next morning, when he stepped into his trousers, something pricked the inside of his thigh. He scratched it. It got worse. He scratched again, and now it was really hurting. What the—? Unbuttoning his pants, he slid them down.

There were little white furry things caught in the hairs of his leg. He pulled one off and held it up to inspect it. Damn it to hell. A thistle, and now he itched like a son of a gun. The men burst into laughter. Wearing only his drawers, Eli marched out of the bunkhouse, across the stable yard out into the back pasture where there was a stream. He stripped out of his drawers and stepped into the water.

"Nice maypole you got there, Knowles," Buck called.

"With family jewels like that, it ain't surprising you ain't got no family."

"Hey, Slick, is that all the bigger they grow things back East?"

"With nuts like that, better watch out for all the squirrels."

He laughed along with them in hopes he'd soon be one of them and they'd give it up but all it resulted in was more laughter. Marching back to the bunkhouse, he chucked the pants into the trash bin.

His best trousers. There would be no way to ever get all those thistles out. He was down to one cheap pair of pants and two shirts, one of which he'd have to pick out all the stitches at the cuff before he could wear it again.

"So what are you gonna do...?" Joey said that evening as he passed by Eli sitting on the wooden stump outside the bunkhouse too exhausted, and too depressed to go inside for dinner.

He peered at the oldster from between narrowed eyelids. "About what?"

"About them idjits giving you the business. You gonna just take it?"

He sighed. "What else can I do?"

The man stared down at Eli, his face twisted like he were puzzled. But he wasn't. So what was going on?

"I dunno. Up to you, I guess. Wouldn't want to make them mad at you or anything, right?" the old man said. "Not when they're having so much fun, and all, right?"

Eli mulled that over. "You mean, it's a game? Of one-upmanship?"

"Yup. Give them back better'n what they gave you and you'll be one of the men." With a smack of his lips, the oldster walked off.

"Huh." Give them back more than what they did to him. That was a tall order. There were six of them and one of him. Did he need to pay each one of them back separately? That might take a while. No, the trick was going to be to find some way to pay them back as a group. Or better yet, find a way to get back at Jinx since he was the ringleader.

Another day passed, dinnertime arrived, and the men gathered for their evening meal, talking about this, that and the other thing that he only half listened to because he was having trouble staying alert after a night only half sleeping for fear what they were going to do to him next.

"Did you see that spider Joey kilt in the kitchen this morning. Damned thing was as big as a dinner plate. Must of set some kind of record," Buck said.

Jinx's fork stopped halfway to his mouth. "A spider? How big? Where was it?"

Buck grinned. "What's the matter, Jinx, you afraid of spiders?"

The other man glared. "I ain't afraid of nothing, least of all an itty-bitty spider," he said but the look in his eyes made a lie of his assertion. His eyes were filled with terror.

"Sure you ain't. Remember when that big ol' spider come down from the rafters and landed on your shoulder?" Palm arched and fingers spread to imitate a spider, Buck laid his hand on the other man's shoulder and finger-walked his way up to Jinx's neck. "You screamed like a girl!"

"Cut that out," Jinx yelled and knocked Buck's hand away.

Buck laughed and wiggled his fingers, spider-like, at Jinx. "Woooo, watch out, Jinxy boy, the spider's gonna get you."

Instead of answering, Jinx picked his plate up, filled with beef covered in gravy, and pitched it at Buck. It hit Buck in the chest, splattering food on the man beside him. With a howl, that man jumped up and chucked his plate at Jinx but missed and hit Zeke, another man, instead. Zeke scooped up a handful of mash potatoes and flung them at Jinx after which it became a free-for-all, with beef and gravy and mashed potatoes flying through the air.

Ducking, Eli picked up his plate and hurried outside to finish his meal. Settling on the log by the front door, he ate his meal slowly, mulling over what he'd witnessed, thinking.

Well, now... Setting his plate aside, he walked out to the barn, picked up a bucket and a shovel, and walked out to the far fence where he checked under rocks and dug a few holes. Half an hour later he was done with his task. After covering the bucket with a board he found in the barn, he left the bucket up in the loft, climbed down the ladder and returned to the bunkhouse for the night.

⁂

She took her time riding into San Antonio, using the ride to work out the kinks in her plan. The more kink-free her plan was, the less likely her father could derail it, and history said he'd try. He never did much that took exerting himself, including mental exertion, but when confronted with opposition, he dug his heels in like a mule.

First stop, the hotel where she changed into something a little more respectable, still pants, but her good pants and a frilly blouse, after which she ambled to her next stop.

"Tillie. Hi, how are you?" the lady at the front desk greeted her when she entered. "What can I get for you today? Dickens? Hawthorne. We got in a new book by that Mark Twain fellow called *Huckleberry Finn* all about Tom Sawyer's friend. Very entertaining. I think you'd love it."

"Hi, Eva, thanks but not now. Maybe later. I'd take something else by Scott, if you've got anything."

Eva grinned. "Somehow I knew you'd say that. You and your knights in shining armor obsession."

Tillie grimaced. Yes, it was a bit of an obsession but not one she would apologize for. A girl needed to have something to dream about.

"I think I have just the thing. *Waverly*. It's set during the Jacobite Rebellion of 1745 about a British officer whose regiment is sent to the Scottish Highlands to defeat the Scots but he falls in love with a Scottish girl. Have you heard of it?"

"No, I haven't. It sounds perfect, Eva. Do you still have a copy for me to borrow?"

Rising, the librarian walked to a back room and came back carrying a thick tome. "I thought you might say that so I've been saving it for you," she said and handed it to Tillie. "Anything else?"

"Yeah," she said and went on to explain what she needed.

The librarian screwed up her mouth in thought but walked her to the back of the library where she pointed out several bookshelves that held the required material. After Eva went back to her front desk, Tillie pulled out the books she wanted and, placing them on a table nearby, she sat and began going through them. Each time she found a picture she wanted, she pulled out her knife and cut it from the book. She felt terrible cutting up a valuable book but justified it in her mind by promising herself she'd replace them. Once her task was complete, she carefully placed all her clippings into an art folio she'd brought for that purpose and walked to the front desk.

Eva sat back in her chair. "All done? Did you get what you needed?"

"Yes, but here's the thing. If anyone, especially my father, asks if you saw me, you didn't. You haven't seen me in weeks, right?"

"Why... I mean..." Eva started then stopped and grinned. "Oh, yes, of course. I haven't seen you since at least April," she said.

"Oh, and I may have done a little damage to a few books... Uh, tell how much to order new books and I'll pay you for them. I wrote down the names of the books."

Eva lifted a brow. Tillie sent back a sorry face.

"Go away, Tillie," the librarian said with a roll of her eyes. "So I can pretend I haven't seen you."

Hugging her portfolio close to her, she left, satisfied she was well on her way to thwarting her father.

Next stop was the stationary store where she bought what she needed. Going back to her hotel room, she spent an hour cutting and pasting, after which she went to a local photographer, a young fellow she was familiar with because she'd hired him to take picture of the quarter horses she put up for sale.

"You want what, Miss Tillie?" the photographer asked. He gazed up at her, his eyes worshipful.

She smiled back at him. It was obvious Sam had a bit of a crush on her, which she usually discouraged but a little flirting didn't hurt. "Like I said. I want a photograph of this."

"Gosh, Miss Tillie, it don't make no sense to me to want a picture of a picture. But it's your money, I guess."

She grinned. "Yes, it is. How long until you can be finished?"

"Couple of hours, say. Come back at lunchtime and I should have it ready."

"I need four copies," she said and handed him enough money to pay for his services.

"Four copies?" the young man said, his voice squeaking. "Oh, better make it one-thirty instead."

She held up four fingers. "Yep. And, by the way, if anyone asks if I've been here..." She leaned an elbow on his counter, propped her chin in her hand and batted her eyelashes, a trick she'd seen those floofy girls use but one she'd never tried until now. "I haven't been. You haven't seen me since Christmas, right?" she said, and winked.

He blushed bright red and nodded. And nodded. And nodded. His Adam's apple bobbed as he swallowed. "Sure thing, Miss Tillie. I haven't seen you in a coon's age."

"Promise?" she said in a low, throaty voice, still pretending to be one of those girls.

He smacked a hand over his heart. "Swear on my Mama's grave. I won't tell a soul."

She patted the young man on his other hand. "Thanks, darlin'. Next time I'm in town, let's be sure to grab lunch together."

Even his ears were beet red.

Sure she'd taken care of that problem, she gave him a coy smile and left. Turned out those floofy girls were good for something, after all.

She ate a leisurely lunch at her hotel. Afterwards, she spent a few hours browsing some of the shops on Houston Street. Moving on to Sanger Brothers department store, she bought a few new shirts, a yellow plaid—she did love yellow—a green check and a solid blue chambray.

On her way out of the store, something attracted her eye. She let out a small gasp at the sight of the mannequin dressed in a gown the color of buttercups in the entrance to the ladies formal wear department. The gown featured a close-fitting bodice with blonde lace insets, enormous sleeves that puffed from shoulder to elbow that became tight from elbow to wrist, but what particularly caught her eye was the skirt. Bustled, of course, but the details were a work of art; over the top of the bustle, the dressmaker draped lace that cascaded down to the floor like a blonde waterfall. Tiny iridescent beads were strategically sewn on the rosettes of the lace while also scattered randomly on the skirt. An underlay of the same beaded lace peeked out from under the beaded hem. It was gorgeous, dramatic, exquisite. It shimmered like sunlight bouncing off water.

She'd never seen anything like it.

Closing her eyes for a moment, she imagined herself, clad in the golden gown on a dance floor, twirling and spinning to the music of a Strauss waltz in the arms of a man. The man was tall—taller than she—broad shouldered, dark haired. And when she looked up the face she saw was...

Eli Knowles!

Heavens to Betsy! What was she thinking? The man was a stranger. And her employee. Worst of all, he was the most irritating man she'd ever met. Besides which, she didn't dance. She didn't wear dresses. She wasn't one of those floofy girls whose only goal in life was to catch a man.

She heaved a sigh. Because she loved this gown. She didn't need a ball gown covered in fancy lace and beads but she wanted it anyway. She might even want a man's arms around her…someday. Just not Knowles's. And not right now either. She turned to walk away.

"That dress would be stunning on you," a voice said from behind.

Unable to stop herself, she devoured the dress again with her eyes. "No," she said, flicking a glance at the saleswoman, but even she could tell her *no* sounded more like a *yes*.

The woman gave her a smile that said *so you say but you're going to try it on anyway, aren't you?* "Mrs. Jacobs," she introduced herself and held out her hand. "I'm the manager. You're Tillie Buchanan, isn't that correct?"

She shook the other woman's hand. "That's me," she answered and the next thing she knew she was in a dressing room with a young assistant helping her into petticoats, and the dress.

"Let me button this up. Lucky you, you don't even need a corset, your waist is so trim. And your…ahem…" She gestured at Tillie's chest then finished buttoning the back and fluffed the draping over the bustle. "Don't need any help there either. Nice and perky. Come on, now, let's go out so you can see in the mirror." The girl opened the door of the dressing room.

She walked out, feeling both constricted and free at the same time. She wasn't used to being so bound up on top but neither was she used to having her legs not encased in trousers. It was a peculiar sensation.

"Oh, you look marvelous. That dress was made for you," Mrs. Jacobs said. "It doesn't even need any alterations."

I bet you say that to everyone. But then she saw her reflection in the mirror and caught her breath. The woman knew her business. The color made Tillie's hair shine like liquid gold and made her face, which was tanner than a woman's face should be, glow pink. The puffed sleeves drew attention to her chest. Goodness. She had a chest. She'd never realized she had a chest. The lace bodice tapered down to her waist making it seem miniscule in comparison to the flare of her hips.

She had a shape. A real honest to goodness shape. A woman's shape. In her shirts and trousers she'd always appeared to be straight up and down, like an arrow, but in this dress...

She was a woman.

Spinning around, she scanned the back view in the mirror. The rear view of her was as spectacular as the front. She was a woman, a curvy, scrumptious woman. She stared, unable to believe her eyes. Tears welled and a lump closed her throat.

Mrs. Jacobs let her look for a long time before finally giving her a gentle push in the direction of the dressing room. "Margaret, help the young lady out of the dress, if you please. Miss Buchanan, I'll have the dress charged to your account and delivered to your hotel, shall I? You're staying at the Menger, correct?"

She didn't know how it happened but somehow she'd found herself leaving the store, walking towards the photography shop, clenched in her hand a sales receipt for one buttercup colored beaded dress.

Holy cow. She'd bought a dress, and not just any dress, a ball gown. What in the world was she thinking? For what that dress cost she could feed all ten horses in the barn for a month. She could hire another hand and pay him for six weeks. Hell's bells, it would pay the stud fee for that quarter horse stallion of Mark Schneider's she'd wanted to cover Daisy next spring to produce another foal.

The dress wasn't altered. She should take the dress back. But the strains of The Blue Danube lilted through her mind until she could almost feel strong masculine arms holding her and...

No, she wouldn't return the dress.

She opened the door of the photography shop. "My pictures ready?"

Reaching under the counter, the fellow hurriedly grabbed a cardboard folio and laid it on the counter, then slowly opening it, excitement sparkling in his eyes like he was unveiling the Mona Lisa.

She grinned. "Perfect. Exactly what I hoped for."

He gulped. "Oh wow. Thanks, Miss Tillie. It was my pleasure. Uh...what're you gonna use it for?"

Her grin got wider. "It's a big secret. But keep an eye on the Express for the next few days and you'll find out." After paying for her photos, she slid them into the folio. "Don't forget now. Nobody but you and me needs to know about these pictures, right?"

His eyes wide, he drew a cross over his chest. "My sacred word, Miss Tillie."

"Good," she said and left. Next stop, the printers. The girl at the counter took the picture and the words she wanted printed on the flyer without a word, or a scintilla of curiosity at the odd-looking animal in the photo.

"Seven dollars," she said. "Come back at five."

Figuring to make good use of the free time, she headed to the newspaper office to give them the announcement she'd written. She got an odd look from the ad rep when he read her words announcing a knight's quest but it didn't stop him from taking her money and promising to run it on the front page before the weekend. Next, she hired a young man to take the train to Dallas to place the same ad in their paper. She decided to skip Houston. She didn't much care for Houston. They were more interested in growing cotton than growing cattle. That done, she revisited the printer and collected her ten flyers. At that point, it was after six, so she ate a late dinner at the hotel and went to bed.

The next morning she took the train to Austin. After dropping her submission off at the Austin Statesman offices, she visited Dave Gault, a local rancher who'd bought several of the quarter horses she'd trained when she'd first taken over the management of the ranch at sixteen. They spent a half hour discussing breeding stock, ranch business and the price of beef. In the end, they shook hands on a deal for him to buy two cutting horses if he liked them once he tried them out. After arriving back to San Antonio on the late train, she made one more stop at the newspaper office.

"Is the paper ready yet? Did they get my ad in?" she asked Sarah at the reception desk. They'd gone all through school together so Sarah knew Tillie and her tricks from way back.

"Yes, it's all printed and ready to be delivered in the morning. I put an advance copy aside for you." Amusement danced in her eyes. "Want to see it?"

Tillie held her hand out and a freshly printed newspaper got slapped into her palm. She upfolded it and there it was, front page, bold as brass, the announcement she'd given them.

Laughter bubbled in her chest. "Thank you!" she said and tucked the newspaper inside the cloth bag she'd used all day. Nearly giddy with glee, she returned to the hotel, gathered up the belongings she'd left with the hotel concierge, including her new ballgown, loaded up her horse and started for home even though it was growing dark.

She'd been gone two days which was plenty of time for her father to get up to all kinds of mischief, so, despite the late hour it was best to get home tonight. It was dark by the time she arrived. The bunkhouse was dark and the house lights were off so she slipped quietly into the house. After stashing the box holding her new dress in the back of her closet and piling a load of old clothes on top to hide it, she undressed in the dark and went to bed to get a good night's sleep. Tomorrow was sure to be an interesting day.

Chapter Six

The morning sun was lipping the horizon when Eli quietly entered the barn, climbed the ladder to the loft and retrieved the bucket he'd set aside. After checking to make sure the contents were still inside, he sneaked into the bunkhouse through the back door where he joined Joey in the kitchen.

The old man eyed the covered bucket Eli set on the floor. "Something special for breakfast?" he asked, quirking a brow.

"A little treat for the men."

"Mmm," the older man said and scooped fried potatoes into a bowl and put a lid on it to keep them warm. "Take this on out to the table."

Eli obeyed. Through the wide doorway, he could see the men getting ready for the day. Ignoring them, he reentered the kitchen.

"Here, eggs."

Eli set the bowlful of eggs on the table and returned.

Joey handed him another—empty—shallow dish. "To put the sausages in. Make sure to put the lid on tight. To keep them warm, you know," he said, his voice not changing an iota from his previous instruction. He jerked his chin towards the grilled sausages still on the stove. Not sure what the man was about since the old man usually filled the other bowls, Eli hesitated.

"Go on. Fill it up. And don't forget to add your special treat," Joey said. Whistling a tune under his breath, he turned his back and began to clean up the mess he'd made with cooking, clanging the pots and pans loud enough to wake the dead.

"Oh, and so's you know," the old fellow said over his shoulder. "Sausage is Jinx's favorite so he always gets first dibs."

Eli stared at the old man, at the shallow dish in his hand then the old man again. Mingled with Joey's racket came the sounds of the men sauntering into the dining area.

"Git to it," Joey said, his back still towards Eli.

Well. With a grin, Eli picked up the frying pan holding the sausages, dumped them into the dish, picked up the bucket and also emptied that into the dish. He quickly slapped a lid on top and carried it out to the dining area where six men now sat, hungry expressions on their faces.

"'bout damned time," Zeke said.

"I'm starving," said Jud. He banged his knife on the table.

"Hope Joey made pancakes fer breakfast today," Beau, a young inexperienced hand, said.

Eli shook his head. "No, eggs and hash browns. Oh, and sausage."

"Those are mine," the foreman bellowed, and pointed to the place in front of him. "Put 'em right there."

"Your wish is my command," Eli answered in a meek tone. He put the dish down and stepped back.

Six pairs of hands reached for various bowls at the same time but Eli only watched one man, Jinx, who lifted the lid, grabbed a fork and stabbed it into a sausage.

Something big and black and long legged leaped out of the dish. Another big black thing—this one hairy—crawled over the lip of the dish. And another. Jinx's eyes went wide. The fork in his hand clattered to the table.

He leapt to his feet with a piercing scream.

"Spiders!" he shrieked. "There's spiders in the sausage!" He sprinted out the door of the bunkhouse, his screams trailing behind him.

Matching screams shrilled from the other men. Benches were propelled backwards and thudded onto the floor as they scrambled to flee. Plates fell off the table, spilling food everywhere. Shoving each other to be first, the men erupted out of the front door into the yard.

Apparently Jinx was not the only one not too fond of the long-legged creatures.

More spiders hopped out of the bowl. Eli backed up to stand against the wall, counting spiders as they fell off the lip of the bowl and crawled across the table top. He'd found thirteen of the little buggers, two of them rather large tarantulas, but so far only five spiders were visible. What wasn't visible were the six men. They were all gathered outside, huddled together for protection. Glaring at Eli through the open front door, the foreman shook his fist at Eli.

Eli waved.

"You son of a bitch! I'll get you for this."

"You already did," Eli called back.

Jinx glared. "You'll pay, city boy. It's only a matter of time."

An uneasy frisson rippled up Eli's spine but he pushed it away. What could the man do, trip him? Already did that. Soak his bed? Jinx had done that too.

Joey ambled out of the kitchen. "How many of those critters do we gotta round up?"

"Thirteen."

"Well, I'd better git to catching them else we'll have baby spiders everywhere. You go on out there and make peace with Jinx. Best to tell him yer even now."

Prepared to defend himself if needed, he fisted his hands at his side and walked through the door to where the men were clustered together while uttering little peeps of fear and laughter. He stopped in front of them, silent, waiting for their response, ready to fight or flee, depending on how many wanted to beat the tar out of him.

"Got us good, city boy," Buck said, and held out his hand. Eli blinked at it, then slowly reached out and took it. Buck grinned. Eli grinned back.

"Spiders. Ugh," Beau added. "At least you didn't put them in our beds." He punched Eli lightly in the arm. Zeke laughed. "Now, if you put them in Jinx's bed..." He smirked.

Jinx rounded on Zeke and slammed his fist into the other man's face. "Fuck you!"

Zeke stumbled backwards. "Son of a—"

"Hey! What in the Sam Hill is going on here?"

The group turned. Six hats were hastily yanked off six heads and held by their sides.

"Nothing, Miss Tillie," Jinx said, his mouth curling up in an ingratiating smile.

Eli held his breath. Damn. Talk about terrible timing. His hardheaded boss with the amazing rearend was back in time to see the mayhem and havoc he'd created with his stunt.

She swept her gaze over the men, her upper lip curled and suspicion in her eyes. He swallowed against the nausea crowding up his throat. His joke might be enough to cause her to let him go with only twelve dollars to his name.

He held his breath, unsure which of the men would rat him out.

"If nothing's going on then why are you all standing out here, wasting time?"

Buck laughed. "Oh, there was a slight problem with the cookstove. Flue got plugged and there was a lot of smoke so we came outside here while Joey fixed things up proper."

Jinx swung his gaze to Buck, glaring, but said nothing.

She tapped her foot, staring at the group while the group stared back, expressions of complete innocence on their faces. Except for Jinx. He side-eyed Eli, murder on his face. Eli gazed back, careful to keep his face impassive. It seemed he might have made some headway with most of the men but he'd have to watch out for the foreman. He'd dealt with men like Jinx before. They never forgot a slight, never forgave anyone they perceive wronged them.

The door of the main house opened and Tillie's father exited. He stood on the porch for a moment, stretching and surveying his domain. Eventually, he spotted the group outside the bunkhouse. Stepping down off the porch, he joined them.

"What's going on, daughter?"

She waved to him "Oh, good, you're here, Pops. Perfect."

He squinted at her. "Perfect? What's perfect?"

"I'm about to announce my quest to find that husband you ordered me to find. I thought it only fair the hands be included."

Eli slanted a look at the girl. A husband? Her father was ordering her to get married? Interesting.

Buchanan pursed his mouth. "Well, I don't know as I'd want one of them for a son-in-law but you're the one who has to sleep with whoever wins so I guess it's up to you."

Walking to the porch, she picked up a folder that was sitting on the railing and carried it with her to stand in front of the group again. From the folder, she pulled out a square of paper and unfolded what appeared to be a page from a newspaper.

"Okay, well, now that you're all here, you can read my announcement which will be in the paper this evening." From one trouser pocket, she extracted a nail then, from her belt loop, she detached a small hammer and used it to nail the newspaper page to the wall of the bunkhouse.

The men crowded around. Eli followed more slowly and stood behind them to view the paper. He was taller than the others so, although he couldn't read the fine print, he was able to see the headline. He squinted at it. What in the world?

"What's it say?" Zeke, who was only about five feet tall, asked, hopping up and down so he could see over the other's shoulders.

"What's a knight?" from Beau.

"What's a quest?" Kermit said. "Is that like a question only not as much?"

"Miss Tillie," Buck said, scratching his head. "What's it say? I don't read so good."

She rolled her eyes. "Fine, let me read it," she said and reached to pull the paper off the wall again but Jinx beat her to it. Yanking it from the wall, he thrust it at her but his fist hit the folder she held and it went flying.

"Jinx. Watch out!" she yelled and bent to gather up the dozen sheets of paper scattered on the ground. Eli quickly knelt and picked up the paper closest to him.

"Gimme!" She grabbed for it.

Eli's gaze went directly to the photo. What the hell? He jerked his gaze up to meet hers.

"Give me back my flyer!" she said, lunging forward, reaching for it, but Eli held his hand out, holding her off so he could study the picture on the flyer.

"Give it back!" she hissed but he ignored her. Instead he read the words under the picture, something about a quest and finding the animal in the picture, but truthfully, none of it made sense.

He looked at the picture again. Equicam...emu? What the hell was an equicamemu? He'd done a fair amount of traveling, been to zoos both in the United States and Europe, and he'd never seen anything like it. What the hell was this? The truth dawned. Equine. Camel. And some kind of bird like that ostrich he'd seen pictures of from Australia. Right. An emu. He bit his lip. If he didn't, he feared wild laughter would escape. The sly minx.

"This isn't—" he whispered. In his distraction, he leaned closer and she snatched the paper out of his hand.

"Keep your mouth shut," she growled under her breath. Blazing from her eyes was the promise of death if he did any different. Holding his hands up in surrender, he backed away. She stuffed the flyer back into the folder, snapped it closed, and walked back to her place in front of the men where Jinx handed her the newspaper clipping he'd torn off the wall.

She held the clipping in front of her so she could read from it. "Hear ye, hear ye. To all the gallant Knights of the realm," she said, delivering the words like she were acting out Hamlet on the stage. "Let it be known that the realm of Buchanan Hollow Ranch has proclaimed there shall be a Knight's Quest for the single men in the kingdom of Texas to win the hand of the fair Lady Matilda Buchanan, and her dowry, Buchanan Hollow Ranch."

Several of the men gasped. A low buzz of conversation followed. Eli slid a look towards Jim Bob Buchanan. Did the man know this quest of his daughter's was a farce? Based on his expression, which was smug and self-satisfied, he didn't but Eli would bet anything he owned—which right now wasn't much but that wasn't the point—that there were a lot more reasons for Tillie to be smug than Buchanan.

"Let it be known that notification of our Quest has gone out to all the Knights residing in the Land of Dallas/Fort Worth, the Land of San Antonio and the Land of Austin and shall officially begin this Saturday, May 16, 1891, at noon. Per the rules, all Knights must be single."

The hands muttered to each other with confusion on their faces. Jim Bob beamed his approval.

"All Knights must be between the ages of twenty-five and thirty-five. Lastly, whoever shall wish to compete in our Quest must first register their intent here at Buchanan Hollow Ranch on the appointed date and must submit an entry fee of twenty dollars."

More confused questions rose from the ranch hands.

"Now, because you all work for Buchanan Hollow, I'm going to give you an early peek at the rules of the Quest." Unsnapping the folio, she pulled out one of the flyers and began reading.

"To win the Quest, all Knights must abide by the following rules: Number one: The Knights must find and bring to the Lady Matilda Buchanan the animal shown on the official entrant flyer which will be handed out to all qualified participants on May 16, 1891, the day the Quest shall begin."

Buchanan glared. "Now hold on a minute—"

She glared at her father. Buchanan snapped his mouth shut. Her glare shifted to Eli, who was unable to stop the wide grin that spread across his face. After a second, the corners of her mouth curled up, almost like a cat who succeeded in catching a sneaky mouse.

She returned her gaze to the announcement. "Number Two: as stated, all entrants must be single and between the ages of twenty-five and thirty-five. Number Three: The Knights have six weeks from the commencement of the Quest, May 16, 1891, to bring said animal to Buchanan Hollow Ranch. All submissions after June 27th shall be null and void."

"Tillie! What in the heck are you doing!"

"Let me finish," she snapped at her father. "Number Four: If no challenger is able to find and bring the required item by the deadline, the Quest shall be null and void."

Buchanan squawked. "Stop. Stop right there, Miss. This here isn't a competition. You said you were going to hold a competition. A competition is like a rodeo or like that. Where's the rodeo? I was counting on a rodeo. Or...or... a spitting contest." To illustrate his point, he hawked a glob of spit a good ten feet.

Her lip curled. "You set the time frame but the agreement was I could pick the nature of the quest. This is what I chose." She took a deep breath, lifting the front of her checkered shirt making Eli's head spun.

"And one other thing. No one here is to mention this to anyone off Buchanan Hollow. Anyone who discusses the details of my quest will be fired."

She dusted off her hands and resumed watching the men who stood around her. "But I'll give a discount to any of you who want to compete. Ten dollars entry fee which I can take out of your pay over three months."

"Tillie," Buchanan protested, his voice squeaking. "C'mon, girl. We need to talk about this."

Ignoring him, she slipped the flyer and the newspaper clipping back into the folio and strutted away. Holding back his laughter, Eli tilted his head, admiring the sway of her slender hips, the tilt of her proud chin. And the intelligence in that wily head of hers.

She's up to something. Jim Bob drummed his fingers on his desk while he stared out the window. He didn't know what that something was, but he knew his daughter and recognized that look in her eye. The question was, what? The bigger question was how to find out. Finding out seemed straightforward enough but with Tillie, it was never straightforward.

Most father's would outright confront their daughters and demand an answer, but Jim Bob was smart enough to realize demanding anything from his daughter would only result in a refusal along with the possibility she'd sabotage his life in ways he wouldn't like.

He knew this because it wouldn't be the only time she'd done it, the first time being almost ten years ago when she announced she was taking over the running of the ranch. He'd flat out said no, no way, no how, wasn't happening. The next day, he'd awakened to find every shirt, every undershirt, every pair of drawers he owned, dyed pink.

"Tillie!" he'd roared and waited while she sprinted across the yard and barged into the house. She stopped dead in her tracks when she saw him. "Oh. Son of a preacher, Pops."

He'd waved a hand at his pink shirt.

She'd seemed puzzled. "Um, shoot, I must have thrown my new red shirt into the wash tub, not realizing the tub was full of all your whites. Looks like the red dye bled."

He remembered glowering at her and the innocent smile she sent back. "No, you can't manage the ranch." Sixteen was too young to manage anything, he'd thought at the time, and anyway, she was a female. Girls didn't manage ranches.

"Well, the pink'll come out eventually," she'd told him and walked out the door.

A few days later she sabotaged his hair. Now Jim Bob purely loved his hair, he did back then and he still did now. He loved how thick and wavy it was which is why he let it grow down to his shoulders. He even loved the fact it was pure white. Most men, their hair got a dull gray when they aged, but not Jim Bob Buchanan. His hair was a snowy white so he made sure to take extra good care of it. He even bought special shampoo—like the ladies used—that he shipped in from back East that came directly from France. Gotta keep it clean and shiny, after all.

That morning he'd washed it, using his French shampoo. When he looked in the mirror, his hair was bright blue.

"Goldarn it! Tillie!"

She'd skidded into his bathroom on her bare feet—back then she never seemed to wear shoes. Her mouth fell open. "Son of a gun, Pops, your hair is blue." Her gaze went to the counter. "Oh, no. Jeepers, I'm so sorry. It's my fault."

He'd glowered.

"It was an accident, Pops. I borrowed your special shampoo to wash Dixie—you know, that white mare. A buyer was coming to see her yesterday, so I borrowed your special shampoo and poured a bit of laundry bluing into it to get her extra white. Somehow, I must have handed Inez the bottle of bluing instead of your special shampoo when I asked her to put it back in your room so—"

She shrugged. "Just an honest mistake."

Jim Bob knew his daughter, after all, he'd raised her for sixteen years, and he'd known it was no such thing. "Cut it out, daughter," he'd told her. "I'm not changing my mind and the next time you dye any of my clothes or my hair, I swan, I'm going to disinherit you."

"So I can't manage the ranch?"

"No!"

It took three washings to get it back close to his own white hair.

Third time occurred a week later. He vividly remembered that morning because who could forget a morning like that? He'd awoken and got ready for the day after making sure his newly delivered shirts and underthings were all right. He'd reckoned his daughter took his threat seriously but with Tillie, even still being wet behind the ears, you never knew. To be on the safe side, he double and triple checked his special shampoo, his shaving soap, his cologne and his face cream. He even checked his clothes before he put them on. Everything seemed fine so he'd concluded his daughter was done throwing her little hissy fit. At sixteen, there was only so much she could do to get her way, especially when dealing with her older and smarter Pops.

So when he sat down to breakfast, he'd figured she'd given up and there was nothing more to worry about. He'd read the newspaper and ate a long, leisurely breakfast after which he'd decided to take a ride into town to visit one of his lady friends. Maybe Flora. She had those big titties and he'd been in the mood for something substantial to hang onto.

He'd walked back to his bedroom with the intent of changing into something a little more go-to-courting style. He remembered vividly how his gut had rumbled. Like something he ate didn't set well. He entered his room. And his stomach had rumbled again. Inside his belly—and boy howdy, did he remember this, even after ten years—his gut had twisted painfully.

What the heck had he eaten that got things so stirred up? He was real careful about his gut and what he ate since spicy food and anything dairy gave him problems the likes of which he didn't want to have. Inez never served him anything with cheese or milk in it, and sadly no chili peppers. But the pancakes and the omelet that morning tasted no different from his usual.

His gut had protested again. And again. Oh. Shit! Really shit! Definitely shit!

He remembered racing to his bathroom, jerking his pants and drawers down, throwing himself on the crapper, barely making it before exploding. He didn't remember much about the rest of it except wanting to die.

After thirty minutes or so, when he was sure he would live, he'd fixed himself up, left the bathroom and stomped out to the front porch. And this part he remembered vividly.

"Tillie!" he'd bellowed.

She'd sauntered up, her fresh young face guileless as a new-born babe's. "Yes, Pops?"

"What'd you do?"

"Me, Pops?" she'd asked, all innocence. "Why, what's wrong?"

He'd scowled at her. "I've got the..." He cleared his throat.

She'd cocked her head. "You've got the...?"

"The...you know. The...the...I ate something..."

"The...?" she said again. Then her eyes had widened with realization. She made a sad face, her lower lip protruding far enough for a bird to perch on. "Ooooh. Darn, Pops. I'm so sorry. I told Inez to take the day off to see her grandchildren in town and that I'd cook breakfast. I always put milk in my eggs to make them fluffy. I must have got your eggs mixed up with mine."

It wasn't only his gut in danger of exploding. His head was too. His jaw worked and he'd forced himself to swallow the words on the tip of his tongue.

"You all right, Pops?" she'd asked.

He'd look daggers at her.

"So do I get to manage the ranch?" she'd asked next, the look in her eyes all those years ago was like the one he'd seen today out at the bunkhouse. Which was how he knew she was up to something now. Which was also why he realized it wouldn't him do any good to ask her now what that was.

Yep, that was almost a decade ago and nothing had changed, certainly not Matilda Rae Buchanan. Still stubborn as a mule and mean as a rattlesnake.

He was mulling over the past for a bit, comparing it to the present, when inspiration struck. There was one person he could ask. He stuck his head out the window. "Hey, you! Knowles. Get in here. I've got a question."

The man rose from where he sat by the bunkhouse cleaning tack, walked across the yard and entered the house.

"Yes?"

Jim Bob chewed on the inside of his cheek, formulating his question before deciding, the heck with that. He was the boss. He'd ask any old way he pleased. "What's Tillie up to?"

The other man's eyes went wide for a second before all expression left his face. "What do you mean?"

"You know what I mean. I saw that look she gave you and I saw you look back. So, tell me what she's up to."

Knowles's mouth arced down in a you-got-me expression. "I've got no idea. It's that I could tell she was having fun so I watched her."

Jim Bob studied him for a second. Sadly, it wasn't like the old days, back when there were things like thumb screws and the rack to get the truth out of people. This was modern times and, unfortunately, torture went out with the Middle Ages. Too bad.

"Fine. Forget I asked. Go on out there and saddle my horse for me. I'm going into town.

Chapter Seven

Tillie stared after her father as he rode out of the gate. She wasn't a hundred percent sure where he was going and why, but she could take a guess. He figured she was up to something—which she was—and thought he could find out what it was by asking around town—which he wouldn't. No one would tell him a thing...

At least it's what she hoped.

She swallowed. The idea that he was poking around in her business and might find out about her scheme made sweat break out and her stomach ache. Maybe she should ride after him, talk him out of going into town. No, because then he'd really suspect she was pulling a fast one which would only make him more determined to thwart her.

Anxiety skittered along her veins like ants crawling over her skin. This wouldn't do. This wouldn't do at all. Fretting never changed anything. But damn the man. What was it with men, anyway? Why did they have to spoil everything? Pigheaded, selfish, obnoxious...

Her gaze went around the stable yard and landed on Slick. "You! Oh, you...you...you man, you!" She stabbed a finger at him.

His mouth dropped open and his eyes went wide.

"You damned man. Just like my father. You all think you're perfect."

He blinked.

"Well, I got news for you. You're not perfect," she said. She said it out loud but what her mind, and her body was saying was this man was a prime example of male perfectness. Even dressed in a cheaply made shirt with his too long hair and his stupid citified shoes he was perfect. Her aggravation too much to keep inside, she stomped her foot. A puff of dust flew.

A smile twitched the corner of his mouth. His gaze drifted over her from her head to her toes and back up again. One eyebrow lifted. "Yes, ma'am. Whatever you say, ma'am."

Damn him. He thought it was funny. Irritation welled inside until it seemed her head would burst. Grrrrr. She downright hated his perfectness.

So why did she have this overwhelming urge to touch him? Why did she find his lips so enticing and her fingers ache to caress that magnificent chest of his. She thrust her fists onto her hips and scorched him with a glare. This time he flinched. Good. Maybe that would put a dent in his perfect armor.

"Slick. Get over here. I need your help," she said. Dave Gault, the rancher she'd made a deal with while she was in Austin was scheduled to come today to try out the horses they'd discussed. He'd be here in a few hours so there was lots to do to get ready.

Her newest ranch hand—and she used that term loosely—walked over to join her, his face wary, his stride nearly a crawl. *Yeah, that's right, be afraid, you...you...you man!*

"I noticed you talking to my father a while ago."

He dipped his head, his expression wary.

"What did he want?"

He took a deep breath before answering. "He thinks you're up to something with your quest. He thinks I know what it is."

She squinted at him. "And do you?"

"Miss Buchanan, it's not my job to question what you're doing. I'm only here to work," he said with a straight face. But there was a knowing twinkle in his eyes. Because he'd seen that photo.

Damn him.

"That sorrel gelding out in the pasture, the one usually in the third stall, Laredo, he's the one with the white blaze and four white stockings. Bring him in and brush him down and put him in the crossties so he can't roll and get dirty again. When you're done with that, bring in that bay usually in the back stall, the one named Frontier. Same thing."

With a last, amused, look, he strode out to the field. She watched him stride away, his long, strong legs moving over the ground at a fast clip, his shoulders thrust forward aggressively, his narrow backside flexing. Damn. Even from the back he was perfect.

She turned away, determined to put the man out of her mind. She should be getting ready for Saturday, the day her quest began. But what if no one showed up to compete? What if it was a complete bust? A knot formed in her chest, making it hard to breathe. What would she do? What would her father do? Would he use it as an excuse to jimmy her into a marriage with someone of his choice or would he give her a chance to come up with another way to find a husband?

Drat. Husbands were nothing but a nuisance. Look at her father. He'd been a husband once upon a time and according to everything her mother told her; he'd been a rotten one. That was probably why she decided to up and die when Tillie was eight. It was the only way her mother could get away from the man.

From what she could tell from observing her schoolmates' husbands after they got married, husbands mostly drank too much, spit and farted too much, and cheated on their wives. Even Eva, the librarian, such a lovely woman, her husband visited a regular girl at one of the bordellos in town every Saturday night.

Tillie didn't need that. If she could find a man who didn't drink to excess, kept his bodily noises and fluids to himself, and who treated her like an equal partner in life, she might consider marriage. A knight, someone noble and honest and true, like Ivanhoe. But until then...

Shaking her head, she went into the house. Inez, their housekeeper straightened from where she'd been cleaning the tile floor. "Inez, where did my father go?"

Her shoulders lifted. "I don't know. He did not say. You know he never tell me anything. He's afraid I'll tell you."

And he was right. Which was why Inez was her secret weapon. "Well, if you find out, please tell me. He's cooking up some kind of chicanery for sure."

"Maybe it is time I clean your father's office. His drawers...very messy. What you think?"

Tillie bit back a smile. "Yeah, I noticed that. Go right ahead. Make sure every drawer is nice and tidy."

"Si. In the meantime, I'll bring you some lunch, okay?" Inez said and hurried off.

Now that was settled, it was time to prepare for Saturday. She needed to copy the list of rules for each knight to receive in addition to her flyers with a description and a picture of the animal they must find, plus she'd needed to keep a log of who'd paid the entry fee. It wasn't like she needed the money from the entry fee but having to pay to compete would separate the non-serious lazy bums seeking a handout from those who might know a thing or two about hard work.

Not that it mattered in the long run. She didn't plan on handing over the control of her ranch, and her body, to some man. She giggled and began writing. The rules were few, short and to the point, and an hour later ten lists were written out, more than she probably needed. She couldn't image too many men would be interested in such a cockamamie scheme because what kind of idiot would go off on some vague, undefined quest with no guarantee that, in the end, they'd get anything in exchange except a waste of time.

Inez knocked at her door. "Miss Tillie, there is a man here to see you. About your horses, yes?"

Rising, she walked outside to find David Gault and two other men waiting near the barn talking with Slick. Gault greeted her with a few pleasantries before asking to see the horses.

"Slick, bring out Laredo."

"Of course," he said and walked inside the barn. A few minutes later, he came out leading the sorrel by its halter.

Gault strolled around the animal, eyeing the gelding up and down, running his hands along the horse's front legs checking for heat, and picking up each hoof. "Can I see him trot?"

"Slick, trot him up to the far corner of the corral and back," she said.

Gault watched the horse's actions. "Good hindquarters, they track well," he said. "Moves nicely."

Damn it, so did Slick.

"I'd like to try him out, see how he reins," was Gault's next request.

She nodded to Slick who took the horse back into the barn. A few minutes later he exited the barn with the saddled horse. Gault mounted and reined the gelding through the gate she held open leading into the corral. He trotted the animal, moved into a canter, first on the right lead, next a flying lead change to the left, and took the gelding through a number of short stops, canters from a standing position and sharp turns. Done, he exited the corral, dismounted, and handed the reins back. "I like him. I'll take him. Let's see the other one."

Without a word, her newest ranch hand walked back into the barn and they went through the same process with Frontier, the bay. In the end, Gault said he'd take both horses.

"Where's your pa?" he asked. "I'll write him a check."

Irritation flared. "He's not here. You can write the check to me."

"Hmmm. Don't know that I like that idea. Where's your pa?" Gault repeated, scratching his chin.

"He went into town."

Gault stared down his nose at her. "Well, then I believe we should wait until he comes back to talk business."

She held in her aggravation. Men. "I have no idea when he'll be back. He took a valise with him so he's probably staying overnight. Even if he were here, I'd still have you write the check to me."

The rancher cocked his head. "That's not what we did last time. Last time I wrote the check to your father and that's what I expected to do today."

Her irritation changed to anger. "Yes, you did write a check to my father last time but I was sixteen and not legal. And when you did, he promptly lost the money in a card game. These are my horses, I'm over eighteen, so this time you're writing the check to me."

"Well, now, pretty lady, it's fine for you to show me the horses and all but you need to let us men handle the finances."

Red hot fury rose. She opened her mouth to blast the man but before she could articulate the words that seemed stuck in her brain, Slick interrupted with, "Mr. Gault, Miss Buchanan raised these horses, she trained these horses, and she owns both these horses. She manages this ranch and the six hands who work here without any help from her father. Are you saying that she doesn't have enough sense to handle a check because she's a woman?"

She snapped her head around to gape at the man. What in world? She quickly whipped her head back to see Gault's reaction.

A wave of red flooded the man's cheeks. "Well, I never said that—"

Her tongue finally came unstuck. "You did say that. You told me you would only write a check to a man."

Gault stared at Tillie. His mouth opened, closed it, and he screwed it up into a tight little bud. She glared back. If she hadn't left her Webley Bull Dog in her bedroom, trying to be polite, she'd have shot the man where he stood.

"Now, Miss Buchanan. Don't get yourself all worked up. I'm sure we can work something out. I came all the way from Austin. Don't want to come all this way for nothing so how about this; I'll take the horses home with me and stop in San Antonio on my way through town and give your father my check." Taking Laredo's reins, he started to hand them over to the man closest to him.

Slick wrapped a hand around Gault's wrist, stopping him. "No, you won't take the horses with you, not without paying for them."

"Now see here—"

"No, you see here," Tillie snapped, deciding it was time to take a stand. "You don't leave this property with those animals without paying for them. And at this point, I think cash only would be in order." Damn the man. Damn all men for their stupid misogynistic belief that women were nothing but pretty ornaments whose job it was to agree with everything a man said and have a dozen babies. She slanted a look at Slick, because somehow, it seemed he didn't quite fit into that category.

"What!" Gault sputtered. "Cash! Nothing was said about cash. Last time I wrote a check and it was fine."

Yeah, and last time I wasn't quite so canny to men's bullshit.

Slick coughed into his hand. She nodded, giving him permission to do what he saw fit. Retrieving the reins from Gault, he said, "You heard the lady. Cash. Or leave without the horses."

A muscle ticked in the rancher's jaw. He scowled at her with a cold blue stare but eventually, he walked to his own horse, dug through his saddle bags and pulled out a wad of cash. He walked back to Tillie. She held her hand out, palm up, and he counted out the payment.

"Fifty, one hundred, one hundred fifty, two hundred, two fifty, two sixty, seventy, eighty, ninety..." He glared at her and slapped the last bill in her palm. "Three hundred."

"Thank you, Mr. Gault." She turned to Slick. "Slick, take the saddle and bridle off both horses, please, and put their halters back on." At the order, a slow smile spread across Slick's face and he began unsaddling Frontier.

Crossing her arms over her chest, she said, "Oh, and Mr. Gault, you can have the halters, no charge," and smiled. She could almost hear the ranch owner's teeth grinding. Slick quickly finished unsaddling the two horses, slipped on halters and handed a lead to each of Gault's men. With a snarl, Gault mounted his horse, and the party jogged away.

"Hmmm. Guess I won't be selling any more horses to Mr. Gault," she said once they disappeared around the bend.

Slick pulled a rag from his back pocket and wiped the sweat from his face. "Do you care?" he finally asked.

She paused to think about it, anger simmering inside, both at Gault for thinking he could bamboozle her, but more at her father for being right, because damn it, this was what he'd been talking about. Men not believing a woman could do business as well as a man. Men thinking women didn't deserve the respect that a man was automatically given. Which didn't mean she was going to change her ways. No sir. It was men who would have to change theirs.

"Nope. Why sell to a shyster when there are plenty of other buyers who will deal honestly with me?"

She walked back towards the house but the entire time she was mulling over the incident in her mind. Inez motioned her into the dining room, where lunch was laid out. Tillie ate, not thinking much about the food, alternately fuming over the Gault incident, mulling over Slick's unprecedented defense of her, and worrying about what her Pops might be doing in town. Could be he was seeing one of his regular ladies but more likely he wanted to find some evidence that would pull the rug out from underneath her and spoil her quest.

Well, let him look. She'd covered her tracks well. She hoped.

But despite her father and his shenanigans, and her naughty thoughts about Slick, her work never stopped. She finished eating, threw her napkin on the table and walked back out to the stable yard. The man was back on the stump, cleaning more tack.

She stood for a minute, watching him, still wondering. Who was he, with his dudish Eastern clothes and his fancy shoes? Where did he come from and why was he working here on Buchanan Hollow? More importantly, what kind of man was he that he defended her right to receive direct payment for her work even though she was a woman? Heck, it was almost like the man believed she knew her business. None of the other hands would have done what he did. Most men would have agreed that her Pops should handle the money. They wouldn't have contradicted Gault, even knowing that Gault was wrong, even knowing that Tillie ran the ranch and that, if her Pops got his hands on that check, the money would be gone in a flash for something other than ranch expenses. So why did Slick defend her?

And why did looking at him make her tingle in places she had no business tingling? And why, almost every minute of the day, did her thoughts somehow drift to his bluer than blue eyes. And why did she want to kiss that oh, so kissable mouth, that defended her like he thought she was something special?

She didn't get it. Was he trying to butter her up to take advantage of her? Shoot, there she went, thinking bad thoughts about the man for no call but why was he here if he was on the up and up? Maybe because he was running from the law. If so, it was the excuse she needed to get rid of him because the last thing she needed was some scheming man with nefarious plans—and a beguiling smile—mucking up her plans. But if he was an evil guy, how come he defended her?

Chapter Eight

Today was the day. Her announcement would run on the front page of San Antonio Express, the Dallas Herald and the Austin American-Statesman and now the day had arrived. All morning long the hands worked to get the place ready for the event, hanging bunting from the overhang above the wide porch and putting a fresh coat of paint on the barn door. Tables were set out that would eventually hold barbecued ribs, corn on the cob and beer.

A tingle of nerves jolted through her body but she didn't know why. She'd gone over her plan in her mind and on paper a dozen times and assured herself it was flawless.

Except Pops was back. His presence ran the risk of ruining everything, the proverbial fly in the ointment. As usual. Still, he hadn't said anything so apparently Eva kept her secret, and other than herself, Eva was the only one who knew that the animal pictured on the flyer was nothing more than a product of her imagination.

Still, whatever Pops did in town the other day, it apparently wasn't enough to discovered the truth about her scheme. If he did, most likely he'd have already shut her down.

"Miss Tillie," Jud yelled from his perch on top of the front gate. "Riders coming."

"Son of a gun," her father muttered, shaking his head in disbelief. "Seems like your dumb plan worked."

Everyone in the yard watched the cloud of dust approaching, signaling more than one rider. The cloud got closer...and closer...and closer. She blinked. At least a dozen men were in the midst of the cloud.

Okay, she'd expected around ten so she could handle a few more. But right behind the first group was another crowd of men—at least half a dozen. And behind them, were more men, along with one lone shay driven by a man barely seen over the back of the horse. Before she realized it, almost thirty men and their horses were milling around the stable yard.

Holy Toledo. She never thought this many men would show up. This wouldn't do at all.

Slick edged up behind her. Leaning, he whispered, "Do you want the men to take hold of all those horses? Someone's liable to get kicked in this crowd if we're not careful."

She hesitated so she could gather the thoughts rampaging through her brain like a manic squirrel then answered, "Um. Sure. Have the men release everyone's horses out in the field."

Nodding, he waved to Buck and Kermit, told them what Tillie said, and began to walk through the crowd gathered in front of the house so they could tell her Questers to dismount. Horse after horse was led away, their bridles removed then turned loose in the back pasture.

Seeing the crowd, sweat broke out on her forehead. What was she supposed to do with all these men? This was way more men than she'd planned on, way more than she wrote instructions packets for, way more than she wanted in her competition. Bull balls. She would have to winnow them down somehow. She needed to come up with a criteria, and fast. But how?

She walked up the three steps onto the porch. The crowd of men rushed to stand at the foot of the steps and stared up at her. The hands all retreated to stand near the corral. She grimaced. Darn, she forgot about them. That meant there were even more men who might join.

"Any of my men want to compete too?" she called, hoping they'd decline. "If so, come on down here with the rest of the men."

A flutter of talk broke out among them before Beau shook his head. "Nah, Miss Tillie. No offense, but none of us has a hankering to get hitched to you. We value our skins, you know?"

Laughter broke out. "Okay, that's fine." More than fine, she thought, her gaze traveling to Slick standing near the corner of the porch. For a second—just a brief second, mind—she wondered what it would be like if Slick was to join the competition for her hand in marriage. A vision of his bare chest popped into her head, along with the memory of what she'd seen that night in the water trough. All that glorious maleness. What would it be like to have *that* in her bed? Heat traveled up her neck and her breasts tightened.

"Miss Buchanan, when are you going to tell us the details of this competition?" a man in the group shouted, bringing her back to the present.

"What do we need to do?"

"Are you paying for our expenses? Looks like we might have to do some traveling and traveling ain't cheap, right?"

"When I win, when do we get married?" a tall fellow with a handlebar mustache and a smarmy smile yelled.

"Hey, who says yer gonna win," another man snarled.

"I say. You don't stand a chance," Mustache Man retorted, running a hand through a headful of luxurious black hair.

"What, because you think you're better than me?"

"I know I'm better than you."

"Are not."

"Am too."

"You're full of shit," was the reply and the next thing fists started to fly. Dust rose, blood flowed and a lot of shins got kicked.

"Problem, sweetheart?" Jim Bob snickered.

Yeah, she had a problem. Her father! This was all his fault. Pulling her hat off her head, she smacked him across the chest. He laughed out loud. She smacked him again. "I'll kill you later," she growled. "Slick! Make them stop!"

He blinked then comprehension flashed in his eyes. Grabbing Zeke by the collar, he dragged him towards the brawl while yelling, "Buck. Jud. Kermit. Over here!" and even though he wasn't their foreman, they all obeyed. There was something about his voice, and his stance, that screamed leader. She watched, mesmerized, while he waded into the fray and took charge. Lordy, lordy, those shoulders.

Her daydream came to an abrupt halt when Jinx yelled, "Hey. What the hell you fellas doing? He ain't your boss," over the bedlam but the other men ignored him and joined the melee.

The brawlers were finally separated and things calmed down. She huffed out a hard breath and stepped forward again so she could view the men who were here to 'win her hand' and her ranch. Blonds, redheads, dark-haired. City men, cowpokes, a few expensively dressed ranchers. Short, tall, skinny, fat, old, young...

Her gaze locked onto a fellow standing to the back, his chin tucked into his chest. His brown eyes met hers from under a mass of stringy blond hair. If he was a day older than fourteen, she'd eat her hat.

"You," she snapped, and pointed to a spot directly in front of her. He slinked forward, lower lip protruding. "How old are you?" she asked.

"Twenty-five, like the ad said." His voice cracked.

Like hell. Reaching out, she ran a finger along the smooth, baby fine skin of his cheek. "You don't even shave yet. Go home to your momma. Come back when you shave and I might hire you."

With a whimper, he disappeared into the crowd of men, headed towards the pasture to retrieve his horse. Her father chortled again. "Now, now, daughter. Don't send him away yet. He might be a good prospect. Start 'em young, bring 'em up right, hee hee hee."

She whacked her father with her hat again. "Shush, old man!" He giggled some more and crossed his arms over his meager chest, a look of unholy glee in his eyes.

Slapping her hat back onto her head, she observed her unexpected crowd again. A bunch of these fellows needed to go but how? She scratched her head, idly watching the boy ride past on his way home.

Of course. Why didn't she think of that sooner? "All right, fellas. Here's what I need you to do. Anyone younger than twenty-five, stand over here." She pointed to the left. Five or six men shifted to the spot she indicated. "Anyone older than thirty-five stand there." She pointed to the right. A dozen men shuffled to the right, leaving about twenty men in the center.

She squinted. Most of the men in the center group were strangers, so she was trusting them to be honest about their age, but a few were locals like the fellow in front whose real name was Roscoe but got called Cackle because of his red hair and his odd clucking laugh. He also sported a wattle under his chin that wobbled when he talked, and wrinkles on his face like an un-ironed sheet. "Cackle Brown, there is no way in hell you're younger than thirty-five."

He stuck his chin out, making the wattles wobble. "Am so."

"You are not."

"Am too."

She scowled at him. "Then what's your birthday?"

"February Twenty-Ninth, Eighteen Twelve."

Eighteen-Twelve? That made him... "Holy cats, Cackle. That makes you seventy-nine years old!"

"Nuh uh. I was born on February Twenty-Nineth, so's I only have a birthday every four years which makes me..." He stopped to count on his fingers as he tallied up the years.

Tillie tallied faster. "If that's so, that makes you only twenty and change. Either way, you're not eligible. Go home."

She glowered when she heard a snort of laughter behind her from her father who nudged her with his shoulder. "Hey, don't dismiss him yet, daughter," he whispered. "He might be just the perfect husband; old enough to know what's what but too feeble to take advantage of the knowledge."

If it was the last thing she did, she would make her father pay. But not yet.

Kicking at the dirt, Cackle made a face. "Well, shucks, Miss Tillie. Can't you give me a chance? I can do the quest. Whatever a quest is. What *is* a quest?"

At this point, everyone in the crowd started to laugh. She slapped a hand over her face. "No. Go home," she repeated. "And those who aren't in the middle group, you go home too."

Grumbling, the men on the left and the men on the right trickled away, retrieved their horses, and rode off. Tillie examined the remaining men. She only wrote out ten flyers, and she really didn't want a slew of men tearing all over Texas trying to complete her quest. The more participants, the greater the chances someone would figure out her scheme and expose her. She needed to find another way to narrow the field a bit more.

"We've been here almost half an hour, Miss Buchanan, and you've told us nothing. Isn't it time to tell us what the details of your competition?" Mustache Man asked.

"Yeah, tell us what we have to do," another fellow said.

"Yes," several more men shouted. "Or we're going to have a problem."

Left with no alternative, she picked up the folio she'd set on a nearby bench and pulled out the copy of rules she'd written out earlier. She handed it to the nearest man. "Pass this around." No way was she going to hand out the official entrant flyers with the photo until she'd reduced the pack. No telling what the losers would do with the information. The question still remained, though, how to reduce the pack?

The sheet of paper slowly made the rounds so each man could read the rules.

"We're supposed to find some animal that we don't even know what it is yet and bring it back to you?" a dark-haired man dressed in an expensive blue suit said. "How do we know it's not some animal we can't possibly bring, like, say an elephant?" He stared up at her, his mouth screwed up into a tight line, his eyes skeptical.

A short, rather rotund fellow poked him in the side. "Hey, you doubting the lady?"

"No, I'm doubting this quest."

Mustache Man fiddled with the diamond stick pin on his tie. "Yes, how do we know this 'quest' is a real thing?"

Damn. She needed to shut them up. They would ruin everything with their doubts and questions. "I promise the quest is a real thing." Of course it was a real thing. What wasn't real was the animal.

Dark Suit Man curled a lip. The crowd began to grow restless, some of them grumbling that it was a scam while others defended her. If she wasn't careful, her quest would fall apart in front of her and her father would use to force her to marry someone will she or won't she. The good news was, she'd figured out a criteria to eliminate a few of these yahoos. Over the heads of the men waiting for her to speak, she caught Slick's eye. He gave her a wry, half-smile and a shrug. Some help he was. Fine. Let the games begin.

"Gentlemen, line up in front of me, please."

The men hurried into place. "Now, I've decided only ten men will compete in the Quest so I need to eliminate some of you."

A protest erupted. She held her hand up. "Sorry, gentlemen, but it's my quest so it's my rules and that's what I've decided. To that end, I'm going to ask each of you a question or two that will help me make my decision."

They all subsided, most looking irritated and unhappy.

She stepped down from the porch and stopped in front of the first man, the Doubting Thomas in the Dark Suit who was eyeing her with disbelief and a curled lip. "What's the capital of England and who's their president?" she asked him.

He sneered at her. "London, of course, and England doesn't have a president, they have a queen and a prime minister."

She pointed to her left. "Go stand over there."

With a smirk at the other men, he strutted over to the place she indicated. "When did the Civil War begin?" she asked the next man, a short, rotund fellow with bright red hair.

"Well, pretty sure it was before I was born. Eighteen-Fifty?"

She pressed a finger to her temple, a pained expression on her face. "How many months have twenty-eight days?"

Red blinked. "Uh, one? February? Right?"

"Over there," she said, pointing to the right. He hurried over to his spot.

"Name the three branches of the US government?" she asked Mustache Man, the next man in line.

"Judicial, executive and legislative. Correct?" he said with a smirk.

She nodded and asked a second question. "What has a head and a tail but no body?"

The man opened his mouth to answer but stopped and thought for a moment before answering. "A coin," he said smugly.

"To the left, please."

She moved on to the next man, a tall slender fellow dressed in an expensive black suit who stared at her blankly when she stopped in front of him. She snapped her fingers in his face but the vapid expression didn't change. She poked Unconscious in the shoulder and he woke up—more or less "How many feet in a yard?" she asked.

He took a minute, his gaze darting here and there before answering. "Uh, well, there's twenty-two folks in this here yard and they all got two feet..." He peeked over his shoulder at a man behind him leaning on a crutch. "Well, except him. He's only got one foot so that makes...um...forty-one?"

She bit her tongue to keep from laughing. If they were counting actual feet, the answer was forty-five, but that wasn't really the question anyway. The man was all suit and no brains. "To the right, please." No need to ask this one a second question.

Another man stepped forward. Not a bad looking man, tall and broad shouldered with a face that wasn't slack jawed like the last one. "A farmer owned seventeen cows. All but six died. How many cows survived?" she asked him.

The man's face lit up. "Ooh, ooh, I know this. Eleven!"

She sighed. "Okay. So what's the capital of Washington, D.C."

He pursed his lips, thought, scratched his head and gave up with a shrug of defeat.

"To the right, please," she said.

She asked questions of the next few men in line and finally found three more to join the group on the right. Over thirty men had arrived to join the quest and she was scraping the bottom of the barrel to find...well, the bottom of the barrel.

At this point she was on stupid overload, so she sized up the remaining men based on their appearance including two who appeared to be twins because, why not, and sent them to the right and sent the remainder to the left. Glad the painful process was completed and hopeful she'd guessed correctly, she mounted the porch again. Her father clapped his hands together. She glared at him but couldn't tell if he was happy or mad about her actions. Slick, on the other hand, looked like he was about to strangle on his laughter.

"Thank you, everyone. I've made my decision about who will compete for my hand in marriage, and for Buchanan Hollow."

A murmur swept through the waiting men, the ones on the left, including the Doubting Thomas in the Dark Suit, preening like they'd won a gold medal, the ones on the right appearing resigned to going home. She pointed at the preeners. "Gentlemen, thank you for your time and trouble in being here today. Before you leave us, please help yourself to the beer and eats we've set out on the tables over yonder. Have a pleasant ride back to wherever you came from."

"What?" one of the men shouted. "You're dismissing us?"

"But I got both my answers right," another protested.

"Me too. This ain't fair."

"We all got our answers right. What's going on? Why were they selected..." Mustache Man pointed at the other group who cringed like rabbits face-to-face with a wolf when they realized that Tillie was keeping them while sending the preeners home. "...and we weren't?"

"To repeat, gentlemen. This is my quest and I set the rules." And her rules were, no intelligent men need apply. "Given your complaints, I suggest we skip the refreshments. Please get your horses now."

A few of the dismissed men ran to the food table and gulped down some beer before joining the rest of the group who left, all of them complaining loudly. Tillie aimed a smile on the men who remained. They gaped back at her, bewilderment written on all their faces.

She rubbed her hands together in satisfaction. Because she had exactly what she needed for her quest; the ten dumbest men in Texas.

Chapter Nine

Eli studied the men the devious minx selected. What a motley bunch of no-hopers. Why in the world did she pick these ten over the other men she'd sent home? Her discards all seemed intelligent, several were better than average in the looks department, and one or two obviously were well off. For the most part, any one of them would be an ideal husband for most women.

Versus the ones she'd asked to stay; a balding man no taller than five feet tall with beady little eyes and a short piggy snout. There was also a young strapping fellow wearing an expensive suit who seemed obsessed with a handful of coins he'd pulled out of his pocket. Mumbling loudly, he'd count them into the palm of one hand, frown, dump them into the palm of his other hand and count them again, each count resulting in a different amount. Eli didn't know what was so difficult. There were less than ten coins.

Next to the coin counter stood a well-built and darkly handsome man but when the fellow opened his mouth to beam a smile at Tillie it exposed the fact he only possessed two teeth. At least the remaining teeth were the ones in front where it counted.

Next was the tall, thin man who, based on the grime on his work-roughened hands and the ring of dirt around his collar, probably hadn't bathed in a month.

Then there was the slack-jawed fellow leaning against the porch, scratching his chest. And scratching. And scratching. And scratching. Holy hell. Eli hoped the man didn't have fleas. Fleas were known to jump from body to body and they weren't picky about the body they jumped to. From what he could see, not one of the men standing in line could tell their asses from their elbows. Dumb as stumps.

Understanding struck. He smacked his forehead. Of course. Dumb was the point. The last thing she wanted was someone smart enough to do some research and find out that there was no way they would ever win her hand in marriage, and the ranch.

Which didn't mean every one of them wouldn't do their darnedest to win. Because, unlike Eli, they were all perfectly fine living in Texas.

Texas. He hated everything about the state of Texas. The heat was unbearable and the flies intolerable. As if to prove the point, a horsefly landed on his neck and bit him. Son of a bitch. He slapped at it and it flew away. And if the flies didn't kill him, Tillie would with her so-called chores, while Jinx made it his mission in life to find more ways to make his life miserable in spite of the fact Eli had reached a détente with most of the other men.

The yard finally empty of all the disqualified suitors, Tillie climbed the stairs onto the porch and stopped in front with her father who stared at his daughter, his mouth crooked to the side as he chewed on the end of his mustache. It was obvious he was irked that he hadn't figured out the method behind his daughter's madness.

Eli, on the other hand, possessed a well-honed sense of the ridiculous and knew exactly what was going on. Not wanting to miss a minute of the imminent farce, he casually ambled closer to the porch so he could watch the upcoming action.

Picking up a flyer, Tillie shouted, "Hear ye, hear ye," reading once again from her flyer. "To all the gallant knights of the realm."

"Gosh, did you hear that?" one of the men whispered loudly. "We're knights!"

"Do I gotta wear armor? Might get kind of hot wearing armor."

Shorty with the piggish nose poked the man closest to him. "What's a realm?"

"Hush up," the man said, and elbowed him in the shoulder. "I wanna hear."

Tillie made a face but continued her speech with, "Let it be known that the kingdom of Buchanan Hollow Ranch has proclaimed there shall be a Knight's Quest for all single men in the kingdom of Texas," using the same theatrical tones as last time. She continued to read, finishing up with, "All knights have until June 27th which is six weeks from the commencement of the Quest, May 16, 1891, to bring said animal to Buchanan Hollow Ranch. All submissions after that date shall be null and void. Lastly, if no challenger is able to find and bring the required item by the deadline the Quest shall be null and void."

After a few seconds of silence, tepid clapping broke out. None of the men seemed excited. Most looked confused.

"Okay. That's done," Tillie said, and descended down from the porch. "Knowles, get over here."

Eli rolled his eyes. Hooray for him. He'd been promoted from *Hey you* and *Slick* to Knowles. The only fly in the ointment was he wished it could be Knight instead of Knowles. Or even better, Eli. But that was a futile wish.

She handed him a small black book, a pencil and a slim stack of flyers. "Come with me and take down these fellows' names and where they're from and that they paid. Once a man pays, you can hand him a flyer."

Yes, ma'am. Nothing he'd like better, a front row seat to all the incipient insanity. She stopped at the first man, the tall, rather gawky fellow he'd noticed earlier who was missing most of his teeth.

"Your name, please?"

"Thorenthon. Thamuel Thorenthon," he said, spraying spit everywhere.

With a grimace, she wiped the spit off her face with her sleeve. "Thamuel Thorenthon, right?" she asked, this time standing a good three feet away.

"No. Thamuel Thorenthon," the man said with a scowl. And more spit.

She gave Eli the side eye, confusion clouding her lovely light blue eyes. "Uh, okay. Write that down. Thamuel Thorenthon."

"No! I thaid Thamuel Thorenthon. Thorenthon. Are you thtupid!"

Eli bit the inside of his cheek. This was shaping up to be more fun than the vaudeville show he'd gone to last December. "I think he said Samuel Sorenson. Correct?"

The man stomped his foot. "Of courthe that'th correct. It'th what I thaid, ithn't it?" More spit flew in his fury.

Tillie winced. "Got it. Samuel Sorenson. Welcome to my Quest. That'll be twenty dollars please," she said through clenched jaws, and held out her hand. Thorenthon—rather Sorenson—dug into his pocket, pulled out a twenty-dollar coin and handed it to her. "Knowles, write his name in the book."

Eli took the coin, stuck it into his pocket, and wrote the man's name down and the address Samuel also provided.

"You. Next in line. C'mon up," she said, pointing at the man who looked like water hadn't touched him in a month of Sundays. The man strolled up to stand in front of the now rather irate Tillie.

Whoa. Eli took a giant step back, out of sniffing distance, and waited to see what the Great Unwashed might offer.

Tillie's hand flew up to cover her nose when the smell caught up with her. Eli shook his head in amusement. Good thing nobody would win this quest because he couldn't see Tillie living with, much less bedding, any of her so-called '*knights*'.

"Name?" she said, her voice nasal because she was pinching her nostrils shut.

"My name is Horace Aker and I'm here to win this here quest and win me a nice wife. Lost mine last year—rattlesnake. Real sad—she was a good woman, hard worker, not much in the looks department though. Or the smarts, neither, now that I think on it since she should of known better than to walk barefoot through the garden—so I bin wanting a new one. Laundry ain't bin done since then."

Obviously. Eli took another step backward.

"Hear that, Tillie," Jim Bob called. "Once he gets himself a wife, he'll probably clean up real good. You might even like him."

She ignored her father.

Without being asked, the man reached down inside his pants—not his pockets, his pants—fumbled around for a moment before pulling out a crumpled wad of bills. "Twenty dollars, you say? Here you go, my entry fee." He peeled off a one-dollar bill from the wad and handed it to Tillie. "One." She recoiled when the bill hit her palm. The dollar was filthy dirty and shiny with...something that was most likely inside the man's filthy drawers.

Aker peeled off another bill. "Two." He slapped it into her palm. She cringed again. "Three." Another bill was handed over. He peeled off a fourth, prepared to hand it to Tillie but she jerked her hand away and held it up.

"Hold on, Mr. Aker. You don't need to count out the twenty dollars. I trust you. Why don't you give it all to Knowles here so he can record it."

Aker shook his head. "Oh, no. I couldn't do that, little missie. Didn't your pa ever teach you not to trust anyone when it comes to money? I gotta count it out so's you know I'm not cheating you."

"I trust you. Really I do," she said, her jaw locked. "Knowles, take his money. Now."

Wishing he wore those gloves he'd thrown into the tack room after the last time he'd cleaned stalls, Eli gingerly took the rest of Aker's money between two fingers, not sure what to do with it. He certainly wasn't putting it in his pocket.

"Set the money on the porch," she hissed out of the corner of her mouth. Carefully, he set the wad of bills on the top step where Jim Bob immediately scooped them up and shoved them into his pocket with a guffaw. Shaking his head, Eli made a mental note to check on Buchanan in a few days to make sure he wasn't sickening with something vile and fatal.

After writing down Aker's name and address, he waited while Tillie motioned the next man forward. It was the short rotund fellow who hemmed and hawed and stammered his way through offering his name and his money. The next few men gave their information and paid their twenty dollars without much trouble and moved to the side to wait.

She reached the last two men. Tall, dirty blond hair, bucktoothed, baby-faced. And exactly alike except for the silver toothpick dangling from the mouth of the man standing closest to her. Before she could ask, the one on the right held his hand out.

"Howdy. I'm Bert."

A second later, his look-alike twin thrust his hand out. "And I'm Bert."

"Um...You're Bert?" Tillie said, gazing at the man who'd introduced himself first, her face screwed up in bewilderment.

The man plucked the toothpick from his mouth. "Yep!" he responded and handed the toothpick to his twin.

"And you're Bert," she said to Bert Two who took the toothpick and stuck it between his lips then nodded.

Eli shoved a knuckle in his mouth, pushing back the laughter that threatened to erupt. It didn't stop Jim Bob's though. The man slapped his knee and howled. Tillie glared at her father but he only let loose another string of loud *hee hee hees*.

She swung back around to face the Berts. "You're both named Bert."

"Yep," Bert One said. "Saves time. Means no one ever has to figure out who's who."

Tillie pressed a palm to her forehead.

Eli bit his lip. Oh, if only he owned a camera to capture the expression on her face. It was priceless.

"And you both want to compete in the Quest?" she mumbled.

Bert One reached into his pants pocket and presented a twenty-dollar bill with a flourish. "Here's Bert and me's entry fee."

Tillie stared at the bill. "Bert...and you...both?"

"Yep. Bert and me, we always do everything together, like now. It—"

"—saves time," she finished for them. "I get it, but it's twenty dollars each."

"Well, now, I don't know how that's gonna work," Bert One said and nudged his brother who handed back the toothpick to his twin who popped it between his lips. "Us always doing the same thing together and all. Don't make sense to pay twice."

Her nostrils flared. "There are two of you. Two people, two fees."

Bert One—or was it Bert Two—gawked at her.

"Okay, listen," she said from between clenched teeth. "When you ride the train do they charge you one fare or two?"

Bert whichever scratched his head. "Well, now, that's kind of a difficult question. See, when we ride the train, we buy one ticket but we sit in different cars. Bert here shows the conductor his ticket and gets it punched. Then when the fella comes to my car, I remind him I already showed him my ticket and hold up an old ticket that done got punched before. Works every time." He nudged the other Bert who grinned and said, "So the question is, if Bert and I win, when can we all get married 'cause our sis wants us back on the farm by September to pick the corn."

Jim Bob issued a shout of laughter and fell to his knees, gasping out a string of *hee hee hees*. Over by the corral, the ranch hands were giggling like lunatics. Eli turned his head, afraid the expression on his face would set Tillie off like an angry volcano.

"*We...*" she said, pointing first at one Bert then the other. "...are not getting married. If, by chance, one of you brings in the winning animal, I'll marry that man."

Eli gulped down his laughter. No she wouldn't. Because no one was going to win this contest.

"But...but...but..." one of the Berts stammered. Eli was pretty sure it was Bert One. "See, here's the thing, Miss Tillie. Bert and me, we always do everything together. If we find this critter you want, we'll find it together which means we're both the winner so that means we both get to marry you," he said, apparently the more dominate of the two, therefore the spokesman.

Under her freckles, her face flushed red. "There's only one of me and it's against the law for me to marry two people. It's called bigamy."

"It's against the law?" Both Bert jaws dropped.

"Yes, and it's also against the law to buy only one ticket and use it for two fares. That's called stealing."

Bert One scratched his nose. "I dunno. This might be a problem. So, um, 'scuse us for a minute, Miss Tillie." He poked his twin who removed the toothpick from his mouth so he could whisper something into his brother's ear. His brother whispered something back. This went on for a minute while Tillie stood, arms crossed, toe tapping, an expression of vexation on her face.

The whisper finally stopped and Bert One spoke. "Okay, so here's what we're gonna do. If we win, I get you for the first year—"

The lady's mouth fell open.

"Then Bert here—" He jerked a thumb at his twin. "He gets you for year two. And I get you back the next year."

"No!" she practically howled.

Eli could no longer hold back his glee. It rolled out in great gusts, a low counterpoint to Jim Bob's high pitched *hee hee hees* which made him laugh even harder. Good lord, he really needed that. He couldn't remember the last time he'd laughed.

Twin faces fell in twin disappointment. "No?" a Bert asked, although Eli wasn't sure which one it was. Not that it seemed to matter.

"I am not a breeding mare that you trade off to the highest bidder."

The whispering commenced again. Eli wiped his eyes, still chuckling. Too bad they didn't have some kind of moving picture camera to capture the scene. It would be worth a million bucks.

A Bert held a hand up. "Okay then, if you're gonna be that way about it, I guess we'll draw straws if we win. You won't know the difference anyhow."

Tillie clenched her fists. "I need something to drink." Spinning on her heel, she stomped up the stairs and flew inside the house, slamming the door behind her.

"Hee hee hee. Think she'll give it up now?" Buchanan asked Eli.

Giving up was probably what Jim Bob was counting on, but if it was, he didn't know his daughter like he thought it did. Even only knowing her for a few weeks, Eli was already aware she possessed a stubborn streak a mile wide. So he shook his head no. Sure enough, two minutes later, she reappeared on the porch and took her place next to Eli. He inhaled, the scent of her usual scent of soap and fresh laundry making him nearly dizzy with lust. He also got a whiff of something alcoholic, probably bourbon. He didn't blame her.

She heaved a sigh. "Knowles, pass out the flyers."

Walking among the small crowd, he handed them out.

"So this here thing in the pitcher is what we have to bring back?" the Great Unwashed asked.

"It is," she answered.

"I never theen nothing like thith before. Are you sure it'th real?" Samuel Sorenson asked next.

Eli bit his lip. Of course it wasn't real. Only a dummy would think it was real. *But that's why you were picked. Because you're a dummy.*

"I ain't never heard of a ...eecua... whatchamacallit," another said.

"Where does this thing come from? It don't look like it's from Texas."

Tillie tugged her hat down over her glaring eyes. "Okay, that's it. No more questions. Either you want to participate in the Quest or you don't. The deadline is six weeks from today, which is June 27th at five p.m. However, that doesn't mean you can't come back sooner if you believe you have found the animal described on the flyer. Thank you, gentlemen, you're dismissed."

"Golly," one of the Berts said, scratching his head. "I think she's mad."

"Naw, she can't be. I think she's in a hurry to marry one of us," the other said. "So we better get our horses and get to looking for this thing on the paper."

They toddled off to the pasture and retrieved their mounts. Eli grinned to see them ride by, surprisingly one on a bay, the other on a gray horse, instead of sharing one animal. Minutes later, their exodus was followed by the other men. The show over, Jinx and his crew retreated into the bunkhouse since they'd received the day off in exchange for their help with the quest, leaving only Eli, Tillie, and Jim Bob.

Jim Bob stroked his long luxurious mustache. "Well, daughter, you couldn't have picked a dumber bunch of fellows if you tried," he said, staring after the last of them.

If you only knew.

"If those fellow are what you want, it's your bed. I just hope you enjoy lying in it."

A frisson of something—anger, dislike, sympathy, or possibly a combination of all three—crawled up Eli's spine. Why didn't the man leave his daughter alone?

"Course, if you don't, I'm sure I can find a bed for you to lie in." Under Jim Bob's luxurious white handlebar mustache, a smirk lurked.

Tillie's hands flexed into fists then, without another word, she jumped down off the porch and stomped into the barn.

Chapter Ten

After Tillie stormed off, Buchanan didn't say anything for a bit, just continued to thoughtfully finger his mustache. Not having received a dismissal, Eli wasn't sure if he should stick around or sneak away in hopes he could avoid questions he couldn't answer. Unfortunately, he wavered too long.

"So this equicamwhatchamacallit thing. How likely is it that one of those dummies will find one before the deadline is up?"

Eli stared at the sky like he was considering the question but he wasn't considering the question at all, he was avoiding Buchanan's eyes. The man was a fool if he didn't realize his daughter was playing a trick on him but Eli wasn't about to tell him the truth.

Buchanan watched him, one eye narrowed, the opposite eyebrow cocked in suspicion. All right, so maybe the man wasn't a fool after all.

"Well..." Eli finally said, dragging out the word, seeking an answer that would satisfy the other man but not rat Tillie out. "I guess...those men have as much chance of finding an equicamemu as anyone." Or no one.

"Hmph." Buchanan tapped his fingers on his thigh. "That daughter of mine. Sometimes I wonder... Does she think she'll be happy marrying one of those stupid fellas so she can be in charge of the ranch?"

Eli coughed to give him time to frame a sentence that was an answer but not an answer. "I...uh...think she'll make the choice that will make her happy." Which was not getting married at all, from what Eli intuited.

Buchanan rocked back and forth on the high heels of his western boots, sucking loudly on his lower lip. "Well, if there's one thing I can say about my daughter, it's that she's too smart to do something not in her best interests. Which is why I'm wondering what she's really got in mind."

Eli nearly swallowed his tongue. "Uh..."

Jim Bob stopped rocking, stopped sucking on his lip to stare down at Eli. "What's Tillie got you doing the rest of the day?" he asked abruptly.

"Uh...nothing. She gave us the day off because of the quest."

"I want you to go into town."

Why hadn't he decamped when everyone else did? "Go into town? What for?"

"Want you to do a little snooping for me."

Hell's bells. Trapped. "Snooping? What kind of snooping?" A quiver of anxiety niggled its way up his spine.

Buchanan huffed. "Into this idiotic quest of Tillie's, what did you think, son? I know that girl and she's slipperier than a bar of soap. She's got some kind of scheme going on and I want to find out what it is."

Eli's heart sank. He didn't have to investigate to know that Buchanan was right. "Um... I'm not sure why you think I can find anything out if you couldn't."

A mischievous sparkle gleamed from Jim Bob's eyes. "If she's up to something, somebody in town will know what it is. The problem is, they're all on her side and won't tell me a thing. Now you, on the other hand, folks in town have never met you and you're a right good-looking fellow with a nice way about you. Stands to reason if her lady friends know, you might be able to charm a little information out of them. And as for the gents, well, men seem to like you too and might let slip a fact or two."

The memory of a few feet thrust out to trip him and his thistle-filled trousers put the lie to Jim Bob's assertion that men liked him. "I don't think your daughter will let me go into town."

The mischievous gleam hardened into determination. "I'm the boss around here and if I say you can go into town, you go into town."

The term boss was another misnomer on Jim Bob's part, but who was Eli to correct him?

"You might need some cash. To grease a few palms or whatever. You got any money?"

He shook his head. The rancher reached into his pocket and pulled out a wad of cash. Eli took a step back. It was the Great Unwashed's wad.

"Oops, sorry." Jim Bob reached into the other pocket, pulled out a wallet and extracted two bills. He laid them in Eli's palm. "Here you go. This should do."

Two fifty-dollar bills. A hundred dollars. He stared at them for a minute, thoughts racing. A hundred dollars would be enough to hire someone to find out if Morgan was after him. A pang went through his chest at the thought he might be able to go home.

Or a hundred dollars could buy him a train ticket...somewhere away from here because he could already see that if he stuck around here much longer, he was headed for trouble. Because the thought of his hands molding themselves around Tillie's hearts-shaped backside invaded his sleep every night. Memories of her eyes, the pale blue surrounded by the almost black ring, popped up every time he let his guard down. Her sweet, sassy mouth made his lips burn to kiss her. The desire to talk with her, be with her, increased with every day that passed.

Talk about stuck between a rock and a hard place. In the end, he took the money. He wished he knew what he was going to do with it.

"You can use my horse Rusty. He's in the barn."

Eli trudged toward the barn. His chest hurt. Was he getting sick or was it because he was about to betray someone he'd grown to like, or even more importantly, grown to respect?

It was dark and quiet inside the barn except for the murmur of a human voice joining with the sounds of horses shuffling through their straw bedding, and their massive teeth grinding up their food. He looked around but didn't see Tillie. Stepping carefully, he edged his way up the aisle until he reached the pregnant mare's stall.

"—don't want to get married right now, Daisy."

He stopped next to the closed stall door.

"No matter what Pops says, I don't need a man. I can do fine by myself."

A minute passed while she said nothing and Eli didn't move. The mare nickered and made a whuffling sound that made her owner giggle.

"Lucky you. You don't have some man telling you what to do every second of every day." She paused. "My apologies, Daisy, that's not quite true. I didn't give you any choice about that old stallion, Rex Maximus, did I, and now see. You're pregnant. But it's different for me. It's not exactly like Pops is forcing me. I mean, he could be like some fathers and beat me or lock me up and starve me... He blusters and yells and makes a big fuss but he won't hurt me. But the thing is...this time I think he's serious. It seems like no matter what I do, I'm gonna end up married even if I don't want to."

"I don't know though. Maybe I'm being stubborn and stupid. Would it be so bad to be married? Other women seem to like it just fine," she said and sniffled a wet sounding snuffle. "It's that I don't want some man telling me what to do and telling me all I'm good for is sitting in the house tatting doilies. I hate tatting and sewing and sitting around. I need to be out doing things."

A long time passed before she spoke again. "But it might be nice to have a husband, children. Someone who...loves me. Really loves me for who I am. If such a man exists." She sighed. "Damn it, I don't understand what's going on in my head. I mean, I spent a whole bunch of money on a dress. A dress, Daisy. A formal ball gown dress. Why in the Sam Hill would I buy a ballgown? I've got no use for a dress like that." The horse nickered again and Tillie laughed, a quiet laugh that was more sad than real laughter.

"And I'm feeling all these things. I go to bed every night and I feel these things I've never felt before. I ache. I...I...I want to be touched. In certain places. Places I don't...can't... The devil, it's so frustrating. Why am I having all these feelings?"

It got quiet again. "It's that man! That...that...darned city slicker!"

Eli jolted. Oh damn.

"It's his fault. He makes me so mad. And...and other things... Oh, Daisy, I don't know what to do. I wish my mother was still here," she wailed and the sound of a tiny sob reached him.

Sweet Jesus. Strong, indomitable Tillie was crying. It made his heart clench. He wanted to take her in his arms and kiss her to make it all better, but he couldn't. She would hate him if she realized he'd heard. His inclination was to comfort her, but that thought was squashed by the need to protect her.

Pressing his back against the wall of the stall, he slid towards the outer door. He took a deep breath, trying to regain the equilibrium he'd lost when he heard her sobs. When his heartbeat slowed and his mind steadied, he deliberately banged his shoulder against the metal framed door and called, "Miss Buchanan. You in here? Your father sent me to get his horse."

He walked slowing into the gloom of the barn, giving her plenty of time to erase all signs of her weeping.

The door to Daisy's stall opened and she stepped out. Under her freckles, her face was pale, and her eyes were puffy. A pang went through him. Once again, his arms ached to hold her, his hands itched to stroke her hair but he pretended he saw nothing.

"Pops sent you for his horse?" she asked, her voice rife with suspicion. Her voice was hoarse with unshed tears.

Hells bells. What a dummy. His mind spun quickly through a dozen reasons why he would need a horse before lighting on, "Uh...he heard from...uh...Zeke, yeah, Zeke, that..." His mind hit a snag before he remembered. He pointed at the patch on the seat of his pants he'd sewn on to cover the hole someone ripped in them when Eli hung them up to dry after the foreman pushed him into the water trough.

Damn the man. Even after all this time, Jinx was still out to pay Eli back for the spider incident. Just yesterday, he sprinkled chili powder on Eli's stew when Eli turned his back for a second. It nearly burned his tongue off when he took a bite.

"He saw this patch and...anyway, I don't have any extra pants to replace them so he said...um...I should go into town to get a few new items of clothing."

Her mouth twisted. She didn't trust him, and why should she, because, after all, he was lying.

"He said to take his horse?"

He stared at his feet. "He said take Rusty. I assume that's his horse. And gave me an advance on my pay to buy what I need." It was another lie, damn it, right when she was beginning to trust him. "I believe payday is next Friday so I can pay you back then?"

She jerked her head at a stall towards the back. "Go on, there's Rusty. But be back by dark."

With a quirk of his lips that he hoped resembled a smile but probably looked more like the spasm of a dying man—which was how he felt—he rushed into the stall, pulled the horse out and tied him up in the crossties. She watched every move he made, sending little pinpricks of nerves up his back while he retrieved the saddle and bridle from the tack room, and tacked the horse up. Done, he led Rusty outside. She followed.

"If you need clothes, go to Sanger Brothers. Get what you need and put it on our account," she said, her face turned away while she rubbed her hand up and down the blaze on the horse's face.

"I can't take money I haven't earned," he told her, hiding the fact that her father handed him a hundred dollars. Because that hundred dollars was not for clothing, it was for bribes.

"Consider it a loan then, not a gift. You can pay back whatever you spend out of your pay when you get it at the end of the month," she said gruffly.

He swallowed the lump in his throat that threatened to choke him. Today was almost too much, the ups, the downs, the laughter he'd experienced watching her make mincemeat out of her Questers, her father's derision and his determination to sabotage his daughter. Witnessing her despair. And her kindness. He faced her, seeing the traces of her tears still on her face, anger and sympathy rioted.

"Miss Tillie?" a voice said from behind him. He jerked around. Jinx. Of course. The foreman's small eyes gleamed maliciously as he sneered at Eli before transferring his gaze to Tillie with a smile. "This man bothering you?"

Eli stiffened, his dislike, once again, rising to the surface.

"No, I'm fine, Jinx. No need to worry."

Jinx transferred his gaze back to Eli, his eyes narrowed in suspicion. "What are you doing with Mr. Buchanan's horse, Slick?" he demanded. "You trying to steal a valuable animal?"

Eli clenched his teeth against the furious words he wanted to hurl at the bully.

"He's on his way into town to buy some new duds," Tillie interjected. "And to pick up a few things I need."

Jinx swung his gaze back to Eli. "Going to town? Did I give you permission to go into town?"

Eli opened his mouth to answer, a few choice words on the tip of his tongue but Tillie beat him to it.

"Mind your business, Jinx. My father gave him permission to borrow the horse, and I gave him permission to go into town." She eyed him up and down. "Don't you have work to do? Day's not over yet, you know."

For a minute, the two of them faced each other, Tillie's face set in stone, the muscles in Jinx's jaw flexing with anger. "I thought you gave us the day off."

"I changed my mind. Seems like you don't have enough things to do to keep you out of other people's business. Seems like I need to find some work for you. Why don't you ride out to that back section of the north pasture and move the horses there to the pasture by the creek."

The other man's jaw hardened. "Sure, I'll get right to it." He pushed past Eli, knocking into Eli's shoulder as he did, and strode out to the nearby pasture to retrieve his own horse.

"Better go, Slick," Tillie said once Jinx was out of sight.

There were words Eli wanted to say but they were stuck in his throat. Instead, he checked the girth again. There was no reason to check the girth, he knew it was cinched perfectly but he couldn't make himself mount and ride away.

"Well, go on," she said, her voice rough. "If you're going to be back by dark, you need to leave now."

He stood facing the animal for a minute, his emotions still in turmoil. He wanted to hug her, hold her tight, say he would make it all better. At the same time, the hundred dollars Buchanan gave him was burning a hole in his pocket. With that money he could be away from here, away from Tillie and the burning desire he felt for her. It could also put him an additional fifteen hundred miles further away from Morgan.

"See you later," she said.

He didn't answer. He couldn't. All he could do was swallow his overwhelming, inconvenient emotions, mount and rein the horse towards the outer gate with its tall posts that held up the wooden sign with the name Buchanan Hollow carved into it.

He cantered underneath, an almost irresistible urge to look back at her flameing through him but he resisted it because if he did, he would race to her side and kiss the living daylights out of the woman. So he didn't turn around, didn't wave goodbye. He simply kicked his horse into a gallop and kept going.

San Antonio was only a half hour's ride from Buchanan Hollow so he soon found himself riding up the main street of town, making note of the different establishments until he found a livery stable to leave the horse.

He wandered slowly past several shop windows, his mind half on the business Buchanan tasked him with, the other half pulling him in a completely different direction. He should probably talk to a few folks, ask some questions but every bit of him didn't want to prove to her father that she was a liar. Still...

Where would Tillie have gone to implement her crazy scheme? Where did she get the pictures of that non-existent beast, her equicamemu? The animal was part horse, part camel and part that strange emu thing. She must have cobbled it together from several pictures.

After getting directions, he found a bookstore and went inside. "I'm looking for some information," he asked the clerk at the front desk. "Do you carry picture books?"

"What kind of picture books. For children?"

"No, with photographs of animals."

The clerk shook his head. "Nope, we mostly carry novels and such like, not reference books. For that you should go to the library. Two streets that way—" She pointed. "And make a left."

He exited, stopping outside to ask himself whether he really wanted to find the answer. The crowd of people eddied around him, intent on their destination.

"Hey, watch where you're going," someone yelled.

"Fuck off, asshole," someone else yelled back.

Startled at the foul language, Eli peered over his shoulder in time to see a man wearing a wide brimmed brown hat that shaded his face lift a single digit at the heckler before disappearing around the closest corner. Something niggled in the back of his mind but the thought disappeared.

He dismissed the incident and walked the short distance to a large gray stone building with four massive pillars surrounding the doorway. Inside, an attractive brunette manned the front desk. Heeding Buchanan's advice, he gave the woman his best smile.

"Can you help me?" he asked. "I'm interested in books with photos of animals."

The smile faded. "Animals? What kind of animals?"

"Any kind. I'm hoping to find some books for..." He paused, realizing telling the truth might not be such a good idea. "For my eight-year-old nephew. He wants to be an animal doctor. I thought some books on animals might help."

She pursed her lips and pointed towards the back. "In reference. Aisles twenty-four and twenty-five."

He followed where her finger pointed and found himself between two rows of shelves filled with books. Holy cow. Where to start? Paging through all these books would take hours, and he didn't know what he was looking for anyway. He walked back to the front desk. "Has anybody but me come in asking for something similar?"

The pursed lips reemerged, along with a suspicious squint. "No. Why are you asking?"

"No reason. Uh, thanks for your time," he said and left. Possibly Tillie found photographs at the library and used them to create her flyers but really, did he care?

Nope. He couldn't care less about the why and the how, and even less about reporting his findings to her father so the man could throw a wrench into the spokes of her wheel. Buchanan might be the person who initially hired him but Tillie was the one who would decide if he stayed. She was also the only one he would miss if he needed to leave. Regardless, he was done.

Asking for further directions, he began a short walk. It being Saturday, a prime shopping day, the walks were crowded, forcing him to sidestep around the people blocking his path. Some people stared at him. The back of his neck itched, like someone was watching him. Glancing over his shoulder, he saw no one who seemed a threat so he kept going until he reached his destination but the tingle continued to bother him.

Western Union. Almost a month had passed. Was Morgan still searching for him? Did he dare? Was it safe? He dithered for a moment. His sister must be nearly frantic not hearing from him. In the end, that's what decided him. "I need to send a telegram to New York City. How much?"

"Ten words, two dollars and seventy cents."

He pulled out several one-dollar coins, the few dollars left from his brother-in-law's contribution. Taking the form the clerk gave him, he wrote out his message.

No worries. Am safe. Will wire again soon. Ulysses.

He waited long enough to see the clerk tap out the message. Now, only one more place to visit. After receiving instructions, he made the long walk out of the downtown area of the city until he reached Hoefgen Street. Stopping outside the two-story stucco building, he searched until he found what he sought, a large blackboard hanging on the wall outside the main entrance. He walked over to stand in front of it and stared at the information written in chalk.

East Bound 10:45 am 1:36 pm 5:21 pm
West Bound 9:13 am 12:22 pm 4:56 pm

He checked the clock hanging on the wall over the doorway. Four-sixteen. Reaching into his pocket, he pulled out the two bills Buchanan gave him. The pros and cons flitted through his mind. There was danger in staying here. He felt it. The creeping sensation that Morgan would somehow track him to Buchanan Hollow never left him. He looked at the bills in his hand again. A hundred dollars. Should he stay? Or should he go?

He didn't know.

Chapter Eleven

The sound of hooves thundered in her ears as Buster galloped up the hill. Dust swirled, and trees whipped by in blur of green. Reaching the top, Tillie yanked hard on the reins, causing the horse to sit back on his haunches and dig his front hooves into the ground when he skidded to a halt, his sides heaving.

She threw herself from the saddle and ran a few steps further up the hill, just far enough to not scare the bejasus out of the horse when she spread her arms wide and screamed a scream that was long and loud and filled with her frustration.

Then, because it felt so good, she screamed again.

Buster flared his nostrils so the pale pink inside showed and gave her a horsey glare.

She glared back. "Are you judging me?" she demanded. "You'd better not be judging me, horse, because I'm entitled. If you were forced to put up with the shit that I'm putting up with, you'd scream too."

He bobbed his head if to say, *I agree, only don't do it again.*

"Fine. Thank you. Sorry for alarming you." After a pat on his sweaty neck, she turned away and started up to the top of the hill so she could view below the long, low white house, the barns and the sheds and the green pastures that nurtured the horses and the cattle that kept the place profitable.

All the things that were supposed to be hers, but now might not be. Unless her plan worked. It had to work because she didn't want to get married, or more accurately, she didn't want to be forced to marry. Marriage was fine for other women but she wasn't like those floofy girls, content to get married and step aside so some man could take over the reins of the ranch while she sat on her tuffet and gave birth to a slew of babies.

At the idea of babies her thoughts jerked to a halt. Babies. Did she want babies? The image of a baby with dark, almost black, curly hair and Texas sky blue eyes, popped into her mind.

Ooooo. It was him. That man. Again. Always invading her thoughts, like some poisonous species of plant, creeping into her mind when she wasn't expecting it. All this...this...waffling, this mental anguish and stupid daydreaming was his fault.

She walked back down the hill, fought her way through a thicket of laurel bushes until she reached a wide stream. Sitting on her favorite rock, she pulled off her boots and socks and dropped her feet into the crystal-clear cool water.

Ahh, that was better. She leaned back on her elbows and closed her eyes. Being here, enjoying the coolness provided by the trees, and the quiet of the woods, always helped her think more clearly. And what she thought about, of course, was Knowles. Because he was a problem.

The man was too sure of himself, too handsome, too...too...manly. But worse than that, was the fact that somehow he'd guessed. She'd seen it in his eyes, she'd seen it in his smile. He knew her plan was full of baloney. He'd guessed her quest was a fake, which meant too many things could go wrong, not the least of which was if that damned city slicker blabbed what he knew.

She sat up. The man needed to go, for a number of reasons, not least being her sanity.

Yep, that was the ticket; get him gone, off Buchanan Hollow Ranch and out of her life. No more broad shoulders to distract her, no more bright blue eyes to mesmerize, no more knowing smiles. What would it take to convince him to leave? Pay him? Cold hard cash? That worked for most people. Money talked and people walked. But somehow she sensed money didn't talk very loudly to Knowles. Seemed like he was one of those honorable types who would resent someone trying to bribe him. A real Ivanhoe. The fictional man she dreamed about and wished existed in real life.

If she couldn't pay Knowles to leave, perhaps she could bribe him to keep it all to himself. She's heard the other hands were making his life miserable so he might be motivated by having somewhere to hang his hat besides the bunkhouse. Or the promise of an easier work load? Not that he complained much. Or at all.

So then what? What else did she have to bargain with?

Herself?

A hot flush went through her. Is that what it would take? And if it did, how would she go about it? She knew the mechanics, no one raised on a ranch could be ignorant of how babies were conceived, but how did one go about seducing a man? Surely it wasn't wham, bam, thank you ma'am, like with cows and horses? So if not, where did one start? Simply walk up to him and say, "How about it, Slick? Wanna trade some quick sex for a little silence? Only you'll have to ignore the fact that I don't know what I'm doing."

Ugh, lying with a man to buy his silence sounded too close to prostitution for her liking. It was wrong, despicable, dishonest, and probably a host of other not-so-nice adjectives, but at the thought of that lean, muscular body joining with hers, heat flashed through her, making body parts she usually ignored rear up and bark.

Apparently, while her mind said no way, her body had a completely different opinion. She fanned herself with her hat.

Probably the safest route was to try to change Pops' mind. She'd done it before and was pretty sure she could do it again.

Pulling her feet out of the stream, she put her socks and boots back on and walked back to her horse. She mounted and started down the hill toward home. It was growing dark, so time to take care of evening stables, and to make sure all the hands were doing their evening chores.

And time to make a decision about Slick. He should be back from his foray into town by now. At the reminder, a creepy crawly worm of desire spiraled up her spine and sweat broke out on her forehead. Damn the man. Why couldn't he be ugly?

Lights were on in the house when she reached the barn. Leading Buster inside his stall, she untacked him, putting his saddle and bridle away. Finding a curry comb in the tack room, she brushed him down, put fresh water in his bucket and a scoop of oats in his feed trough and shut him inside his stall. After giving Daisy a pat and a carrot and checking to see how close she was to delivering, Tillie walked up the aisle, checking on the other horses to make sure the horses were all bedded down properly.

Except they weren't. Rusty's stall was empty. She pulled her watch out of her pocket to check the time. Ten minutes after seven. Why was Rusty not in his stall? Was Slick not back from town? Leaving the barn, she walked around behind the barn to the bunkhouse. After knocking, she poked her head inside. "Is Slick here?"

Zeke shook his head. "Nope, we ain't seen him."

"Last I saw him, he was riding your pa's horse headed into town," Jud said.

"Well, he's not back," Tillie said sharply.

Jinx snickered. "Yeah, and I wouldn't count on you seeing him, nor that horse of your pa's ever again."

"What do you mean?"

Rising from his seat at the table, Jinx strolled over. "I mean, I saw him in town heading towards the railway station. If I were you, I'd contact the sheriff 'cause I don't think yer ever going to see that horse again."

He'd left? He'd stolen a horse, her father's horse, and took off? Inexplicably, her heart sank. Wasn't that what she wanted, to have him gone, taking with him the threat of his blowing up her plan?

Wait... if he was taking the train, why would he steal a horse? It wasn't like he could take the horse on the train. Something didn't make sense.

And why was Jinx in town? "What were you doing in town?"

His upper lip curled, almost a sneer. "You gave us the afternoon off, remember. No reason I couldn't go into town."

She shook her head. "No, when you smarted off to me, I asked you to go out to the back section and move the horses to the north pasture."

Something sparked in his eye, something she didn't like. He'd always been a good employee, but lately, she'd begun to wonder if she should keep him on. The problem was, getting rid of Jinx would leave her without a man to manage the crew on a day-to-day basis.

She'd have to keep an eye on him. "Next time I tell you to do something, you do it, got it?"

The almost sneer morphed into a supercilious smile. "Yes, ma'am," he said. "Whatever you say."

Yes, she'd definitely need to keep an eye on him.

"Um, excuse me," a low, husky voice said from behind her. She whipped around to see Slick, looking tired and rumpled and grim.

Her heart leapt, relief filling her for two seconds before relief was replaced by anger followed by a quick surge of what could only be called lust so powerful it nearly knocked her over. "Where the heck have you been?"

"Town," was his response. One corner of his mouth crooked up in what might be a smile but really wasn't. There was no amusement in his eyes, only a look of defeat. A twinge of sympathy pinged but she dismissed it. She couldn't afford sympathy. She couldn't afford that hot tingle racing through her blood either, which didn't mean it wasn't there.

"You were supposed to be back by dark. It's almost dark so you're late. I don't accept lateness." Even when she said it, she wanted to slap herself for being so nasty. Why was she so angry? Why was she scolding the man for doing something most of the hands did on a regular basis?

She sucked in a breath. Maybe because it was possible the man was in town enjoying manly things, things that roused a green slime of envy in her breast. It wasn't fair that some other, undeserving floofy girl got to enjoy all his manliness.

Or was she agitated because she wondered if he didn't plan on coming back at all. The idea made her short of breath, which made her mad all over again. "It's going to be a long day tomorrow. Get some rest," she ordered, and left.

Damn it. Damn it, damn it, damn it. The man was making her crazy, and she couldn't afford any additional crazy. She had enough crazy in her life what with her Pops and his efforts to sabotage her life with this marriage thing.

All ten of her quest knights were out there seeking something that didn't exist but that didn't mean the danger was past. Her father was still digging around, hoping to find holes in her scheme, ready to pounce at her slightest mistake.

Stomping into the house, she stormed into her bedroom and slammed the door shut behind her. Stripping down, she slipped on her nightgown and fell into bed. She'd read *Ivanhoe*. Maybe that would reassure her.

It didn't. It only reinforced the fact that there was a man out there who was getting ready for bed, probably stripped down to his drawers, that she wanted. A man she shouldn't want but wanted anyway. She was in so much trouble.

Ivanhoe having not done the trick; she blew out the lamp and went to sleep. Or tried to, because her sleep was rife with dreams of broad shoulders, a tight butt, and bright Texas sky blue eyes.

It was officially the second week of her quest, too soon to expect anyone to show up with results, which was fine with her since every fellow who returned to Buchanan Hollow was one more chance her fraud would be exposed. After over a week of nearly sleepless nights, she woke up early, tired and sluggish.

Strangely, somehow, overnight, her unconscious mind realized that the best thing to do was to make sure Knowles spent his time away from the house—and her. Maybe her female bits would stop begging for attention like a dog in heat.

Right now it was time to do what she should have been doing all along, which was managing her ranch instead of spending time on this stupidity. Her heritage. And her inheritance, she reminded herself. If she didn't get her ass going and take care of things, the success—or non-success—of the quest wouldn't matter for a hill of beans because the ranch would fail.

After her Eli-filled night, she spent the next day trying to avoid the man who was the star of all those dreams. Interestingly enough, he seemed to be avoiding her too, which, perversely, irritated the bejasus out of her to the point that she found herself trying to get a rise out of him even though she'd promised herself she would ignore him.

"Clean the latrines," she said the day after he was back from town. She could see the steam practically coming from his ears but he'd smiled and answered, "Yes, ma'am, Miss Buchanan, ma'am," saying words that should have been respectful but weren't quite because a gleam of deviltry shone from his eyes.

"Food not good enough for you?" she'd sniped when he declined to eat the refried beans Joey served one night. Not that she blamed him; Joey's refried beans tasted like shit. And gave her the shits.

"No, ma'am, Miss Buchanan." Another gleam and a smirk. "Simply not hungry. Ma'am."

"You're looking tired. Not sleeping well?"

"I'm sleeping fine, Miss Buchanan, ma'am. Best mattress I've ever slept on. Ma'am."

He'd taken it all with a smile and a knowing look in his eyes. It was war but she wasn't sure who was winning.

Eight days since the Quest started. Maybe today would be a better day, or more aptly, maybe she'd be a better person. She walked out to the bunkhouse ready to be on her best behavior for a change. The men, including Slick, were leaving the bunkhouse when she arrived.

"Jinx, you're still working out in the south pasture, right?"

He gave her a look from under his lashes that seemed to say, *I'm not stupid. Even if you are.* A whisper of unease curled up her spine but she quickly dismissed it.

"Okay, take Jud and Zeke with you. Pretty sure there's still a few calves that need castrating. Round them up and bring them in."

Spinning around, Jinx left with the other two. "Kermit, go check the windmill out by Duggan's Creek. Beau said there's a big puddle forming out by the trough so there might be a crack in the pipe. Take some piping with you and fix it if it needs it."

Scratching his armpit, the hand muttered sourly, "Oh, goodie. My favorite thing. Let me get a shovel," and turned to leave but Tillie added, "Take Slick with you. You might need some help. Even though he's useless at most things, I know he can dig."

Apparently, so could she. And that was a pretty nasty dig, come to think of it.

Slick leveled a flat stare at her—which made heat flood her face—and followed Kermit into the tool shed.

"Buck, you can ride the fence line in the south pasture. Hitch up the wagon, load a spool of wire into it and a post or two in case those dumbass cows have knocked any over."

Done giving orders, sure her orders would be obeyed, she went back inside the house to eat.

Her Pops was at the dining table, busy shoveling eggs and biscuits into his mouth while reading the San Antonio Express.

"Says here you got the state of Texas all in a tizzy with this quest thing of yours." He bit into a sausage.

Tillie made a face. So far she'd not seen hide nor hair of any of the Questers. For a while she'd wondered if they'd all decided it wasn't worth the effort and walked away without saying a word but now it seemed it was official—they were still on the hunt. Damn. The Questers might be dumb as rocks but most of them were smart enough to realize winning the contest meant winning a ranch and winning her. At the thought, her stomach roiled sickly.

She shrugged even though she didn't feel all that dismissive inside, more apprehensive and pissed. "If people are in a tizzy, that's their problem, not mine." She smiled a thanks at Inez when her breakfast plate loaded with huevos rancheros, grilled tomatoes, refried beans and several tortillas was placed in front of her. Forking the eggs and beans into the tortilla, she took a bite.

Her father jabbed a finger at the newspaper. "So, says here two of those fellows got on the train, said they were heading down south to Meheeco to find that equi-whatever thing you want them to find and bring back. What do you think their chances are, going down there and all?"

Taking a sip of coffee, Tillie squinted at him over the rim of the cup. What was the old buzzard up to now? He wore that sly expression, one she recognized starting from the age of five when she figured out her father had more dirty tricks up his sleeve than a card shark.

"Whether they find the Equicamemu or not is up to them," she answered blandly. "Time will tell." It sure would, and she couldn't wait to see all the disappointed faces when they returned empty handed.

He stared at her. She stared back, smiling a smile that said, *gotcha, old man.*

"Well, personally, I don't think they'll find anything down south of the border."

"Oh, yeah? So...if you're so smart, where would you look?" she responded. Picking up another tortilla, she spooned eggs and beans into it, folded it over and shoved it into her mouth, casually gazing out the wide window at the corral next to the barn like she didn't have a care in the world when she was really a bundle of nerves wondering what her father was thinking.

He didn't answer. Good. Maybe now she could get some peace and quiet. Still avoiding his eyes, she allowed her gaze to drift over to the water trough. It was empty. Of course it was empty. It was daylight so no fancy pantsy city slicker would be sliding his manly body into the trough for her viewing pleasure. Heat rushed to her face.

"Fact is, I think no matter where they go they won't find a darned thing," her father said, jerking her out of her thoughts.

She whipped her gaze around to view him, a dozen responses spinning through her brain. "Why's that?" Okay, that wasn't exactly the stellar response she thought it was. Truthfully, it was pretty stupid because it opened the door for him to accuse her of cheating. Which she was, but that was beside the point. The point was, her entire life depended on making people believe her lies.

"Well..." he said hesitantly. He skated his fork back and forth through the pile of eggs on his plate, taking his time answering, probably to torture her. Or...maybe he didn't have a valid reason for his doubts, simply a bunch of suspicions. "Seems like not too many people have heard of this *equicamemu* thing. I never heard of it, and I even asked at the library and they didn't know what I was talking about either. Seems like someone ought to know what that thing is and where someone could find it, don't you think?"

She blew out a silent breath of relief. Nothing but a lot of suspicions and no real facts. So she'd give him some facts. Sort of. "Ever hear of a platypus?"

Her Pops squinted at her. "Uh, no."

"Weird little thing from Australia. A mammal that lays eggs. Has a bill like a duck. And it's back claws are poisonous. How about a chinchilla?"

He shook his head.

"A cute, furry rodent from South America in the Andes Mountains 'bout the size of a squirrel. Just because you haven't heard of them doesn't mean they don't exist. I'm sure if my questers do a little research, they'll figure it out." Or not. Under the table, she crossed her fingers because she was lying and it seemed the thing to do.

He shook his head. "No idea. Those fellows you picked don't seem too bright."

She smiled at him. The last thing she wanted to do was let slip the fact she'd picked them for their stupidity.

He slumped back in his chair, his smile gone, his visage downcast. He took a bit of eggs, chewed, and narrowed his eyes while he thought, obviously working on some scheme. She could always tell when he was hatching a new one because he got this certain expression on his face, like now. Minutes passed. Tillie ate and tried to ignore him but it wasn't easy. For Jim Bob Buchanan, thinking entailed a lot of mumbling and finger tapping and throat clearing. Sadly for her, it didn't usually entail a lot of actual analytical thought. In this instance, however, she was glad for the fact.

"Which is why I invited your cousin Orson to visit," he interjected abruptly into the silence.

"What!" she shrieked.

"Now, now, don't get your petticoats in a twist." The expression on his face was bland but the gleam shining in his eyes was pure deviltry.

"I don't wear petticoats, and you know it," she growled then realized she was letting him sidetrack her. "Why in hell's half acre would you invite Odious for a visit? Don't you remember what happened last time he was here?"

The last time Orson visited, he'd let the stallion she'd brought in to mate with her best mare out of his stall, and the randy thing enjoyed a grand old time with Meggie, an eleven-year-old broken-down nag she'd taken in out of pity when the owner threatened to put her down. After that, her idiot cousin entered the hen house to get a couple eggs, upset the hens so much they'd attacked him and didn't lay eggs for a week. A few days later, he'd gone for a ride and gotten lost. When he didn't show up for dinner, everyone was forced to ride out in the pouring rain to find him. When they finally found him, he was waiting out the storm in the bed of the widow lady a few miles down the road. He didn't appear happy to be found. There were other things too numerous to even think about.

Gazing up at the ceiling like he had nothing much of importance on his mind, which was most of the time, only not today, her father answer, "Well, now, sugar pie..."

Sugar pie. When he started calling her pet names was when she needed to seriously start worrying. "No. Tell him no."

"He's your cousin. You haven't seen him in a while. Time to get reacquainted."

"What are you up to?"

His entire life revolved around food, naps and his mistresses. Oh, and his get-rich-quick schemes, which never came to fruition. He put his hand over his heart and assumed his I'm-as-innocent-as-a-newborn-baby look. "Why, Tillie. Are you accusing me of something nefarious or something?"

"Or something," she growled.

"I believe he's got plans to come real soon," Pops said, taking another bite of sausage and grinning at her wide enough she could see his molars in addition to a few chunks of meat. Ugh.

"Either uninvite him, or...or...else." Shoving her chair back, Tillie stood. "I'm not hungry anymore, and I've got work to do." Grabbing her hat off the side table, she jammed it on her head and headed for the exit. She slammed the front door behind her.

She stopped by the bunkhouse to make sure all the hands had left to do their jobs to learn Joey wasn't well so it fell to her to take care of the horses in the barn. First thing was to check if her mare was ready to deliver. The mare's teats waxed up two days ago, a sign she was close. Lifting her tail, Tillie saw vaginal discharge which would indicate she would probably be give birth in the next twenty-four to forty-eight hours. She couldn't wait. Daisy was her best mare, and the stud was the best stallion in the county, but more than that, she loved the mare and couldn't wait to have a foal from her.

Giving the mare a pat, she retrieved a pitchfork and the wheelbarrow and began cleaning the stalls. Time passed and she got into a rhythm—shovel, toss into the wheelbarrow, shovel, toss, shovel, toss. It was mindless work so she shut her mind off, trying not to think about the Orson's possible arrival or the tall, strong body of a certain man who was always in the back of her mind.

⁂

Jim Bob speared another chunk of sausage, stuck it in his mouth and stared up at the ceiling while he slowly chewed. Well, like usual, that conversation hadn't gone quite the way he intended. It almost sounded like she was threatening him. Like that time when she dyed his hair blue and gave him the runs for a week. Given those head-to-head confrontations, he wasn't eager for another one because the girl was now almost ten years older and smarter than last time, so no telling what she'd do to him now if he got crosswise with her.

If only the people in town had dropped a hint about Tillie's scheme so he could shut the entire idiotic thing down. But no, people in town seemed to have an affection for her so their lips were locked up tight.

He still didn't understand how come people in town liked her so much but not him. Wasn't he the one who schmoozed with the mayor and the city council? Wasn't he the one who spent gobs of money in town, most likely keeping all those snooty merchants dressed in silk and diamonds? And wasn't he the one who was a man, meaning the fellow with a deep voice and a still working cock, even at sixty-two?

That was the important detail right there. He was a Man which meant he should be able to do whatever he damned well pleased, including getting his daughter married and protected. She believed she could take care of herself fine but she was a woman, a slender hundred-and-ten-pound woman, and if some skunk of an evildoer decided to take advantage of her, there was no way in hell Tillie could protect herself. For her own good, she needed a man in her life, a husband so she was safe. She needed a man to help her manage the ranch, even if he did nothing more than what he, Jim Bob, did; make sure Tillie got a fair deal when men tried to cheat her.

And now that he thought about it, she needed a man to make a few babies. He wanted the Buchanan name to live on. The problem was, Tillie was female. If she married one of those dumb yahoos, by rights her offspring would carry the name of whoever she married. He wasn't all that crazy about that idea. Did he want his grandkids going through life with a name like Aker or Williams or God forbid, Trinkenschuh, when there was an outstanding name like Buchanan? Problem was, only a male Buchanan, like Orson, would be able to carry on his name.

Well, doggies. Sometimes the answer was right in front of a man but he didn't see it until it reared up and slapped him in the face. He invited Orson to visit because he'd figured Orson was the perfect threat, either get married or Orson gets the ranch. However, no one ever said Jim Bob Buchanan needed to be slapped more than once. Because there was Orson. Unmarried Cousin Orson who already came equipped with the last name Buchanan.

Nope, Orson might not be the perfect choice for a husband but he was a Buchanan and that stood for something. Anyway, it was too late to uninvite him. He was already on his way and would likely arrive in a day. He swallowed the last of his sausage and stood up, walked to his study where made himself comfy on his chaise lounge, laid his hat over his face to keep out the light, and settled in for his nap. Once he rested up a might, he'd ride into town and get a few things done.

Chapter Twelve

Ye gads, it was hot. Did it ever cool off in Texas? It was the end of May, it was nine o'clock at night, and it was still hotter than hell. Eli reclined onto the thin, rock-hard mattress with a sigh and closed his eyes. His bones hurt. His muscles ached. He was exhausted both physically and mentally. Around him he could hear the other men brushing their teeth, stripping out of their clothes, discussing the events of the day while they got ready for bed. Per Jinx's orders, their conversations didn't include him.

He never thought he'd admit it, but he was lonely. Back in New York, he'd been busy with his practice. He and Ned became good friends over the years, and frequently went sailing together on Sundays. He had his sister and his father. Here he had nothing, and no one.

Sometimes he woke up at night craving someone to talk to. Annoyingly, sometimes the craving was for one specific person and for much more than someone to talk to. He'd wake up at night, hard, needing relief and unable to achieve it when there were six other men within arm's reach. Of course, from what he heard in the dead silence of the night, he wasn't always the only one with unfulfilled cravings.

An alarm jangled in his mind. His craving was dangerous. Much as he might like to, he could never act on it. He rolled over onto his side and tucked his arm under his head. Better to leave before things got out of control. But how? Tempted though he was to keep Jim Bob Buchanan's money, he'd handed the two fifty-dollar bills back to Tillie's father the minute he returned from San Antonio, leaving him with only the few dollars from what Ned gave him. Ten bucks, all that remained after sending that telegram, wouldn't get him far.

Squeezing his eyes shut, he forced those thoughts out of his head and told himself to go to sleep. And shortly, he did.

"Slick."

Huh? He groaned and rolled over, already falling back to sleep. "Slick, wake up. I need you."

"Shoo," he mumbled, and swatted at the annoying buzz in his ear.

Something—someone—grabbed his shoulder. "What the—" he exclaimed but was cut off when a hand clapped over his mouth.

"Hush!"

He wrenched open his eyes then threw up a hand to shield them from the bright light of the lantern next to his head. Over the top of the glare from the flame, he could see the gleam of Tillie's eyes.

He shoved her hand aside and sat up. "What's going on? What time is it?" he growled, keeping his voice low to avoid waking the other men. Rubbing the sleep out of his eyes, he surveyed the long white nightgown she wore and her long blond hair hanging loose around her shoulders. The woman was the next thing to naked. Okay, not naked, the nightgown covered her from her head to the tips of her pink toes that peeked out from under the gown, but damn, she wasn't wearing real clothing and he knew damned well she wore nothing under the gown. Even in the dim light, he could see the points of her nipples and the dark pink areola surrounding them through the thin cotton. Unwanted, inappropriate heat rushed to his lower half.

"Shh," she whispered. "It's a little after three in the morning. Get dressed and come outside."

His brain still fogged from his abrupt awakening, he blinked for a minute, trying to orient himself.

"Quick." Like a ghostly apparition in her white gown, she wafted out the door. The light of the lantern disappeared when the door shut behind her.

It took two minutes to tug on pants and a shirt and lace up his shoes. Quietly shutting the bunkhouse door behind him, he whispered, "What's wrong?"

She bit her lip. "You said you worked in a hospital back east, right?"

He nodded, the motion tentative because if her father was ill and she was asking him to help, that presented a problem he wasn't sure he wanted to be involved in.

"So you might know something about giving birth?"

Cocking his head, he stared at her. What was going on? She certainly wasn't pregnant, so then what was it? He gave her another tentative nod, more unsure than ever.

"I need your help," she said, her words falling out of her mouth in a rush. "My mare, Daisy, the one who's in foal? The foal is coming...her water broke but nothing is happening like it's supposed to and I've walked her and she's obviously in distress and I don't know what else to do and I think the foal is turned the wrong way. Please, is there anything you can do to help?" The hand holding the lantern trembled, making the light bob and dip. "She's in the barn. Please come."

At least it wasn't someone having a heart attack, or worse. "Come on," he said over his shoulder as he quickly strode into the barn and pulled open the door to the mare's stall. The mare was on her feet, swaying, her coppery hide dark with sweat and her distended belly heaving. Her breathing rushed out of her body harsh and labored.

Entering behind him, Tillie hung the lantern high on a hook overhead then approached the mare, her steps slow and careful. She reached out to take hold of her halter. "Shhh, Daisy, shhh. Eli is here to help you. It's okay. You're going to be fine."

He took a long shuddery breath. He knew nothing about horses giving birth. "Isn't there a vet nearby?"

"No, the closest one is in town, a half hour away."

By which time the mare, and her foal, might be dead. He ran a hand through his hair. "How long has she been in labor?"

"At least four hours. I came out at nine to check and she seemed fine, no signs of anything happening, so I went back to the house and got ready for bed. But for some reason I woke up a few minutes ago and I thought I should check on her again and she was like this and I can see it's not progressing and she's struggling. She's already given birth to three foals and she always gives birth quick with no problem but..." She stared at him, her eyes filled with anguish, her voice trembling with her fear. "I can't lose her. She's... I...She's my..." She stopped, her tears choking off the words.

He ran a hand over the mare's belly. She flinched and moved away, stomping her hooves in agitation. Walking behind the mare, he managed to lift her tail enough to see she wasn't close to giving birth. With a high-pitched whinny, she twisted around and nipped at her side.

Damn it. He wasn't sure if he could help. He didn't know anything about horses. All he could do was try. "I need clean water, a lot of water, and soap. And a couple lengths of rope," he told Tillie. Somewhere, someplace, he'd read that, for large animals like horses and cattle, sometimes in a difficult birth, the baby needed to be physically pulled out of the mother with a rope looped around the baby's feet. He hoped the mare wouldn't require it. Still, best to be prepared. "And rags, lots of clean rags."

She dashed out of the stall.

He took a deep breath. In his practice, he'd delivered dozens of human babies, almost all of them with no problems. There's been a few times when the baby was positioned feet first so needed to be turned. The mechanics were probably the same but how did he know for sure? Could he do this? The horse groaned again, her head drooping. He needed to try. Taking a few steps to reach her head, he gently rubbed a hand over her long face several times. She slowly blinked, her glazed eyes showing her weariness...and what he feared was a sign she'd given up.

"I've got you. Don't give up on me. I'm going to help you," he whispered. "At least I hope so" he said, leaning forward to blow in her nostrils to accustom her to his scent to calm her. Like she understood, she sighed and buried her head against Eli's chest. *Help me*, she seemed to say. *I trust you.*

Believing she'd allow him to examine her now, he ran his hands over her belly again. He could feel the muscles bunch and relax before contracting again. She let out a low guttural groan. He pressed his hand into her taut belly and tried to determine where, and how, the foal lay inside the enormous body of the mare.

Tillie rushed back in; a bucket filled with water carried in each hand. She set them down. "I'll be right back with the rope. How long do you need?"

"One long enough to tie back her tail, and another about six feet long," he told her. Tillie thrust a bar of soap at him and ran out again. Unbuttoning his shirt, he stripped out of it and hung it over the stall door. He soaped up his hands, arms and shoulder, using the clean water from a pail to sluice off the soapsuds.

Tillie appeared in the doorway again. And jerked to a halt, the ropes hanging limply in her hand. She gawked at him, her gaze fastened on his chest. "Um... You don't have your shirt on," she mumbled, her voice raspy, her eyes like dinner plates in the light from the lantern.

"I only have two so I can't afford to ruin this one. And I won't be able to do what needs to be done if I have a shirt on."

She nodded her understanding but her gaze darted to the left, to the right and left again, almost like if she didn't know where to look.

"Tillie," he said, for the first time using her name when she continued to stare off in the distance instead of the usual Miss Buchanan. "Pay attention. I need your help. Tie her tail out of the way. I've already washed up so I don't want to touch anything."

Blinking, she collected herself and quickly tied the mare's tail to her halter.

"I think the foal is hind end first. I'm going to try to push it back into the uterus so I can turn it around. Hold Daisy's head and keep her still. Don't let her try to lay down or she'll break my arm."

Fear evident in every line of her face, Tillie took the mare's halter, holding tight while she caressed and whispered to the animal.

He closed his eyes for a moment. He'd done this kind of maneuver before for human babies but this was not a human. He wished he knew more about horse anatomy, but he didn't so he attempted to visualize what lay inside that huge body. Hell. Why did he feel so useless?

The horse groaned again. Realizing he couldn't delay any further, he took one last breath and, his fingers curled slightly to avoid scraping the lining of her cervix with his fingernails, he slid his hand inside. Another low moan issued from the mare. Her muscles tightened forcefully on his arm. He caught his breath and stopped, unable to proceed any further. Damn, that hurt, more than hurt, it was excruciating. Nothing he'd ever experienced with a human mother ever felt like this. But nothing to do but keep on. The contraction relaxed. Gritting his teeth, he continued until he reached what felt like the hindquarter of the foal stuck in the birth canal.

He took another breath. Okay, he knew what to do now. This wasn't so different from a human baby. Another contraction hit. He clenched his jaw, waited for it to end then, carefully, teeth gritted, using ever bit of strength he could muster, he pushed, and tugged and maneuvered the small horse back into the mother's womb. Her contractions continued to squeeze painfully around his arm but at last that part of the job was completed.

Now to turn the foal so it was head first. He moved cautiously, feeling around until he was sure where the foal's head and all its legs were. Okay, good. Next step. An inch at a time, stopping every few minutes to wait out the painful contractions, he moved this leg and that leg, manipulating the little body until the foal's head and legs were correctly positioned.

Slowly, carefully, he extracted his arm, shaking it to relieve the ache. Now, hopefully, nature would take over but if not, there was always the rope. He stepped back.

"What's happening? Is she all right? Why did you stop?" Tillie blurted.

He shook his head. "I turned the foal. I'll only use the rope if I have to. For now we wait." And hope that he'd done everything correctly. Sliding down the stall wall, he sat. After a minute, she joined him.

The mare uttered a high-pitched whining sound. Her head bobbed. She shifted on her hooves then circled several times, moving more energetically than previously.

"Is she okay? Is something wrong?" Tillie asked, alarm showing on her face.

He peered at her from the corner of his eye. "You're the horse person. You tell me."

Some of the tension left her. "No, no, of course. She's fine. This is normal. This is what should have happened all along."

A few minutes passed. Her brows creased with worry. Even with a frown on her face, she was still beautiful. "When did you start managing the ranch?" he asked, hoping it would take her mind off the mare's pacing.

She went back to studying the mare. "When I was sixteen."

"Sixteen? You were sixteen? That's young. Why did you want to manage this place? Most girls that age are searching for husbands, not managing ranches." His admiration for her went up several notches.

She took so long to answer, he thought she wasn't going to. But finally she said, "My father was running it into the ground. He doesn't have a clue how to run a ranch and hates to listen to advice." Daisy groaned, long and loud and Tillie straightened, her fists clenched while she waited for something to happen. But the mare let a breath out and relaxed so she continued.

"Then, when my mother died, he didn't care anymore." She went silent but he figured there was more to the story so he held his peace.

"My mother said he was always slapdash about taking care of things but she kept him on the straight and narrow. Made him take care of things outside while she paid the bills and such."

She kept quiet for a long time then, and he thought that was the end but then she said, "Once my mother wasn't here to control him and his spending, he went crazy with the money. Doubled the size of the house. To impress people. He's always wanted to impress people."

Not knowing what to say, he tentatively put his arm around her shoulders. She tensed for a moment, then slowly, unbending a bit at a time, leaned against him. Her head snuggled into his shoulder. His heart skipped a beat and hot blood rushed through him. The side of her breast nestled against his ribcage, the heat of her body seeped into him so he wanted to lay her down in the straw and make love to her. But he did nothing. Except burn.

"I didn't realize at first. I was too young, but then things started falling apart and finally I couldn't help but notice. People, merchants, in town, stopped giving us credit." She drew in a shaky breath.

He ached for her. For the most part, his life was easy. There was always enough money, friends, family, to support his father after his own mother died.

"Even then he didn't want to let me take over. Pissed him off something fierce. I had to...uh...basically torture him into letting me take the reins."

"Torture?" He had visions of being strapped to the rack, an old medieval torture device.

"I dyed his shirts pink. I dyed his hair blue." She paused, then emitted a snort of laughter. "I gave him the runs. That's when he gave in."

Christ, the woman was diabolical. He'd be sure to never cross her.

She yawned and snuggled closer. He tightened his arm. Peeking down, he saw her eyes were closed. And now he could look his fill. He could count the freckles on her nose, thirteen. He could study the shell of her ear, curved and delicate. Her chin was pointed, her jaw sharply outlined. Her cheeks sported a pale pink blush. Her lips...oh, my lord, her rosy lips were made for kissing.

His heart thudded; his blood raced. Things were going on in his trousers that shouldn't be happening. Biting the inside of his cheek, he focused on the mare. She paced. Then stopped. With a long groan, she hunched her back.

"Tillie. Wake up. I think it's happening now."

She sat up abruptly and leaped to her feet.

The mare shifted her back end, her back hooves tap-dancing on the floor of the stall and gave a grunt. Another groan, long and high-pitched, and a tiny hoof appeared, followed quickly by another hoof, then a small wet head, ears flattened against its head.

Another grunt and the foal slithered out and dropped into the straw with a soft *plop*. It lay without moving, still wrapped in the birth sac.

Tillie threw herself down next to the foal and tore away the thick coating that covered the foal's head. "Come on, baby, breathe," she said. The foal lay still. "Breathe, damn it, breathe," she demanded, her voice cracking. She stroked her hand along the tiny horse's neck.

Lowering her head, the mare nudged the foal with a whuffle. Still, the foal remained motionless, its little chest not rising.

Eli grabbed a clean rag. Dropping to his knees, he quickly swabbed out the foal's nostrils, at the same time gently pushing on the foal's ribcage. But nothing happened. Tillie whimpered. Fear and anguish hammered through him. Save the baby. Must save the baby.

The baby. It needed air in its lungs, that same as a human baby. Leaning over, he opened his mouth wide and placed it over the foal's nostrils. He puffed lightly, paused and puffed again, still pressing lightly on the foal's ribcage. "Tillie, watch how I'm pressing his side. You do it."

After watching him for moment, she took over, allowing him to use all his concentration on breathing for the foal.

Puff. Pause. Puff. Pause. His heart pounded. Fear prickled through his veins like hot lava.

"Come on, baby," Tillie said, begging the foal to breathe.

Puff—

A hoof moved. A leg twitched. Its chest rose and a wheeze fluttered from the foal's small body. Seconds later, the foal rolled up onto its belly, its long legs sprawling in all directions. It blinked and shook its little head. Goop flew.

Eli sat back on his haunches. Thank God. Pulling himself to his feet, he walked over to the pail and plunged his hands into the water. He scrubbed his hands, arms and chest with soap. Finally, picking up the bucket of clean water, he poured it over his front to finish the job.

Tillie stood next to the baby, hands outstretched to catch him if needed, while the foal struggled to its feet. It wobbled a bit, staggered but steadied itself. Its fuzzy little tail waggled.

"It's a colt. I have a colt. You saved him. Thank you, thank you, thank you," she cried and launched herself into Eli's arms so hard he reeled backwards and banged up against the stall door. It flew open, sending them both spiraling into the aisle.

"Oof." Overwhelmed, there was nothing to stop his momentum. He stumbled and fell flat onto the dirt floor with Tillie plastered to his front.

He groaned. Jesus, his back. Grimacing, he took a deep breath and felt...a warm, soft feminine body draped across his. He opened his eyes. Tillie's face was two inches from his, her eyes nearly crossed as she stared at him.

He stared back, not daring to breathe. She didn't breathe either. Heat flared in her eyes. Her lips parted. The tip of her tongue darted out and slid over her lower lip. Then her lips were on his, soft and hard at the same time, slightly parted, hesitant, unpracticed, which contradicted the needy groan that escaped from her mouth, a sound of frustration and pleasure, mirroring his surging desires.

He flattened his hands on either side of her skull and held her in place, pressing her mouth harder to his, using his tongue to lick her lips open so he could taste her. Her hands fell to his chest and touched lightly, tentatively, exploring the expanse of his body with her fingers, making his skin quiver. He was on fire, burning up inside with need. He wanted to touch her, devour her, be inside her. But no. He couldn't. Her unpracticed kisses, her tentative touch, told him she knew nothing about a man and his body and sex.

He groaned, lifted a hand and gently pressed her shoulder, pushing her away. "Tillie, stop."

"I need...I want..." She draped a leg over his thighs and thrust against his hip and groaned.

He jumped as if struck by a bolt of lightning. "Tillie, damn it, Tillie. Don't do that. You don't know—" Every nerve in his body lit on fire.

"I want...kiss you," she moaned. "I want...I need...I want... something...I..."

She didn't know what she needed, but Eli did. Which didn't mean he should give it to her. She didn't realize the possible complications. She had no idea that if the worst that could happen, happened, that he couldn't be here to care for her. "Tillie, stop. You don't know... we shouldn't..." But holy hell, he wanted to.

"I ... I want...I need... Eli, please...Touch me. That's all I want."

He caressed her breast, fingering the nipple till it stood erect.

She gasped. "Oh, yes. That feels good."

His head buzzed, he burned and shook and wanted. Through the cloth of his pants, her fingers molded the shape of him, tantalizing, ratcheting up the flame higher and higher and her moans and her little whispers and her breath on his cheek was so perfect that his heart could hardly hold the magnificence of her. He needed her, he needed to touch her and hold her and absorb her into the essence of who he was. Unable to help himself, he slid his hand up under her gown, caressing his way up her sleek thigh until he reached her buttock. Lord help him, she was so soft. So perfect.

With his other hand, he reached for his belt. And the mare let out a loud nicker.

Fuck. What the hell was he thinking? He stopped, his fingers still wrapped around the second button, preparing to undo it. "Tillie. No. We can't." He lifted his weight from her, preparing to rise.

One of her arms wrapped around him, held him locked in place. "Yes. Yes, Eli, please. Don't stop. Don't stop. It feels...I want..."

Desire shot through his body, like lightning in a stormy sky, white hot, sizzling. He slanted his mouth over hers, tasting her, inhaling her essence. He wanted her, Jesus, how he wanted her.

But he couldn't. He didn't dare. But then her plump lips nibbled at his mouth, his cheek, and his ear, and again her hand touched him through the fabric of his trousers. And then, her fingers slid a button out of its buttonhole. Then another. And another. Until he sprang into her hand.

A jolt of electricity shot through him and all rational thought vanished. This was wrong, so wrong, but he couldn't stop. But he could be careful. Rucking up the hem of her nightgown, he bared her to the waist and slipped his fingers lower until he found the damp core of her. She was wet and soft and achingly feminine.

His entire body caught fire, ready to explode like a roman rocket. Legs trembling, he stroked her wet folds, seeking the tiny bud until he found it. He kneaded, rubbed, stroked, using her natural dampness to ease the way.

Her breath came out in uneven gasps and moans. Her hand squeezed his cock tight. Her legs clamped over his hand. "Eli. Oh God, Eli." Her cry came out high on a gasp. "Please."

He wanted to stroke and thrust and hold the miracle that was Tillie Buchanan until she bucked and howled and came apart in his hands. He wanted to fill her the same way she filled his heart. But he couldn't. He shouldn't. His fingers worked her, caressing the bud buried in her folds.

Rubbing against him, she whispered, "Yes, that, Eli. Please do that." Her hand tightened on his cock so hard his eyes rolled.

Yes. He thrust a finger inside her and she jerked and shook and screamed, a small shrill sound that pierced him to the core. And he erupted. In her hand. Against her stomach. Pumping, pulsing and hot until there was nothing left to give. Gasping, his head fell back.

She lay atop him, not moving, not speaking. After a moment, her hand slid from between them and lifted to his face where she pressed it against his cheek. "Eli," she said. Only that. Simply Eli. He had no idea what it meant. Was it a recrimination. A thank you? A sign that for once, she acknowledge him as a person worthy of notice?

They lay tangled together for a long time, neither moving, not speaking about what happened. But like all good things, it must, and did, come to an end. With a muted grunt, she rolled off him, stood, and busied herself smoothing down her nightgown, her gaze on everything but him. When minutes passed in silence, he buttoned his trousers and rose to his feet.

Say something, he wanted to tell her, staring at her back. But she didn't. Instead, she walked into Daisy's stall and shut the door. He heard the sounds of her washing up and the door opening again. "He's nursing. I think he'll be fine now. I'll check him in the morning." Unhooking the lantern from the overhead hook, she walked out of the stall, shut the door behind her and strode out of the barn, leaving Eli in darkness.

He blew out a breath. What the hell happened? She'd left, and without saying a word. His heart still pounded from the exertion, from the pure rush of making love to the beautiful, enigmatic, stubborn woman who seemed to want him. And then didn't. He'd made love to Tillie, and she'd walked away like she considered what they'd done was no more important than mucking out the stalls. Why? Was he the only one who'd felt something momentous, something that could become something special?

He didn't know and she was no longer here to ask the multitude of questions swirling through his brain. Using a clean rag, he cleaned himself off then waited a minute, two minutes, five minutes thinking, hoping she'd come back but she didn't. Finally, confused, resentful but replete, he left the barn and went back to his bed.

It took forever to fall asleep.

Chapter Thirteen

What in the Sam Hill was she thinking? She'd attacked Eli Knowles. She'd launched herself at him like a mad bull charging a waving red cape. She kissed him, she'd sucked on his tongue, she'd touched his...his...hard...smooth...whatever. The man must believe she was...was...something she was not.

Embarrassment flooded her in a red-hot wave. Her skin crawled with mortification. She wanted to die. Why? Why, why, why? Yes, she had an itch but for heaven's sakes, she'd gotten itches before. That's what her hand was for. But her hand never made her feel like that. The man was the master of touch. His fingers should be enshrined in a museum right next to all those famous renaissance pieces of art. His lips should be bronzed and save for posterity. It made her shiver and burn even to think about what he'd done to her body. Complete and utter annihilation of her senses.

And it was all her fault. She'd asked for it. The heck with asked; she'd demanded it.

Grabbing her pillow, she jammed it over her face. She'd never be able to look at him again. Her cheeks burning, she rolled over onto her stomach and screamed into the mattress.

Because, damnation, she wanted more of the same. But that could never...never...never happen again. She'd broken her own rule. And she'd made a fool of herself.

Okay. Maybe it wasn't completely her fault. Maybe it was the excitement over the survival of the foal. Yes, that was it, it was an aberration, a mistake, a teeny-tiny booboo never to be repeated. Yep, it was an error to be ignored like it never happened. Everybody made mistakes. She was only human after all. Oh good, now she felt better. Everything could go back to normal, right? Rolling over, she prepared to go to sleep.

But wait. Something wasn't right. She cast her mind back over all the little details of their tryst. Okay, yes. Kisses. Touching. Tongue sucking. And groping, lots of groping. And rubbing on places she'd never been rubbed before...

She sat bolt upright in bed. By the good lord Harry. He didn't finish the job. He'd stopped!

She flopped back onto her mattress. Why? Didn't he like her well enough to finish? Was there something wrong with her that he didn't want her? Well, fine, lots of people didn't want her, including her father, since it seemed like he was busting a gut to get her married.

Fine, if that's the way he felt, fine. She didn't need him. Pushing aside her hurt, she rolled onto her side, closed her eyes and told herself to sleep.

Only she couldn't. Three sleepless, agonizing hours later, the sun shone in through her window and told her it was morning. She crawled out of bed. No point in putting off the day. There was work to do regardless of having to face a man who'd put his hands, and mouth, all over her last night. Who she'd put her hands all over him in return.

Pulling on her clothing, she jammed her feet into her boots, tucked her pistol into the holster on her belt and headed to the dining room. Her father was already there, stuffing bacon into his mouth per his usual.

"Heard you and Eli helped deliver Daisy's foal last night."

She jumped a foot. Did he know what happened in the barn late last night? "A colt." Her voice trembled. She grabbed a muffin off a plate Inez put in the middle of the table and skedaddled out of the dining room before he could ask any other questions. No point in giving the old buzzard an opening.

The men were already drifting out of the bunkhouse and heading to the north pasture behind the barn to catch their horses. She went into the barn to see the foal who was perky and nursing lustily from his mother. He was going to make a fine stallion someday.

Walking back outside, she said, "Beau, we've still got those calves that were born late that need castrating. We need to do that today. Bring them in and put them in the smaller corral." She needed to keep moving, keep talking or she would sink into a pit of self-pity and abject need.

Beau gave her a two-finger salute. "Sure thing, boss."

"Jud, you'll stay to help with the castration," she added.

"Awww, Miss Tillie," the man whined. "No, c'mon, again? You know I hate castrating the poor critters."

Tillie jammed her hands on her hips. "Jud, someone needs to help and you're the one who—"

"I'll help," said a voice behind her. Flame whooshed up her spine, curled into a hot ball of *gimmee* before descending a bit lower.

Tillie turned. Slick. Naturally it was Slick. Of course, given what happened last night she probably shouldn't call him Slick any more. Eli seemed much more appropriate to call a man who'd kissed her breasts.

Or how about Sir Lance-my-spot. Or Ivan-oh-oh-oh. She'd decide later, after she cooled off. She let out a hard breath.

He stared at her, his eyes questioning.

"Uh...no, that's all right. Jud will..." she stammered.

"Jud's gone," the man said with a quirk of his mouth. "Ran like his tail was on fire the minute you weren't looking."

Tillie whipped her head around. He was right. Jud was nowhere in sight. The coward. "Well, geezwax."

"I think you're stuck with me."

Stuck wasn't exactly the word Tillie would use. She didn't know what word she would use though. Fortunate? Blessed? The luckiest woman in Texas, which was five words but so what? The memory of last night rose up in her mind and nearly did her in. Between her legs, heat swirled, dampness collected, and an ache built while her fingers tingled, wanting to touch the man's firm muscles, his silky hair.

Hell's fire, it was too much. She felt too much. She wanted too much. Did he want too? No, of course, he didn't. He appeared calm and collected. She could really learn to hate the man. If only he weren't so devastatingly attractive. If only he didn't make her feel things she'd never felt before. If only the fire between her legs would go out.

"Do you know what castrating a calf means? Can you handle it?" she muttered, hoping he'd leave once he realized what they were about to do. A lot of men, like Jud, were squeamish about the process.

"You're going to snip off his testicles. I think I can handle it fine." The quirk grew into a full-fledged grin.

So much for that. He was staying, which meant she would continue to burn. And how come he didn't seem to be hot and bothered like her? Gritting her teeth, she said, "Fine. So's not to waste time, while we wait for the boys to bring in the calves, we can turn out the horses in the barn and clean the stalls. You go ahead and get started. I'll catch up," she said. What she'd really like to catch was her breath because she didn't seem to have any. The man was potent.

"Sure thing. I'll get started." Wiping his hands on a rag he pulled from his back pocket, he walked into the barn.

Damn him. The man was an iceberg. Here she was, ready to burst into flames, and he walked away like last night never happened. The ache of rejection resumed, why she didn't know. Wasn't it better if he forgot about last night? She wished she could do the same.

The man was like fine whiskey, completely additive, and unfortunately, it appeared she was an alcoholic, which was a bad, bad thing, because alcohol was highly flammable.

Rather than go into the barn—temptation was alive and waiting for her in the barn—she headed back inside to the dining room. Even sitting down with her father and his prying, suspicious questions was better than being alone with Eli Knowles with his potent lure. Lucky for her, when she entered, her father was gone, probably sleeping off his breakfast in his office, so she was able to help herself to some vittles. He'd left his newspaper behind so she picked it up and thumbed through it while eating. Anything to delay having to return outside.

Most of the articles on the front page was news about the latest Kentucky Derby. She viewed the photo of the winning horse, Kingman. Not good for much of anything except running fast. She'd take her sturdy quarter horses any day of the week. She flipped through the rest of the paper, halfway wanting to see an article about her quest, like the one Pops showed her, mostly glad she didn't. Keeping it quiet was better.

The panicked bleating of baby cows reached her. Beau and Zeke were back. Rising, she grabbed one last muffin, shoved it into her mouth and walked out to the stable yard.

And there he was, waiting to set her on fire again, temptation on the hoof, Eli Knowles.

Boy howdy, she wasn't going to last the day at this rate. "Open the back gate to the corral so the boys can send in a couple of calves," she told him through dry lips and a raspy throat. Once he walked away, she gathered up her tools from the barn and washed them thoroughly.

With his help, two calves were soon shooed into the corral. Between the two of them, they cornered one terrified animal. "You'll need to flip him onto his side and hold him while I snip." Eli flipped it, she snipped, swabbed some phenol on the cut, and he let it go. She and Eli moved on to the next calf, then the next, all done with little conversation, and no eye contact, but the entire time they worked, her hands shook and her body burned with wanting to touch him. And to have him touch her.

Why, oh why, had she agreed to let him assist?

She shoved her addiction from her mind to focus on the job. It was hot, dusty, dirty, smelly work. Her back hurt, and her hands cramped from holding the snippers. "Want to try?" she asked him after she'd been at it for an hour, holding out the tool.

With a smile, he took them and went to work like he'd done the job for years. Each calf was castrated quickly, efficiently, and with minimum trauma. Eli must be exhausted, she certainly was, but he worked without complaint. Soon, eleven calves had their masculinity removed.

"That's the last of them, Miss Tillie," Zeke said, and closed and locked the gate.

She straightened. "Take a break, Zeke." Picking up the bucket filled with dirty water, she said to Eli, "Help me clean up all the tools. When we're finished, go out to the goat's pen and feed them. Joey's ailing a bit so I don't want him having to ride out there. You can use Rusty again."

"Yes ma'am," he said, again with that hint of amusement that said he was making fun of her.

He strode over to the water trough and pumped some water over his hands while Tillie dipped her tools into the bucket of water she'd set aside for that purpose. Her back ached and a throbbing had begun behind her eyes. And her stomach was about to shake hands with her backbone she was so hungry.

Once the task was done, she walked into the house where her father was waiting at the dining table, a plate filled with fried potatoes, fried chicken and fried squash in front of him.

"That stuff's going to kill you, you know," she told him.

He grinned. "We all gotta die sometime. In the meantime, I'm going to enjoy myself."

Which meant he would continue to cat around with his three ladies, eat too much, drink too much, and look for ways to make her life miserable.

Her father tossed the denuded chicken bone over his shoulder. It landed in the base of a potted orange tree. "So heard from any of your questers yet?"

She shook her head. She wasn't sure whether to be happy or disappointed by the fact.

"Too bad. Maybe one of them will get lucky and find your equithingie. What do you think?" He smirked, eyes twinkling with malicious glee.

The urge to drive a knife into his heart surged but all she had was a butter knife. "I'm sure someone will," she said, playing the game she was determined to win.

Gaze lifted up to the ceiling, he chewed up the bit of potato he'd shoveled into his mouth, almost like he was truly considering her rebuttal. Which he wasn't. His goal was to torment her, and he was succeeding. "Well, no matter. Even if they fail, Orson should be here anytime now."

With that dire prediction, he shoved one last bite of chicken into his mouth, picked up his newspaper, and walked out. "Gonna go do some work in my office," he called on his way down the hall. Sure he was, after a three-hour nap.

"You were supposed to tell Orson not to come," she yelled after him but he didn't answer.

Tillie snatched up a fried drumstick from the plate Inez set on the table. Tearing off huge chunks, she swallowed them without chewing followed by the roll she stuffed into her mouth. It sat like a pile of rocks in her stomach. After all, why wouldn't it? She was a liar, a cheat, and a fake and trying to fend off her father's efforts to get her married at the same time lusting after one of her hired hands. It was nothing more than she deserved.

Throwing the rest of her roll onto the table, she stomped out of the house and, after making sure Eli wasn't there, she entered the barn. Saddling Buster, she galloped out of the stable yard. Time to visit her favorite hill.

Eli put away the snippers, scrubbed out the water pail and left it in the supply room. His back was killing him, so were his hands although they were beginning to develop callouses. He deserved a break but he'd been ordered out to feed the goats which, thinking about it, he was more than fine with the chore. Pulling Rusty out of his stall, he tacked him up and led him outside to mount.

Reining his borrowed horse out of the stable yard, he rode to the pen. The goats were waiting eagerly by the fence, their yellow eyes on him like two dozen imps of Satan. He fed them, checked the pen to make sure there was no way they could get out, or get hurt on anything then returned to his horse.

He mounted to return to the house then paused to stare at the low gray-green hills in the distance. So far he'd been safe here, but he never knew if, or when, that could change. If he needed to run, it would be important to know which direction. Tillie gave him no tasks to complete for the rest of the day and the other hands were all out on the range doing ranch hand stuff. Now the afternoon was free. Why not use it to scout around a little? It seemed unlikely that Morgan could track him down to some out-of-the-way ranch but Eli couldn't be sure. Better to know the avenues of escape. Reining Rusty away from the house, he rode towards the low mountains.

The sun beamed down on his back, for once not too hot. The sky was a clear cerulean with a few puff balls of clouds. The sense of freedom was something he hadn't felt in a long while, not since he left New York in April. After riding across the wooden bridge spanning Duggan's Creek, the brush-covered land began to slope upwards. The brush gave way to dense trees, cedar and oak and sycamore. Other than the sound of birds, and the rustle of the wind in the tree branches, it was quiet, something he hadn't enjoyed since he'd arrived on the ranch. Rusty seemed to be familiar with the area so Eli allowed him to pick his own way until they came upon a well-worn path. They kept to that. The trees grew thicker, the shade denser, the quiet more intense.

Soon Eli wasn't seeking places where he might hide if necessary, or paths of escape, he was simply enjoying the solitude. Although, possibly solitude wasn't the best thing right now, because being alone gave him too much time to think, and what he was thinking about was Tillie.

What in the hell was he thinking last night? It was only by the grace of God, and the sound of a horse nickering, that he didn't complete the act of making love to the woman. Every muscle in his body, every fiber of his being wanted to be inside her. He'd wanted to scoop her up and carry her to a soft bed with clean sweet-smelling linen and make her his, not only for the night, but forever.

But what a fatal mistake that would have been. Even now, he shuddered at the thought of what might have happened if he'd done what his body wanted. What if he got her with child?

A child. A boy. Or a girl. With blonde hair and a nose covered with freckles and a bossy attitude to go with his or her sassy mouth.

He yanked the horse to a stop. Son of a... What was he thinking? He couldn't have feelings for her. Cold sweat erupted on his body. He couldn't. He shouldn't. Was he in love with her? Being in love with her, remaining here to make her his wife, to have children, wasn't possible. It was too dangerous.

The urge to flee shuddered through his body. What was he going to do? He'd had a chance to run the day he traveled into San Antonio but he'd stupidly decided to stay. He told himself at the time it was because he needed to wait until he was paid but now he realized it wasn't that.

Dread, and something like horror, wrapped around his heart as the truth struck him. Damn it. In spite of his reservations and the danger, it seemed likely he stayed because of Tillie.

Rusty shuffled his feet and snorted, waking Eli out of his trance. Too many questions. Too much doubt.

Throwing himself off the horse, he ran up the path towards the summit of the hill, trusting Rusty would stay but not sure if he cared. He kept running until the horse was left far behind and his chest heaved with exertion. Finally, unable to run any further, he stopped. Putting his hands on his knees, he bent over, gasping until he caught his breath.

When he could breathe again, he straightened. It was dim under the canopy the trees created. And quiet. Except for the sound of water flowing to his right. After his run, he was thirsty. A drink of water might clear his head.

Seeing a path leading towards the stream, he took it. The air grew cooler and the sound of water grew louder. The path ended on the edge of a bank that hung several feet above a wide stream rushing over rocks and fallen logs on its way down the mountain. From where he stood, there was no way to access the water but uphill he could see a place where it appeared that the bank gradually flattened to the same level as the stream.

Since the overhanging bank was too treacherous to walk on, he returned to the path and walked uphill until he reached another path that led to the stream. Breaking through the last bush in his way, he reached the wide, pebble-strewn bank and stopped.

"Eli!" came from his left.

He spun to face the caller. His breath caught in his lungs. Tillie stood hip-deep in the water, naked as Venus rising from the sea. Spying him, her hands flew up and covered her breasts, the ones he'd fondled and caressed last night but in the darkness, never saw. Well, now he'd seen them, and they were beautiful, glorious, like a feast laid out in front of a starving man.

Honor dictated that he shut his eyes, that he turn his back, but he couldn't make himself do it. His feet were rooted to the ground, and his gaze fixated on the vision of her.

She stared back, her blue eyes wide and fearful, her arms crossed tight over her chest. But while he watched, the fear in her eyes bled away. Her lips parted then tilted upwards in a tentative smile.

Time passed. Seconds. Minutes. Hours. He didn't know. And neither moved. The only sound was the rasp of his breathing and the splash of water rushing past.

Her eyelashes fluttered. His heart fluttered. Then, slowly, one of her slender white arms fell away and exposed the round globe of her breast, the rosy pink of her nipple. Then the other arm fell away. She stood, hands by her side, bared to his eyes, proud, defiant, daring him to look.

And he looked. Oh, how he looked. And wanted and yearned and burned. Then, because he couldn't stop himself, he stepped one foot into the water, and the next. The water lapped over his shoes, his ankles, then his knees until it surrounded him to his waist. The chill water sent a shiver through him but it didn't douse the burning of his cock.

And then mere inches separated them. Even in the cool of the stream, he felt the heat of her, smelled her clean scent. Her eyes rose and met his and in them he saw that same dare, making him aware that it was his move. All the reasons he shouldn't make that move swirled through his brain but his body wasn't listening to his brain. His body had other ideas.

"Tillie, you are so beautiful. So perfect." He ached. Everything he was as a man wanted her.

Staring into his eyes, she thrust her shoulders back and her chin out.

And he was lost. Dipping his head, he pressed his lips against hers. Her breath gusted out, an acceptance, but her hands stayed at her side. Caution. She would allow him to be the aggressor, to be the one who made the decision to move forward or retreat.

Placing a hand on a breast, he carefully flexed his fingers, remembering the texture of it from last night, remembering the weight and the softness and the hard nub of her nipple. Despite the coolness of her skin, his palm burned from the mere touch. Inside his trousers, he was hard, throbbing, ferocious with desire.

He groaned. She sighed, and for the first time, touched him. Her hand caressed his chest, sliding over his nipple hidden beneath the thin cotton of his shirt so his skin quivered and his body shook with excitement. She hadn't touched him like this last night, so softly, a mere caress. He would remember if she did.

She moaned. "Eli. Touch me more," she whispered and he ached to do so but her request brought back the memory of his regret and the fear of the danger that loomed, dark, amorphous, and feral.

Yet he still wanted her. What was fear in the face of his desire? Nothing. What was regret? Something for another day.

But...what was honor? His heart, his emotions battled with his brain, his heart shouting yes, you want this, you can do this, you can find a way, and his brain, his logical, science-oriented brain, snarling, don't be a fool. You know this would be her ruination. And yours.

But right now, this moment, he wanted to be a fool. He slanted his mouth over hers and touched the tip of his tongue to her lips. They parted and he entered, tasting the sweetness of her mouth, the rough edge of her teeth, the slickness of her tongue, determined to absorb every bit of her that he could.

Before it was goodbye.

Before he surrendered to his brain.

Which finally said, "Stop," and he stepped away. But even that one small step was excruciating.

"No," she whimpered. "Eli."

"Yes. I'm sorry. I can't. I shouldn't. You shouldn't." He gazed down at her and could only hope that she saw the helplessness and the despair in his eyes. Like before, they stared into each other's eyes, not speaking. Slowly her defiance ebbed into resignation, and her pride became sorrow. Her lips flattened and her shoulders sagged.

"Fine. Then leave, Eli."

He swallowed, heat burning the backs of his eyes then he swung around and waded back to the stream bank. He was soaked to the skin from the waist down, his pants clinging to his legs, his shoes probably ruined. Still facing away, he stood on the bank, dripping, regretting, and bowed his head.

"I'm sorry, so sorry. But I can't. It's not right," he said. "You know it's not right."

"Right? What's not right about this? What's not right about our wanting each other, about our feelings?"

The muscles in his throat tightened, making it hard to speak. "You. Me. Us..." He cleared his throat. "Together. Becoming..." He couldn't finish.

"How would you know what's right for me or what's wrong?" she said, her voice shrill with distress. "How do you know what I want? Do you care?"

He squeezed his eyes shut. "Tillie. Hell yes I care. I care so... But..."

"But? But, but, but, that's all you can say?"

The anguish in her voice was a knife to his heart. If she only knew. If she had any idea how much he wanted to wade back into the water and take her to places she'd never been. He wanted her. He wanted to make her his. He wanted to pay her the homage she deserved. She was glorious. She was everything. The things he felt for her. He... he... oh, God help him, he loved her. His heart shredded.

He forced the ache away. "Tillie. If I...do what you want...I'll hurt you."

She snorted. "Big deal. After riding astride since I was two, I doubt there's anything left there that could hurt me."

Against his will, a chuckle broke out. The woman never minced words. It was one of the things, among many, that he... He closed his eyes again and took a deep breath because even thinking the word was new and frightening even though every second that passed made the word, the idea, the emotion, more real.

He loved her.

"Not that. Damn, Tillie. There are other ways to hurt someone. Other ways to cause you untold pain. I wish I could explain."

She said nothing for a moment. Then, "Like what? Tell me?"

He shook his head. "I can't. Not now. Maybe someday. If I can. Maybe never." With that, he walked away until the sound of water was no more. Then he ran. He raced down the path, tripping over tree branches, sliding on gravel, feet squelching in his shoes, wet pant legs slapping against his shins until he reached his horse. Scrambling aboard, he spurred him down the trail. The horse lurched, slid and nearly fell to its knees.

Idiot. Eli pulled him back to a trot. The last thing he needed was for the animal to break its leg. And Eli to break his neck.

Letting Rusty pick his way the rest of the way down the dirt trail, they reached the flat lands. Once there, he kicked the horse into a gallop. Maybe the wind would blow away his regrets. Maybe he could outrun his guilt. God help him, he wanted her. He wanted to stay and make her his. The idea of staying, of having her for his own, having children, of building a life together was like putting opium in front of a man who was addicted. He craved her with every fiber of his being. But he couldn't stay. It was too dangerous.

But the thought of leaving, of never seeing her again, tore his heart from his chest.

Behind his back, the sun edged to the top of the hills as afternoon waned. The horse galloped on, breathing hard, lathered in sweat. He urged the animal faster, faster, but no matter how fast or far Rusty carried him, guilt followed him. And so did the realization that he needed to leave before he did something irretrievable.

When he drew closer to the house, he slowed the horse to a walk to give him time to cool down. A horse, sweaty and breathing hard, would be noticed and the last thing he needed was to be noticed.

The ranch hands were back from their work, sitting around the bunkhouse gossiping and smoking. Zeke and Beau tipped their heads his way in greeting when he dismounted, but they were careful not to let Jinx catch them at it.

Jinx broke away from the group. "Where the hell you been?"

Eli clenched his jaw. He was caught unprepared to throw out some lame excuse but being unprepared in the future could cost him his life. What an idiot. "I went to the goat pasture to feed the goats like Miss Tillie said."

"It shouldn't have taken you three hours to do that."

What could he say? "No, I rode around a bit, checked out the windmill that served that section and lost track of time."

Ice shone from Jinx's pale blue eyes. "You know, I've getting damned tired of you getting special treatment and doing whatever you damned well please."

Cleaning the latrines twice a week? Shoveling shit out of the stalls every morning and every evening? Crawling around on his hands and knees pulling up weeds? Special treatment? If that was special treatment, he'd be interested to see what abuse was. But he held his tongue.

"Sorry," he said, nearly choking on his anger. "It won't happen again."

Baring his teeth like a wolf, Jinx stared at Eli, the promise of death in his eyes. It sent a shiver up his spine. Money or not...it might be time to leave.

Chapter Fourteen

She'd been rejected. She'd offered herself and he'd flat out rejected her. Again. Why? They—whoever they were—said don't buy the cow until you've tried the milk, or something like that, so she'd showed him the milk, even let him have a little taste of it, and yet he'd still decided not to buy the cow. It was enough to make a girl think there was something wrong with her.

After using her shirt to dry herself, she pulled it on then tugged on her pants and socks, growling and muttering threats. If she'd had a stick handy when he'd spouted that nonsense, she'd of whacked the tar out of him. Unfortunately, she didn't have a stick, so firing him would have to do instead. The minute she got home. Soon. The minute she saw him.

She shoved her feet into her boots and began the uphill climb to reach the wide, grassy area where she'd left Buster.

Maybe offering the milk was the problem. Maybe, because she offered herself so freely, he valued her no better than a mongrel. Well, shoot, if that wasn't a mixed metaphor, she didn't know what it was. It showed how confused she was, but none of that mattered. What mattered was Eli hadn't wanted her, and he'd offered the lamest excuse that she'd ever heard.

Buster trotted down the mountain, surefooted as a mountain goat. Reaching the flatlands, she kicked the horse into an easy lope. She had a firing to get done, sooner rather than later.

Despite her decision, doubts continued to assail her. He said if they made love, he would hurt her. For the love of Mike, what kind of bull-pucky was that? But he said there were other ways to hurt a person. What ways? How?

She dismissed from her mind the tone of his voice when he muttered all those excuses. So what if he'd sounded tortured when he said the thing he didn't say? Or tried to say. Or couldn't find the words for. Heck, she had no idea what *she* was trying to say much less what Eli meant.

Maybe he wasn't rejecting her. Maybe there was something else going on that she didn't know about. His kiss seemed...honest, was the only word she could think of to describe it. They seemed honest and sincere. She didn't have much experience—okay, hardly any—but she'd been kissed by a low-life or two before she'd learned a good knee to the nuts warned them off so she recognized a varmint when she kissed one. Eli didn't seem like a varmint.

Tillie wasn't a woman who placed much credence on a hard cock. Any old bull or stallion could get hard. They felt nothing but the urge to mate.

No, it was Eli's kiss that told the tale. His kiss was an honest kiss, one that spoke of caring. His hands held her gently, his touch reverent. And no one could fake the sparkle in his bright blue eyes. So maybe she shouldn't fire him after all. Possibly she should wait and see.

She slowed Buster to a jog and arrived back home to see Eli and Jinx facing off. "Jinx, what's going on?"

"Slick here's been sneaking off doing gosh knows what when he's supposed to be working," Jinx answered angrily, jabbing a finger at Eli.

Eli said nothing, his face stiff like he was waiting for her to throw him to the wolves.

Like she would do that, not after that kiss, at least not until she'd figured out yet what it meant.

Dismounting, she released her horse in the corral and walked to join them. "Sneaking off? You mean because I told him to feed the goats then check the water levels in the ponds out in the north field? Is that a problem, Jinx?"

Eli's gaze flew up to her face. She ignored him, focusing her eyes on Jinx, daring him to dispute him.

Anger snapped in the ramrod's eyes but he seemed to sense he was treading a fine line so he only said, "No, not a problem. I...didn't know."

"Good. Then we're done here," she said with an internal sigh. More and more lately she really wondered why she wanted to run this outfit. Sometimes it was simply too much work.

Her thoughts jerked to a halt. What the hell was she thinking? The ranch was everything to her and she wasn't giving it up for anything. But sometimes she needed a break. Sometimes she wished she had help. Or at least a broad shoulder to support her.

"Hey, Miss Tillie. Look there. Riders coming," Beau called.

She looked and sure enough, a cloud of dust was approaching. One of her Quester? Geezwax, she hoped not. The figures inside the cloud became clearer. Huh. Not riders. The cloud of dust grew larger, the figures drew closer and now she could see what was coming. A carriage.

With a clatter and the snap of a whip, the vehicle passed under the Buchanan Hollow sign and raced into the stable yard. "Whoa, you damned nags, whoa," the driver yelled. He cracked the whip again and hauled back on the reins. The horses, a team of four, bucked and kicked and neighed their displeasure. "Sons a bitches. Hold still."

The men standing outside the bunkhouse drew closer, ready to help, alarm on their faces watching the horses' antics.

The team finally calmed. The vehicle, a monstrous thing painted red with gold trim, rocked to a halt. The driver, a lean fellow with a handlebar mustache wearing a black Stetson hat, leaped down from the driver's seat. Clomping to the carriage door, he pulled it open. For a minute, nothing happened, then a foot poked out and settled on the small step. The foot wore a red leather shoe that was barely visible under the tan spats with gold buttons. The foot was joined by a leg. Another leg exited followed by the rest of the man, at which point, Tillie was treated to the full splendor of the passenger when he stepped onto the ground.

A purple velvet jacket. Purple and yellow checked pants. A canary yellow waistcoat. And a tie the most virulent shade of green ever inflicted on human kind.

Beau whistled. Jed snickered. The rest of the hands simply gaped.

"Good heavens," the Rainbow said, giving a visible, and exaggerated, shudder. "What a dreadful journey. Worse than I remembered. The dust. The smell. The road. Why, oh why, did I ever leave New York City?" His fat upper lip curled in a sneer, he flicked a pudgy hand over the purple jacket, removing any dust that had the temerity to land on him.

Oh. Dear. God. No. Please no. Tillie dropped her head until her chin hit her chest. Why? What did she ever do to deserve this?

Eli edged up next to her. "What—I mean, who—*is* that?" he asked in a voice that spoke volumes about his shock.

"That, my friend, is my cousin Orson, also known as Odious. The man my father will leave my ranch to if I don't find someone to marry from my quest."

Jinx's head whipped around at her words but he didn't say anything. Instead, he watched Orson still brushing dust off his jacket. A curl of unease rippled through Tillie at Jinx's expression but she dismissed it. She'd pretty much made a decision that, come payday, he was history so the ramrod's thoughts about Orson, or anyone, for that matter, weren't worth spit.

"Why would your father leave the ranch to him?" Eli asked.

Why? That was a good question. Because her cousin was as useless as an extra nipple on a man's chest. Maybe her cousin was changed since she'd seen him ten years ago, so she checked him out again. Nope, still the same beady black eyes, the fat lips, pointy nose and chubby cheeks.

"He thinks threatening to leave it to Odious will motivate me to pick someone," she muttered. "I can promise you it won't."

Reaching inside the carriage, Orson extracted a hat, dark purple with a turquoise band, and settled it on his head. He tapped it, once, twice, making sure it was firm then sauntered up to Tillie. "Tillie, my dear cousin. So lovely to see you again." Opening his arms, he tried to hug her.

Tillie shot her hands out in front of herself. "Stop right there."

"But Cousin Matilda. We haven't seen each other in ever so long. Ten years to be precise. And we're dear, dear cousins after all. Of course I want to greet you properly with a hug and a kiss."

"Consider me greeted," she gritted. Too bad they couldn't have waited another ten years for his visit.

Odious tapped a finger on his chin, clucking his tongue in a derogatory tsk. "Well, I see not much has changed in the last ten years." Apparently she didn't pass muster. But if passing muster meant wearing purple velvet—she'd pass. She managed to give him a tight smile.

He cocked a brow. "My bags?" he said. No one moved. Most likely still stunned by the extravagant panoply of colors on his person. After a moment, his gaze flitted over Tillie's shoulder. "You, boy," he said to Eli. "Get my bags from the carriage."

The sudden blast of silent fury radiating from Eli made her jerk her head around to stare at him. She mouthed *no* and he clamped his jaw tight.

"Of course, whatever you say," he muttered in a low voice filled with resentment.

"Sir," her cousin said in a snide tone.

Eli's Adam's apple bobbed visibly as he swallowed his words. "Sir," he finally muttered and began walking to the back of the carriage. With the driver's help, he unloaded a carpet bag, then several leather satchels. Lastly, a trunk was thrown down from the roof of the coach.

Tarnation. How long did he plan on staying?

Tucking the carpet bag under his arm, and carrying the satchels, Eli started back to join them. Jinx spun around, like he was about to leave, then stumbled. Tilting sideways, his elbow caught the carpet bag tucked under Eli's arm and it went flying. It hit the ground, burst open and clothing spilled out.

"You oaf. My things. My beautiful shirts. And my...my...undergarments. Silk," Orson yelled at the same time that Tillie shouted, "Jinx. Watch what you're doing."

"If anything is damaged, you'll pay for it, do you hear?" her cousin continued, still shouting. "Pick them up. Everything. All of it."

Anger flashed from Eli's eyes but he only said, "I'm sorry....sir. It was an accident," and stooping, gathered the spilled items and put them back into the carpet bag. Standing, he held out the bag but instead of taking it, the other man squinted at Eli.

"Do I know you? You look familiar," her cousin said and lifted his chin so he could peer down his nose at Eli, not an easy thing to do since Eli was at least four inches taller.

A muscle spasmed in Eli's cheek. "No, you've never met me," he growled.

"Hmm, I'm certain I recognize you from somewhere. Where are you from?"

Another small spasm before Eli said, "Philadelphia." Tillie now knew for sure that was a lie because Jinx had made a point, probably thinking it would get Eli fired, to inform Tillie about the telegram Eli sent to someone in New York City the day he went into town. So why was Eli lying?

"Not New York?" Orson continued.

"No." Eli's jaw grew tighter. Tillie held her breath, hoping he would hold onto his temper. If Eli even lifted a finger against her cousin, she wouldn't put it past him to have Eli arrested.

"Perhaps you've visited New York? Have family in New York."

"I said no," Eli snapped. "I've never been to New York."

"Well, I'm certain I shall remember sooner or later." Dismissing the mystery, Orson turned his attention to Tillie but she ignored him. Instead, her eyes were on Jinx who was staring at Eli, his lips drawn tight in suppressed anger. A trickle of unease went down her spine. What was going on with Jinx?

Taking advantage of Tillie's distraction, Odious wrapped an arm around her shoulders and gave her the hug he'd threatened early. She shoved him away. "Stop that!"

"Purely a friendly greeting between cousins. Who might become something much closer," he said under his breath with a smirk.

Setting her fists on her hips, she glared at him. The dislike she'd felt for him ten years ago was back with a vengeance but unfortunately that opinion didn't seem to be shared by her father who bustled out of the house, arms wide. "Orson, my boy."

"Uncle J...um...Ji...um..." Odious hesitated; the words seemingly stuck in his throat. Finally he forced out, "Uh, Uncle James."

Okay, so the name Jim Bob didn't exactly align with Orson's upper-class ideas of what were proper names. In his world, proper names were James and Lawrence and Theodore, not Jim Bob.

"Hey, Miss Tillie. Someone else is coming."

What the heck. She could see another billow of dust in the distance. Eli stepped closer, and the fire between her legs reignited, along with the longing in her heart.

Soon a figure materialized inside the cloud, a dark figure on a horse with another form close behind. Tillie squinted. "What in the world?"

The horse and rider...and the other thing, whatever it was, trotted into the yard and stopped. The big hairy thing trailing behind also stopped.

Eli slapped a hand on his forehead. "Oh boy, it's the Spitter."

Tillie slapped a hand over her mouth to hold in her laughter. "Thamu...I mean Samuel," she finally managed to greet the visitor. "You're back." Regrettably. Because she'd really hoped all ten of her questers would have given up by now.

"I brung you the winning animal." Dismounting, Samuel led the beast forward. Tall and furry with funny spatulate feet that weren't quite hooves but weren't quite paws either, on the ugly scale, it fell somewhere between a gargoyle and the proverbial mud fence.

"Here you go, an equica-whatever, jutht like you thaid," he said and extend the lead rope to Tillie.

She stepped back. Nope. Not hers, not now, not ever.

Pops stared at the beast, gnawing on the chicken leg in his hand. "Welcome back, sir. I see you brought us something. What you got?"

"It's a camel. A Bactrian camel," Eli said quietly before Sorenson could speak. "Two humps instead of one."

Her father took his time checking the beast out, chewing on his chicken leg while he did. "You sure it isn't one of those equi-thingies?" he finally said, wink, wink, nudge, nudge. Tillie shoved her own elbow into his middle, the smart aleck. He responded with an "Oof" and a "Now, now, that wasn't nice, daughter." His voice was all wounded, but the sly glint in his eyes was pure deviltry.

"You thaying thith here ith a camel?" Samuel asked. He yanked the animal's head down so they were face-to-face. Big camel eyes with long lashes met Samuel's lashless blue eyes. The camel made a strange sound unlike anything Tillie ever heard, part groan, part grumble, part growl and stomped a foot on the ground. It didn't look like a happy beast.

Orson chose that moment to intrude in that creeping, odious way he had, like sludge seeping under the door, gross and smelly and unstoppable. He poked a finger into Samuel's chest. "You heard the lady, you big oaf. Are so you stupid you don't recognize a camel when you see one?"

Samuel's face flared red with anger. "Who you calling thtupid..." he shouted, and spit flew out of his mouth. And landed on Orson's cheek.

"How dare you!" her cousin yelled and shoved Sorenson. The man flew backwards and crashed into the camel. Who bellowed. Roared. Then spit. A big fat wet blob of camel goop. Right into Orson's face.

"Bloody hell!" Jumping up and down, Odious swiped at the slobbery green goober thing hanging from his nose. "You idiot. You moron. You imbecile." He took another swipe at the mess. The glob of spit caught on his fingers. "Ugh! Ugh, ugh, ugh." He shook his hand, trying to fling the glop off. It flew through the air and landed on Jim Bob's pristine white shirt.

"Son of a bitch," her father roared, his hands slapping at the wet while around him the hands howled with laughter.

Tillie covered her mouth with a hand, trying her darnedest to hold in her laughter but it wasn't easy. This was almost as good as the day she dyed her father's hair blue.

Not liking the commotion, the camel stomped its feet and bawled its displeasure. Its head bobbed and weaved and its eyes rolled wildly and warned of something heinous to come.

"Sorenson," Eli snapped. "Get ahold of that beast before it hurts someone."

Pouting, Samuel tightened his hold on the tether and, after a tug of war, managed to pull the camel's head down, forcing it to stop dancing. Once the camel was under control, he faced Tillie. "Tho thith ithn't a equi-thing like in the picture? Tho I didn't win?"

"Nope. And nope."

"Tho what am I thuppothed to do with thith thing? I can't keep him. I live in the thity and the feller I got him from don't want him back."

A wave of despair washed through her. Why in the world did she ever think it was a good idea to start this quest thing. It almost seemed like it would be easier to marry whoever Pops wanted.

Eli tapped her on the shoulder. "Let's put him in with the goats," he said. "Hopefully goats and camels get along." Taking, the tether from Samuel's hand, he retrieved his horse, mounted it and rode away, the camel gallomping behind him.

Holy cow. Was there ever anything more awkward and ungainly than that camel galloping. What was God thinking?

After a bit more grumbling, a lot of dirt kicking and one last look filled with sadness and regret, Samuel mounted his horse and rode off. Ignoring the sight of his receding back, Tillie scanned the crew of men still hanging around watching the comedy. "All of you, get back to work," she growled.

"Tillie—" Jinx growled.

"Miss Buchanan," Tillie corrected, her chin thrust out. She'd pretty much had it with the man.

An angry gleam showed in Jinx's eyes. "Miss Buchanan," he repeated, sarcasm underlying the words. "A word to the wise. I'd be more careful if I were you. Not every man takes rejection so easily," he said then strode off to retrieve his horse. Within minutes, he was gone. It was past time to do something about Jinx. But she had no idea what that would be.

After a long, uncomfortable pause, Beau said, "Well, time for supper," his voice a squeak, and fled into the bunkhouse. The rest of the crew raced after him.

Silence followed everyone's departure "Well, glad that's all settled," her father said. He threw his arm over Orson's shoulder and dragged him in the direction of the house, talking while they walked. "So glad you could make it, son. Been looking forward to it. How are your folks? Still alive, of course, or at least they were last I heard. That's good. Folks dying? Not a good thing. How was the trip? Any difficulties? No? Good, good. So, we've got lots to talk about, hope you brought enough clothes to stay a good long time..."

Tillie rolled her eyes. If the clothes Orson brought were anything like what he wore now, they'd all be blind by the time he left.

"Big changes since you were here last, my boy, and lots you need to learn. First thing tomorrow, we'll give you a tour of the ranch. Oh, wait, I got things to do tomorrow, so I won't be along for the tour. Tillie can take you around, she'll be happy to show you everything, right, Tillie?" her father shouted over his shoulder.

Till lifted a fist and showed it to her father. She wanted to show him something else but she was nominally a lady and ladies didn't do that. But, boy, was she tempted.

Opening the front door, her Pops ushered his nephew inside. The door shut. Then opened again. "Dinner's in half an hour." The door shut. Then it opened again. His head popped out. "Wear a dress," he shouted. The door slammed shut.

Like hell.

Chapter Fifteen

Eli dragged the large, smelly, reluctant camel to the goats' pen. He took a moment to watch while the species squared off against each other; twenty small but pissed off goats defending their territory against one camel with feet big enough to take out several goats in one fell swoop. Shaking his head, he rode off, hoping they wouldn't kill each other the minute he was gone.

But whether they did or didn't, it wasn't his problem. He had bigger issues. Tillie's cousin was from New York City. There were almost three million people living in New York and yet, somehow, her cousin thought Eli looked familiar. How? Eli was sure he'd never met Orson Buchanan before, nor did he remember the man's name which was uncommon. Was it possible her cousin saw a photo of Eli in the newspaper since Eli often attended society events. Or...

A wave of fear surged up his throat, nearly choking him. He squeezed his eyes shut for a moment and took a deep breath. Or was he one of Morgan's men, sent to find him? Was Orson waiting for some kind of proof that Eli was the person he was hunting? Or was he waiting for word from Morgan to complete his mission?

He shook his head. No, that didn't seem likely. The puzzlement on the man's face was genuine. He truly hadn't identified Eli. At least, not yet.

But how long would it be before he did remember? And if he did, what would he do about it?

The terror that always lurked under the surface suddenly erupted, making his heart pound and the tips of his fingers go numb. Christ. He should have used that hundred dollars Buchanan gave him and taken the train as far as a hundred dollars would take him. But he hadn't. Thoughts of Tillie and that night in the barn kept him here.

He was a fool. A fool for Tillie. He should have left when the opportunity presented itself but he hadn't. He'd stayed because... because...

He'd stay because...damn it, because he loved her.

Standing in the stream this morning while she gazed up at him with complete trust in her eyes, the answer slammed into him, nearly overwhelming him. He loved her. He was *in* love with her. He wanted her. He wanted a life with her, children with her, to grow old with her. He wanted to die, old and gray and feeble, with her by his side holding his hands so her beloved face was the last thing he saw before God took him. He ached with the need to have her in his life.

But it could never happen.

He couldn't breathe. Reining Rusty to a halt, he bent over the saddle horn and shook and gasped and shed tears that wrenched the breath from his body until his lungs were on fire. What was he going to do? What could he do?

His head ached, his body ached. His very soul ached.

Eventually the tears ran out because there were only so many tears in a man. He pulled himself together and kicked Rusty in the direction of Duggan's Creek a few hundred yards ahead. Dismounting, he led the horse down the embankment to the water and let him drink while Eli rinsed the tears off his face. At his feet, the cool, clear water of the creek rushed by, the same creek as the one on top of the mountain that he'd waded into to reach Tillie. Those moments with her were the most life-changing moments of his life, more than the day he graduated from college, more than the day he got his medical license. More than the day Morgan's son died under his care.

Damn the man. Damn him for his cruelty, damn him for his vicious nature that meant he'd never let even the smallest slight go by without seeking revenge.

And yet, bless him, because if Eli wasn't forced to flee New York City, he would have never met Tillie and that would have been a tragedy beyond compare.

What was he going to do? He didn't know. If only there was a way to learn if Morgan was after him. Possibly he could send another telegram but that was risky. Due to his haste the day he fled New York, he hadn't really taken the time to explain to Helen and her husband what happened. He'd mentioned Morgan but given them no details which meant any telegram he sent would need to include the kind of information, including his Morgan's name, which could alert him. If only Helen owned that new invention, the telephone, but even if she did, most likely no one here in San Antonio had one.

Remounting, he started the ride back to the ranch. Even if Morgan wasn't after him, would Eli be able to stay? Tillie's father seemed determined to marry her off to her cousin, the Odious Orson. And then there was Jinx. Somehow, he'd made an enemy of the man. Imagine if Eli were to marry Tillie, the hatred that would engender. From what Eli heard, Jinx worked at Buchanan Hollow for the last eight years. Would Tillie be willing to let the man go in exchange for marrying a man she barely knew, a man who hadn't even told her his true identity?

He reined Rusty to a stop again. Damn it. He hadn't even thought of that. Another problem. He wasn't who he said he was. Lie after lie, justified to keep himself safe, but still lies. Would she forgive him? Would it change her feelings for him? Some women would understand, and his gut instinct told him that Tillie was one of them, but many women would not. There was no way to tell for sure until he admitted the lies and then it would be too late.

The headache that was a low throb behind his eyes before now burst into full bloom. He needed to find someplace dark and quiet where he could close his eyes and block out all the unbearable thoughts that wouldn't leave him alone.

If that was even possible. He kicked Rusty into a trot and completed his ride back home.

Putting Rusty back in his stall, Eli curried him down. Once done, he walked out of the barn but stopped next to the water trough and gazed out at the sunset. Gorgeous. Vivid orange, coral, pink, purple. New York didn't have sunsets like this. This was a Texas thing, one he was growing to appreciate. There was beauty in Texas. Different than New York but beautiful in its own way. The blue bonnets alone where enough to make a man fall in love with the state.

He took a deep breath. The air smelled sweet, not like the smell of burning coal, horse manure and the human waste that pervaded the air in New York. He chuckled. Take away the flies and maybe Texas wasn't so bad.

The sun finally slipped below the horizon and the windows in the house glowed gold with the light of multiple lamps behind the shades. Occasionally a black shadow would walk past the window. He wondered if one of them was Tillie, but he couldn't tell for sure.

If it was, what was she doing? Was she enjoying herself entertaining her newly arrived cousin? No, he was certain that, even if she was entertaining him, she wasn't enjoying it.

What was she thinking then? Was she thinking about this morning? Was she remembering how they kissed. Did she still feel his hands on her breast, his lips on hers. Was she remembering the depth of desire that shown from his eyes? His cock hardened and heat burned through him at the memory. He took a deep breath and forced his pulse to return to normal.

Did she regret that he'd walked away? Had anger replaced the wanting or did she still want him? Even the mere thought that she might still want him, made him throb with desire.

A dark form walked past the window again, and this time he could tell it was her. Knowing she was there, beyond reach, was torture.

With a sigh, he walked back into the barn and climbed the ladder to the loft. There was no way he would be able to sleep in the bunkhouse tonight, not burning the way he was.

Dinner was another level of hell.

If she could have figured out a way to avoid it, she would have but there couldn't. And, infuriatingly, it was worse than she'd expected because Warren Trinkenshuh, Pops' attorney showed up too.

Jim Bob scooped a forkful of refried beans into his mouth. "So Tillie has this quest thing going on, like I told you. Seems kind of foolish to me but she insisted. You know how womenfolk are. They got their whims and their little rebellions. Us menfolk only need to wait it out until they get over it."

Lips pursed in sanctimonious agreement, the attorney nodded. "Well, your will has been written to hopefully quell any such feminine notions."

Tillie growled and thrust her fork into her peas so hard one skittered off the plate and landed in the attorney's lap. He blinked and carefully plucked it up using his thumb and a finger.

The sparkle in her father's eyes told Tillie he knew her thoughts. "Now, daughter, I realize you think you're going to pick someone to marry from that bunch of..." Lips pursed, he paused while he searched for a word. "...brave and heroic knights," he finished with sarcasm. "And that's fine if you do. But if none of them succeeds—"

Her hands curled involuntarily into fists. Too bad her hands weren't around Pop's neck when they clenched. "Pops, it's only been a couple of weeks," she protested, realizing even as the words came out of her mouth that her argument was specious. A week? A month? A year? It wouldn't matter. Nobody was going to win the quest.

Jim Bob waved her comment aside. "If things don't go well with your quest, I want to make sure the fellow who might be my heir gets a gander at what he might inherit so's I can get him up to speed, so to speak. That's why I invited Orson for a visit." He squinted at the attorney. "Warren, why don't you explain to Orson what I did with my will."

"Of course," the attorney said with an unctuous smile.

Gripping her knife, Tillie banged the haft down on the wooden table.

The attorney squeaked. His gaze darted to Tillie, over to her father then back to Tillie. Eyes wide with terror, he slunk down into his chair. "On the other hand, maybe you should explain it, Jim Bob. Much easier for everyone if it's explained in layman's term," he said, his voice coming out in a hoarse whisper.

Tillie smirked. At least the man was smart enough to realize he should be frightened.

Jim Bob grinned. "Well, sure, why not. It is my will, after all. So, Tillie, Orson, here's the deal," he began and went on to lay out his plan. Once the quest was completed, if she wasn't married to one of the questers, she had three months to find a husband, he didn't care who it was, but whoever it was, needed to be willing to change his name to Buchanan. At the end of three months, if she was still unmarried, she would marry Orson or Orson would inherit the whole kit and caboodle.

"So, given my decision," her father said. "I can't expect the boy to step in cold. Not fair to him to ask him to take over without knowing what he's doing. That's why you should give Orson here a tour of the place tomorrow. Get him up to speed, show him the ropes. Teach him all the tricks of the trade." He grinned at Orson. "The ranch is doing well, my boy, thanks to Tillie. Even though she's a woman, she's done a bang-up job."

Her hand tightened around her knife. What was the penalty for patricide if the person wielding the knife was female and had a solid reason for the murder?

Across the table, the attorney shrank lower in his chair, pale with fright. On the other hand, her father and Orson seemed completely oblivious. "Indeed, Uncle James," Odious said. "Imagine what could happen if I applied a bit of masculine competence and intelligence."

Her father clapped his hands together. "Now you're thinking. Why, Buchanan Hollow could become the biggest spread in Texas."

Orson slid a sly glance in Tillie's direction, his odious smile oozing across his face. She could almost see the dollar signs imprinted on his eyeballs. She needed a plan, and fast. "Orson, whatever you're thinking, you can unthink it right now. I'm going to find a husband before the deadline." She pointed a finger at her father. "Hear that, Pops?"

Gazing up at the ceiling like he had nothing much of importance on his mind, which was most of the time, just not today, her father answer, "Well, now, that's fine and all, but here's the thing. None of those fellows you picked for your quest are named Buchanan and I have a hankering to have a grandson named Buchanan before I go to that big ranch in the sky."

Okay, now she got it. It was all about the name. Her father didn't give a rat's patootie about the ranch; never had, never will. All he cared about is making sure his name carried on.

Orson's odious smile reemerged. "Women shouldn't be in control of a large concern like Buchanan Hollow. Everyone knows women's brains are smaller than a man's. It's been proven that too much thinking on the part of women leads to brain fevers and female maladies. And to be in charge of a bunch of crude, uncouth cowboys? Tsk. So unlady-like. A true lady would be in the home taking care of things more suited to a woman. Sewing, cooking, tending to her children. A real woman would be clad appropriately in a dress" He scanned her up and down. "Which you don't seem to be wearing."

Tillie looked at her blue jeans and her dirty boots. Very unlady-like. Like she cared.

"Orson, I don't wear dresses, especially for some no-account skunk like you. And I don't need some pantywaist woman-chasing jackass coming in here and telling me how to run a ranch I've managed for almost ten years."

"Which is why you're going to take Orson here on a tour of the ranch tomorrow and start teaching him everything he needs to know to run the place," her father interrupted.

"Pops—"

"No arguments, Matilda. I mean it."

A black haze of anger clouded her mind. "So let me see if I've got this straight. The only way this ranch will succeed is if a man's in charge, do I have that right?"

Across the table, the attorney slid down another inch until his chin rested on the table cloth, but her father simply beamed and nodded.

Tillie gritted her teeth. She could almost hear her teeth cracking. "Well then, if I'm so inept because I'm a woman...then I don't see what little ol' me has to teach Orson. He's a man, he's so smart, let him figure it out."

"Tillie!" Pops bellowed.

"Tsk. Manners, Tillie, manners. No need to be unladylike," Orson said, a tight-lipped sanctimonious smile tilting the corners of his mouth.

Throwing her napkin on the table, she jerked to her feet. "You know what, Orson, you can stuff it."

Orson gasped. "Now see here—"

"And Pops, that applies to you too because I've about had enough of your crap." Stomping out the front door, she slammed it behind her.

Which left her standing on the front porch with no place to go. Stupid. She quietly opened the door again, tip-toed in and crept to her bedroom. She sighed. Well, geezwax, sneaking back inside kind of ruined the point of her little snit fit. Heaven help her if either of those dad blasted women despising misogynistic men find out she hadn't left. To make sure they didn't find out, she locked her door. Donning her nightgown, she slid into bed and picked up *Ivanhoe*.

But after fifteen minutes of trying, she was still on page one-hundred seventy-two. Because how was she supposed to get excited about a fictional hero when she had her own hero right across the stable yard. Who didn't want her.

※

Tillie woke very early a few mornings later with a heavy sense of dread. According to her father's orders, ready or not, willing or not, today was give Odious-a-tour day. She'd somehow managed to evade the task for three days by disappearing before sunup but yesterday her luck ran out and her father cornered her before she could leave for the day and delivered his edict. Damn the man. Her father never got out of bed before ten in the morning. What did he think he was doing, getting up practically before the sun rose? It was a trap. Anyway, he'd dropped the hammer on her; take Orson for a tour. Or else.

The idea of spending the day with her cousin was worse than all the previous nights when she'd tossed and turned, her mind whirling with a kaleidoscope of the sweet moments she'd spent with Eli.

How was a girl supposed to get a good night's sleep when all she wanted was to have her hero's hands and his lips on her again, when her body remembered his touch on her bare breast, and the jolt of electricity it caused. She still felt the heat of him standing so close to her while the chilly stream water swirled around her waist, another erotic sensation. And the knowledge that she was bare to his gaze, everything revealed for his eyes alone. Texas sky blue eyes that held a maelstrom of passion.

And the fierce kisses they'd shared that night in the stables when his hands touched her lower down and built a fire in her. And the memory of the explosion raging through her body like a tornado, wreaking havoc with her mind and her heart and her ability to resist. It was nothing at all like the half-assed spasms she occasionally gave herself when she couldn't take the itch one minute longer.

Doomed. She was doomed. With a sigh, she climbed out of bed. Opening her closet, she pulled out her dirtiest Levis, her rattiest shirt and her oldest boots and put them on. She was being forced to spend the day with her cousin but that didn't mean she must make it pleasant for him. She tucked her pistol into her holster. If all else failed, she could always shoot the son of a bitch.

Prepared as she'd ever be, which wasn't really prepared at all, she walked to the dining room, on tenterhooks because she fully expected that Orson would be there stuffing his face like last night. But hallelujah, the room was empty.

Right. Of course it was. She'd forgotten. Orson never got up before ten either. Yay, a reprieve. Of a few hours. The nausea resumed. Why? Why was Pops so set on her getting married? Why was he now so certain it should be Odious? Even the thought of her cousin's hands on the same places Eli touched so tenderly made her cringe. The only way she'd ever let Orson's soft little hands touch her body was if she was dead. Yeah, dead would be best.

But since she wasn't ready to die quite yet, drunk sounded like a great idea. Maybe the alcohol would blot out the sound of Orson's nasal voice. Striding to the liquor cabinet, she pulled out a bottle of something, she had no idea what it was since the only alcohol she typically drank was wine, tilted it to her lips and gulped down a big slug.

Gah! Geezwax, how did men drink this stuff? Her tongue, her throat, were about to burn up. Holding up the bottle, she checked the label. Tequila. Eighty proof. Lord, no wonder. She grit her teeth and waited for the fire to go away. Eventually it did, but interestingly, it was replaced by a sense of…something. She wasn't quite sure what it was, just something that made her feel like nobody better get in her way.

She took another sip. Hmmm. More heat spread through her. This was even better the second time. Tilting the bottle again, she gulped down another mouthful. The heat, the sense of hey-it's-me-against-the-world-and-the-world-is-gonna-lose grew. Wow. Now she understood why men drank. She felt like she could take on Odious with one jab to the nose. Curling her hands into fists, she held them up and admired them. Fists, prepare to meet a nose.

Okay, she was ready to take on the world now and nothing was going to stop her.

Exiting the house, she stood on the porch for a minute and surveyed her domain, because yeah, it was her domain. Maybe it was her father's name on the deed but this place was hers and it was going to stay hers, no matter what. She was tired of being treated like she was some kind of subservient slave, of having to toe the line because men said she should be a lady. Men who said her only goal in life was to have kids and to stay out of men's business.

Screw that.

Her head buzzed with her thoughts, and the alcohol. Why was she letting her do-nothing, know-nothing father tell her how to run her life? It was her life and, by the good lord Harry, she was going to live it her way. Hell, if she wanted, she might even go to the courthouse come November and vote. Of course, they'd throw her out kicking and screaming but at least she'd have shown them she had balls.

She grimaced. And that was the problem and the story of her life, the lack of balls, or at least the right kind of balls.

Well, she was sick to death of men telling her what she could and couldn't do. From now on she was going to do whatever she wanted. Her eyes drifted to the left where Eli knelt behind the small corral pulling loco weed. Hoo daddy. Balls or no balls, she was going to do what she wanted and have what she wanted. Starting with him.

"Eli," she bellowed.

He rocked back on his haunches and cocked a questioning brow at her.

"Saddle your horse. You're going into town with me."

He jumped to his feet, not even questioning the order, and followed her into the barn where she saddled and bridled her horse while Eli saddled Rusty. Leading her horse into the stable yard, she mounted up and Eli quickly followed her example. Together, they galloped under the Buchanan Hollow signposts out onto the main road but slowed to a walk when their horses started to labor.

Eli pulled up next to her. "Any particular reason we're going into town?" he asked.

"Ride now. Talk later." He'd find out the answer soon enough. She kept her face blank, giving nothing away but the alcohol in her body and the memory of last night's dinner drove her on, determined to live out her fantasy.

Over the last ten years she'd made fun of the girls in town, calling them silly and floofy and declaring she had better things to do than spending all her time trying to land a man. But the truth was, no man ever really shown an interest in her. They were mighty interested in her possessions, but none were interested in her, or so it seemed.

Well, enough of that. She wasn't waiting around for some no-good yahoo to decide he wanted her. She would do her own deciding. Half an hour later, she steered her horse into an alley behind the Menger Hotel. The back of her neck tingled from Eli's gaze behind her. Her nipples tingled, between her legs she burned. Her lungs felt tight with anxiety and anticipation.

Harvey, the stable owner, tall and burly with a big grin, came out to greet her. "Staying long, Miss Tillie?" he asked.

Dismounting, she handed him the reins. Next to her, also Eli dismounted. Even standing several feet away, she was aware of Eli's scent, a hint of black soil from the garden where he'd been working, sunshine and something unique to him, like a trace of lemon. Fire spread through her veins.

"I'm not sure. Maybe a few hours," she told Harvey, but her mind wasn't on the stable owner, nor was her body. They were both focused on Eli, the man standing next to her. She clenched her fists to stop her hands from grabbing his face and kissing the life out of him.

"No problem. I got plenty of room so come back whenever you want." Harvey led the horses away.

Tillie pointed a finger at Eli. "You. Come with me." Wow. That felt good.

One of his eyebrows went up, questioning. Her response was to crook a finger then lead the way through the alley. She'd promised herself she would take what she wanted, and by God, she was going to do it. Soon they reached the back door of a large three-story building. She pulled the door open, walked through the large kitchen where the staff stared at her, startled, along a long hallway, and started up the servant's stairs.

"Tillie—"

"No talking." Another flight. Behind her, she could hear him breathing. Stopping on the third landing, she opened the door, peeked out into the hallway. Empty. She tugged him through the open doorway and raced down the carpeted hall until they reached a set of double doors. Her father's suite. No one used the suite except her father for the trysts that he thought no one knew about but everyone did.

Bending, she stuck a finger inside a small rip in the carpet and extracted the key to the door. She thrust it into the keyhole, twisted the handle and the door opened.

Dragging Eli inside, she slammed the door shut. Then she threw herself at him so hard they fell against the door with a crash. Fierce desire was eating her up. She wanted him, and she wanted him now. Yesterday, in the creek, and that night in the barn, had only been a taste of what they could do together.

"What's going on? What's this all about, Tillie?" His hands were on her hips, like firebrands. "What are we doing here?"

"We're here for me. It's about me taking what I want for a change. It's about me standing up and being a man." She grabbed his cheeks between her palms. And kissed him. Hard.

He pulled back. "What? What are you talking about." A flicker of amusement gleamed in his eyes. "Don't know that I'm interested in kissing a man."

"Oh, shut up. You know what I mean." This time she grabbed him by the ears before mashing her lips on his.

The kiss went on. And on. And on. Until they both pulled away, gasping, so they could breathe. But damn, that kiss was one for the record books. Her whole body was on fire. The minute she had time to recover, she was going in for seconds because the man had lips that could conquer the world. Pressing her chest against his, she lifted her face, making him aware that she was ready for that second round.

But instead of kissing her, he cupped his hand around the back of her head. "Tillie, tell me what's going on."

She stomped her foot. "It's about me taking charge of my life. It's about me being me. I'm sick of people telling me how to live my life. I'm tired of doing what men tell me to do. I'm tired..." She stopped, gulping down the lump of tears in her throat. "I'm tired of men telling me I'm not enough, that the only way I'll ever be enough is if I subjugate myself to a man."

Something hot flared in his blue eyes. "Your father said that?"

"And Orson. He said...I don't dress right...I'm not...womanly..." The pain of her admission built up in her chest like a thunderstorm, threatening to erupt if she wasn't careful.

His jaw hardened. "Tillie. Don't let Orson, or your father tell you you're not woman enough. You're more than enough. You're a beautiful woman, but more than that, you are an amazing woman. You are smart, and caring and competent. I've never met a woman like you."

The words were like aloe on poison ivy, soothing and healing. And hope began to flood her heart. She bit her lip, trapping in her mouth the words begging for reassurance.

"Tillie, you have no idea how much I l...li..." He seemed to stumble over the word. "How much I like you. I like everything about you. I like your beautiful hair, like spun sunshine. I like the dusting of freckles on your nose that are like fairy dust. I like your voice. It has this low raspy quality that sends shivers up my spine. I love your wily mind. I love your perverse sense of humor. I love how you stand up for yourself, like right now. You make me laugh all the time even when I have nothing to laugh about. You have no idea how much I need to laugh sometimes."

Somewhere in the back of her mind she realized his litany of likes now morphed into a listing of loves but it didn't matter because she'd already leaped into his arms and wrapped her legs around his waist. "Kiss me, damn it," she said. "Make love to me."

His arms tightened even further, pulling her snug against his body. She could feel him even though their clothes. He was hard.

A spark shot through her, so hot it set her body ablaze but even more, it lit a fire in her mind. Her imagination went wild thinking about his long, hard body over hers, in hers.

"Tillie, damn it. I want to. But I can't. Nothing's really changed from before... But I want you so much." Releasing her legs, he allowed her to drop back to the floor.

But it wasn't over. His hand roamed over her, touching everywhere, and everywhere he touched, it electrified her. Heat and fire and sizzle skipped through her body, like lightning striking. His hand cupped her breast, his thumb sliding over her nipple. More lightening. Her knees weakened.

"Eli, everything's changed. I've changed. I'm taking control of what I want, and what I want is you," she whispered, and pointed over her shoulder. The effects of the whiskey she'd drunk only an hour ago made it easier for her to tell him what she wanted but it wasn't whiskey what made her want to make love with him. It was him, and the warmth in his eyes and the gentle caress of his hands on her. There was such kindness and caring and desire radiating from him.

"Tillie, I want to, please, you have to know how much I want this but I could... it could result in..." Fear and uncertainty and desire rippled across his face.

"Then we'll have to be careful." Other than the night in the barn, she'd never touched a man intimately, but that night taught her a lot. She now knew what she wanted from a man...this man.

And she also knew how this man wanted to be touched. How he came undone when she kissed his mouth, touched the rippling muscles. Touched his manhood. During their last encounter she'd been a bit timid, a bit shy but she was done with that. This was the new her, the woman who decided what was right for her. Rising on her toes, she kissed the corner of his mouth. Her toes tingled and between her legs she felt scalded.

She ran her tongue along the seam of his lip. He gasped then moaned.

Yes. She must be doing it right. She wasn't sure, it was all new but the sensations where the same—better—than the night in the barn so it must be right. This was what she wanted, the heat, the sense that she was the one in charge of her life. It completed the circle of her life, knowing who and what she was, first with the ranch and now with a man.

More assured, she rubbed a thumb over his nipple. His face twisted into a look of agony. "Tillie. Ah, Tillie. Don't..." His voice trailed off.

There was more. She knew there was more. Did she dare? Under her hands, Eli shook like a terrified animal. Yes, she dared. She wanted this. She wanted to make him want her. She let her hand slide down his stomach, hesitating briefly grasping him through his trousers.

"Don't," he groaned, but he didn't touch her the way she wanted. But he didn't move away either. She burned for him but he still stubbornly held out and she was beginning to lose courage. If he didn't do something soon, she didn't know how much longer she could do this.

"Eli. Please. This is what I want," she pleaded.

"Okay, okay. We can do what we did in the barn. No more. That'll be enough. No further. I'll make you feel better than we'll stop. Tell me to stop and I will. We can do what we did in the barn and you'll still be a virgin and you'll be safe," he said and before she respond, he picked her up and was striding over to the bed. He carefully laid her onto the duvet and followed her down, his lips on hers. His hands stroked, touching her everywhere, leaving sparks behind while, one piece at a time, clothing came off.

After a brief hesitation, her hand got busy unbuttoning and tugging off his shirt. There was an awkward moment when she pushed his trousers off over his hips when they got stuck on his shoes but he toed them off onto the floor, his eyes never leaving hers, his lips traveling across her collarbone, her cheeks and to her ear where he whispered sweet words.

"You are so beautiful. I've never met anyone so beautiful." She wasn't, she wore pants and walked like a man and sometimes swore like a man. There were thousands of women more beautiful than she was. But she loved hearing it anyway.

He nipped her earlobe, making her moan. Lips. She had lips. The man deserved her best so she was damned well going to make the most of her lips. She nipped and sucked and kissed every bare inch of his body until he was quivering and moaning.

"See. This is what you want, right?" His hands caressed her, touching her breasts, her nipples, roaming over her shoulders to her neck until every inch of her shivered with need. Between her legs, she throbbed and dampened in preparation for his entry. But it was only his hand that touched her there, only a finger that entered.

With a squeal, she dug her heels into the bed. She burned. She hurt. She wanted. He thrust his finger in and out and then his thumb found the place buried between the lips of her femininity and, with a cry, she exploded.

God in heaven. This was what she wanted, this and the rest of it. Because this was just the beginning. The appetizer. "Eli," she panted.

"Good. Good. Sweet Tillie. That was beautiful. See, that's what you needed." Stroking her hair back off her forehead, he placed a gentle kiss on her cheek, his eyes brimming with warmth. With a groan he lifted, prepared to roll off.

What! No, not again! He wasn't going to do that to her again. She grabbed him around the neck and pulled him back down. "Don't you dare leave."

"What? What are you—"

"We're not done," Tillie whispered, determined he wouldn't leave her.

"Yes, we are. We're done. You—"

She twined her legs around his waist, trapping him. "I did but you didn't and I want it all. Don't leave. Make love to me now," she said.

"Tillie, this shouldn't happen. Nothing's really changed."

"I want this," she said through gritted teeth. "I want you. I want to make love with you. I don't care that you say it's wrong. It's not wrong; it's everything that's right."

"Tillie." He closed his eyes for a moment, his mouth drawn tight. "If I do...I could...you could... So, no. Still no... damn it, I want to though."

Damn it to hell. He wanted to. And so did she. Tightening her arms, she pulled his head down and kissed him, using all her want, all the desire in her to tell him the answer was yes.

He moaned. And she took it the next step and twined her legs around him, locking them over his buttocks. Now he was trapped. "Please," she said, begging.

His chest rose when he took a deep breath. "Tillie. Ah, God...don't..." he said, concern darkening his face.

"Don't? No, it's don't stop. I want you. I want this. Please," she said softly. Threading her hands through his hair, she kissed the corner of his mouth, his ear, the tip of his chin, until he quivered and shook and moaned.

"Hell, Tillie. We shouldn't. I shouldn't. But God help me, I want you so much," he said. His hips moved, back and forth, back and forth, his hard cock stroking her at the very heart of her until she was on fire.

Wishing she knew what else to say, what else to do, she whispered, "Then take me," and pressed her core against his hard cock. "Please. Make me yours."

"I am yours. Always and forever," he moaned and surrendered to the inevitable. There was a moment when she didn't think her body would stretch that far but the moment passed and her doubt was replaced by something so intense she thought she would fly off the mattress.

"Tillie. Tell me it's okay," he whispered, his breath coming out harsh and fast.

She closed her eyes. "It's better than okay. It's perfect."

His hips flexed, and he thrust into her again until he was seated to the hilt, hard and slick. And then there was nothing but heat and wetness and his lips on hers. His breath became hers, their hearts beat together as one.

The sounds filled her ears, their moans, the harsh breathing, the sound of his hips slapping against her, the wet slide when he withdrew and thrust back in.

Rising up on his arms, he stared down at her, his gaze intent. *Watch me*, his gaze seemed to say. *Watch what you do to me. See how you unman me.* His chest heaved. Sweat dripped off his face that was pulled tight. The arms holding up his body quivered.

Her inner muscles tightened. The friction. The heat. How had she ever denied herself this? How would she manage to live the rest of her life without this if he spurned her afterwards? She shivered, her legs shaking. Her thoughts spun, round and round. This was what she wanted. This man. This feeling.

He groaned. Rotating his hips to another angle, he thrust, hitting spots she had no idea existed. His gaze drilled into her, lightning focused. *Look at me when you come.*

She ached. She recognized the ache, she'd experienced it before, but not like this. She needed what Eli was giving her to make it better. Her body tightened, coiled, like a spring waiting for release. And then it was there. Hard. Searing. Going on and on forever. She cried out. Her soul rose up and answered his and she knew she would never be the same.

"Yes," he moaned into her neck, his hips still working. "Yes. Tillie. I...I...ah God!" Another groan, and he jerked out of her. Rolling to his back, he held himself while he spent.

Her body still shaking from her climax, she watched, fascinated. Of course she'd seen horses and cattle mate, she could name all the body parts and where they belonged, but this was different. He was completely bare, both in body and in who he was as a man. She'd seen him at his most intimate moment. Pride filled her. And almost.... disappointment.

"You pulled out,"

He turned his head so their eyes met. "Holy hell, you know why. You told me to be careful. I had to be careful. Otherwise it could be disastrous."

She did. But the fact she'd told him not to get her pregnant didn't make her regret it any less, it only increased it. It said something about his plans. Children were not in the picture. Marriage was not in the cards.

They lay together, silent, and caught their breath. Finally, he rolled off the bed and walked to the wash stand. Dipping a cloth into the water basin, he wiped himself down, rinsed out the cloth and returned to her. Using tender strokes, he wiped her clean.

"Tillie. If I could...I would...I..."

Her lower lip trembled. She wouldn't cry. She wouldn't. Tillie Buchanan didn't cry. "Never mind. I had..." She started to say she had fun but stopped herself. Having fun did not begin to describe what just happened.

His hand caressed her cheek. "Tillie. I..." He briefly closed his eyes. "If you don't remember anything else, if you don't believe anything else...." He bit his lip. "Believe this. I love you."

Her heart leaped for joy, then wrenched painfully. Remember? *Remember* was said because the speaker was aware they wouldn't be around to say the words again.

Sliding off the bed, she gathered up her clothing and dressed. Her words of love stayed where they were, in her mind, because what good would it do to say them? A long-term man was not part of her plan anyway. She'd keep him for as long as he'd stay, then let him go.

"We should start back home. I was supposed to take Orson on a tour today. Pops will be wondering where I got to." She forced back the tears.

"Of course."

Not looking at each other, not speaking, they tidied the room and left, locking the door behind them, and putting the key back in its not-so-secret hiding place then walked back to the stables and retrieved their horses.

The ride back was quiet. And awkward. Every so often, she caught him peering at her but he would instantly glance away. Then he would catch her peeking at him and then quickly ignore her stare.

They rode under the Buchanan Hollow sign and entered the yard to see the entire crew gathered in a circle staring and muttering about something in the middle.

Dismounting, they approached the crowd which parted to reveal one man and... something. Tillie couldn't tell what it was. Just something with four legs covered in a blanket.

"Oh boy," Eli muttered in a voice that spoke volumes about his dismay. "It's the Great Unwashed."

Sure enough, it was the fellow who kept his money inside his underdrawers. She shuddered in revulsion.

Unwashed held out the end of a rope that was attached to the something small and four-legged. He grinned. "Am I the first? Did I beat everyone else? Did I win?"

Too stunned to speak or even think of a good lie, she grimaced. "Uh...well..."

"So I'm not the first?" His grin faded.

Tillie shook her head. "No, Mr. Aker."

Aker squinted at the four-legged thing on the end of his lead. "So someone else won."

"No, nobody has won."

"So someone beat me here...but they didn't win?"

"Uh, yes. I mean no." There would be no winning, only disappointed Questers.

The door to the house opened. Her father exited and walked over to join them. "Good looking critter you got there, mister," he said to Aker. "Might be you won, right? When you figure on marrying my daughter? I always heard June was a nice month for a wedding. Course it's already almost June so that might be mite difficult to pull off."

Tillie slapped Jim Bob with her hat. She was sick to death of her father and his snide remarks. "Go back inside, you old fart, and mind your own business," she growled then stabbed a finger at Eli. "And you stop laughing," she told him because he was snickering under his breath.

She inspected the Great Unwashed who lifted a hand to scratch his neck, leaving behind a slim track of clean white skin under the dirt. Ugh. It was too warm for a hot bath but she was taking one anyway the minute she got rid of the man.

"I don't get it. Someone else was first but didn't win. So then I must be the winner," Unwashed said, a smile breaking out on his face and revealing those missing teeth. Tillie swallowed. It was almost too bad he wouldn't be able to win. With a little money he might be able to get dentures.

"No, you didn't win. That's not an equicamemu." She wasn't sure what the thing on the other end of his tether was, but it wasn't an equicamemu. The animal was small, standing only about three feet tall, with slim legs and dainty hooves. It possessed a horse's head, so definitely horse-like, but underneath a heavy blanket draped across its back rose an enormous hump—definitely not horse-like.

Behind her back, came another series of *tee hees* from her father.

The door to the house opened again and Orson walked out, today dressed all in pink and violet. Skipping down the steps, he walked over to stand next to Tillie. "For heaven's sake, now what? Another one of your Questers?" he said with a sneer.

Like she didn't already have enough problems. "This is Horace Aker, one of the Questers. He brought his..." She stopped because she really didn't know what to say about what Aker brought.

"His what, Tillie? His equi whatever? It's a fake." Sticking a finger under the blanket draped over the animal's back, Orson lifted it and peered underneath. "Why, that's nothing but a pony he's tied some rags onto its back. He's trying to cheat us. See," he said and reached out to yank the blanket off.

The tiny horse didn't like it. With a squeal, the creature bucked, bucked again. The strap securing the blanket came loose and it flew off, revealing a large bundle of wool tied to the horse's back.

"There! Look at that," Orson yipped and yanked on the bundle. And the tiny horse bucked again, kicking out with its back feet, and catching Orson. Right in the...in the...

Orson fell to the ground, howling, his hands cupping his masculine parts.

Nobody said anything for a minute. Tillie covered her mouth with her hand. One of the ranch hands snickered. Eli muttered, "That's got to hurt," and Unwashed gaped, his face the perfect picture of shock. A bellow of laughter came from her father.

The laughter rolling from her father finally faded. Orson continued to moan and writhe on the ground. All eyes returned to the Unwashed and the little horse that no longer looked anything like an equicamemu, merely a tiny little horse. Aker's eyes fell. He scuffed the ground with the toe of his boot. "Guess I better be on my way," he said. Grumbling under his breath, he led the miniature steed out through the front entrance and down the road.

Jim Bob gave one last snicker. "Well, it wasn't much of a horse anyway, daughter. More like half a horse. Or maybe a quarter of a horse." He snorted and poked Tillie in the side. "Haw. A quarter of a horse. Get it? A quarter horse. Tee hee hee."

Tillie didn't respond because the comment wasn't worth responding to. It would only encourage more inane jokes. Instead, she peered down at her cousin still thrashing about on the ground, moaning and holding his parts. "Sure, Pops, I get it. But that thing about Buchanan grandchildren? You might want to rethink that," she said, and pointed to where Orson was cupping himself.

The grin fell off Jim Bob's face. Leaning over the moaning Orson, he hissed, "Oh, stop your whining, boy. Get up and be a man." He straightened and stalked into the house.

Chapter Sixteen

The stable door creaked open and Tillie walked inside. And Eli escaped out the back door. Running around the corner, he raced towards the far side of the back paddock.

Holy cow. He took a deep breath. That was a close one. He'd been dodging and hiding for several days so he was getting pretty good at it but she'd nearly caught him this time. Sure, he was being a coward but he needed to do whatever he could to avoid her because all he needed to do was see her and his heart drummed fiercely in his chest and his entire body yearned to have her again and the next thing he knew, he'd be all over her, unable to stop, and run the risk for a second time that he could create a child.

And that must not happen. So he needed to stay away from her. For both their sakes.

He'd tried. Oh, lord God, how he'd tried to not make love to her but it seemed predestined. The look on her face when she came, her smell, her lips on his. Once she touched him like that he was a goner and he'd surrendered.

And now he ran and hid like a coward. Shame spread though his body, hot and prickly. He'd surrendered. After promising himself he would stand firm, he'd yielded. He was a fool. A weak fool, because when her lips touched his, when her hand gripped him, when her eyes begged him to give her what she wanted, he couldn't help himself. He'd fallen.

His body had fallen, but worse, his heart did too. Against all wisdom, he'd fallen in love with Tillie. How could he not? She was everything he ever wanted. Strong. Determined. Smart, and not afraid to show it. There was nothing about her that he didn't love. And didn't admire. He respected her desire to be in charge of her own life, to go against society's norms so she could live her life the way she chose. All she wanted was the same thing that men took for granted.

Sadly, life wasn't fair to women. Why shouldn't she be free to run this ranch, to earn money of her own? To make love to a man she wanted...loved.

But that man couldn't be him. Stupidly, he'd given into his own weakness and made love with her which was why he was ducking and hiding; so he didn't give in again. He couldn't take the chance that making love to her could result in a child. The very thought that he might have to flee Buchanan Hollow and leave her pregnant sent a cold shiver through him. Everything she desired, worked for, would be destroyed if she became pregnant with an illegitimate child.

He pressed a hand to his chest, his heart pounding from his run, and from the regret and anger at himself. He shouldn't have yielded. He should have stayed firm. But he'd wanted that one time, that one glorious time, so he'd have that memory to take with him and treasure for the rest of his life.

Which only solidified his belief that he should leave before he gave into temptation again. But damn, she was making it difficult.

"Eli?" he heard her call. He kept going, past Daisy and her new foal, and around the other side of a clump of bushes in hopes it would hide him.

"Eli Knowles, I see you. If you don't get your rear-end back here within two minutes, I'm going to fire you."

A snort of laughter escaped. Stopping, he spun around to face her. Setting his fists on his hips, he yelled, "What do you want?"

She mimicked his pose. "What do you think I want?"

He sighed. That's what he was afraid of. "I know what you want, and I'm not giving it to you."

She chuckled. "Okay, how about you give me half of what I want?" she said, striding through the grass towards him.

"What exactly does that mean?" Damn him for a fool, he was so tempted. His cock hardened in anticipation of the thing he was going to deny it.

She stopped ten feet away. "A kiss. That's all I want is a kiss."

"Hah. A kiss is not half. More like ten percent. Half would be much, much more than a kiss."

A smile spreading across her face, she twirled a strand of hair around a finger and peered at him through her lashes. "Well, maybe more than one kiss. Maybe a hug or two."

Damn, she was flirting with him. "Still not half," he said then squeezed his eyes shut. Hell and damnation, he was an idiot.

She took another two steps forward, close enough that he could see the freckles sprinkled on her nose, and an enticing hollow above her collar bone he'd love to lick. "Well," she said, drawing out the word. "I guess you could touch my breast..." She touched a finger to the body part in question then took another step closer. Only a few feet separated them now. "And I could touch your..." She licked her lips, a look of unholy glee shining in her eyes.

He inhaled sharply. She was killing him.

She grinned. "Your hand."

He let out a gust of air and took two steps that closed the gap a little further. "Lips only. That's all. Ten percent."

Her lower lip went out in a pout but she nodded. His heart hammering, he leaned forward, being careful to leave six inches of space between their bodies, and gently pressed his lips to hers. Fire raced through his body; his cock strained against the front of his trousers.

She parted her lips to provide easier access so he took it by slipping his tongue into her mouth. Against his will, a moan tumbled out. She matched it with a moan of her own. Lips molded together, tongues touched, taste and passion was exchanged, and yet, other than their lips, they didn't touch each other. Sweet Jesus, this was heaven.

Knowing it must end now or things might get out of control, Eli finally pulled away. It was like losing a part of his body.

She gazed up at him. Her eyes held a plea for more. "Eli."

He shook his head.

"Why not? We're adults. I want you. You obviously want me. So why not?"

He shook his head. "We can't. It's not right. We can't risk it."

Red splashed across her cheeks. "Stop saying that. You keep saying the same stupid thing. It's ridiculous. There's nothing to stop us from taking what we want. Is it because we're not married? Is that the reason? Are you one of those men who believe a good woman shouldn't have sex unless they're married and if I do, I'm not a good woman anymore? I'm defiled? I'm a tramp?"

"No. Don't say that. I don't think that. I don't think that at all. We already did... uh, you know, and how I feel hasn't changed. I admire you. I respect you. I..." He squeezed his eyes shut for a second, not willing to remind her that he'd already said he loved her. That would seal their fate.

"I... Never mind. What I believe is that you have every right to choose your own course in life, your own path, and not get reviled and insulted for it."

The expression on her face froze. "What do you mean?"

The need to explain himself pressed hotly in his throat. "I mean, you are entitled to the same respect as any man for being who you are. I would never want to force you into some archaic, bizarre concept that society expects of you simply because you're a woman. Be yourself, Tillie, because yourself is magnificent."

Her eyes clouded up then a tear slid over the edge and slid down her cheek. Biting her lip, she inhaled a shaking breath. "Then what's the problem? If it's not me, than what is it? Why?"

He pressed his fist to his chest because it hurt to breath. "It's me. It's my problem."

"I don't understand you. You say I have the same right to choose how I live same like a man. Well, I chose you, but you keep telling me that making love with me wouldn't be right. It's making me crazy because I don't understand. Am I breaking some unwritten rule you believe in? Are you one of those honorable men who, in spite of what you just now said, still want to protect us little women? Is it one of those honor and valor and slay the dragon things, like those knights in shining armor in *Ivanhoe*? You're determined to protect me from myself, is that it?" She took a deep breath, her lips trembling.

Something inside him collapsed. Heaven help him, if she only knew how ironic her statement was. She was breaking his heart. He couldn't be what she wanted. He'd die to be the knight she wanted but he couldn't. Real knights didn't run off and leave their ladies abandoned. He shook his head.

All the fire and hope and wanting bled off her face. "Why?" she whispered, her voice flat.

Such a simple question. And one that he wasn't sure he could adequately answer but she deserved that he at least try. "Tillie, there are things I haven't told you, danger—"

"Miss Tillie!" The shout carried over the expanse of the field. They both watched Zeke run to join them. He skidded to a halt. "You got more of your knight fellows that just come."

Her eyes widened. "More? Geezwax. Which ones now?"

"The twins fellows," Zeke said, panting.

"Oh boy," Eli muttered. Reaching out, he took her hand and together they ran towards the stables. Sprinting around the corner, they found, once again, the Buchanan Hollow ranch hands gathered in a circle surrounding someone. The circle parted, and sure enough, it was Bert and Bert. Identically blond haired, buck-toothed, and baby-faced. And on their identical baby faces were identical scowls.

Putting a hand to her chest, Tillie took a deep breath but before she could speak Bert beat her to the punch.

"You lied to us," the Bert said, and taking his silver toothpick from between his lips, poked it at her, like a scolding finger.

Tillie's face lost all color. "Uh..."

The ranch hands took the usual giant step back, not wanting to get in the middle of another of Tillie's little conspiracies. Eli took a step forward, his natural instinct to protect her taking over before he remembered she wasn't some frail flower who would wilt under a man's aggression. He reined in his desire to smash a fist into Bert's face and simply said, "Watch what you're saying to Miss Buchanan."

Bert the second moved forward to stand next to his twin. "But she lied."

"Yes, lied," from the first Bert.

"Lying is wrong," Bert number two said.

"Lying is a sin," number one picked up the thread again.

"Commandment number nine says you shouldn't bear false witness against your neighbor. Ain't that the same like lying?" Number two thrust his chin out, crossed his arms over his chest and stared at Tillie as if daring her to dispute his comment.

Eli was already aware her little quest was a complete farce but how did the Berts find out? The words, "Please explain," hovered unspoken on his tongue but he bit them back. If he wanted to claim he respected Tillie for who she was, he needed to let her handle it.

"What are you saying I lied about?" she said.

Bert's—Eli wasn't sure which Bert it was at this point, not that it seemed to make much difference—eyes narrowed in a glare. "You done told us that you was gonna marry whoever brought back that there equi—thingie but now we hear your Daddy has brought in some fellow from back east that yer gonna marry."

Tillie let out a huff of breath. Relief, Eli was sure. "Okay, now look, Bert. That's not true. Yes, my Pops invited my cousin to stay for a while, and yes, he's made it clear he would like me to marry my cousin, but the answer is no, I'm not going to marry Orson. The Quest is still in process and so far no one has brought me the winning animal." She crossed her arms over her chest and scowled at the two Berts while tapping her foot.

Bert—whichever one—fingered his chin. Eli could almost see the wheels spinning in his head. "So yer not gonna marry this fellow Orson."

"No." The answer was emphatic. "So if you still want to win, go out there and find my equicamemu." Behind her back, Tillie's fingers were crossed, an indication she'd lied. But what had she lied about; the fact that the Berts would never find an equicamemu or that she wasn't going to marry Orson?

He shouldn't care which, but he did, and his heart took a nosedive.

A long silence reigned while Bert One tapped his chin, thinking, and Bert Two picked his teeth with the silver toothpick he'd snatched from his twin's mouth. "Okay, fine," Bert One said. Dragging his brother to their horses, they mounted and rode off.

Eli swatted at the fly buzzing around his head. "Too bad the animal you invented wasn't something with long sharp teeth," he murmured. "Then we could always hope the something would eat them."

Tillie chuckled.

The Berts finally disappeared from sight and miraculously, with little fuss.

※

Good luck and good riddance was Tillie's thought. Incredulity that she believed her quest was a good idea was her second thought. The entire thing started out as a way to foil her father's unreasonable demand which was why she'd picked ten of the dimmest men in Texas. None of them were ever serious contenders. But even if they were, she still wouldn't have chosen any of them. On the other hand, there was Eli.

But he seemed a little—well, a lot—reluctant. She still needed answers. "Eli," she said, meaning to get a few but he was gone, along with everyone else. Son of a...

She fisted her hands on her hips. Now what? Why wouldn't the man stay put? Why wouldn't he answer her questions?

Her thoughts went back to their previous conversation. He'd said something, something like... "It's me. It's my problem." Then he'd said something else... oh, yeah, something like danger...uh, dangerous? What did that mean? Was he saying he was in danger? Or did he mean he was a danger to her? Her heart stopped. Would he hurt her? No, she didn't believe that. He would never hurt her. Then what else could it be?

They really needed to talk. She checked inside the barn but all the stalls were empty since all the horses would be in the back pasture at this time of day. Damn the man, he'd been running and hiding from her for the almost a week. She wanted some answers, and she wanted them now.

She snapped her fingers. Of course. He'd gone back out to the pasture. To hide again. Like a coward.

Opening the back doors, she walked back out into the back pasture. A half dozen horses meandered back and forth, nipping at the lush green grass and behind them, far to the back, was Eli along with Daisy and the foal. She strode out to join them but the minute he saw her coming, he spun around, prepared to run.

"Don't you dare," she yelled. Gosh darn it, they were right back where they started before the Berts arrived.

He stopped. "What, Tillie?" he asked. Stress tightened his face, and tension made his shoulders rigid but at least he waited.

"I have a question."

He nodded, trepidation on his face like he expected her to hit him over the head with a two-by-four.

"Why are you avoiding me?"

"Tillie, for heaven's sake," he said, which was no answer at all.

Okay, so she might have to dig a little deeper. "Is there something wrong with you?" She deliberately made the question vague because, truthfully, she didn't know what she was asking. She didn't know that she really wanted an answer either, not if the answer was yes.

His eyes widened and his jaw dropped. "No! Dear lord, why would you think that?" He ran a hand through his hair, an expression of exasperation and embarrassment on his face.

"Well, doggone it, Eli, it's the only explanation I could think of. Then tell me why. I need to understand."

He looked away from her, not speaking for long minutes, before heaving a sigh. "Tillie. Okay. Fine. I...I...I... Something happened. Back where I'm from. Someone died. And...I was blamed...and..."

Her heart sank in her chest. "Did you kill someone? Is the law after you?"

"No, Jesus, no. Not the law. The opposite. A man who has no respect for the law."

Fear raced along her nerves, making her fingers tingle and her breath clot in her throat. "And this man, he's after you?"

"I don't know. I have no way to find out. But knowing him, he won't rest until he finds me." He ran a hand that shook through his hair, despair shadowing his eyes.

Tillie's fear began to recede and determination took its place. "Then let me help. Let me do whatever needs doing to find out."

Alarm sparked in his eyes. "No! Lord, no, Tillie. Don't. It's too dangerous. He's rich and he has people and connections and he's utterly ruthless. Even the slightest hint, the slightest whisper of where I am, and he would hear of it and be here in a flash. It would put you at risk, your father at risk." He laid his hand on his chest, his breath coming out harsh and fast. "Tillie, please don't. I can always run, hide, but you and your father, you're vulnerable. I couldn't bear it..." He stopped and looked at her, his eyes pleading.

Seeing his horror, his fear, she could do nothing but give in. "Are you going to run now? Leave?" *Please say no.* Why she wanted that she couldn't say. It wasn't like she wanted a man in her life, much less one who stuck around forever.

Bowing his head, he took a long, shaky breath. "I should. God help me, I really should. But..."

"But you don't want to leave, right? So stay, then, Eli. I'll help however you let me. We can figure it out." She bit her lip. What was she doing, asking him to stay like she was one of those floofy girls in town, desperate for a man? She wasn't. It was simply that she like him, wanted him. He was a complicated man, with many hidden layers so what was not to like? She liked his sly amusement, that he stood up for what he believed but mostly the fact that he viewed her as a person, not simply a woman.

The fact that she enjoyed being with him, that she loved what they did in her father's hotel suite and wanted to do it again, meant nothing. Telling him she wanted him to stay was all part of taking charge of her own life, right?

"I'll try. But I can't promise." His shoulders sagged, his eyes were flat, a man completely defeated.

Seeing it, something inside twisted painfully, like a signal that life was going to change irrevocably in ways she wouldn't like.

Work. Whenever she was sad or depressed, it was always work that saved her. She simply needed to stick to her plan; defeat her father's nefarious scheme so she could live her life the way she wanted. After all, wasn't Eli the one who said, 'You have every right to choose your own course in life, your own path, and not get reviled and insulted for it. If that included enjoying Eli, then that's what she'd do.

She wished she could figure out why the idea of that hurt so much.

Pushing the thought aside, she said, "If you go into the tack room there's a small halter hanging on the wall, small enough for the foal. We can start halter training him."

After a half hour working with foal, Tillie removed the halter and started back to the barn. Eli followed but jerked to a halt when she yelled, "Eli, stop!" then pulled out her pocket revolver.

Bang!

He jumped a foot. "Holy hell, Tillie, what was that?"

"Rattlesnake," she said, tucking her pocket pistol back into her belt and walking on like nothing happened because when it came to snakes in Texas, nothing did. His eyes wide, Eli followed behind her, skirting a wide circle around the dead rattler.

The hands working the fences that afternoon were beginning to return by the time they reached the barn. Careful not to give the impression they were together, they didn't touch, they didn't look at each other. Jinx dismounted from his horse and watched them, his eyes cold under knitted brows. It made a shiver run up her spine.

Eli shot a look at her. "What's his problem, anyway?" he murmured under his breath.

"No idea, but it would be smart to stay out of his way." She clenched her teeth. She really wanted to fire Jinx but he was her father's hire way back when so she'd need a solid reason to let him go. Which she didn't have. Yet.

Still pretending to ignore Eli, she said, "I'm going inside. Stay away from him," and walked into the house.

Searching for her father, she poked her head into the dining room. Other than when he went into town to visit one of his lady friends, he spent most of his time in his two favorite places, the dining room where he liked to eat, and the study where he liked to nap. She found him in the dining room where he was busy scooping refried beans into his mouth.

"More of your questers?" he asked.

She nodded, irritated at his snide tone.

"No teeny tiny shrunken horses, no ugly things what spit, no dragons, no what did you call it, plateepuses?"

Smart ass. "If there were, I would have told you." But that day would never come.

He shook his head, tsking. "You're running out of time, girl. Only a few weeks left and so far three of your questers have come back here with nothing to show for their time." Picking a slab of bread, he tore a hunk off it and chewed. "Now, it's time you did what I asked and start teaching Orson what he needs to know. That's an order."

The *or else* was left unsaid but it was there. "Fine." Spinning around, she marched down the hall to Orson's room. Who, now that she thought about it, she hadn't seen in several days, not since the day the Great Unwashed showed up with his pony. Giving a quick rap on the door, she pushed it open.

Orson was lying on the bed. She jerked to a halt. What in the holy hell? From the waist up, Odious was properly clothed, wearing a white linen shirt, a pink brocade vest and a red ascot tie at his neck. But below his waist, he wore... oh dear. Nothing. Except for a cloth draped across his hips with his hands folded on top.

He glared at her. "What do you want?" he said, his words sulky.

"Uh..." She was having a hard time not staring. Unlike Eli's long, muscular legs, Orson's legs were short and skinny and bowed. And hairy. Wow, were they hairy. Ugh.

"Well?" he demanded.

"Uh, I came say we could take that tour of the ranch Pops wants. We could ride out tomorrow morning if that works for you."

Actual flames shot from his eyes, or at least that's what it seemed like. "A tour? You think I can take a tour? You think I can ride a horse with this?" he screamed and yanked the cloth away from his hips.

"Holy Toledo," she gasped and slapped a hand over her eyes. Dear lord, she did *not* want to see that! It couldn't be real, could it? It was large. Huge even, and dark purple. It was like a giant eggplant sprouting between his legs.

Still holding her hand over her eyes, she said, "Okay, well, I guess we'll do the tour another day then," then spun around and fled. She managed to hold in her reaction until she was outside but the minute she jumped off the porch she bent double with laughter. The good news for her was there wouldn't be a tour for quite some time.

Chapter Seventeen

Two more peaceful days passed where she didn't have Orson dogging her heels, glaring while also trying to slide his wet lips over her mouth and pushing her into corners with his flabby body. No, he was still hiding in his room where, she assumed, he was nursing that enormous eggplant she'd accidentally viewed. Not that she really care. The more time he spent babying his booboo, the less time he spent bothering her.

The downside was that Eli was also still avoiding her. She'd hoped him telling her about his past would change things but it didn't. She was beyond frustrated. And anxious. And she was... She took a deep breath. Okay, time to admit it; she in a dither she wanted him so badly. Every part of her ached to have his arms around her, his lips pressed to hers, him inside her, hard and hot and thrusting until she exploded and the itch went away.

There, she'd said it. She was officially one of those floofy girls. Ugh!

The ache for him was only intensified by the worrying and fretting and wishing that there was something she could do to help him but she couldn't think of a single thing that wouldn't put him at risk.

Unfortunately, the next day it all went to hell in a hand basket. Odious, apparently threatened by her father, emerged from his self-imposed exile.

"Yes, yes, I'm up but for God's sake, why? Only birds get up at this hour. I am not a bird. I am a man and I need my sleep. I should be in bed. I shouldn't be walking with my injury. And that mattress is doing my injury no good. I shall need something more comfortable if I'm to stay much longer." He sat gingerly in the chair next to Jim Bob.

Inez entered the dining room and set a plate in front of Orson loaded with steamy refried beans, scrambled eggs and tortillas. A cup of coffee was set next to his plate.

"What is this," Orson exclaimed, viewing the food. Picking up a fork, he scooped up a heap of bean and held it out. "Bloody hell, this looks like something my dog would leave on the sidewalk."

"Orson," her father interrupted. "Ladies present."

Orson made a sour face. "Yes, of course. Ladies." He threw a sneer Tillie's way.

Tillie sneered right back. How dare he insult Inez's cooking. "Don't like our accommodations? Go back to where you came from. This is not New York City. We don't sleep until noon here. We get up and start work at dawn."

"Not if I have anything to say about it," he muttered under his breath, shaking the beans off and stabbing a chunk of eggs instead. "Speaking of dawn, what was that...that...thing, screeching outside my window before the sun rose. Whatever it was, if I hear it again, I shall shoot it with my pistol."

A rooster. What kind of fool had never heard of a rooster?

Her father bit off a chunk of ham. "Never mind all that. You're finally up and about. Time to take that tour," he said. "Tillie will take you around, show you everything we've got. Listen to what she's got to teach you and everything should be Jim dandy."

Well, how about that. Maybe her father was on her side after all.

Orson tugged his shirt cuffs far enough that a half inch showed beneath his purple coat sleeve. "Of course, Uncle James. I'm eager to learn all there is to know and take the heavy burden off poor Tillie's shoulders once and for all so she can finally become the lady she was meant to be."

Her father clapped his hands together. "That's the spirit, boy. Get out there and take charge."

Tillie hurled her toast at him. Butter side facing forward, it landed on Jim Bob's chest and stuck, but after a moment, it unstuck and slid down his front and landed in his lap. He picked it up, raised it to his mouth and took a bite.

Grinning at her, he said, "Tsk, tsk. Your aims needs a little practice. Back in the old days, you would have got me in the face," and took another bite.

Back in the old days, she would have put a tack on the seat of his chair. She glared at him. He simply smirked back and finished off the toast she'd thrown.

"Well?" Odious said, interrupting their silent feud. "Are we to take this tour or not?"

Tillie pretended she didn't hear. Maybe if she ignored him long enough, he'd return to his hideout for another few days.

But nope. "Tillie. Take him on the tour. That's an order," her father said, and this time there was no amusement in his voice.

"Fine. Half an hour." Leaving most of her breakfast uneaten, she exited the house. Outside, the men were getting saddled up to leave for the day. Eli saw her coming and began striding away.

"Eli," she called. "Stop." He did. His back was to her but she could visualize the expression on his face, one of exasperation and resignation. He turned to face her, but his face was expressionless.

"I'm taking Orson on that tour of the ranch my father wanted."

He nodded. "I'll saddle Buster. And Chessy? For Orson?"

"Don't worry about Buster and Chessy, I'll take care of them. You saddle Rusty."

"Rusty? Why?"

"You're coming with us. I need a buffer. Good lord, do I need a buffer," she said and led the way into the barn. The fact that she craved his company went unsaid. While Eli saddled Rusty, she took care of Buster, then Chessy.

The horses ready, Tillie led the way out and found Orson waiting, dressed in English jodhpurs, riding boots and a cobalt blue hacking jacket. And talking to Jinx.

Both turned. Their conversation abruptly stopped. Both sets of eyes widened, then both sets narrowed. Unease briefly flitted across Orson's face before it settled back into its usual petulant frown. Jinx crossed his arms and ignored her.

What was that about? "Jinx, you're supposed to be supervising the crew cleaning out the water lines from the windmill to the tanks. Why are you still here?"

His lips tightened into a hard line. "Sure." Gathering the reins of his already saddled horse, he mounted and, spurring the horse into a fast trot, left. Tillie shook her head. It was getting harder and harder to tolerate Jinx's insolence.

"Well, should we be off?" Orson said. "I'm a capital horseman, so I want a horse with a little spirit. I'll take that one." He pointed to Buster who was tossing his head and dancing with eagerness to get going.

Tillie kept her thoughts to herself and only said, "No, Buster is mine. You get Chessy. He's an easy ride. Treat him right. If you so much as harm a hair on his hide, I'll skin yours and hang it on the barn wall."

Orson's lips crunched up into a tight ball but he didn't respond. Instead, he languidly stared at Eli. "You, boy, what's your name again? I've forgotten."

"That's because I never gave you my name in the first place," Eli said through tight lips.

"Mind your manners, boy," Orson snapped. Running his gaze up and down Eli's tall, well-built frame, he tapped his chin with a finger. "You do look so familiar. Why is that? Who. Do. You. Remind me of? Hmm." More chin tapping.

A chill ran down Tillie's back. "We should get going while it's still cool," she quickly said to distract her cousin.

Orson heaved a sigh like the weight of the world was dropped on his shoulders. "Well, never mind. I'm sure it will come to me eventually. So let us be off. But there are three horses. Why are there three horses?"

"Because Eli is coming with us."

She might as well have said Genghis Khan was accompanying them. Orson's face reddened, and his cheeks swelled. "What? I do not ride with the paid help. He stays here."

"Orson—"

Lifting a hand to stop the protest, Eli murmured, "No, it's fine, Tillie. I'll stay here."

Orson huffed. "That would be Miss Buchanan to you." Stepping closer to Tillie, he laid a proprietary hand around her shoulders. His grip said *you belong to me*, a frightening thought if she'd ever had one but it was better that Orson believed Eli was nothing more than a hired hand. Better that Orson didn't learn about the day they'd spent in her father's hotel suite so she said nothing, simply slid out from under his grasp the minute his fingers relaxed.

"Fine. Eli, why don't you do your usual work in the barn."

With a nod, Eli led Rusty back into the barn.

Not waiting for Orson's agreement, Tillie mounted and trotted off, trusting that her cousin was behind her but not really caring, and headed towards the goat pens. The cattle were spread all over hundreds of acres but the goats were in a small enclosure, so it made sense to head there first.

They rode silently for a while then Orson said, "Good lord. I don't understand why anyone lives in this benighted place. All the dirt, and dust, and bugs," in a whine that scraped her nerves raw. He swatted at something buzzing around his head. "The bugs. Heavens, cousin, why don't you people do something about the bugs?"

Even though she hated to, Tillie agreed about the bugs. But she said nothing because what could anyone actually do about bugs?

Two minutes later, "Egad, why is it so hot? If it continues to be this hot I shall surely expire."

Then, "You must do something about that woman, the one who cooks, although I don't believe what she does can legitimately be called cooking. Those beans. Nothing but mush. Revolting. And the meat. Stringy. Completely inedible. And the spice? I do believe she's trying to kill me. Well, we shall have to find someone to replace her, someone who can cook fine cuisine."

Tillie's hands tightened on her reins. "Inez stays," she bit out then spurred her horse a little faster, hoping itt would help her escape. *Think about making love with Eli. Maybe that would help.*

Reaching the bridge over Duggan's Creek, they clattered across. A few minutes later they reached the goat pen. Like every other time she visited, the kids were bouncing around like rubber balls. On one side of the enclosure the adult goats were bunched together. On the other side, the camel stood alone, monopolizing the hay and feed that was intended for the goats. Drat, something would have to be done about that.

And somehow, Orson thought it was his job to do the something. Reaching inside his coat, he pulled out a derringer, took quick aim and pulled the trigger.

"Tarnation," Tillie shrieked and tightened her reins so Buster didn't bolt.

The camel jumped a foot, bellowed then stampeded in the opposite direction, breaking down the wire and split-rail fence, and galloped towards the distant hills. The goats mwa'd, danced around, then, seeing the large gap in the fence, followed him, thirteen adult goats, tails held high, and eight kids, all running pell-mell for the hills where there were trees and bushes and all kinds of nooks and crannies for them to disappear into.

"You stupid son of a—" She bit her tongue, realizing if she went on, she was going to say something she shouldn't.

Her cousin's mouth curled in disgust and said, "The devil take it, I missed the damned thing."

"—bitch!" she said, deciding to finish her sentence. "You idiot. You moron. You utter cretin. What the hell were you thinking? What's the matter with you? Are you stupid or something?" She was on a tear and couldn't stop. "Those goats are valuable. They're fifteen percent of our annual intake. Those kids can be sold for a lot of money or could increase the productivity of the herd. You...you...you...I'm so mad I'm could spit!" Or shoot the stupid jackass.

"Like what that creature did to me? He spit on me. Disgusting. If I see him again, I will shoot again and next time I won't miss."

"It's not your right to do anything," she yelled.

Tucking the gun back inside his coat, he muttered, "Not yet. But it will be," and reined his horse back in the direction they'd come from.

Tillie watched him leave, a chill settling in her stomach. She didn't like the look on his face, she didn't like what he said, she positively didn't like that Orson somehow got the idea that their marriage, and his inheritance, was a done deal.

But for now, there was a pen to repair and goats to find, something she needed help with. Several men were repairing fences in the far north pasture so she rode that way until she found Kermit and Zeke.

"Hey Miss Tillie," Kermit said, putting down the hammer he was using to nail barbed wire to a fence post.

"Hey boys. There's been a little problem at the goat enclosure. You can leave this for tomorrow. What I need can't wait. Bring the wagon and come with me."

Kermit mounted his horse while Zeke climbed up to the seat of the buckboard with his horse tied to the back and followed. With three of them working, it took an hour to repair the fence, then leaving the wagon, they rode into the hills and began searching for the goats. By the time five o'clock arrived, they were all three hot and tired and hungry but managed to capture all but two of the goats, one billy and one nanny. Capturing them would wait for tomorrow.

"Hey, it's dinner time. Time for you men to go home."

"You coming too?" Zeke asked.

"After I make sure the goats are secure and their water is fresh."

The two men rode off, leaving the wagon behind for the next day's work. Tillie checked the pen again, watched the kids bounce around pestering the adults and finally left for home.

By the time she rode into the yard, it was after six and all the hands were inside the bunkhouse cleaning up for dinner. Except Eli. He was pacing in front of the barn, back and forth, head downing and muttering something Tillie was too far away to hear but when he saw her, he rushed forward to meet her. She dismounted.

"What happened? Orson came back without you hours ago. What did he do to you? Why did he come back without you? Are you all right?" His words came out in a rush.

"Eli, stop. I'm fine."

He clapped a hand over his mouth and blinked his eyes shut for a moment. "Heaven help me, Tillie. I thought something happened to you and that son of a bitch, your cousin, wouldn't say. I was scared stiff and I couldn't even go look for you because Jinx ordered me to stay here." He ran a shaking hand through his hair. "Bloody hell, Tillie, what's the matter with that man that he wasn't worried? What's the matter with your father that he wasn't worried?"

Warmth flooded her chest at being told that someone cared enough to worry, because usually nobody did. Everyone assumed she could take care of herself. Besides, she always had her Bull Dog pocket pistol strapped to her belt, so the thought that someone might be worried never occurred to her.

She laid a finger across his lips. "Shh. I'm fine. We had a little disaster, all of Odious's making, so I needed to fix it. It took a while."

"What did he do? Did he hurt you?" Eli asked, and laid his hand, still trembling slightly, against her cheek. It was warm, and calloused after weeks of hard work, and felt like heaven against her skin.

Closing her eyes, she allowed herself to lean into it. The thought crossed her mind that this was a sign that the days when Eli ran and hid from her, when he was determined to freeze her out, were over. The thought that she was beginning to rely on Eli threw her but she dismissed it. Everyone needed someone, even her. It didn't make her a helpless female. "Come with me while I put Buster away and I'll tell you about it."

Together they walked into the barn. Replacing Buster's bridle with a halter, she put him in the crossties and unsaddled him. While she brushed him down, she related how Orson shot at the camel and how the goats escaped so she'd spent the day rebuilding the fence then tracking them down.

"That bastard. He could have accidentally shot you. Or one of the goats. Or, I guess, the camel. Speaking of which, what happened to the camel?"

Shooshing Buster into his stall, she closed the door. "No idea. We couldn't find him. And I'm not wasting any time looking for him. Far as I'm concerned, it's good riddance."

Eli snorted. "Better it should be good riddance to your cousin," he said, amusement in his eyes. Then, the amusement faded and hunger crept in until his eyes were hot blue flames. "Tillie. I was nearly frantic with worry."

His arms went around her and he backed her until she thumped against the wall of the stall. Sliding an arm under her butt, he hoisted her up, his mouth still on hers, devouring her, stroking the crease between her lips with his tongue until she parted them and let him in. He wrapped her legs around his waist. His jeans-clad hips pumped against her core, a crude facsimile of making love. He moaned, a long-drawn-out sound that struck at the heart of her and lit her on fire.

Kiss followed kiss, thrust followed thrust, moans blended together, while inside the tension grew and grew and grew until she exploded. Seconds later, he followed.

They remained leaning against the wall, still locked together, trembling in the aftermath as they struggled to catch their breath. Eli let out a sigh, his warm breath gusting against her neck. "Mmm." He kissed her, nibbled her jaw, her ear. "I..."

"You... What?"

He chuckled. "I need to go visit the creek to clean up. Unless, of course, you say it's okay to use the trough."

"No!" She smacked him in the shoulder then, unwrapping her legs, lowered herself to her feet. They stood there for a moment, staring at each other, both wide-eyed with simmering desire as well as amusement at their lack of control.

Then his smile disappeared and his expression went serious. He cupped her cheek with a hand. "I love you, Tillie. I love you."

Something inside shifted. Like a fossil buried for eons that was suddenly uncovered, the feeling was so new she didn't know what to do with it. It made her weak, and vulnerable and stupidly female.

And loved. Tears burned the back of her eyes. He'd said it once before but then never repeated it so she'd figured it was something said in the heat of the moment. "Does that mean you're staying?" she whispered. At least until they tired of each other.

He took a moment to answer. "Tillie. I want to. You have no clue how much I want to. But I can't promise. All I can promise is I'll try."

Hard facts, unwanted. "Will you at least try to find out if that man is still after you?"

Taking a strand of her hair, he wrapped it around his finger and tugged. "I'll try. That's all I can do."

"We could hire an investigator."

"No, it's too risky."

It wasn't the first time he'd said that and she was getting tired of it. "So what are you going to do then? Sit around doing nothing except praying that this fellow, whoever he is, doesn't catch up to you? Wait forever while he could be dead and no longer a risk and you never realizing it because you're afraid to investigate."

He inhaled sharply and snapped, "I'm not—"

"You are," she answered sharply. "I'm not saying you're afraid for yourself. I understand you're afraid for me, and Pops, but I can't live wondering if we'll ever have a life together. I don't want to spend the next thirty years sneaking around in the barn."

Sadness filled his eyes. "Tillie—"

"No. I'm going to—"

The sound of the barn door opening stopped her words. Orson strode in. He stopped. Stared at them. Nobody moved. His eyes narrowed, the hatred shining from them lethal. After staring coldly at them for a moment, he spun on his heel and left.

"Damn it." Wrenching herself out of Eli's arms, Tillie rushed out the door, hoping to avert the catastrophe. But Orson was nowhere in sight.

Pulling back the corner of the lace curtain, Jim Bob carefully peered out at the scene taking place in the stable yard. Rat-a-tat-tapping his fingers on the window sill, he stared at Tillie and Eli Knowles, the hand he'd hired a month or so ago, and hadn't thought much about since, standing so close together it was a miracle either of them could breathe. While he watched, Tillie lifted her hand to Knowles's face and ran a finger across his lips.

Fingering his mustache, Jim Bob twirled the ends between his fingers. That sure was a lot of touching going between someone who was supposed to be the boss of the other someone. It wasn't exactly what he'd planned. His plans focused on Orson.

Why was it his plans never went the way he wanted them to? Tillie's plans always did but for some reason, which he could never figure out, something always went cock-eyed any time Jim Bob planned anything more complicated than a Saturday afternoon frolic in bed with one of his dollies.

All he'd wanted was to protect his daughter from crooks and con artists and fortune hunters. Somehow or other that urge led to this quest thing which was now completely out of hand as evidenced by the fact that his life had been invaded by a motley band of misfits and losers plus he was now the not-so-proud owner of an ugly, useless camel.

In the beginning it seemed to be only a small hiccup in the grand scheme of things, which was why he let her get away with it, but knowing his daughter the way he did, a hiccup had the potential to grow into a major volcanic eruption that could wipe out entire cities if he wasn't careful. So he'd invited dear cousin Orson to visit, figuring the fellow could be useful in a couple of ways; either as a threat or a husband, one or the other, either one, he didn't care.

But now it seemed like it was going to be neither. First of all, Orson wasn't the man he hoped. Of course, Jim Bob wasn't the man his parents hoped either but he could never be bothered to change that. Why change a good thing?

But back to the point, Orson wasn't the man Jim hoped for. After spending three days in bed—all right, possibly keeping to his bed was justified—getting kicked in the nuts by a pony was sure to cause some trauma to any man—but aside from that, the man simply didn't have what it took. First of all, there was his wardrobe. What man worth his salt wore purple? Or for that matter, yellow checks?

Jim Bob was willing to overlook the boy's lack of sartorial taste but there was the whining. Whine, whine, whine. That's all the fellow did. His room was too hot, his bed was too hard. The food made him nauseous. The bugs, the heat, the bad roads. The ranch hands were crude and rude, the questers were idiots, the quest was ridiculous and Tillie wasn't ladylike.

That last really smarted. How could he expect Tillie to marry a fellow who thought so low of her? Maybe she wasn't in the conventional way as females went but she was a better man than Orson...and he meant that in the best possible way, of course.

He twitched the curtain a little further to the side. Knowles, the hired hand he'd pretty much forgotten about, touched his daughter's cheek. Jim Bob drew in a sharp breath. Tillie looked... she looked at Knowles like...

Damn, she watched the hired hand like Helen, his wife, looked at Jim Bob when they first met, before he disappointed her and she lost patience.

One of them, he wasn't sure who, took a step forward and now they were so close there was hardly a whisper between them. Some conversation was exchanged then together they led the horse into the barn.

He stuck one end of his mustache into the corner of his mouth and suck. What to do? Knowles was a nobody, a stranger virtually without a past. He might—or might not—be a doctor. Or he could be nothing more than an orderly in a hospital, like he'd said in the beginning.

But worse than that, he wasn't a Texan, he wasn't a cattle rancher, and worst of all, he wasn't a Buchanan. Far as Jim Bob was concerned, his only positive attribute was he was a prize in the looks department. On the other hand, Tillie seemed to like him...or even more than like him. Which must count for something.

Letting the curtain drop back into place, Jim Bob strolled back to his study, settled himself on the chaise and placed his hat over his face. He always thought better after a little nap.

Chapter Eighteen

Problems. Too many problems. Jinx and Orson and her father, every one of them presenting a different problem and she didn't really care all that much about any of them. But it was Eli who was the biggest problem because Eli wouldn't say if he could stay, yet he wouldn't allow her to do anything to help either. How could he live not knowing if Morgan was still searching for him? How could he stand putting his life on hold, living in limbo?

That wasn't living. She needed answers, and action.

Because once she knew the answer, what then? Would they marry? Eli said he loved her but there was nothing said about marriage. And was that what she wanted after all her protestations about floofy girls and being her own man...so to speak.

And speaking of marriage, there was her father who was set on seeing her married by hook or by crook to someone, anyone but nothing was ever said about Eli. No, Pops was set on Orson, who wanted to put his fat, nasty lips all over her face.

Ahh, yes. Orson. She'd spent the last few days doing nothing but ducking and hiding and running from Orson. Every time she went around a corner, there he was, lips puckered. She'd lost count of the number of times she'd slithered out from under his arms, stomped on his toes or run like a rabbit to avoid his flabby, nasty lips.

If it was only his nasty lips that made her stomach upset, it might not have been so bad, but it was more. It was the look in his eyes, one of steely resolve to get what he wanted no matter the cost. So she did her best to hide while, at the same time, try to steal a few minutes with Eli during which she tried to discuss the future and got nowhere.

She felt things she'd never felt before. It was now to the point where she could hardly eat, hardly sleep, for fretting and was nearly working herself into the ground so she didn't have to think. Sometimes she wanted to scream. The problem was, screaming might feel good but it didn't solve anything. Only action would. Stepping into the coolness of the barn, she found Eli mucking out a stall.

"I'm going into town."

Setting aside his rake, he straightened. "For?"

Taking a deep breath, she said nothing for a minute so she could think about what to say. But, really, the decision was easy. "Two reasons. One, Jinx and Orson are up to something and I want to know what it is."

He frowned at her. "How do you know they're up to something?"

"They went into town together. It makes no sense. Jinx is not anyone Orson would normally associate with. It makes me a little suspicious."

"Okay, and what's the other reason?"

"I'm going to hire someone to find out if anyone is searching for you." The decision came to her late in the night. One way other another, it needed to be settled so that Eli could stay, not because he was safe here, but because he wanted to. Because he wanted to build a life here. Because he loved her. Only then would Tillie know that her feelings were worth all the risk.

"Tillie. No."

Or that he would simply break her heart. "Yes. Eli, no matter what, I need to know. You need to know. Somehow, this needs to end. Now, what's the name of this man?"

Closing his eyes, he sighed. Then said, "Morgan. Clevon Morgan. He's a gangster, a thug in charge of dozens of other thugs. I wish you wouldn't." He shook his head. "But I can't stop you. I won't stop you."

"You won't?" Shock made her blink.

"Tillie, I'm against the whole idea. I don't like the idea my troubles could put you in danger." One corner of his mouth lifted in self-deprecation. "If I had my way, I'd build a ten-foot wall around you to keep you safe, but like I told you before, I won't treat you any differently than I would a man in this regard. I respect you too much." He sighed. "And you're right. I need to know too. I've been hiding but I need to stop hiding and start acting." Having made the decision, he told her everything she needed to know about Morgan.

Stepping closer, she slid an arm around his waist and laid her head on his chest, tears pricking her eyes. What other man would trust a woman to find her own path, and maybe his path too. Eli was one in a million. And he was hers.

Neither moved for several minutes but finally Tillie stepped back. She cleared her throat. It wasn't like she was going to cry or anything, she only had a scratchy throat. "Okay, going."

He ran a finger down her cheek and over to her lips. Reaching her lower lip, he dragged his thumb across it. "Be well. Be careful."

Doubts and fears still on her mind, she rode into town. Having never needed anything even close to what she needed now, she had no idea how to find an investigator. Pinkerton agents were the usual people to do this kind of work but she wasn't sure if there was a Pinkerton Agency in town. Not knowing how else to start, she located an attorney, not Trinkenshuh because that would be guaranteed to get back to her father, instead a young man named Tom Garvey.

"I need an investigator, someone quick and sharp, most importantly, someone discrete."

Garvey's brows lifted. He rubbed a hand across his mouth. "Uh, is this a...uh...I mean...a marital..."

"No," Tillie interrupted. "A friend is in trouble. He thinks someone is trying to kill him but he can't be sure because he has no way to check since the person who might be after him is in New York City."

"Ah. Okay. Well, my firm has an investigator. He can send a telegram—"

"No, no telegrams. It might alert the man. The investigator needs to go to New York. And it's imperative that he not let this man find out someone is asking questions. The man is dangerous, very dangerous."

Garvey nodded. "Yes, I see. I have exactly the right person. Give me what information you have and we'll start immediately."

"I don't have much but here's what I learned," she said and gave him the information.

After signing a contract for a month's investigation and working out a plan for how he would communicate any news, she walked around town to see if she could spot either Orson or Jinx but after an hour she realized it was fruitless and rode home.

"I hired a man to go to New York City and ask questions," she told Eli while unsaddling her horse.

He let out a long slow breath. "Okay. Good. Hopefully he'll find something out," he said but what wasn't said was that he hoped her meddling wouldn't put them all in danger.

Several days passed and nothing changed. She worked her usual eleven or twelve hours a day, sneaking in a few minutes each morning to spend with Eli in the barn. They kissed and fondled and stroked each other to the point neither one could breathe then parted, still burning with unspent desire, to do their work. Once or twice she was able to sneak off of an evening but that was difficult to do since Orson watched her like a hawk.

KNIGHT TIME IN TEXAS 263

Three days after she went into town, a rider came out with a telegram. *No News. Stop. Query Still In NYC. Stop. Still Looking. Stop.*

Well, what with the trip to New York City taking almost two days, the investigator hadn't had much time to ask any questions. She showed it to Eli who nodded, the look in his eyes unhappy, and returned to work. With nothing more to say, Tillie did too. Taking Kermit again, she rode out to the goat enclosure because there were still a few goats that needed to be sheared. By the end of the day the wool was sheared and tied the wool into bundles.

By the time she returned home, her father and Orson had eaten and disappeared to wherever they went at the end of the day, so she ate alone and then took a lantern for light and curled up in the wicker chair at the end of the porch. She'd worked thirteen hours straight today and all she wanted was a few minutes to relax and enjoy the night air. The thought of rousing Eli and asking him to meet her in the barn occurred but the lights in the bunkhouse were out and she admitted he was most likely tired too and deserved his rest.

She pulled *Ivanhoe* out of her robe pocket and opened it to the last page she'd read. But, no matter how she tried, it didn't hold her interest so she doused the light then leaned back to simply enjoy the night.

The sun was long set but the air was still hot and humid, making her nightgown stick to her torso. Crickets chirped in the distance, and fireflies flickered their way around the yard. She loved the fireflies. When she was small, she and her mother would trap them in a glass Mason jar and count how many they caught before releasing them.

If only her mother was still alive. She'd know what to do about Pops and Orson.

And speak of the devil. Orson popped his head out of the barn door, startling her. Instinctively, Tillie drew deeper into the shadows. After glancing around, her cousin slithered out through the door in that creepy way he had and slinked towards the house.

Seconds later, Jinx exited the barn through the same door. "Tomorrow," he called to Orson in a low voice.

Her cousin touched two fingers to his brow in a silent salute then bounded up the stairs and into the house, too self-absorbed to see Tillie hiding in the shadows.

Jinx remained standing next to the barn. A light flickered when he lit a match then brought it to his mouth to light a cigarette. The tip of his cigarette glowed orange in the darkness and the smell of burning tobacco filled the air.

Rising, Tillie descended the porch stairs and strode over to where Jinx stood. Seeing her, he stubbed out his cigarette on the sole of his boot and flicked it away.

"Miss Tillie," he said, his tone not quite insolent, but close.

"What were you and Orson doing in the barn?"

He stared down at her for a minute, not answering before the corners of his mouth lifted in a sneer and he said. "None of your business."

Shock ratcheted through her. "What did you say?"

"I said, it's none of your business. It was private, between me and your cousin."

A nasty suspicion briefly crossed her mind but she immediately discarded it. Jinx was known for his tomcat ways, and then there was Orson's widow woman that last time he was here. But, really, it didn't matter. She'd been seeking an excuse to fire Jinx and this was it. "You're fired. Pack your stuff and leave. Now."

His eyes widened. "What? You can't fire me."

"I just did."

"Your pa hired me. He's the only one who can fire me."

"I could drag my father out of bed and tell him what you've said but he'll only back me up. But it doesn't matter if he does or doesn't. I control payroll and if I say you're fired, you're fired because I won't pay you."

He seemed to swell up and the fury that rolled off him was lethal. She was afraid but she didn't let him see it. Instead she stared him in the eyes and dared him to touch her. After a minute, he swallowed then, spinning around, he stomped to the bunkhouse. At the door, he turned. "You're going to be sorry you've done this," he said then went inside. Minutes later, he exited with saddle bags thrown over his shoulder.

She waited while he found his horse in the paddock, saddled it, and rode away. Relief gusted out of her in a hard breath. For a minute she'd thought he was going to hit her. She didn't know what she would have done if he did. Usually she carried her pocket pistol with her but being in her nightgown, she was weaponless. She'd been damned lucky. But at least the problem was solved. Jinx was gone. Now if only she could get rid of Orson. Still trying to decide what to do, she returned to bed.

But, of course, a new day dawned and with it, the same old problems.

"So's you know," she said to her father. She took a bite of tortilla filled with scrambled eggs and hot peppers. "I fired Jinx last night."

Her father dropped his fork. "What? You fired Jinx. He's been here eight years. Why?"

"I can't figure out what was going on with him but he was getting more and more insolent. Last night he told me to mind my own business when I asked him why he and Orson were in the barn together. And he's been sneaking off to town, ignoring his work, without permission."

Pops chewed on his lip. "He do anything to you he shouldn't have?"

His question raised the image of Jinx last night, the anger rolling off him. She hid the shiver the memory evoked. "No, I handled it."

"What are you going to do about a foreman now?"

Good question.

"How about Orson. With a little training, he could step up and do the job."

Was her father insane? "No! Orson will never be foreman." He would never be her bridegroom either but that was an argument for another day.

"What's going on with Orson and you?" he asked. "He seems to like you fine. You're the one with the problem."

"Nothing's going on," she answered even though plenty was. But she couldn't say so because her father would dismiss her concerns. "And nothing will go on."

Jim Bob tapped his fist on his chest and burped then took a sip of coffee. "He'd be a fine catch for any young lady. Of course, he's not quite so good looking like that Knowles fellow. Knowles is a strapping young thing. Mighty fine looking and a hard worker too. But a nobody. Now Orson, on the other hand, might not be so strapping and handsome but he's a somebody. He's a Buchanan. But I understand that he's still a kind of a stranger to you. So you might want to try him on for size. You know, to see if the two of you fit. You know, if your Questers fail."

Tillie's stomach lurched. She looked up from her plate to glare at her father to find him grinning at her, a sly twinkle in his eyes. "What, you want me to take a sip of the milk before I buy the cow?" she asked.

He tee-heed. "Well, now, he's not really a cow."

"No, and neither am I. So mind your own business." Good golly, she was echoing Jinx.

Tossing her napkin on the table, she left the dining room and stomped out of the house. What was going on with her father? Suggesting she sleep with Orson. Comparing him to Eli. Her father's sanity was never screwed on too tight but now he'd finally lost his marbles.

She found Eli in the barn. By himself. With no one around. She smiled. "Notice anything different around here?" she said and kissed the hollow above his collar bone exposed by his open shirt.

He groaned. "No, why?" His breath gusted out in pants when her fingers threaded through the hair on his chest.

"Jinx is gone. I fired him."

He pushed her away, staring at her in surprise. "You fired him?"

She nodded, smiling. "Yep. He smarted off to me last night so I fired him." She related how she'd caught her cousin and Jinx in the barn and what Jinx said to her. "Which means he won't be around to bother you anymore. Might make staying around Buchanan Hollow a little more tolerable. For now, I'm the only one who will be telling you what to do. Starting with this." She undid the top button of his shirt and widened the gap and exposing the hair on his chest. She stuck a finger inside and stroked. "How do you like that?"

He dipped his head until their lips met and murmured, "I like it a lot." He kissed her. Kiss followed kiss, breath mingled, and the heat between them rose until the sound of someone approaching the barn door reached them. They sprang apart. Tillie quickly moved to the back of the barn, saying, "If you could finish painting the shed out back, that would be great. I'm going out to search for that danged camel and the goat I'm still missing."

Throwing a satisfied smile over his shoulder, Eli walked out the rear door of the barn. Tillie saddled up Buster and rode off. Hunting through the brush was boring work that took no brain power so she spent her time trying to decide what kind of future she wanted with Eli.

At the end of the day she rode home for dinner, physically, mentally, and emotionally exhausted. Orson was already seated at the table. And he was already filling the air with his complaints about the food, the uncomfortable mattress, the heat, the bugs. The boredom, good heavens, Texas was so boring.

Like you?

Her father, of course, ignored it all. Then, "And that foreman of yours," Orson whined. "Where is he? I needed him to run into town for me and he's nowhere to be found?"

"I fired him," she said. Orson's face paled. The urge to yell *hah!* was on the tip of her tongue but she held it in.

So did Orson for the rest of the meal after which he locked himself in his room. Tillie spent an hour or so on the porch enjoying the evening air and the fireflies then she went to her bedroom and undressed. Once again she picked up *Ivanhoe* and tried to plunge herself into the exploits of the hero but with her own hero to worry about she couldn't muster up any interest in a fictional man who lived six hundred years ago. Clicking off the oil lamp, she closed her eyes and told herself to go to sleep. After a bit, she rolled onto her side. Ten minutes later she rolled to her other side. Then she flipped onto her back and stared up into the darkness at the ceiling.

Phooey. Reaching out to her nightstand, she picked up her clock and held it up to the moonlight streaming in through her window. Two-thirty. And she needed to get up at five.

She sighed, rolled onto her stomach and tried again to sleep but it wasn't happening. Flipping back the covers, she shoved her feet into her felt slippers, grabbed her robe hanging on the hook behind the door and slipped it on. After belting it, she carefully opened her bedroom door and sneaked out, down the hallway, through the foyer and out the front door.

May as well go check on her foal. He was almost three weeks old now and growing like a weed but the more time she spent with him, the better. If he was going to be a good mount, she needed to make sure he trusted people.

After entering the barn, she flip-flopped in her slippers to Daisy's stall. Opening the top half of the door, she observed the colt lying in the straw, his eyes shut while his mother loomed over him, asleep. Hearing Tillie, she opened her eyes and nickered softly.

"Hey Daisy," Tillie whispered. "Hey Junior." She still hadn't decided on his official name yet. To some degree her choice depended on whether she left him intact as a stallion or gelded him, and she wouldn't make that decision until he matured a bit. In the meantime, she simply called him Junior.

The foal struggled to his feet and clambered over to see her on his long gangly legs. "Hi baby," she said and reached out her hand to stroke him when a sound interrupted her. She spun around. And the world went dark.

"Help!" she yelled, and grabbed at whatever was over her head, muffling the sound of her cries and making it hard to breath. She yanked at it, tugging, pulling with one hand while jabbing behind her with her elbow.

"Oof," someone said.

She kicked and scratched and jabbed, wiggling, screaming but the arms around her tightened, capturing her arms. "Let me go!" Her breath came in hard pants, the fetid smell of whatever was over her head making her dizzy. With a hard tug, she freed one arm. Reaching back, she clawed at her captor.

"Ouch! Dagnabit! Cut that out."

"Don't let her get away," someone yelled.

"I'm trying but she's really strong."

Damned right she was strong. Fear made her heart hammer and her breath short but she would never give up. Making a fist, she punched backwards into the man's face.

"Ow! My nose! Stop that, Miss Tillie. Yer hurting me."

Oh my stars! It was Bert! She redoubled her efforts, punching, scratching. Kicking. One of her slippers went flying so she used her bare foot to kick the man between his legs.

"Stop that!"

"Hit her, Bert. Hit her and knock her out." The other Bert. Dear lord, it was both Berts. Apparently they didn't take no for an answer.

"Nuh uh, I don't wanna do that. She's too perty to bruise. I'll use that stuff the doc guv us when Ma was sickly," he said. The mouth of the sack opened wide and a hand reached inside. She struggled, trying to bite the hand but a cloth was crammed over her nose and the smell assaulted her and her senses swam. She struggled. Her legs felt weak. Couldn't breathe. And then, it all went black.

When Tillie woke up she was lying on a hard mattress and there were three faces staring down at her, two Berts and one blonde bucktoothed baby-faced female-type Bert.

"Oh, good. Yer awake. We was getting worried. We was afraid we mighta killed you or something 'cause you was asleep for hours," one of the Berts said, then pointed at the female version of himself. "This here is Bertina. She's gonna watch you, make sure you behave while me and Bert go into Macdona."

Tillie blinked blearily at him. Bertina? Macdona? What?

"Now, it might take us a couple a hours or so but that's no problem, it'll give you plenty of time to decide which one of us you is gonna marry."

It was after seven in the morning and so far Eli couldn't find Tillie anywhere. Normally, at this time she was already issuing orders to the hands gathered in the stable yard after which she would walk into the barn like she had business there. Which she did, just not ranching business. It was one of the few times he and Tillie could be together without Orson interrupting with his hateful glares since seven a.m. wasn't Orson's time of day.

Where could she be? Was she sick and still in bed? The thought sent a shaft of panic through him. Jogging across the yard, he leaped up the steps onto the porch and banged on the door. He heard steps and the door was opened by the tiny housekeeper, Inez. "Have you seen Tillie?" he asked.

"No, señor, she did not come to breakfast this morning."

Damn it. Not waiting for permission, he pushed his way inside. "Where's Buchanan?"

The housekeeper pointed to the dining room. He strode inside to find the man eating and reading a newspaper. "Where's your daughter?"

Jim Bob frowned. "Out working, I suppose, like always."

"No, she's not."

"She's not? She's always out working." He folded his newspaper.

"Well, she's not today. Nobody has seen her." Eli thought for a moment. Something wasn't right. "Where's that nephew of yours?"

Rising to his feet, Buchanan led the way to Orson's room. Eli shoved the door open. Orson lay spread eagle on the bed, naked as the day he was born with a bottle of Kentucky bourbon atop his hairy stomach held there with one hand while the other hand was cupped around his nether parts.

Eli grabbed the bottle, tossed it aside and punched Orson on his arm, hard. "Wake up, you idiot."

Sputtering and cursing, Orson lurched upright. "What. What's going on? Who are you? What are you doing? Why are you in my bedroom? Get out. Whiskey, where's my whiskey," he said while fumbling around in the blankets for the bottle.

Eli slapped him.

"Ow!" Odious pressed a hand to his assaulted check and stared up at Eli, his mouth gaping in shock. "You hit me!"

"Where's Tillie?"

"Tillie? I haven't seen Tillie. Why?"

"She's missing," Eli said grimly. The way Orson hounded Tillie, Eli's bet was that her cousin had something to do with it.

"Missing? Missing? How missing. When? Where? What are you talking about?" Orson yelled with a look of total confusion. Damn it, it seemed Eli's suspicious were wrong, it wasn't Orson.

"Where's her bedroom?" he asked Buchanan next and followed the man to her bedroom. They opened the door and peered inside. It was empty, the bed unmade.

"She always makes her bed in the morning," Jim Bob said, worry in his voice. "Oh, and damn. Look there. There's her gun." He pointed at small pocket revolver lying on her bedside table. "She never goes out to work on the range without her pistol. Something's happened to her."

Not waiting for any more discussion, Eli left the house and rejoined the crew outside. "Something's happened to Miss Buchanan. We need to search. You, Zeke, search all the outbuildings. Beau, Jud, go to the north pasture, see if she went out there and had an accident. Kermit, Buck, check around the rest of the property. I'm going to check the barn, see if she took her horse out this morning."

Striding inside, he walked down the aisle towards Buster's stall. Hearing Eli, the horse poked his head out of the stall door. Eli stopped. Holy hell. At the foot of Buster's door lay a bright pink lump. He took a step closer. Fuck. It was a woman's bedroom slipper, probably her slipper.

Fear clenched his heart so hard, his head spun. He bent over, hands on his knees to keep from passing out. That's when he saw it. A glint of silver half buried in the dirt. Picking it up, he straightened and stared at it.

The barn door opened and Jim Bob hurried in. On his heels was Orson, obviously hastily dressed, yet even in his rush, he'd managed to don a fresh pink shirt, and a maroon ascot neckcloth in a counterpoint to his maroon and tan striped trousers and jacket.

"What's that you got?" Buchanan asked.

Eli studied it. Something jogged in his memory. What was it? The image of blond hair and a wide grin with a toothpick barely hanging onto a lip popped into his head. "It's a toothpick," he exclaimed. "It's that silver toothpick of the Berts. The Berts have her. They've taken her somewhere." He thought for a moment. "Where's that little black book Tillie kept for the quest? When I took their Quest entry, I wrote down where each participant is from."

They rushed to the house and dug through Tillie's desk until they found her book. "Macdona. Where is that? How far?"

"Ten, eleven miles south and east of here. I'll take you," Buchanan said and ran towards the barn.

Orson panted along on their heels. "I'll come too," he said.

Eli selected a horse and pulled it out of its stall, leaving Rusty for Buchanan. "Why would you come?" he demanded of Orson, already throwing a saddle pad on the horse, then the saddle.

Orson drew back, his expression offended. "Of course I must go to her rescue. She's to be my bride."

Not if I can help it. Eli shot a quick look at Buchanan who stared back and gave his head a little shake no, his eyes wide in disbelief.

Good. Eli readied his horse while a few feet away, Buchanan was already done. Orson, suddenly realizing he was about to be left behind and made to look like a useless fool, pulled another horse from its stall then trotted to the barn door and yelled for help. Beau entered and, with a shake of his head, began prepping the horse.

Eli and Jim Bob didn't wait. Odious would have to catch up. They rode fast, occasionally galloping, then slowing to a trot to rest the horses before galloping again. The pace didn't allow for talking but Eli didn't know what he'd say anyway, his entire focus was on how they were to find Tillie and rescue her. After an hour, they entered the small town of Macdona and stopped the first person they saw. "We're looking for the Bartlett place." Fortunately, they'd discovered the Berts' last name from the entry book Tillie kept.

The portly man dressed in a black serge suit, sporting a trilby hat and a bushy mustache, snorted. "Huh, them. What do you want with those no-account thieves?"

Of course, it only made sense they were known thieves although this was probably the first time they'd stolen a person. "They stole something from us. We want to get it back."

Not appearing to be at all surprised, the man gave them directions a mile or two east. They left town, followed the directions down a narrow dirt road and rode until they saw a tumbled down cabin in the distance.

Pulling out of sight underneath a large oak tree, they stopped.

"What do you think?" Buchanan asked, chewing on the end of his mustache.

Eli dismounted. "Let me go in on foot and check the place out. We don't know if there are more than the two of them or if they're armed. No point in taking chances. If it's safe, I'll wave," he said.

"'fore you go, take this," Buchanan said, reaching into the saddlebag tied to the back of his saddle. He pulled out two revolvers and handed one to Eli. With a nod, Eli tucked it into his belt and stole away. Using the trees for cover, he crept around the back side of the cabin. Once there, he slid along the wall until he found a window. Stooping, he lifted far enough to peek inside.

Sitting on a chair canted away from the window was a woman, tall, blonde and buck-toothed. A female Bert. Opposite her, Tillie sat in the bed, still in her nightgown. Her legs were crossed and she was swinging one leg back and forth and gesturing with one arm while she talked. Realizing that Tillie's captor couldn't see him positioned the way she was, Eli rose to his feet. He lifted a hand. Tillie's gaze passed over him then quickly returned. Her mouth stopped working for a second, but immediately resumed speaking, hands still waving, like she'd seen nothing.

What a woman. This was one of many reasons why he loved her. Catching Buchanan's eye, he waved him forward. When Jim Bob joined him, he whispered, "So far, I only see Tillie and a woman but I'm going to walk around the cabin and make sure there's no one here other than the woman. You stay here. Once I learn it's safe, we can go in and get Tillie."

Buchanan nodded and Eli tip-toed off, peering into the windows around the house, seeing nothing but several unmade beds and piles of dirty laundry until he was satisfied the blonde woman was alone. He tip-toed back.

"No one. Let's go in." Walking around to the front, they climbed up the stairs and pushed the door open. It swung shut behind them.

"Holy shamoly," the woman yelled and jumped to her feet. And grabbed the rifle leaning against her chair. The muzzle rose and pointed at Jim Bob.

Oops. Eli Didn't see that. He took a step to the left so he and Jim Bob weren't one target and studied the woman. Who was really a girl, probably only sixteen or seventeen, her eyes bulging with fear.

She swung the rifle around and pointed it at Eli. Then swung it back to point at Jim Bob. "Don't move or I'll shoot," she said, her voice trembling.

Buchanan drew his own revolver from his belt and pointed it at the woman. She squeaked but Jim Bob's response was to take a step closer to Eli. "Now, young lady, seems we've got a bit of a standoff. Maybe you can shoot me before I shoot you but Eli here—" he said while surreptitiously stomping on Eli's foot to remind him to draw his own weapon. "Will then shoot you. You'll be dead and Tillie will still go free. May as well give it up while you're still alive and kicking. So...what's it gonna be?"

The girl opened her mouth to speak when the door behind them burst open and Orson flew in and stumbled to a stop.

"Bloody hell," Odious yipped, at the same time Jim Bob yelled, "You idjit!" and Eli slapped a hand on his forehead and muttered, "Oh boy, just what we need."

The girl yelped.

In the distraction, Tillie stood and took the rifle out of the girl's hands. "Hi Pops. What took you so long?" She cocked the lever to pop out the bullets and dropped them into the pocket of her nightgown. "Hi Eli," she said next, her tone silky and caressing unlike the impatient tone she'd used with her father.

"I'm here to save you, Tillie," Odious announced, and spread his arms wide.

"Shut up, Orson," everyone except the girl said. Her gaze turned to Orson and a smile lit her face. Ignoring her recent hostage and her rifle, the girl walked up to Orson, only stopping when her chest pressed against his. "Yer pretty. My name's Bertina. What's yours?"

Orson's beady little eyes nearly popped out of his head. He took a step back. The girl took a step forward so they were still chest to chest. "Are you married?" she asked. She gazed up at him, her expression filled with wonder. And greed.

The sound of Orson's gulp was audible to everyone. He took another backwards step, the girl also stepped forward and now Orson was pressed up against the wall with the girl plastered to his front.

Eli flicked a look at Tillie who shrugged and grinned.

And the door opened again and the Berts stepped inside along with a short, shriveled gnome of a man with a bible clutched in his hands.

"What the dickens is going on?" one of the Berts demanded.

"Bert, lookie what I found. Ain't he perty? And see them clothes. Ain't they the most glorious things you ever seen?"

"Bertina, never mind him. We done brought the preacher so's he can marry one of us to Miss Tillie."

Okay, enough was enough. "Tillie isn't going to marry either of you. She's promised to me," Eli interjected. That should take care of that.

"What!" the other Bert yelled. He glared at Tillie. "You never told us you was promised. You said you wasn't gonna marry your cousin."

"And I'm not," Tillie answered. She pointed at Orson who was still pressed to the wall with Bertina glommed to his front. "That's my cousin. I'm not marrying him. Seems I'm marrying this fellow, Eli," she said with smug smile.

"Now hang on a min—" from a Bert.

"Oh, shut up, Bert," Bertina interrupted. "Never mind her. She don't want to marry you so stop." She flicked her hand, dismissing the topic, leaving Bert whichever sputtering. "Let's talk about me fer a change."

"But Ber—"

Bertina stomped her bare foot. "I never get what I want. It's always what you want, always, always, always. Well, this time I'm gonna get what I want and what I want is this feller here."

"What!" erupted from Orson.

Bert One pursed lips. "Well, I guess that's fair. You bin a good sister so if that's what you want, I guess we can get that done."

"No!" Orson squeaked.

Both Berts drew their pistols and pointed them at Orson. "We got the preacher and we got a groom and I say we're gonna have us a wedding," Bert Two said.

Catching Tillie's eye, Eli twirled a finger over his head. *Let's go.* The three of them edged around the perimeter of the room and walked out the door, leaving the Berts holding Orson at bay trapped against the wall with cocked guns and the preacher already leafing through his bible in search of wedding passages.

"No! Stop. Don't leave me. Tillie. Uncle James, come back. Saaaaave meeee." Orson's frantic cries followed them as they all walked back to the big oak tree and retrieved their horses. Eli mounted. Reaching a hand down to Tillie, he hoisted up behind him and they rode home.

Chapter Nineteen

"So, you're going to marry my daughter, huh?" Jim Bob said, rocking his desk chair back on its two back legs.

Tillie examined Eli, waiting for his answer. Despite the touching and the fondling and the heated kisses, Eli still hadn't promised to stay, much less promise her marriage, so she needed to hear how he responded to the question. Because, sometime between when a smelly gunny sack was thrown over her head and when he'd shown up and told the Berts she was marrying him, she'd made her decision. Come hell or high water, she would marry Eli Knowles.

Eli leaned forward in his chair. "Sir, I'd like nothing more than to marry your daughter..."

Tillie's heart surged with joy.

"But I don't know that I can."

Her heart sank.

"I love her. More than I can even describe." Eli stared into Tillie's eyes. She could see the love shining out of his Texas blue eyes. Her heart surged again.

"But it might not be possible."

Her heart plummeted to her shoes. Dang, much more of this and she was going to pass out.

Her father stopped rocking. He studied Eli for a minute then reached down, pulled his Colt .45 from his belt and, resting his hand on the top of the desk, pointed the weapon at Eli. Then smiled.

"Okay. And now you're going to explain to me why not. Aren't you?" The sound of him cocking the Colt echoed loudly in the small confines of her father's office.

After the morning where multiple weapons were drawn and pointed at him, Eli didn't seem fazed at all. What was one more loaded gun, after all? "There are things you don't know, things I haven't even fully explained to Tillie. My staying here, marrying her, could be dangerous for both her and you."

Jim Bob squinted then laid the gun down. He crossed his arms over his chest and leaned back again. "Okay, let's hear it."

Eli kept his explanation short, only explaining that he'd made an enemy of Clevon Morgan when his son was shot and only went into detail to describe the kind of man Morgan was and why he was so dangerous. Listening, Tillie began to understand the terror Eli must have felt for the last months. It made her wonder why he hadn't kept going until he reached China.

Once Eli finished, her father stroked his mustache several times before saying, "So if it weren't for this fellow trying to put a period to your existence, you'd marry Tillie, right?"

"In a heartbeat." His gaze flitted towards her, then back to her father.

Tillie's heart soared.

More mustache stroking ensued while Tillie fidgeted in her seat. She hated the fact that her entire future relied on her *unreliable* father. Long minutes passed. Eli looked calm but seeing his fisted hands in his lap, it was obvious he wasn't.

"Well, good. That's good. The thing of it is, there are a few stipulations."

Like what?" Eli asked, frowning.

"Well, for one there's your name—"

"Pops!" Tillie barked. "Never mind that now. We have other, more important things to take care of."

"Right, right, you're right. The thing is, this is complicated," her father said. "Seems like the best thing for everyone is for Eli here to marry you, Tillie, but that fellow from New York is getting in the way. I need to spend some time thinking about what I have to do to fix things."

Was he kidding? "Pops, I already hired a private investigator who is in New York right now investigating. So far all he's learned is that, as of three days ago, this Morgan fellow was still there but we don't know if he's set other men on Eli's trail. That's what we're waiting to find out. I've done everything that needs to be done so what do *you* think you can do?" she said.

It was only after her father's face fell that she realized she'd implied that he was useless. Well, he actually was, but a good daughter wouldn't point it out. Of course, Tillie gave up being a good daughter about ten years ago so her comment stood.

Rising, Jim Bob tugged his pants up, pulled his shirt sleeves down to cover his wrists and cleared his throat. "Sometimes I have ideas."

Yes, sometimes he did. Almost always bad one, ones that cost her time or money. She compressed her lips.

"I'll think on it," he said, his stiff back and fisted hands demonstrating his indignation. "And now that I consider it, I think I'll do my thinking in town. Don't expect me back for dinner." He walked out the door. They heard him speaking to Inez and then he left.

Tillie released the breath she'd been holding.

Eli pulled her close with an arm over her shoulder. "He'll get over it."

"Yes, he will," Tillie replied. "He always gets over it, usually by spending the money I've made us."

He kissed her temple. A little tingle went through her. His lips drifted from her temple to her ear and nibbled on the lobe. The tingle grew into a spark. Her jaw was next, nibble, nibble, nibble, then his lips slid to her mouth and took possession. Tongues got involved, and teeth and the spark burst into a conflagration.

Well, this was more like it. Throwing her arms around his neck, she threw a leg over his thighs and settled down on his lap. More kisses rained on her face, her neck, her chest until he pushed her away. "We need to stop."

"Why? Are you not going to marry me?" Even when the words flew out of her mouth, she had a hard time believing she'd said them, begging for reassurance like those floofy girls in town. But she didn't care. She loved him and right now, love was all that mattered.

Tomorrow would be different. Tomorrow would be filled with work and responsibility but today she wanted this. All this time she'd fretted and worried about giving up her independence, having a man in her life expected her to change, when the truth was, Eli already proved he liked her for who she was, while any changes she made for him would only be for the better.

And, she suspected, he'd be perfectly willing to make some changes of his own if it made her happy.

He placed a gentle kiss on her check. "I would marry you this minute if I could. But..."

At the serious tone of his voice, she sat up.

"Tillie..." He pushed a lock of hair off her face then stroked his thumb across her cheek. She leaned into it. It felt so good to have him caress her. Sure she was an independent woman, but at the end of the day, sometimes she wanted to put down her independence and be treated simply as a woman.

"Eli..."

His Texas blue eyes were dim, his face somber. "Tillie, if your investigator doesn't find something within the next few days...I'm going to go back to New York."

"What? No!" Her stomach lurched.

"Yes, I have to. I have to find out if Morgan is still after me. You were right. I can't sit here, day after day, week after week, year after year, cowering, waiting and wondering if he's going to show up one day and harm the people I love. One way or another, I have to settle things."

"Eli, no," she protested again, but in her heart she realized he had no choice. Anyway, he didn't need her approval or agreement. He was a man, and was doing what a man needed to do and she needed to respect that, like he would need to respect her decisions if they were to have a happy life together. But she was afraid, so afraid.

She curled up in his lap and tucked her head under his chin. "Spend the night with me, Eli," she murmured.

Tangling his fingers in her hair, he massaged her skull. "No, I can't do that. What if I go to New York and never come back and you were...?"

"You'll come back," she insisted because anything else was too frightening to contemplate.

"Yes, I always will...if I can. But what if I can't? Things happen..."

Even though she tried to stop it, a tear dribbled down her cheek. He needed to do what he needed to do and her whining would only make him feel guilty so she held back her sobs. "Then have dinner with me tonight and afterwards we can sit on the porch and enjoy the night."

"What about the men? It might not be a good idea for them to see us together."

"It's Friday. And payday. The men will go into town tonight to celebrate."

He kissed the top of her head. "Then I'm in."

They cuddled for a few more minutes but the tone was different, quieter, less urgent, almost like it was goodbye. Finally Tillie slid off his lap. "There's still work to be done," she said and after listing a few chores he could do, she left.

Jim Bob was hot with embarrassment. His own daughter thought he was useless. Slowing his horse to a walk, he fingered his mustache, thinking and reviewing his life. Damn. He *was* kind of useless. Because what had he done with his life other than to produce the best daughter a man ever sired, one who spent twelve hours a day working her tail off making Buchanan Hollow one of the most profitable ranches in Texas. And what did he do? He ate and he drank and he slept…a lot. Once a week he rode into San Antonio and played cards with Warren Trinkenshuh, Curtis Lockner, owner of the biggest general store in town, Clem Sanger, of Sanger Brothers Department Store and the mayor where he lost a lot of money that he hadn't earned.

It made him feel bad. A man didn't like to admit he wasn't a real man but other than the fact he had three mistresses that he kept pretty happy, he had nothing else to prove his masculinity.

He kicked his horse forward. If he could solve this problem for Tillie that would be something. It would take intelligence and perseverance and daring. Those were all manly traits, right? He figured the daring would be easy to fake, because even though he'd been shaking in his boots when guns were pointed at him during their rescue this morning, hadn't he given the appearance of daring? And that's what counted, after all, right? Appearance?

And perseverance was easy too. He could be downright stubborn when he wanted to, like when Tillie tried to convince him to let her take over the management of the ranch. Took her three tries before he gave in.

It was the intelligence part that stumped him. He'd always known that he wasn't too smart but usually it didn't bother him. Slick talk and bullshit got him by until Tillie was old enough to take over and after that he didn't need intelligence anymore.

Now he wished he had a little.

Reaching town, he stabled his horse then walked back to East Crockett Street where he stood and thought for a bit more. What should he do? Tillie already hired a private investigator so hiring another might only gum up the works. So what else could he do? This was a puzzle, one he was set on solving because Tillie wanted Eli Knowles and if that's what Tillie wanted, he wanted it too otherwise she was liable to marry one of those dumb bunny questers of hers.

The other benefit was if he could come up with a solution, she'd have to admit he wasn't so useless after all. In retrospect, he wasn't too proud of who he was but he'd sure like it now if his daughter was proud of him. He thought some more but like always, thinking was hard on his brain. Maybe a little liquid lubricant would shake a few ideas loose.

Decision made, he headed for this place where he spent a fair amount of time. The bartender and he were friends, the drinks were cheap, and so were the women. Walking, he greeted a few men he recognized, tipped his hat to the pretty ladies. It never hurt to impress a pretty lady. Stopping at the corner of Bowie and Elm, he waited impatiently for a gap in the traffic before crossing when the sight of Jinx caught his gaze. Well, that was handy. Maybe he could find out more about why Tillie fired him.

He started to lift his hand to catch the man's attention, then changed his mind. Jinx was talking to a couple other fellows, a big man built like a bull and another shorter ugly customer that Jim Bob wouldn't want to meet in a dark alley.

Since the two scary men stood in his path to where he was going, he decided he wasn't going there. Spinning around, he headed towards the Menger Hotel.

"JB, what are you doing in town? Why didn't you let me know you were coming in?"

He spun around and there was Flora, his favorite of all his lady friends because of her big titties. "Flora, hey there. Sorry, darling. Last minute change of plans, you know?"

She sashayed up to him, her satin skirts swishing, and pressed herself up against him. Blood flowed hotly through him, making him sweat.

"Well, now that you're here, we should spend some time together." Her fingers walked up his chest and toyed with his collar.

Tillie's situation flitted briefly through his mind but then Flora rose on her toes and kissed the corner of his mouth and the thought was gone. "What have you got in mind?" he asked and wrapped his arm around her trim waist.

She took his hand and tugged him towards the hotel. "Well, we could start with having the kitchen send up some nice wine and some oysters. You know what they say about oysters."

He could hardly breath for the scent of her perfume making him hard. "No," he panted. "What do they say?"

"Come with me now and I'll show you." She smiled and Jim Bob followed her into the hotel where they did a little of this and a little of that and a lot more of the kind of things Flora was so good at, in fact, she was so good at it that it wore Jim Bob out and he fell asleep.

When he woke up it was dark. He checked his watch. Nine o'clock! Doggone it. He'd made this trip special to find a way to help Tillie's beau get out of that mess he was in and now Jim Bob had gone and fallen asleep and it was too late to do anything.

He shook Flora's shoulder. "Hey, darlin', I've got to head home."

She rolled over with a groan. Her eyes flickered open. "Aww, do you have to? Can't you stay the night?"

"Naw, but you don't have to leave yet. Slip the key into its spot when you leave."

She rolled over and immediately went back to sleep.

Shaking his head, Jim Bob left the hotel and headed for the stables to fetch his horse. He didn't know what he was going to tell Tillie about his trip into town. Actually, he wasn't sure he was going to tell her anything because the trip was nothing but a waste of time. Once more he'd proved useless.

Chapter Twenty

Tillie handed Jud's pay packets to the wrangler. He opened it up, counted it and grinned. "A little extra?"

Tillie smiled back. "You fellows earned it what with the Quest and the camel and the tiny horse and, of course, me being kidnapped." She handed the other envelopes out. Each man counted his money, whooped and raced back to the bunkhouse. Within minutes, all five of them came out dressed in their best clothing, rounded up a horse and disappeared down the road without a thank you or a goodbye. Even Joey toddled off to visit his granddaughter in town.

Not one of them noted the fact that Eli wasn't with them. She held an envelope out to him.

He dipped his chin and smiled up at her from under his brow. "Really?"

"You may need this for your trip," she said. Saying the words made it real, and it made her ache with fear and longing. But at least they would have tonight. Inez left for her home, the hands would be gone until after midnight, and her father was doing whatever her father did when he went into town, his return undetermined.

They would have hours alone and she wanted to make the most of the time. Taking his hand, she tugged him off the porch and into the dining room. "Sit down and don't move. I'll be right back," she said. Hardly waiting to see if he obeyed, she ran to her bedroom. There, she opened her closet door and pulled out that box she'd hidden last month. She lifted off the lid and the splendor of the dress took her breath away the way it did the day she bought it. The beads, the lace, the pleats, it was all indescribably beautiful. But no time to waste.

Throwing her clothes off, she pulled on the dress. The buttons in back were a challenge but she found if she did them up to her waist, she could still get into it and button the rest.

"Tillie," Eli called. "Where are you? What's taking you so long?"

"Coming. Don't move." She tugged off her boots and donned the one pair of ladies shoes she owned. Then she took a deep breath and walked to the dining room.

When he saw her, his eyes widened and he carefully rose to his feet. He took a slow, deep breath, a look of awe on his face. "Tillie. Lord in heaven, Tillie," he said, his voice hushed. "You are beautiful. An angel from heaven." There was a shimmer in his eyes.

Tillie bit her lip, not knowing how to react, or what to say. No one ever called her beautiful. "I am?"

"Yes."

She made a deprecating face. "It's the dress."

He walked around the table to stand in front of her. One hand lifted to gently cup her cheek. "Of course you are beautiful in this dress. Glorious. Stunning. Like the sun coming out on a cloudy day. You have a pretty face, a cute nose, eyes that shine like gems but...you'll still be beautiful when you are eighty, because it's not your face or your form or your clothes that make you beautiful, it's you. You are beautiful no matter what you wear."

Her heart swelled for this man who made her so happy because he loved her for who she was and appreciated her in all her guises. Blue jeans or fancy ball gown, he thought she was beautiful. The effort not to sob out loud was making Tillie's chest shake.

He leaned forward, kissed her cheek, kissing the tears away that she didn't realize she'd shed. Then he grinned at her. "The only problem is I don't see how you're going to carry a pistol in that dress and that's a problem because without a gun, you wouldn't be my Tillie."

"Wanna bet?" she said, and pulled out her pocket pistol from the folds of her dress. "Pockets. I wouldn't have bought it otherwise. Why do you think they call this a pocket pistol?"

He laughed. "Put that thing away before you accidently shoot something, like my toes. Instead, let's eat."

She stuck it back in her pocket "Inez left dinner for us in the oven, roast chicken, carrots and potatoes. Sit, and I'll serve it," she said, and walked into the kitchen.

They ate, not saying much because what was there to say? They couldn't discuss the future because they didn't know what the future held, and Eli didn't want to discuss the past. But talking didn't matter. They were together. After finishing, Tillie picked up the dirty dishes to carry into the kitchen. Eli also picked up several plates. "I'm unmarried. I'm used to doing for myself. Plus..." He smiled. "Don't forget about my kitchen duty with Joey."

"What shall we—" he started to say when a heavy knock came at the door. He threw Tillie a puzzled glance.

She shrugged. "No idea. Not expecting company." Going to the front door, she opened it.

And Jinx burst in, slamming the door open, and pushing her back so hard she tripped and almost fell. Behind him, were two men, a bull of a man and a shorter man with a black mustache and a cruel blade of a mouth.

Eli stepped into the hallway. "Morgan," he said flatly, his face stony.

Morgan? Holy hell, Morgan. Eli's enemy. She stared at the taller man, the one built like a bull. His face was broad, harsh and covered with scars. His mouth was cruel, his bold nose the nose of a man who bullied his way through life. Seeing him caused a shiver to shake her. This was a man with no pity. And Jinx brought him here. The shock was almost more than she could take in.

She glared at her previous foreman. "Jinx. Why are you here? What are you doing?"

A sneer spread across his lean face. "I told you you'd be sorry and now I'm making sure you are." Looming over her, he flicked a finger under her chin. "And, while I'm at it, I'm gonna make sure lover boy here gets his too."

The flick smarted. Bastard. But he wasn't going to do it again, not if she could help it. Carefully taking a step backward, then another, she backed up until she stood in front of Eli. She was shorter then Eli, slimmer, but somehow she felt that standing in front of him would protect him.

"Tillie," Eli whispered. "Stop. Get behind me." He tugged on her arm.

She ignored him. He was doing his Ivanhoe thing again and she wasn't having any of it. "Jinx. How? Morgan. How did you...? I don't understand." She stopped, her chest caught in a vise but she needed answers and was going to get them even if asking put her in danger.

"I always figured there was something funny about ol' Slick here. He just didn't fit." Like a caged animal, Jinx began pacing. Tillie could almost feel the nervous energy radiating off him. Reaching the end wall turned, he started back, brushing against Morgan's thug as he did. The thug growled and reached out to grab Jinx but Morgan laid an hand on his wrist, stopping him.

"But I couldn't figure out what," Jinx continued. "Till your cousin got here. Took him awhile but we got to talking about this and that and I told him about your quest being in the papers and all, and he suddenly remembered where he'd seen him. Seems lover boy is quite the *boon vee bont* about town in New York City."

Eli's hand spasmed in hers and his breathing gusted out sharp and short. She could sense the tension in his body.

"Seems he's one of them high society fellas that gets invited to all the fancy parties what get written up in the papers" Jinx continued. "So then it didn't take but two seconds for your cousin to connect the dots and remember he'd seen ol' Eli here at one of them fancy parties."

Tillie darted a look at Morgan, who all this time said nothing, done nothing. What was he waiting for? Why was he waiting? His silence was ominous, more frightening then Jinx's threats. She turned back to Jinx. "But why, Jinx, why?"

He laughed, his blue eyes filled with malice. "Are you stupid? For the money of course. Five thousand dollars. Which me and Orson were gonna split 'cause it turns out poor old Orson is really hurting for money. Seems he has a bad habit of playing the ponies and his pa uninherited him." Feigning a pout, he tsked. "Of course, now, what with Orson getting married and all and the Berts being his new brothers, I don't guess he's gonna get a share of the money no more."

A red hot haze rage inside Tillie, causing her to tremble. She wanted nothing more than to rip his eyes from their sockets. "You...bastard. After everything my father and I have done for you, you sell us out for a bit of money." The urge to rip his eyeballs out grew but Eli's hand came down on her shoulder, gripping, a warning to wait, to not rile the angry beast. So she leashed her anger.

The traitor snickered. "Oh, it wasn't only for money. There's also you. I'm going to really enjoy having you." He took a few bold steps forward until he stood in front of Tillie then, leaning forward, pressed his lips to hers, hard, smothering, bruising. She pushed against his shoulder forcing him away.

Eli growled and lunged forward.

"Eli, no!" she said and used her body to keep him in place. Son of a gun, she was getting pretty tired of men thinking they had to right to touch her. Sending Jinx a look of disgust, she wiped her mouth.

Jinx grabbed her wrist. "You little—"

Eli yanked her away. "Don't touch her, you son of a bitch." He shoved Jinx, nearly knocking him off his feet.

For a moment, it seemed like Jinx would respond by attacking Eli but then Morgan snapped, "Horton," and Jinx lifted his hands and backed off.

"I'll stop for now. But later? Oh, later I'm going to touch her. I'll touch her plenty wherever, however I want." He speared Tillie with a glance of his icy blue eyes. "Think how much fun you and me can have. All the places I can touch you, bite you, fuck you. And maybe I'll make the city slicker watch, what do you think about that?"

"I think I'm going to kill you, you bastard," Eli said, his voice gravelly with anger.

Tillie's breath caught in her throat. Her father's warning about being a single woman alone with a crew of men darted through her mind. For the first time, she understood his concern. She pressed herself against Eli, terrified for herself, and for Eli who trembled with the need to launch himself at her tormentor. The rage pouring off him was palpable and that made her even more fearful.

"Stay away from me, Jinx," she said, putting on a brave face but she felt a lot braver due to the fact that Eli now stood in front of her.

"I don't think so. It's only a matter of time before you're mine, sweetheart," Jinx said.

Morgan, who'd been quiet until now, simply standing back and watching the interaction, now pushed to the front. "Well, now, Mr. Horton, I haven't quite made up my mind about the young lady," he said. "You never said how pretty she is so I might want her for myself." He turned his gaze to Tillie, his dark eyes cold and soulless. This was a man who looked capable of anything. Now she really understood why Eli ran.

Jinx spun around with a glare for the gangster. "You promised me I could have her. It's the only reason I'm here."

"My, my, Mr. Horton, you received your ten pieces of silver to play Judas. What else do you want?"

"Okay, fine, sure I want the money but I want her. I want what you promised...her."

Morgan smiled. "Well, you know what they say, promises are meant to be broken."

Rage lit in the depths of Jinx's light blue eyes. "You bastard. We made a deal. I don't like men who lie, who break—" he began but never finished because Morgan drew a gun from under his coat, aimed it and shot Jinx between the eyes.

The bang of the gun filled the silence. The smell of gunpowder filled the room. Tillie gasped and clapped a hand over her mouth.

"Son of a..." Eli whispered, gripping Tillie's shoulder so tightly it would leave bruises.

For a few seconds Jinx stood upright, his eyes wide, shock on his face. A thin trickle of blood oozed out of the bullet hole and slid onto Jinx's nose. Then his knees folded and he fell to the floor.

She couldn't breathe. Dead. Holy cow, this man she'd known for eight years was dead, just like that, one minute alive the next minute dead. She swayed then caught herself. She hadn't liked him but she hadn't wanted him dead either.

Nobody moved for several minutes, nobody talked. Her stomach pitched and rolled until she thought she would vomit so she gripped Eli's hand, which shook violently in hers, but she could see his eyes burned with hatred and fury at his helplessness, rather than fear.

Finally Morgan sighed, breaking the silence and gestured to the mustachioed man a few feet away. "Butler, please take out the garbage. It's beginning to stink in here."

His henchman scratched his nose. "Sure, boss. Where you want I should put him?"

"For fuck's sake, I don't know. Wherever one puts garbage. Just get him out of my sight."

"Okay." Butler bent, grabbed the body and hoisted it over his shoulders. "Be right back."

"See that you do. I might need you," Morgan said and took a step closer. His gaze passed over Tillie and focused on Eli. "Now, what shall I do about you, Mr. Man-who-killed-my-son?" the gangster said, tapping his chin with the barrel of his gun. "Shall I make it quick and shoot you where you stand, or should I come up with something more creative?"

Without thinking, Tillie stepped a bit forward until her body created a barrier between Eli and Morgan. The hand gripping her shoulder tried to push her aside. A low growl issued from Eli's throat but Tillie dug her heels in and refused to move. He pushed, she pushed back, all the time glaring at Morgan.

The gangster laughed. "How droll. It seems you have a little protector. It must be love," he said, drawing the word out sarcastically. "Maybe that's the answer, torture the lovely Miss Tillie here. Ah, but I think not. That would be a waste of a perfectly good woman. Besides, I'm not sure you would care, being a coward and all."

Eli lurched forward. She grabbed his wrist and he stopped, but continued to vibrate with tension. "Eli's not a coward," she dared to say. She wished he was a bit more of a coward then she wouldn't be so worried he would go off half-cocked and get himself killed.

"Well, of course he is, dear girl, otherwise why run? So, even though it might offer me some cursory entertainment, I think I'll save you for dessert later. Now, back to the issue at hand, what to do about my old friend here. Hmm." He tapped his chin with his gun again, frowning then a bright smile beamed across his face like this marvelous idea that moment came to him, which, of course, it hadn't.

His gaze zeroed in on Eli. "Maybe I'll start by shooting your leg. Then you wouldn't have a leg to stand on." He guffawed. "A leg to stand on. Get it?"

Haha. So funny. Although Tillie didn't think so. She was growing madder and madder. How dare this pompous ass break into her home and threaten her and Eli. If she had her gun...

Wait...she did. Unfortunately, there was no way to use it without dying first.

So instead of answering, she pressed herself up against Eli and spread her skirts to hide his legs. If Morgan thought he was going to shoot Eli he was going to have to go through her, or at least her skirts.

Morgan sighed. "Oh dear. She's going to play the mother hen, isn't she? Now, child, it's not that I'm not enjoying tormenting your sweet hero, because I am, oh so much...but he's not a hero, only a common ordinary everyday coward. So you'll need to get out of the way." He gazed around. "Where's that man of mine? I need him to remove you, dear. You've become quite the pest."

"Hey, boss, done," Butler said, reentering the room and striding over to join Morgan.

"Good, then your next job is to take the little lady to her room and make her stay there until I'm ready for her."

"Sure thing," he said and stepped forward.

Another figure stepped into the room. "Hey, what's going on?" he said. "Why is—?"

"Pops!" Tillie shouted and then everything happened at once.

"Fuck!" Morgan turned. And fired. Bang!

Her father drew his gun. Bang!

Morgan fell.

Her father fell.

Butler lunged for Eli.

Eli grabbed the thug's gun, forcing it upward. Bang!

Tillie thrust her hand into her pocket, gripped the Bull Dog and pulled the trigger—bang!—not bothering to pull it from her pocket. Well, geezwax. So much for her beautiful golden dress.

Butler grabbed his chest, lurched backwards and fell.

Eli tackled Tillie, threw her to the floor and spread himself over her. "Don't move!" he whispered, his warm breath tickling her ear and sending curlicues of desire through her body despite the danger they were in.

And then it was quiet. Eli continued to lay on her, his weight nearly crushing her. "I can't breathe," she whispered.

"Don't move!" he whispered back so she did what he said, instead lying quietly, biting her lip and wondering if a bullet was going to strike her at any moment. His heart beat wildly while his breath came out in gasps.

But seconds passed, then minutes and nothing happened so she lifted her head to see over his shoulder. There wasn't a soul in sight. She cocked her head to the right and found herself staring directly into Butler's lifeless eyes.

"Yikes!" Holy hell, she'd killed him. She'd killed a man. Who was trying to kill her. Did she care? She wasn't sure but now wasn't the time to search for an answer.

"Tillie, don't move!" Eli said again, pushing his weight against her.

"Eli, let me see." Looking over his shoulder, she saw feet, which were attached to bodies. That were prone on the floor.

"Eli. Look. Everyone's dead!" she said, first with relief and exuberance then horror when she remembered one set of those feet probably belonged to her father.

A groan reached her ears. It was a very familiar sounding groan, one she'd heard many times. "Pops! Tarnation, Pops. Eli, get up. Get off me. It's my father."

He slid off. Rolling over, she crawled toward her father lying in the doorway but the sight of Morgan only a few feet away, stopped her. She looked down. His harsh face was melted into slack folds, and the menace in his eyes now the opaque gray of death.

Well, she couldn't say she was sorry about this man's death either. Another moan came from her father so she scrambled the last few feet to reach him. "Pops? Pops are you all right?" She ran her hands over his torso then his legs. Blood. Her Pops was bleeding.

"Eli! Come—"

"I'm right here." Pulling a pocket knife from his pants pocket, he knelt down next to her, and used the knife to rip a long slit in Jim Bob's pants.

"I been shot," her father mumbled. His face was a peculiar shade of gray-green.

"Pops, oh God, don't die, please don't die." Of course Tillie loved her father but she hadn't known how much until she was in danger of losing him, and all because he tried to save her. "Don't worry, Pops. I'll get a doctor. Hang on."

"Tillie, *I'm* a doctor," Eli said.

She stared at Eli. "You are? You're a doctor?"

Peering at her from the corner of his eye, he said, "Yes, I said that this morning when I told your father about Morgan. Don't you remember?" He removed his shirt and wrapped it around the wound.

No, actually, she didn't. She'd been too busy staring at his lips and thinking about how much she'd love to have those lips touch her in a few unmentionable places. She shook her head.

"Go get me a good sized needle and some thread," he ordered. "And some whiskey." She jumped up and ran into her office to retrieve her medical kit. With the number of accidents the crew seemed to have, she had sewn up any number of minor wounds. She carried it and a bottle of rum, all that was handy, back to Eli. "Is he going to be okay?"

"He's going to be fine. The bullet went through his leg and I've gotten the bleeding to almost stop. All I need to do now is clean out the wound, sterilize it then sew him up." He handed the rum to Jim Bob. "Drink."

"Hey, no problem," her father said and took a sip. He lifted the bottle to take another drink but Eli pulled it away. "That's enough. Alcohol will cause you to bleed more.

A whine burbled out of Jim Bob's mouth.

Using the tweezers in Tillie's medical box, Eli picked bits of thread out of the wound then upended the rum over it.

"Yi!" Jim Bob screamed. Snatching the rum out of Eli's hand, he held it to his mouth. Glug, glug, glug.

Eli shook his head and took the bottle back. "You shouldn't have done that but too late now," Eli said. Taking a square of gauze, he wiped up the blood staining Jim Bob's leg then picked out a few more threads. "You're going to be fine, Mr. Buchanan," Eli said.

"No. No, no, no. I'm not," her father slurred. "I'm dying. I can feel my life all oozing out of me. Tillie, I'm...s...sss...sorry. I've been a...um...bad father. Let you down and now...now... dying and can't make it up to you." A tear leaked out of his eye then another.

Leaning closer to Eli, Tillie whispered, "Are you sure he's going to be okay?"

"As long as he takes care not to get the wound infected, yes."

She patted her father's hand who was acting like a big baby and needed reassurance. "No, Pops, you've been a wonderful father. The best," she said then bent over Eli's shoulder to watch him work. He was quick, sure, his hands moving like a well-rehearsed prima ballerina, using his fingers to find a small bleed and suture it.

"Ow, ow, ow. That hurts," her father—the hero—whined. Once that was done, Eli doused the wound once more, using the last of the rum.

Her father yipped when the rum hit. Another tear dripped down his cheek.

Next Eli laid a thick pad of gauze over it and strapped it down with a long length of gauze around Jim Bob's leg while Jim Bob continued to ramble and whine.

"Tillie, Tillie, I...me...useless. Wanted...be a hero." He sighed mournfully. "And now...it's...last day. And I failed. I need...take care of you. And Flora. Remember Flora? I loooove Flora." Tillie wasn't sure if he was really drunk—it didn't seem like those few sips should do this—or if this was simply her father being her father.

Her father stopped, got a crafty look on his face. "Flora? Coochi coochi." He sounded awfully healthy for a man who was on his death bed.

"Oh boy," Eli murmured under his breath.

When Tillie heard Eli's *oh boy* said in that sarcastic tone she knew her father was going to be fine. She patted her father's shoulder. "You are a hero, Pops. Morgan was about to shoot Eli, and you save us." It wasn't completely true but if it made her Pops feel better, so what?

Jim Bob sat up abruptly. "I did. I am? You mean I was a hero? I saved you?"

"Yes, Pops, you were. An honest to God hero."

"So I'm not useless after all?" His eyes pleaded with her to agree.

That was a tough one because her father was ninety-nine and three quarters percent useless. The fact that he'd managed to play the hero—rather inadvertently—might make up for his past uselessness, but all things being equal, her father probably had another twenty years in him so there was plenty of time for the hero to wear off and the useless to make a resurgence.

Her father inspected the bandage around his leg, poked it a few times, testing, then laid back down. "Well, how about that? Wait till I tell Warren Trinkenshuh and Curtis, oh and the mayor. Why, I deserve a medal. Maybe the city can even throw a parade for me. It's not every day a man shoots and kills a vicious gangster, after all, right?"

Eli got to his feet and held his hand out to help Tillie up. He curled an arm around her waist, ignoring Jim Bob who was rhapsodizing about the parade he wanted to celebrate his heroism.

"Help me up," her father demanded, interrupting them. Eli reached down a hand and pulled Jim Bob to his feet. "Chair please," he said, so Eli swept him up in his arms and carried him to his usual dining chair. "Okay, I'm good. Except bring me that rum. I need a belt or two."

"The rum is gone."

Jim Bob pointed to a cabinet. "Whiskey."

Eli retrieved the bottle of whiskey and handed it to Jim Bob. He took a drink, belched then closed his eyes with a smile. "I'm good. The hero's good. You all can carry on now."

Taking her hand, Eli led Tillie away a few feet. "Are you all right?"

She nodded. "Yes. Is Pops going to be okay? No problem with anymore bleeding"

"He'll be sore but he's going to be fine if he takes it easy for a few days and we keep the wound clean and sterilized."

"Good, then come with me to the barn. I'd like to show you how all right I really am."

A bright light flared in his Texas blue eyes. "Don't you think we should first do something about the...uh..." He gestured at Morgan's body with his chin.

"Nope, I think that's a job for the hero. Pops," she said and gave her father a poke in his good leg with her finger. "Pops, Joey should be back any time. I'll send him in to help so when you're feeling a little more heroic, the two of you can figure out how to take out the garbage." The fact that she repeated Morgan's words was irrelevant. It was exactly what the man deserved.

Her father was still rambling on and on about his parade when she and Eli walked out the door.

Epilogue

"Okay, so now that we're all here, let's get this done," her father said. "No point in putting it off because a man never knows what life might hold for him. At any time, he might be forced to step up and be a hero and almost die. As I very well know," her father said, tottering to a chair and flopping into it.

Tillie shared a look with Eli whose lips were pressed tightly together to hold in his laughter. It was a good thing he found her father amusing because he was going to have a lot of reasons to be amused in the next twenty/thirty years. And Tillie? Not so much. After she realized her father wasn't going to die, and after she gave him his due for being a hero, she was back to finding him exasperating. Still, he was her father so she was stuck with him.

Now that it was all over, she looked forward to telling her grandchildren about the day Morgan almost succeeded in killing Eli, although, not her children because God forbid she give them ideas. Regardless, it was like God watched over them that day because the bad people died and the good people lived.

When the ranch hands returned from their Friday night festivities, Tillie sent Kermit back into town to summon the law. Her father provided a long winded account of the situation (from his death bed, hah hah) while a more succinct one was given by her and Eli after which the garbage was removed permanently.

Eli's nightmare was finally over but it was going to take while for the memory of that night to fade and for her nightmares in which she imagined Eli killed in front of her went away. Eli, on the other hand, struggled with the fact he wasn't the one who was the hero, that Tillie and her father were the ones to save the day.

It was only when she pointed out that he'd grabbed the thug's gun before he could shoot her which gave her the chance to kill Morgan. And, she pointed out, if not for his medical knowledge and quick thinking, her father would most likely have bled to death.

And now, a week later, her father was finally out of bed ready to admit he wasn't going to die. He didn't get his parade but he was still milking the event for all it was worth and basking in his heroism.

"Come on, everyone, we haven't got all day. We need to get this done because this hero needs his food." He clapped his hands together.

Ah yes, food. As far as her father was concerned, with all the important things that were due to take place this day, the food was at the top of his list.

Eli's sister, who traveled all the way from New York once she heard what happened, laid a hand on his arm. "Eli, are you sure about this? Are you sure this is what you want, because now you can come back to New York. Your practice and your patients are still there, waiting for you, and Dad really misses you and your skills."

"Yes, Uncle Eli, come home. We miss you," his niece, Florence begged, taking his hand and tugging on it.

Bending, Eli picked her up so he could speak to her face to face. "I can't, string bean. My life is here now."

"See, Eli, even Flo wants you home," Helen's husband, Ned, said.

Eli leveled a warm look on his sister and her family. "Helen, Ned, this is my home now. This is what I want. Tillie would never be happy away from her ranch, away from Texas and what Tillie wants, I want. And the timing is perfect. My staying means Doctor Peterson can finally retire since I can take over his practice now. Tillie will be free to manage the ranch like she has always done, and I'll still be a doctor with my own practice."

"All right, all right. Enough of that mushy stuff," her father said, snickering under his breath. "Let's get the show on the road."

Tillie shook her head. Eli grinned at her, took her hand and led her into her father's study where Warren Trinkenshuh sat behind her father's desk. They sat in the two chairs in front of the desk while her father plunked himself on the corner of the desk were he could keep an eye on everything and make snide comments. After shutting the door, Ned and Helen and little Florence crowded into a corner.

Warren laid several pages out on the desk and, after clearing his throat, began to read from them. "I, James Robert Buchanan, resident of Bexar County in the great state of Texas, hereby make and declare this to be my last will and testament."

Tillie's heart banged against her rib cage. It was happening. It was finally happening. Today was the day she would learn if her father was going to give her what she'd always most desired. And then, after that, her other desire would be fulfilled, which in truth, superseded the one about to be fulfilled right now.

Warren rambled on with a lot of legalese which she barely paid attention to. Her attention was focused on Eli and his hand in hers, and the fact that tonight would be different from all the nights before. Her heart swelled in her chest, almost making her dizzy with happiness. She couldn't wait.

Eventually Warren stopped.

"Are you done? Is that it?" Everything he said was what she'd expected; when her father passed away, she would inherit the ranch and everything else he owned, blah, blah, blah. She tightened her grip on Eli's hand until heat radiated through her body from anticipation of what tonight would bring.

Jim Bob tee-heed and rubbed his hands together. "Well, no. That's a bunch of mumbo jumbo we needed to get through. Now's the important part. There is the issue of your name," he said, pointing to Eli.

Eli blinked. "My name? What about my name?"

"Pops, what's going on? What are you talking about?"

"Weren't you folks listening? Your name isn't Buchanan. That's no good. For Tillie to inherit, you've got to change your name to Buchanan."

Eli's jaw jutted out. "What? I am not changing my name."

Her father's jaw jutted out even further than Eli's. "Why not? What's wrong with the name Buchanan?"

Rising, Eli stalked over to Jim Bob, leaned towards him so that her father needed to practically bend over backwards or fall off the desk, and said, "And what's wrong with the name Knight?"

"Nothi—" Jim Bob started but Tillie interrupted him.

"Wait. Stop. Knight? I thought your name was Knowles?"

Eli removed his finger from Jim Bob's chest and turned to look at Tillie. "No, it's Knight, Eli Knight. Dr. Eli Knight to be precise."

"It's not Knowles? Since when?" Tillie asked. What in the world? Why did she not know that? How did this never come up? It was like her world tilted on its axis.

"Since forever," Eli said impatiently. "I used Knowles to make it harder for Morgan to find me but my name is Knight."

She began to laugh.

Eli's blue eyes shot fire while everyone else frowned with confusion. "What's so funny?" he asked.

Walking over to join him, she rose up on her tiptoes and kissed him. "Oh, Eli, you have no idea. I always said I never wanted a man but in my dreams, there was always this...this idea. Or more accurately, this ideal. I would only give my hand, and my heart, to a man like Ivanhoe, a man who would be my perfect white knight. And here you are...my perfect knight."

An *aww* came from Helen. A quiet bravo from Ned while Flo bounced around saying in a confused voice, "What's going on? Why is everyone so strange?"

Eli threaded his fingers through Tillie's hair, which Tillie wore unbound especially for Eli. She shivered at his touch.

"Tillie, fair warning, I'm far from perfect," he said then, with a sly smile added, "Ma'am, Miss Buchanan, whatever you say, ma'am," just to prove the point.

She grinned up at him. "You may not be perfect. But you'll always be my knight."

To which her father squawked, "Now hold on a gosh darned minute. He can't be a Knight. He has to be a Buchanan."

Ned and Helen and Tillie all turned to glare at Jim Bob and yelled, "He's not changing his name!" while little Flo ran forward and pushed him off the desk.

"Ow! You little—"

"Pops, stop," Tillie stopped before her father could say something he regretted...or more likely Tillie regretted. "Eli is not changing his name. His name is Knight which is perfect."

"But—"

"Pops, either strike that or I'll be Mrs. Eli Knight of New York City." She glared at her father. He glared back, then his gaze wavered, and then fell. He sighed. "Warren, cross that bit out."

With a grin, Warren drew a thick black ink line across the page.

"Happy now?" Jim Bob said.

She simply smirked. He glowered and picked himself up off the floor.

The door to the office opened and Inez stuck her head inside. "Mr. Buchanan, Pastor McKagan is here." She backed out of the way while everyone, except Tillie and Eli, rushed to be the first out of the room.

They weren't in any hurry to leave, having decided that a bit of fondling, a lot more groping that involved unbuttoned pants and hiked up skirts, and a few kisses here or there, couldn't wait for tonight.

Helen poked her head back into the room. "Ahem. We're all waiting."

They sprang apart. Tillie's skirt was brushed back down while Eli's fingers hastily rebutton his pants before his sister got an eyeful she didn't need. She snorted. "It's not like I haven't seen it before, Eli. I changed your diaper, remember?"

He laughed. Taking Tillie's hand, he brushed past his sister and led the way back to the dining room where everyone, including the food, was waiting. Around them, everyone, even Jim Bob who still looked a bit put out over the name thing, grew quiet as the two of them approached the pastor.

The pastor stood at the front of the room, opened his bible and began. "Dearly beloved..." he said, and went on to say the most important words of Tillie's life.

Tillie closed her eyes and smiled, envisioning all the nights...and Knights, to come. And minutes later they were married, the lady who was not quite a Lady, and her Knight.

THE END

Hungry for more stories in Texas. ***A Wild and Wooly Texan*** *is available now.*

Chapter One

London, February 1891

L   ondon, February 1891
It was the smell of roses and unwashed feet that woke him. Dragging open one sleep-encrusted eye, Lord Algernon Grey stared up at the ruby-colored canopy draped overhead before carefully tilting his head to the right to gaze blearily at the wall. The familiar blue eyes of the third Duke of Stonebridge, the poor sod who lost his head under Cromwell, glared back from his portrait, seemingly critical of his descendant even after two centuries.

Ah, yes. Home, thank the Lord, when he could as easily have awakened in any one of a dozen married ladies' beds, a whore's crib, or even a filthy gutter. Satisfied he was where he belonged, Algernon relaxed and swiveled his head in the other direction, toward the smell of feet.

One slender foot, complete with five dainty toes, rested on the pillow next to his head. He frowned as he dredged through his cloudy memory, trying to match a face to the foot. After minutes of painfully sluggish mental thrashing, Algernon admitted defeat, lifted the edge of the duvet, and allowed his gaze to trail along the length of the slim leg until it joined its owner.

Well, well, well. Deirdre Holmes. Deirdre of the scandalous reputation and even more scandalously clever mouth. Deirdre, whom he tried to lure into his bed for months but she always spurned him in favor of Lord Falkner.

Yet it seemed somehow, in some fashion, he succeeded. He looked at the view, vaguely aware the room hung heavy with the scent of roses and sex, pleased because it meant he hadn't been too drunk to perform, always a concern when one couldn't remember entire evenings.

But, Algernon reminded himself, a man's performance shouldn't matter. Not when one possessed a handsome face, an ancient and sought-after name, and a great deal of parental wealth to support his needs, a happy state of affairs requiring nothing in the way of effort or thought on his part. Indeed, he couldn't imagine anything better than being the third son of the wealthy and generous Duke of Stonebridge.

Closing his eyes, Algernon rested his head back onto his pillow and basked in a sea of self-satisfaction. Alas, his contentment was not to last. With a crash, his bedroom door flew open. The sharp crack of heavy oak on plaster sent a shaft of blinding pain through his brain, making him want to howl. Howling, however, required entirely too much effort, so he moaned instead, and pressed the heels of his hands to his temples in a vain attempt to secure his reeling head to the rest of his body.

The heavy curtains covering the window were thrown back, sending a burst of yellow sunshine into his eyes.

He slammed his eyes shut and held a hand up to block the glare. "Bloody hell! Close the demmed drapes."

"Algernon. Be. Silent," his father growled.

He cracked open one eye, biting back his retort as experience with his father's tirades had taught him speaking would only make his parent angrier. Instead, he'd do as he customarily did, pretend to listen and then, the moment the lecture was over, go about his business as usual. Focusing his bleary vision on the dark silhouette of his father, he leaned back against his pillows, counting the minutes until he could return to the contentment of his own life.

Instead of the usual lecture, a bulging carpet bag dropped onto the middle of Algernon's stomach. He grunted from the weight. "Good God. What...?"

His father held up a hand and smiled a crafty smile which made Algernon swallow the rest of what he intended to say.

"Get dressed, my boy, and come down to the library," the duke said, his smile growing more devious, his thick, bushy eyebrows cocked in wicked satisfaction over his eyes. "I wish to tell you about the trip you are taking."

Texas, April 1891

"Molly Yeager, are you playing with those foolish chemicals again?" The outer door of the pharmacy slammed open.

Molly jumped as the sound of her mother's voice penetrated through the closed door of the small storage room she'd made into her laboratory.

"Oh no!" Grabbing a large cotton towel from her work table, she used it to cover all her precious beakers and glass tubes she scrimped and saved to buy. After a last distracted look, she scrambled off her stool and reached for the door leading out into her shop in order to lock it, but before she could reach it, the laboratory door flew open, banging against the wall so hard the glass beakers rattled on their metal stands.

A dark silhouette, short and round as a Texas tumbleweed, filled the doorway.

"Momma!" Molly smiled weakly and sidled backward until she stood in front of the cotton-draped mountain of glass vials, copper tubing, and Bunsen burners, and prayed Ethel Yeager didn't destroy all of her hard work.

"You *have*," her mother accused, her doughy face splotched purple with anger. She poked a pudgy finger into Molly's breastbone. "How could you? You know I've forbidden you to spend any more of our money on those foolish chemicals when we're barely making enough to get by."

Molly rubbed her sore chest and counted to ten before answering. "I know, Momma. I promise I'm not doing anything you wouldn't approve of." It was a lie but so what. She was the one who taught school all day then worked all evening in the pharmacy she'd inherited from her father to make a few extra dollars, and if she chose to spend a few pennies to accomplish her dream, she would. She simply didn't want her mother to find out. "Anyway, the chemicals I buy only cost a few cents."

"I don't care how cheap the chemicals are. It's a waste of time and money. Why don't you just stick to making headache powders and Bromo-seltzers?"

"Because I'm better than that," she mumbled, distracted as she became aware of a faint acrid odor. She forced herself not to turn and look, but she knew darned well something was burning. "I'm a good chemist and I want to do something important." Something like create a new kind of fertilizer to help the local ranchers improve their grazing land. Though so far without much success.

It wasn't her fault things never went as planned. Her equipment was outdated, and her chemicals were either ten years old, left over from her father's day, or of the cheapest manufacture.

"You're just like your father," her mother huffed. "Determined to make me a laughingstock in this town. And for what?" Her lip curled. "You're a woman. Do you think you'll get paid to work as a chemist?"

Molly dug her fingers into the edge of the lab table, her nose starting to twitch from the chemical smell. "No, Momma. I guess not." But she didn't see why not. Marie Curie did.

"Hmmph. You better not. Because that's not what men want in a wife," her mother sneered. "Maybe if you weren't so smart, someone would have already asked you to be his wife."

"I'm sure you're right, Momma," Molly gritted. The acrid smell got stronger and she tilted her head to peer over her shoulder. She stifled a gasp. A thin curl of black smoke rose in the air as orange flames consumed the towel she'd thrown over her experiment.

Whirling back around, she grabbed her mother by the shoulders and pushed her through the narrow doorway of her lab then propelled her across the wooden floors of the shop to the front door.

She yanked it open. "Bye, Momma," she gasped, and pushed her mother out onto the boardwalk. Slamming the door behind her mother, she locked it.

"Molly Yeager!"

Her mother's bellow followed her as Molly ran through the door into her laboratory and out the back door leading into the alleyway. Grabbing up several tin pails, she dipped them both into the rain barrel and staggered back inside, sloshing water behind her.

She threw a pail full of water over the flames.

Instead of extinguishing it, the fire erupted into an orange ball of fire that billowed over the table, scorching everything in its path, including Molly's eyebrows. She shrieked and grabbed a heavy gunny sack from the pile she kept under the table. Swinging it wildly, she beat at the flames until the fireball flickered and went out, leaving Molly to glower at the broken beakers and bent brass pipes of her experiment.

"Mith Molly. Are you all right?"

Molly yelped and spun around to see a gap-toothed grin beaming up at her from a freckled face. "Tommy. How did you get in here?"

"I camed in with your mother and hid behind the counter."

"Oh." Molly smiled down at him as she absentmindedly licked a finger and slicked down the cowlick on the back of his head. "Yes, but I've told you not to come into my laboratory when I'm working."

"But, Mith Molly," the young boy lisped, ignoring her admonition. "I had to tell you." He pointed a dirty finger at his mouth, which he opened even wider. "See! I lost a tooth."

Molly peered into his mouth. "Good heavens. I do believe you're right. You did lose a tooth. Do you still have it?"

"Nope," he answered, sticking his thumbs into the straps of his overalls and puffing out his chest. "I swallered it." His grin faded to be replaced by a frown. "Do you suppose it'll come out the other end?"

Molly shook her head, regarding his round face with two parts exasperation and three parts affection. Not the sharpest tool in the shed, she smiled to herself, but of all her students, eight-year-old Tommy Brady was the most lovable, as if God blessed him with an unlimited amount of sweetness in exchange for the brains He hadn't given him.

Her student grinned up at her, pleased with his question. Gazing back, a tiny ache unfurled in Molly's chest. She may have given up on being married, but it didn't mean she didn't want to have children. Unfortunately, God seemed to have other plans for her. Her hope was God's plans might get her out of Briar, Texas, and away from her mother.

"What should I do if it comes out the other end, Mith Yeager?" the youngster asked, interrupting Molly's thoughts with his fixation on one particular topic as was often the case.

Molly grabbed him in a big hug. "Well, I'm sure it won't, but if it does, you probably won't know about it."

He frowned as he seemed to consider the possibility. Finally, he nodded his head. "Oh. Okay, but I was kind of hoping I could show it to Joey Clump."

After ruffling his hair, which made his cowlick pop up again, she turned back to her work table and surveyed the damage. Over a week's wages up in flames.

She sighed, because she knew her mother would somehow find out and—she glanced down and saw her charred bodice—make her pay for the cost to replace her dress. The material, old and worn, had almost disintegrated under the heat. Gaping holes rimmed with blackened fabric decorated the front of her dress like giant polka dots. In a few spots, the material had given way and hung in long tatters around her waist, exposing her chemise.

Oh dear. And her mother would know Molly lied. With a grimace, she yanked up the long shreds and tucked them into the top of her chemise to anchor them. She'd find pins to secure the pieces later, before she went home.

"Tommy, find me an empty bucket for this mess." Eager to help, he raced out the door as Molly scraped the soggy ashes and the shards of glass into a pile. Conscious of the recent disaster, she carefully picked up the last remaining beaker filled with chemicals, intending to put it safely on a shelf.

"Hey, Miss Yeager!" a different voice shouted behind her.

She jerked, startled, and dropped the beaker. The chemicals spilled out and mingled with the mess still on the table.

Whoomp! A ball of fire flared up.

"Oh my gosh. Help me!" Molly grabbed up her gunny sack again and lifted it over her head. Without warning, a wall of water hit her, soaking Molly, and leaving behind damp, tattered strands of blue cotton and lots of stringy brown hair dripping onto her chest. With a glare at the water flinger, she walloped the flames until they were out, hopefully for the last time.

"Morty Adams!" she yelled, swinging around to face the older boy. "I've told you not to come in when the back door is closed."

The twelve-year-old bridled at her tone and dropped the empty bucket at his feet with a clang. His pugnacious jaw thrust out and his short nose rose in the air as he scowled at her from beneath shaggy blond bangs. "I ain't a dope, you know. If the cotton-picking door was locked, I wouldn't have been able come in. The door was wide open."

"Don't say 'ain't,'" Molly said as she turned to check the veracity of his statement. Sure enough, Tommy stood in the open doorway leading out to the alleyway, bucket in hand, guilt written all over his face.

Oh dear. "I'm sorry, Morty," Molly offered.

The boy grunted and stuck his hands in the pockets of his faded denim pants, sulking. Then he brightened. "Miss Yeager, you've got to come see what come in on the stage. You ain't gonna believe it."

Grabbing her hand, he dragged her out the front door of her pharmacy, ignoring the fact Molly wore only half a dress, the other half lying somewhere on the floor in the form of ashes. Moving at his slow, thoughtful pace, Tommy followed in the rear.

Morty stopped on the boardwalk and pointed at the stage depot across the street. A mountain of luggage accumulated on the ground as the stagecoach driver threw more suitcases from the top of the stagecoach. Next to the dozen or so valises stood two men, the likes of which Molly had never seen in her twenty-eight years of life.

The closest one—a prissy little man—was short and skinny, with thin legs that disappeared under a jacket too large for his short torso, making him appear to be a child clad in adult clothing. His proper little mustache twitched under his beaky nose as he hopped around, shouting at Ike, the stagecoach driver, to be more careful with the luggage.

Every time a valise hit the ground, the little man wrung his hands and moaned to the other man, "Oh dear. Please forgive him, my lord. He doesn't know what he is doing."

Molly blinked. The Lord? Had God come to town? Unlikely, although the other man seemed to believe he was God as he stood on the boardwalk twiddling his thumbs, nose in the air, while everyone else did the work.

Tall and lean and long-legged, "my lord" wore a black velvet jacket fitting his trim waist and broad shoulders to perfection, a waistcoat of scarlet-and-black embroidered silk, and a matching red-and-black ascot tied in an intricate knot under his firm chin. Three gold fobs hung from the pockets and an umbrella—an umbrella?—in Texas?—hung over one forearm by the hooked handle.

As she stared, he removed his high crowned hat to reveal a glorious mass of pale-golden curls that sprang to life and curled beguiling about his lean face. Beating the dust off his hat on his thigh, the Lord turned to survey the long dusty street.

"Good heavens," Molly exclaimed. "Who *is* that?"

Standing next to her on the boardwalk, unconsciously echoing Molly's earlier thoughts, Tommy answered in reverent tones, "I think it'th God."

Looking at the dusty street of the dismal little town that was to be his home for the next year, or until he could make his father's cattle ranch profitable, whichever came first, Algernon's heart sank in his chest and collided sickeningly with his stomach. Never a good carriage passenger, the trip to Briar, Texas, had been hellacious. He was nauseous almost every mile of the way and staring at the dusty, dingy, brown town he felt doubly ill.

The wide main street was a mere block long. A number of scraggly houses peeked out from behind the dozen or so single-storied businesses lining the dirt street. All poorly constructed, with the paint beginning to peel in long strips from the cracked and splintered wood. Most of the buildings wore some sort of crude hand-painted sign over the door, indicating the nature of the business.

A quick glance told Algernon more than half the establishments were saloons.

Well, good, because he would need every one of them since he intended to stay drunk for at least the next month of his life. Drunk was better than having to deal with this town and the louts who seemed to inhabit it. The way the yokels stared and whispered, one would think they never saw a civilized man before.

Narrowing his eyes in annoyance at their rudeness, Algernon swept a gaze in a one hundred eighty-degree radius around the street, making sure he included everyone.

His eyes focused on—someone—something—he wasn't sure what, across the street. Tall, very tall. Large brown eyes blinked back at him from within a sooty-black oval. Dark-brown hair hung lank onto square shoulders. Underneath the face, he saw some sort of raggedy dress with the front removed to expose a grimy chemise. As he stared in shock, the black oval split and white teeth suddenly gleamed.

Damnation. It smiled at me. He winced and poked Martin, his valet, in the back.

"Yes, Lord Algernon?" Martin responded, turning and bowing.

Algernon pointed with distaste. "There. What is that?" he asked, wondering what kind of place allowed creatures to blacken their faces and run about, half dressed, in public.

Martin glanced across the street in the direction Algernon pointed, pausing in his attempts to make order out of chaos. "I'm sure I don't know, my lord. Shall I find out for you?"

Algernon shook his head, deciding he had no desire to examine the creature any closer. In truth, he only needed one thing: a quick and easy profit from the ranch his father sentenced him to, after which he would leave this sorry excuse for a town and return to London, where he belonged.

"No. No, thank you, Martin, I don't believe I wish to know. Just rent a conveyance and let us remove ourselves to Crossroads Ranch as quickly as possible." He sighed with exhaustion. "I'm sure you are as fatigued as I."

With a nod, Martin scurried off to look for the town livery stable. Algernon waited for his return, standing hot and itchy on the boardwalk as sweat ran down the middle of his back into the top of his trousers, feeling more and more irritable as he tried to ignore the sly smiles, stares, and whispers of the crowd who stood nearby. He took his hat off again and wiped the thin trickles of sweat from his brow.

"Godforsaken place," he muttered to himself, and jammed his hat back on. From behind, something hard poked him in the back. He turned and raised an inquiring eyebrow.

"Oh, I do beg yer pardon, ma'am," the man, one of those Western cowboys from the look of him, said. The cowboy grinned while behind him a crowd of men snickered.

"Quite all right," Algernon answered through gritted teeth, revolted as he viewed the filth-encrusted denim pants, the manure-covered high-heeled Western boots, and the greasy blond hair of the cowboy. A sour smell drifted up to his nostrils, a disgusting combination of unwashed human and liquor.

And the acrid animal smell of cow.

Algernon shuddered, the memory of cloven hooves thundering at his back and the feel of sharp horns flinging his eight-year-old self still vivid even after twenty years.

"Ooooh, did you hear that, fellas?" The rude cowboy thrust out his lower lip in a pout and placed his hand on his hip, simpering. "The lady said it was all right. I just hope I didn't hurt the poor little thing's feelings." His equally uncouth friends roared with laughter and slapped their legs with their bedraggled hats, raising a cloud of dust.

Algernon stiffened at the insult.

"Hey, Slim," another dirty ruffian said, smirking at his unwashed friend. "Would you look at all them pretty yellow curls; just like one of them high society ladies back East."

Slim chuckled. "Well shucks, Frank, I think your right, but I can't see them so good with that there fancy hat hiding them." He knocked the hat from Algernon's head with a sly grin. Then he deliberately laid his foot on top of it, smashing the crown.

"Go on, sweet thing," he smirked. "Pick it up."

His churning stomach, the unexpected attack from the cowboy, and the burning sense of being ill-used by his father all served to bring Algernon's blood to a furious boil. But...no reason to cause a fight. It wouldn't do, his first day here. Teeth clenched, he bent down to pick up his hat. He clasped the brim. And a foot smashed down on his knuckles.

Bloody...hell! He clenched his teeth against the pain and waited a moment for the foot to be removed but, of course, it wasn't.

Well, something must be done about that. "Terribly sorry, old chap," he said and surged upward, yanking his fingers free as he made a fist and caught the cowboy square on the nose with a squishy splat.

A suspended instant of consternation hung in the air while the cowboy blinked at Algernon in surprise. Then his eyes rolled back in his head and he hit the boardwalk with a crash. Silence reigned as the crowd of men stared in astonishment at the fallen Slim, arms and legs sprawled, eyes closed, and mouth opened inelegantly, a thread of saliva dribbling from his mouth.

Puzzled eyes swung back up to stare at Algernon before dipping back toward the prone man. Then there was a collective howl from the group and they all rushed at him at once.

"Fight!" Morty yelled, his eyes gleaming in masculine glee, and leapt off the boardwalk heading toward the melee.

"They're beating up God," Tommy howled and raced after Morty.

"Tommy, stop," Molly called after him, picking up her skirts. She sprinted across the street after the boys. Grunts, groans, moans, and shouts of pain filled the air as she approached. Fists flew, feet kicked, and bodies rolled in the dust. Spectators stood around them, laughing and cheering as they incited their friends to further murder and mayhem.

She forced herself through the cheering crowd of men gathered around the brawling men and stopped next to the younger boy.

"They're hurting Him, Mith Molly," the boy yelled, grabbing hold of Molly's skirt. "They're hurting God. Make them stop."

The simmering violence in the air sent a chill up Molly's spine. She gripped the boy's shoulder and pushed him toward the back of the crowd. "Tommy, get back before..."

Bang! The stagecoach horses squealed and lunged in their traces at the sound of the gunshot. The nearest horse bucked and a thrashing hoof smacked into Molly and threw her to the ground with a bone-jarring crash. The back of her head hit the packed-dirt street with a hard whack. Steel-shod feet flashed over her head. A heavy hoof thudded on the ground then another. With a gasp, she threw her arms over her head to protect herself, her heart thundering in her ears.

God help me!

Suddenly someone grabbed her collar, yanked her to her feet, and shoved her out of the way. She staggered, her head still reeling from the impact with the hard ground. After a moment, she caught her balance, and blinked at the cowboys who'd stopped their fighting and stood around her, mute and red-faced with shame.

"Oh geez. We're real sorry, Miss Molly," one of the cowboys muttered, twisting his hat in his hand.

"Yeah. We didn't mean no harm," another chimed in.

"Any harm," Molly corrected, her voice still shaky.

"That's what I said," he agreed, nodding eagerly. "We didn't mean nothing. It was that Slim Muldoon what started it and we kind of got caught up in the fun. We wasn't thinking you might get hurt." The rest of the men nodded and added their own apologies.

Tommy sidled up to Molly's side and gripped her skirt in a small hand. Molly wrapped an arm around his shoulder. "Well, you should have been thinking," she responded sharply. "Someone could have been injured."

The men stared at the ground, looking embarrassed.

She softened her next words. "But you pulled me out from under the horse and saved my life, so I guess I have to forgive you."

The men looked at each other, shame written on their faces, and scuffled their feet like small boys.

"That weren't one of us, Miss Molly," one admitted in a low voice.

Molly frowned. "Then who did?"

As one, the men pointed behind her. "He did," they chorused.

"Who did?" she asked, frowning as she turned.

And blinked as she stared at the closest thing to perfection she'd ever seen. Even bruised and bleeding, everything about him was mind-boggling, from his large, sleepy gray eyes, slashing cheekbones and strong chin to his chiseled nose and perfectly sculpted lips, never mind the long legs, broad shoulders and tapered waistline, which didn't bear repeating since she'd already admired them more than once from across the street.

"You did?" she whispered.

"Are you unhurt?" he asked. One blond brow rose in question.

Molly blinked, taken aback by the movement. How did he do that? "Oh. Yes, I'm fine. I guess thanks to you, mister."

"My lord," he replied. The eyebrow went higher and disappeared into the shiny blond curls falling over his wide forehead.

The thought of running her fingers through those curls stopped the breath in Molly's chest. She swallowed, realizing she'd let the silence drag on in her admiration as he stared at her, his eyebrow still cocked. She pulled herself together with difficulty. "Well...er, I don't approve of taking the Lord's name in vain, however I suppose it's forgivable under these circumstances."

"No," he corrected. "That is how you should address me. 'My lord.'" He brushed at the dirt on his jacket sleeve while eyeing her from under his long lashes.

Next to her, Tommy jerked in excitement. "Thee, Miss Molly," he whispered in awestruck tones. "He is God."

God? He certainly wasn't God. She grimaced, all thoughts of his good looks and his good deed erased by his rudeness and the fact he was staring at her breasts, barely concealed by what was left of her chemise.

She jerked the bits and pieces of her charred dress up as far as the strands would reach and held them to her chest. "Hah! I don't call anyone 'My Lord' except God." Just to make sure he understood, she added, "And you aren't him."

His mouth fell open. She glowered at him for a moment, her nose raised in the air then spun on her heel and stalked away.

Stunned at her temerity—and the fact she could actually speak English—Algernon watched the woman march across the dirt road, her back stiff and her skirts swishing like an angry cat's tail.

He sucked in a breath. In spite of the tatters and the dirt, there was something beguiling about the sway of her backside. He watched, fascinated, his head cocked, until she disappeared inside one of the dilapidated buildings across the street, and slammed the door behind her. The view gone, he turned to glare at the spectators who still remained on the boardwalk, eyeing him with amusement. Bloody hell, what kind of country was this where the residents mocked a man simply because he chose to dress like a gentleman? In England, no one ever questioned his manhood; in fact, everyone who mattered admired him for being a bruising rider, a better than average tennis player, and a first-rate pugilist able to best his opponent as long as it was a fair fight.

The problem was these country bumpkins didn't obey the Marquess of Queensbury rules. His pride still smarting, Algernon pulled his handkerchief from his pocket to dab at the blood trickling down his chin and sent the bystanders another glare. With a smirk, they all drifted away, leaving him standing alone on the boardwalk. Except for the young boy, who still stood and stared at him, his mouth agape.

"I try really hard, God, honest I do, but sometimes I can't help myself and I just do bad things. Am I going to go to hell?" the boy asked.

Algernon blinked. The boy continued to stare, waiting for an answer, his eyes large and worried.

"Go away, child."

The boy's lower lip went out. "Wath I bad? I'm thorry."

Oh, dear God. Why were little boys so appealing? And why was he such a sucker? Heaving a sigh, he reached into his waistcoat pocket and pulled out a small paper sack filled with horehound candies, his favorite. He'd eked them out for the last month of travel, not sure when, if ever, he'd be able to find more. He stared at the sack for a moment, his mouth watering then thrust it at the child.

"Don't worry...Tommy," he added at the end, at last remembering the boy's name. "God loves all little boys." Tommy stared; his eyes huge. Algernon shook the sack, causing a papery rattle. "Well, go ahead. Take it. You've been forgiven."

His mouth open in awe, the boy slowly reached out and took the sack. His eyes widened when he opened it and saw what was inside. "Thank you, God," he whispered in awe.

"Yes, yes," Algernon answered. "Now go and sin no more." *Damnation.* Had he just said that?

With a quick smile, the boy spun around and raced back across the street while Algernon patted his empty pocket, already missing the comfort he got from his favorite treat. Still, he'd enjoyed the small thrill of pleasure he'd felt at the sight of the boy's excitement, so perhaps it was worth it.

However, time was wasting. It was hot and dusty here on the street, and he was exhausted. Seeing the crowd gathered for the fight had dispersed, he gave a passing thought to locating Martin, because, after all, without Martin, his plans would come to nothing. Upon further consideration, he decided his current needs were far more pressing.

Entering the closest saloon, he extracted a hundred-dollar bill from his wallet, delighting the saloon owner, and bought a case of fine Kentucky whiskey. If he was to live in Texas for the next year, he may as well enjoy it.

Milton Keynes UK
Ingram Content Group UK Ltd.
UKHW020121221024
449869UK00010B/380